FERNEY

FERNEY

—

JAMES LONG

BANTAM BOOKS

NEW YORK TORONTO
LONDON SYDNEY AUCKLAND

FERNEY
A Bantam Book / published by arrangement with
HarperCollins*Publishers*, London

PUBLISHING HISTORY
HarperCollins edition / 1998
Bantam edition / June 1999

Library of Congress Cataloging-in-Publication Data
Long, James.
Ferney / James Long.
p.   cm.
ISBN: 0-553-10844-1
I. Title.
PR6062.05123F4   1999
813'.54—dc21   99-11758
                                                CIP

Bantam Books are published by Bantam Books, a division of Random House, Inc.
Its trademark, consisting of the words "Bantam Books" and the portrayal
of a rooster, is Registered in U.S. Patent and Trademark Office and
in other countries. Marca Registrada. Bantam Books,
1540 Broadway, New York, New York 10036.

PRINTED IN THE UNITED STATES OF AMERICA
BVG   10   9   8   7   6   5   4   3   2   1

To Annie with love

ACKNOWLEDGMENTS

Penselwood is a real village and has, through geographical accident, provided the setting for the major historical events described in this book. It is an extraordinary place and has played a role quite disproportionate to its size or present importance. I have wandered through it many times during the twenty years that this book was in the making. I would like to thank those people who, with very little persuasion, have taken me in and told me parts of the story of their village.

Jock Baker and Michael Shiel wrote an excellent local history booklet which filled in many gaps. The staff at the Somerset County Archive led me through dusty files to the true story of the discovery of Monmouth's drum and much else besides. I have read many books in the course of researching this one, too many unfortunately to list, but I would like to acknowledge one which I turned to often, Keith Thomas's excellent *Man and the Natural World*. The Dovecote Press's superb range of books on Somerset history and archaeology was also extremely useful.

Old friends also played their part. I would like to thank Jane Turnbull for getting me started and David Burnett, George Speake, Charles Freeman and Pam Collin for their help in chasing down odd sidetracks of history.

I would specially also like to thank three people for the enormous support they have given during the course of writing this book: Nick Sayers, Caradoc King and Nick Evans.

FERNEY

I

AS HE LOOKED for the bones of his long-dead wife, old Ferney came close to death. Caught in the traffic jam that resulted, Gally Martin's life changed.

Because of Gally's groan, Mike Martin wasn't looking at the road. Just before the brake lights flared ahead, her sudden despairing sound had made him glance sideways, so that he was slow to spot the looming chain reaction. When he did, his efforts to stop had the car's tyres howling.

It's the same place, Mike thought incredulously. *It's the same damned place.* This was, without any doubt, the very road construction where Gally had been seized by an anxiety attack on their way down that morning. He'd pretended not to notice it at the time, and she'd struggled to keep it inside her as he kept close watch out of the corner of his eye. He was used to watching her fight for control at the sight of even the mildest car accident and knew the roots of that all too well. Gally had been Mike's pride, joy, and constant worry in the short time they had been married, and lately worry had gained the upper hand.

Now he looked across at her and put on a reassuring smile.

"What is it?"

Her face was on the verge of tears, but she tried for an answering smile which crumpled into an apologetic grimace.

"I don't know. It's this place, I think. I'm sorry."

Gally was a poem with a missing verse, a symphony with a few discordant phrases. Mike was used to her terrible nightmares, used to her odd and unpredictable reactions to everyday events. But this felt new.

The cars ahead showed no signs of moving and with every second her distress seemed to get worse. He took her hand and felt tension twitching in her fingers.

"The place? What about it?"

"It's . . . frightening."

"We'll be out of here in a minute. It's just roadwork, that's all." He looked ahead. "There's a truck stopped up there." At least there was no fire. That was always his dread, that they'd come across a car on fire.

"Can we go round it?" Her voice trembled.

There were perhaps twenty cars ahead, jammed into a coned-off funnel.

"There's no room."

She moaned and it tore at his heart. "Okay, Gally, hang on."

He twisted the wheel and drove onto the grass shoulder, seeing the startled face of the passenger in the car in front as they bumped past it. The car's exhaust scraped on a ridge of earth and he looked uneasily ahead wondering what else might be hidden in the tall grass. A sign, pointing down a side lane, said PENSELWOOD.

FERNEY, WHO WAS the cause of the traffic snarl, had been searching the earth for weeks. Passersby, trapped in the immense complexity of their own teeming lives, saw no reason to take notice of an old man and turned their attention back to the road.

Each day of that May, eighty-three-year-old Ferney had walked slowly and a little stiffly down from the hill to the main road to stand, unaware of the traffic, as the digger's metal mouthfuls sliced cross-sections down into time. The spring sunlight would often trick him, splashing some fragment of chalky rock to imitate the smooth gleam of bone. Each time he would turn away, caught between relief and disappointment that, after fifty-seven years, there was still no answer to the cruel mystery.

Ferney's stock of memories had long ago overflowed into dungeons and his expeditions to retrieve them needed careful planning. They required a cue, often tiny but always precise. The shape and colour of a freshly painted window might be enough, or perhaps the felling of a tree on the borders of the steadily shrinking woodland. From such a fixed point he could work carefully backwards, fleshing out the details of the old specific image until it blotted out the present and let him drag the memories up towards the daylight. Down here by the road it had proved hard, because so very little had changed over the many years until modern impatience had its rude way.

His last resort was the sense of smell, always a powerful short-cut, and in this case there was a very particular smell.

He needed to see the smithy again—the smithy that had once stood here beside the road, where the digger's hole was now encroaching. Once a smithy, then briefly a primitive petrol station with a single pump and gaudy enamel advertisements, then a ruin from which stones had been taken piecemeal to serve again in local walls, then nothing, not even a bump at the edge of the road. It was the smithy that obsessed Ferney, the smithy and an older, smaller hole which had been dug behind it. Sitting on the bank across the road from the construction site, he held a horse's hoof-paring to the flame of a lighter, bent his head and breathed in deeply.

The smoke was acrid with hot iron and singed hooves, and its first message was pain in his nose and throat, and as the scent claimed precedence, he looked back at the road and the other sight took over. The road's borders, hacked back for high-speed safety, filled again with untrimmed nature. The outline of the trees was still uncertain, shifting, not sure yet which of the myriad variations of the past years to adopt until he trapped the corner of a roof-line, pulled it into shape and the rest of the details obediently followed.

In a daze, Ferney got to his feet, hanging on to the vision, suddenly sure of his direction. Across the stony track ahead was the low, uneven roof of the smithy and the shed beyond it. He was young, strong, determined. The sense of a girl came unexpectedly, and all at once he was filled with anger fuelled by grief. Cochrane was in there, somewhere in his harsh darkness of iron, earth and anvils, on fire with rum or torpid in its wake. Three times the smith had forced Ferney to a fight. Three times Ferney had swiftly lost to his hammer-hardened muscles. Ferney, who by long practice abhorred violence, had nevertheless been forced to it on occasion by other men's challenges, and it was a very long time since he had last been so completely certain of victory.

Forgetting that all he had sought was the precise placing of the smithy's walls to help him locate that other hole the smith had dug, old Ferney stumbled down the slope to settle a score whose issue had been in no doubt since 1933. Down the track, on the fringe of his vision, a horse and cart moved slowly closer. Two more steps, and where his eyes saw the grassy shoulder, his feet felt anachronistic smooth road. Another two steps and a shrieking wedge of solid, violent air slammed him in the chest, hurled him up and backwards to fall thudding in the long grass behind, piling the years brutally back onto him.

The truck driver wrestled his screaming vehicle to a halt. Trembling violently, he took a long breath and climbed quickly down from the cab, looking fearfully back to the knot of cars and the running roadcrew. He ran, too, his stomach churning and his eyes fixed on the crowd around the thing on the roadside, the thing that must certainly be dead. Even before he got there, he found he had been reprieved. Incredibly, the old man he had glimpsed so nightmarishly almost under his front wheels was up on his feet, angrily dismissing the roadcrew and the gathering drivers, banging the dust from his clothes.

"You missed 'im," said a bedraggled youth in dirty overalls, hefting his shovel. "All you did was blow 'im over. More than 'e deserves, I tell yer. He's a mad old fart. He's always down here, stumping up and down, mumbling away. Totally bloody loony. Maybe now he'll get the message it's dangerous."

The old man was going off without a backward glance. The driver, fright fertilizing his anger, thought of running after him to argue, but his truck was blocking the road, the jam was building up and an impatient horn sounded.

"He must be hurt, mustn't he?"

"Naah. He's all right. Tough old git. Wasn't your fault, was it? You did bloody well to miss 'im. I told you, he's as mad as they come."

A car pulled out of the snarl of traffic and bumped down the grass towards them.

"Some people got no patience," said the youth.

FERNEY ACHED AS he walked off, wanting to be back home, safe. Concerned people from the cars had urged him to sit for a while, suggested calling an ambulance. Intent on their own schedules, none had been quite so well-meaning as to offer to take him home. Once he was on the field path he felt a little better, cut off from their view by the hedge, and he forced his legs to drive him on up the reassuring hill away from the main road against the gravity that grew ever stronger as he got older.

A stupid thing to do, he told himself, to get snared by such old anger. The sorrow was still real, but the anger was as dead as Cochrane. He climbed steadily towards home.

The village of Penselwood defies all attempts to know it quickly, spread out on spidery lanes across the southern end of a steep ridge. Anyone relying on a map would look for the village centre at the church from which six lanes radiate, but they would be disappointed by the open vacancy of that place. Much of the village lies along the lanes that run south and east from the church, but the houses are spread out so that they rarely form anything like a cluster. The spirit of Penselwood is on the prow of the ridge. The roofs of houses show up here and there in little huddles along the lanes, too individual to need any closer association.

At its southern foot, beneath Penselwood's contempt, the road-crew's excavation was changing everything. The hole was now two hundred feet long and fifteen feet deep. The main road known most recently as the A303 was a modern invention, an eighteenth-century turnpike made for the new carriage traffic—but there had always been something here. For more than ten centuries a lesser path had followed the same course through this part of the border land where Somerset, Dorset and Wiltshire meet. In the year that King Edward the Martyr, a deeply unpleasant youth treated far too kindly by the political conveniences of historical distortion, suffered a fatal mugging down the road at Corfe, the clearance of a tangled nest of woodland had allowed the travellers of the time to cut out a long detour. That had been the last significant route change for a thousand years. Since then, the only deviations from the track had been caused by slow, natural things: the patient inroads of a widening stream bend which gradually pushed the route southward for a hundred yards, or the fall of a huge elm, forcing a kink in the track which stayed long after the last of the massive tree trunk had rotted into powder. Even when the track was ripped wider, pounded with crushed stone and cauterized with hot tarmac, the line of the route was only widened, never changed.

The arrival of addictive speed ended that. Highway engineers, plotting to by-pass the villages of Bourton and Zeals, trained to look at these things from a seventy-miles-per-hour perspective, were blind to history and to the beauty of these roads that wandered along their way. Braking distances and visibility angles vectored together to spell hazard in their language where the smaller lane crossed the road. Geometry took over and the hole was the engineers' solution, the rough vacuum into which a coarse concrete underpass would be moulded to solve the problem. Now their plans had been approved, their budgets allocated and the traffic was coned and channelled past the confusion of machinery involved in its creation.

.   .   .

GALLY'S MOOD CHANGED bewilderingly as soon as they left
the main road. As they drove up the lane she lowered the window
and sniffed the air with appreciation.

"This is better," she said. "Much better. Thank you."

"Can you have a look at the map," Mike said. "Find a way back
to the road."

"I'd like to see Penselwood." She lingered over the name. "I've got
a feeling. I think it might be the place."

"I thought you wanted time to stop at Stonehenge?" he said. "It's
been a long day. There won't be time for both."

Gally was not a natural town-dweller and in the three months
since she had lost the baby the search for a country cottage had provided welcome balm to her troubled soul, but it was a search they
conducted in two very different ways. Mike liked to do everything in
an orderly fashion. He would call estate agents, look through the
local papers, read the details carefully and make an organized list of
the possible houses, listing their pros and cons. Gally would ruffle his
hair absently as he showed her the photographs. She'd smile as they
went round the houses, then suddenly, nostrils flaring like a gun dog,
she'd be off up the road, into someone else's drive, knocking at the
door, asking complete strangers if they wanted to sell. Mike found it
embarrassing, but for her sake he put up with it. For her sake, most
people would put up with most things.

Gally at her best irradiated those around her with a transforming
energy, but the source of her light was eclipsed all too often. There
was no malice in her troubles. They were a pain she inflicted only on
herself. Her mother, an elderly and bitter woman to whom Gally's
connections were puzzlingly loose, would turn away from his questions on the rare occasions when they talked at all.

"It was her father's death," Gally's mother had said once and once
only. "It's a thing to forget."

The woman had stared at him with flat, sealed eyes that showed
the depth of denial in her and promised extreme anger if he dared to
scratch at her sores again. Her look filled him with a fear that the
hurt would one day claim Gally entirely. What was it that had made
her shudder at the sight of the engagement ring he had tried to give
her? What was it that brought her nightmares?

"I have bad dreams," she had told him when they first went to bed
together. "You mustn't mind."

Distracted by the excitement of the moment, he had taken no real notice until shocked awake in the early hours of the morning by the thrashing, screaming figure at his side.

"It was the boilman," Gally had sobbed as he held her and tried to calm her, but she wouldn't answer any questions and for the first of many times he let her push it grimly aside rather than risk hurting her by demanding she explain.

That was the bad side; but the good side was so good that, when his mind sprang back into the private world of organized intellectual thought from which she so often dragged him, it made him feel dry, dull and only half real. Gally was illogical, unpredictable and overloaded with intuition, but she had a sure touch with people.

He thought back two years to the moment when he had first noticed her—only two astonishingly full, vibrant years, a monsoon that had ended his drought. She had flowed as she walked off the London streets into his classroom, her dark chestnut hair in liquid motion round a wide, smiling face. "Hierarchies and social order, the evidence of the Domesday Book" had been the subject of his lecture. Most of the students arrived as they always did in little knots, twos and threes, keeping their buzz of twentieth-century conversation going until the moment when he could compel their silence and unroll a thick layer of medieval history as sound insulation across the lecture theatre. A few who lived only in the cerebral world came in by themselves, moving quickly with downturned eyes to isolated places where they would perform fussy rituals with their pens, impatient for him to start.

Gally, too, entered alone, not at all furtively but with total assurance, looking round at all the people who were clearly strangers to her with an open, interested air which said she knew exactly who she was and why she chose to be there. He was quite sure she'd never come before because he would certainly have noticed.

At the end of the lecture, she had come up to him to talk and she had shaken his beliefs. She had stood nearby, waiting her turn as a handful of students, more eager to make an impression than to gain knowledge, advanced ill-thought-out ideas and misunderstood his answers. When they'd all gone, she finally spoke.

"Would you mind if I said that people aren't quite like that?" she had said.

"What?"

"It was very good—your lecture. I enjoyed it, but you were describing lists, not people."

He'd frowned and wished immediately he'd smiled instead. "We have to rely on our sources. Domesday is the best record we could hope to . . ."

"No, I know, and I really liked listening, but I just feel it's a mistake to make it sound like the people stepped out of its pages, all fitting neatly in columns. It's like someone in a thousand years' time trying to describe us now when all they've got to go by is a train timetable."

His surprise at this unaccustomed temerity was kept in bounds by the fascination of staring into her huge eyes. She'd touched on what he knew was his weakest spot, an academic tendency to see imperfect archives as more than the broken fragments of a skeleton. He tried to hold his ground.

"You have to remember that society was a whole lot more rigid then. There wasn't room for much divergence."

She just smiled and shook her head and said with total certainty, "People don't change. There are all sorts now and there always have been."

"They didn't have much cultural elbow room to be different. Not until the fifteenth century or so."

"How do you know it changed then?"

"We've got letters from then on."

"Ah. It's the letters then, isn't it? That's what changed. The evidence, not the people."

He was impressed by her challenge even if he didn't quite see what she was getting at. "You aren't a student here, are you?"

She had put her hand to her mouth in sudden alarm. "Oh no, I hope you don't mind. I sometimes just pop in to lectures if I'm passing. I love history, you see. Isn't that allowed?"

That removed the only barrier to asking her to lunch with him and he'd been warming himself in her flame ever since. There had never been any doubt on his part. Frozen photographs rarely caught her beauty, but life showed it: she was always moving, leaving behind a warm trail of returned smiles.

Mike wondered almost constantly what *she* saw in *him*. Perhaps it was history. He responded to her passionate need to discuss what came before, understood it and could stoke the fire with facts. History was soothing to her, sometimes indeed the only way she could be calmed when the unexpected terrible sadness would strike. At her hospital bed after the miscarriage, she had wanted him to tell her old tales of kings and queens.

The offer from Georgetown University had seemed to him like a miracle. It had been in the air for three or four months, but he hadn't mentioned a word to Gally until he knew it was firm. Washington seemed a perfect solution for them. He'd tried to prepare the way, shifting his tales from British to American history, but those stories failed to hold her interest. When he told her outright that he had been offered the teaching job he had always dreamed of, she tried to fake it, tried to pretend there was nothing she would like more than to go to America with him, but the nightmares redoubled and her anxiety during her waking hours was so terrible to see that in the end he asked her outright if the thought of moving scared her. After a long silence she told him that yes, it did.

He'd turned the job down without saying another word, but a small, bitter, irrepressible voice kept telling him he had just given up the best chance his career would ever be offered. It was a heavy, heavy blow to him, and he tried not to mind when it became clear that moving was just exactly what she *did* want as long as it wasn't away from England. He didn't understand the sense of that, but he went along with it because he had never expected to be offered the delight of love and this was nearer than he could have hoped of getting to it, despite the price he had to pay.

So they had started on a quest in which he felt largely a passenger. The villages they visited in search of the haven she needed had been judged by their role in history and almost always found wanting. Only old cottages would do and the ones that came nearest were the ones where the owners could tell a tale or two of their past.

They came to a junction of lanes. "I think we ought to go home," he said. "It's going to take ages to get back to London."

"Just this one, I promise. Penselwood's down there, it says. I want to see Penselwood."

"If you'd said that before we wouldn't have wasted all day round Castle Cary," he grumbled. Then it struck him: "Penselwood? I know that name. A battle?"

She smiled happily, knowing she'd won as he signalled a left turn into the lane.

They did a slow tour of spread-out houses without ever being sure they'd found the centre of the village. There was one "For Sale" sign, but the tiny cottage behind it had carriage lanterns and bottle-glass held in by plastic window frames and they didn't stop. They turned and came back to where the road forked.

"Nothing there," said Mike, relieved that she hadn't decided to knock on anyone's door.

"Try down here," she said, pointing down the fork. "It probably goes back to the main road anyway."

He could see no reason to suppose that was true, but he did what she asked. They went fifty yards down a narrow curving lane and she said, "Stop a minute."

"What for?"

"I don't know. I just want to look."

From anywhere else but that precise spot they might not have noticed it, or so they both supposed at the time, and if they had not their life would have been sharply different, but as soon as Gally got out of the car she saw the ivy-covered silhouette of the chimney poking up behind the trees.

"There's a house in there," she exclaimed in delight. "Right where I wanted it to be."

"A house?" Mike said as he got out to join her. "Where?"

To the north, beyond a sparse screen of trees, pasture stretched uphill. A trio of beeches, tangled with ivy, almost hid the house. Gally was already at the gate, a rotten, slimy thing held by roughly bent wire and twine. There was a small clearing beyond, perhaps a farmyard once, and Mike followed her through, feeling like a trespasser, envying her ease.

The cottage was not much more than a shell, and a green, wet-looking shell at that, though the roof was still on. Long and low, the jumbled lines of its random stonework told of many changes and additions over all the busy years. Stone lintels topped window holes filled only by ivy and from the middle of the house a buckled, wooden latticework porch jutted out, tilting down from the weight of the vine that had massed on it. The door was a sheet of stained plywood, held in place by a diagonal plank that spelt out closure and abandonment. Everywhere there were vines, wild bushes and saplings, nature's demolition team patiently inching apart the mortared joints of man's temporary work.

Gally turned slowly right round with her arms outspread, then hugged herself and jumped up and down. "It's perfect," she declared. "This is it."

Mike felt a cold shudder that started at his chequebook. "It's a ruin."

"That just means no one's had a chance to spoil it."

"It will cost a fortune to fix."

"How do you know?"

"It's not for sale."

"Well, you can't have it both ways. If it's not for sale, it won't cost a fortune. Look," she said. A line of flowers he didn't recognize was pushing its way through the dirt. In front of them, a row of half-round tiles edged what had been a flower bed.

"Come on," she said, grabbing his hand and tugging. "Let's look inside."

The plywood sheet where the door had once been was no obstacle. It was nailed to a rotten frame that crumbled as she pushed it.

"Hang on," he said. "I don't know if we should . . ."

"It's all right." She sounded excited. "No one's going to mind."

It seemed to him suddenly that going inside would be a good idea. The desolation they would find there would persuade her this was not the comfortable country haven she craved and for which they had searched all these past weekends. That overcame his scruples about trespassing, but once indoors he soon found the house was not on his side in this matter. Under the vegetation the roof was obviously still good. It still felt like a house. Gally stopped in front of him, seemed about to speak, but then moved on. They were in a passage that ran the length of the building, filled with green half-light that filtered past the ivy in the empty windows. Four large rooms opened off it. The floor was covered by decaying domestic jetsam—tiles, yellowing gardening magazines and a discarded boiler, red with rust. Below each window there was an arc of damp on the stones, very clearly defined, where the house had said, "Stop, that's far enough." Apart from that it was dry, damaged by intruders, not by weather.

"Oh dear," he said. "It's a bit past it, isn't it?"

Her voice had soft wonder in it. "Poor thing. It's been so brave. All it needs is some love and care."

They went on into the room at the end and he heard her give a small, sad groan. Here the house had suffered its death wound. The far wall was bulging, cracked and crumbled, roof timbers sagging into a gap, unsupported as the gable leaned outwards. In the near corner, steps led down into the darkness of a cellar. Gally moved towards them and the floorboards creaked and cracked under her. Before she got to the first step her foot caught a lump of plaster lying on the boards and it shot forward into a hole, but instead of an eventual thump there was an immediate splash. Mike knelt to a broken board, pulled it out of the way and peered down. Six inches below the boards, black water glinted, sullen, cold and disconcerting.

"It's a stream," he said, aghast. "It's running water." He stood and stepped back, heard a footfall on the boards behind him and knew instantly with a rush of shaming fear that where there had been two of them there were now three.

He turned and his fear veered into embarrassment as he found himself face to face with an old man, gazing at him with grim, questioning suspicion. Two clear eyes locked on his, challenging his presence with disconcerting authority.

2

GALLY FELT SAFE inside the house and though she turned quickly when she heard Mike's gasp, she was not nearly so startled by the old man's sudden presence as he was. When they shared their impressions afterwards she found herself unable to tell Mike the complete truth. They both saw the same man, and on a physical level they both recorded the same information. He was shorter than Mike, a shade under six feet tall, and if his age had started to shrink him, so far it seemed only to have condensed his vitality into a more concentrated form. He looked fit and weathered and his eyes of seafaring blue had escaped the watery weakening of the years. They burned from a face that was tanned and sculpted by the wind over strong cheekbones and a square jaw. Hair flecked dark amongst the grey might have led you to guess his age at somewhere in the sixties and miss the target by a score of years.

Mike saw an authority that made him feel callow, tongue-tied and defensive. Feeling they had been caught where they had no right to be, his own uncertainty sketched a fierceness onto his image of the man's face that, by any objective standard, was certainly not there. Mike felt like an urban intruder. The man who stood staring at him looked as if he owned the place—and not just the house, perhaps, but everywhere round about.

Gally was a searcher of faces. In London she would scan crowds restlessly, incessantly, in shops, on the underground or simply walking down the street. In the first few seconds of Ferney's appearance in her life, she decided there was more to find in this man's face than in any she had ever seen before. Afterwards, when she had time to sort out the tumult he raised in her, she remembered patience coupled with strength; a philosopher king with a sword in one hand and a book of verse in the other. That sounded fanciful enough, but what she really couldn't tell Mike was that a certainty had come bursting into her the moment she'd seen him that this was someone important whom she had been hoping to see for a long time, as if a favourite uncle had finally returned from years abroad.

The old man said nothing and Gally recovered her wits first. "I'm sorry," she told him. "We were just being nosy. Is this yours?"

He continued to weigh her impassively, then his gaze softened a fraction. "No," he said. "Not now."

She smiled at him. "I love it," she said. "It's just . . . well, beautiful."

He looked around, sniffed and looked back at her, searching her face.

"My name's Gabriella Martin," she said, "and this is Mike, my husband."

He just nodded and continued to stare as if used to disappointment.

"And you are?" she prompted, gently.

"My name," he said, with an odd inflection that said other definitions of himself were possible, "is Ferney."

She knew as soon as she heard that name, as a certainty and no longer as a whim, that this was someone she would like very much. Astonished at this, she fended him off with words to give herself space. "It's so sad it should be left to fall apart," she said. "Do you know whose it is?"

"I do. It's private property," he said and she waited, but that was all.

"I'm sorry," said Mike. "Look, Gally, I think we should go and . . ." but the old man's head lifted sharply.

"Gally? Who's Gally?"

She laughed. "That's what I'm always called. I'm sorry, Mike's right. We shouldn't be here."

"No, no. Who gave you that name?" the old man said and she couldn't tell whether it was excitement or anger in his voice.

"I . . . well, I think I gave it to myself. It was all I could say when I was very little." She looked at him in surprise. "I'm sorry if we're trespassing. We ought to go."

But suddenly he didn't want that. "There's no need," he said and now his face relaxed. "No one will mind. Mrs. Mullard, she has the rights to this house now. She lives way down by Buckhorn Weston— never comes up here these days. You look round all you like."

"It's just that we want to buy somewhere in the country, you see. Mike's away a lot and I don't want to bring up a family in the town."

The old man stared at her, seemingly transfixed. "You're having a baby?"

Mike froze inside, watching to see how she would respond. Since the miscarriage, babies had been landmines, surrounding them on all sides. Every casual reference had the capacity to hurl Gally into a deep pit of sadness. Every diaper advertisement or passing baby carriage could trigger tears. Now, to his utter astonishment, she laughed at the old man's interest.

"No, not right away. It's just an idea at the moment."

Ferney was still looking hard at her and a slow smile that seemed to stretch long disused muscles spread across his face. For a moment, until he blinked hard, his eyes caught the light with a faint sheen of tears.

Mike never understood the effortless process by which Gally and the old man stitched it all up between them without, it seemed, using conventional conversation at all. Ten minutes of half-sentences and oblique words left him nothing more than a baffled observer. At the end of it they said goodbye to Ferney at the gate and the old man ambled off up the lane. Mike tugged the gate closed, the rotten string that stood in for a hinge gave way and the whole gate sagged sideways, twisting, diamond-shaped, into the hedge.

"There," she said triumphantly, "you've broken it. Now we'll have to buy it."

He was on the defensive, irritated at being somehow excluded. Certain that she would want to talk about the possibilities, he was preparing a relentlessly logical defence but instead, when they drove off, she went into some sort of a dream. They joined the main road at the same construction site, but this time it had no effect on Gally. That was a relief to him and he left well enough alone. In the end his lecture notes muscled themselves back into his thoughts and all the way to London his mind barely left them except for odd, unguarded moments when it drifted briefly to America and what might have been.

IT WAS THURSDAY before the subject came up again and then she only said, "You're okay for Saturday, aren't you?"

"What for?"

"Houses."

"The tarted-up toolshed at Donhead? I read the brochure. I thought you didn't like it."

"No, not that horrid thing. We're going to Buckhorn Weston."

The name rang no bells. "I haven't seen that one."

"It isn't a one. It's a her. We're going to see Mrs. Mullard. I've written to her."

And so it was that very much against his better judgement they found themselves pulling up in front of a secluded and ramshackle house, flanked by disintegrating outbuildings in paddocks fenced by rusty chicken wire. Mrs. Mullard was an old vixen, an English gentlewoman gone wild, as gnarled as a briar root, and she didn't miss a trick. The door, covered in convex scales of fossilized green paint, was whipped open before they knocked—the curtains had been twitching as they pulled up outside—and Gally was drawn in by a bony hand before she'd had a chance to say a word.

"Come and sit down," commanded the old lady. She would not have been much over five foot two if she stood straight, and her arched spine lopped a further four inches off that. The room into which she led them had its parched floorboards half-covered in patches of linoleum. She settled herself into the one complete article of furniture, a cracked brown leather armchair, and smiled questioningly while Gally and Mike perched on the unpadded frame of an old sofa. Mike expected Gally to say something, but she just smiled back and he felt, with sudden panic, a need to take the initiative.

"We were at Penselwood last weekend," he began, "and—"

"Eggs," said Mrs. Mullard. "I expect you're wondering how we live. It's eggs." She turned and with a stentorian bellow that gave the lie to her apparent octogenarian fragility, yelled "BESSY!"

A grey, slack-mouthed woman, less old but more aged, appeared at the door. Mrs. Mullard wagged a finger at her. "Go and get an egg, Bessy."

Gally stared after Bessy as she departed and Mike watched Gally, as ever, for signs of an unexpected problem, but she seemed on top of the world today, in charge of herself. She'd thrashed awake only once the previous night, then gone back to sleep quickly, though he'd had more difficulty in doing so. Bessy shuffled back and the egg she carried in her large hand was passed around for their solemn inspection.

"Perfect," said Mike. "Lovely brown colour and, er . . ."

"We've got fifty hens now," Mrs. Mullard said.

"We just went to Penselwood by chance," he persisted. "We didn't—"

"Oh yes! Penselwood," she said. "I don't expect you know why it's called that, do you?"

"No."

"There used to be a tunnel from the church to the big house, you know." Mrs. Mullard paused. Mike looked at her expectantly. She beamed. He waited. Gally had said nothing since they arrived and Mike felt he had to go on.

"We happened to see your cottage," he said in a rush. "At least someone said it was yours."

"Riding gloves," she said. "That's another thing we do. We make riding gloves."

Gally leaned forward then and said, as though carrying on some earlier conversation, "Ferney mentioned you might feel the time had come for you to pass it on."

"That's what he said to me."

"You've talked to him?"

"He walked over to see me yesterday."

"Walked?" said Mike. "It's miles."

Mrs. Mullard frowned at him, then turned back to Gally. "I always wanted to get it nice again myself, but sometimes there's no talking to that man." She looked cross for a moment, but then a wry little smile creased her face. "Perhaps he's right. You'll make a better job of it and anyway it's drier here. You can ask him about that, the old rascal. You'll have to undo all that."

Gally nodded as if this made sense. "You're happy about doing this, are you?"

"I suppose I must be."

Mike had lost control again, barely able to believe the speed with which peculiar alliances were being forged all around him. "I'm sorry, I'm not quite with all this. Are you saying you'll sell the cottage to us? Because we'd have to get a survey done and a few things like that."

Mrs. Mullard's face slowly crumpled. She bent farther and farther forward until he was looking at the thin crown of her head, and she began to wheeze. He watched in alarm and then a gout of laughter burst out of her and another and another, an altogether too powerful physical experience for her ancient, tiny frame, as dangerous as boiling tar in a porcelain cup. "A survey?" she eventually gasped. "A survey?"

Gally looked at Mike with an attempt at a straight face. "I think what Mrs. Mullard means," she said, "is that a surveyor will tell you it's a complete ruin and we already know that."

"Yes, yes," said the old lady as the spasms subsided, "but the wall-paper in the end bedroom's very nice, one and tenpence a roll. It should clean up well. Don't let him start digging. That's the main thing. He was always digging. If you take my advice you won't let him near the place at all."

Gally nodded. "It will be all right."

"He'll want to know about the money," said Mrs. Mullard, nodding towards Mike but otherwise treating him as if he wasn't there at all. "I'll write."

TWO DAYS LATER she did write, and what she wrote came as a surprise to both of them, delighting Gally and depriving Mike of his best argument against buying.

"We ought to pay her more than that," said Gally over breakfast. "I don't think we should take advantage of her, do you?"

"I doubt anyone's ever managed to do that. You're the only one who thinks it's wonderful. She knows the place is a ruin and so do I."

"Anyway, we can definitely buy it."

"Just hold on. We can't rush in like that. God knows what it would cost to fix it up. We need builders' estimates, all that sort of thing."

Gally said nothing, looking out of the kitchen window at the west London traffic. Then she tried another tack. "Did you say there was a battle there?"

He looked up from Mrs. Mullard's letter. "Huh?"

"At Penselwood."

"Yes, there was. I looked it up. It's a bit before my period."

"When?"

"Er, seventh century some time—658, I think. Cenwalh, king of Wessex. Also called Cenwalch. Came back from exile, thrashed the Britons at Peonnum, or Peonnan as it's sometimes spelt. One of the turning points of British history, when the Saxons pushed out the Britons. Only thing is, Hoskins insists Peonnum wasn't Penselwood after all. He says it must have been farther west, somewhere much nearer Exeter, though I must say that doesn't seem to square with the Anglo-Saxon Chronicles."

When he focused on her again, Gally was staring at him with a touch of wildness in her eyes. She sighed as if pushing off a sudden pain, then nodded firmly.

"I bet it was Penselwood," she told him. "If we lived there, I'm sure you'd be able to find out."

GALLY GOT HER way and things happened quickly. On a balmy morning in June, without the need for an alarm clock, she shook Mike out of bed at sunrise, pushed his exploring hands gently but firmly away and had him dressed, breakfasted and in the car like some giant schoolboy in the hands of a ruthlessly efficient parent.

"We'll be far too early," he complained. "The caravan's not coming until midday."

"Aren't you excited?" she demanded. "I can't wait to get there. It's ours. Tonight we'll be staying in our very own cottage."

He glanced across at her as he wove in and out of the early morning traffic heading for the M3 and her happiness rubbed off on him. "Not exactly in it," he said, "just outside it, maybe, if the van turns up."

"It will," she said.

They talked then of how it would be, camping out on their new doorstep, of the logistics of water, gas and chemical loos. They'd made this journey four times in the brief month that the purchase had taken and some central doubt still gnawed at him, a doubt he didn't want to take out and examine for fear it might solidify in the light of reason and refuse to go away. It was a muddled doubt all about his centrality in Gally's life, a small, intricate, demanding universe of two. This new venture seemed already to have brought her more peace and happiness than he had seen since they first met, but he was worried that it might be a pipe-dream, that the reality of Penselwood might disappoint her so much that it would provoke a dive to new depths, depths where he might no longer be able to reach her and coax her back, and that was the most frightening thought he knew.

Mike's parents had equipped him perfectly for life in an ivory tower. His father had only spoken to him in awkward mono-syllables as if to a complete stranger. In his patchy, clouded memory of his childhood his mother had been warm and loving once, but that had congealed into a disapproving resentment of the world that had failed her. By the time he was eighteen she hated everything including, to his bewilderment, him. She was almost mad.

Gally had dazzled Mike with the undreamed possibility of love, joy and friendship, although she had warned him straightaway that all was not as simple as he hoped. Confronted and appalled by the evidence of the disabling desperation that would ambush her, he still believed he could help. Her terror seemed to him to be only a thin layer over the essential Gally, a coat of camouflaging paint that he could, given time, rub off. It proved to be persistent paint. The miscarriage had brought the chance of therapy and the counsellor, seeing them both together at the start, took the obvious cues from Mike's prompting. Nightmares? What were they about? Burning. Mike supplied the answer when Gally proved reluctant and what could the counsellor, a wise woman with a creased, warm face, do but embrace such an obvious trauma? Seeing her father die as the flames burst through their twisted car, restrained by the men who had pulled her clear as she fought helplessly to get back to him, was certainly the stuff of nightmares.

For all Mike's hopes, the counselling never even scratched the surface of Gally's troubles. She took it all politely, thanked the woman for her time and her help and went right on having the nightmares. And yet Mike believed he was getting better and better at handling it, that he could usually hold and cajole her back. Life in the country, from her reaction so far, promised much, but it also threatened. He would be farther away, less able to help, and he feared her ability to get through each day without his watchful presence.

Gally glanced at him and perhaps read something of his doubt. "Am I rushing you?" she asked softly.

"No more than usual."

"You'll see I'm right. It's going to be just perfect."

"I don't know what we're getting into," he replied slowly. "Maybe we won't like the people. We haven't really looked at the village at all."

"We can soon fix that," she said briskly. "That's just a treat to come. I'm certain you'll like it." Then she looked at him more gently. "I wish you could feel it like I do. It's like home already."

"I'm sure I will," he said, not totally truthfully.

The process of buying the cottage had brought, unasked and surprisingly unexpected, a name for their new home—Bagstone Farm. The name had disconcerted Mike, with all its implications that the old house carried with it a long history, a known niche within a working community that its camouflaged dereliction had allowed him to ignore. Easier to think of it as just "the cottage," a hidden, forgotten place in which they could start again, a clean slate. Gally didn't see it that way. She'd felt the name was the final perfect touch, repeating it over and over again as she shuffled through all the photographs they'd taken, drawing pictures, planning the slow healing of the injured building.

They were at the village by ten-thirty and, following an instinct that all Mike needed to put him right was something with a touch of age about it, she persuaded him to drive straight to the church, certain it would work some magic on him. It was small and stout, just a nave, a chancel and a low, square tower.

They walked up the path to the porch, Mike slightly ahead as Gally lingered over the gravestones.

"Look at the carving," he said as she joined him outside the door.

"The lamb and the lions," she said without thinking as she obediently looked up.

He laughed. "Not from where I'm standing. Why do you say that?"

She blinked and the stone panel swam into her view like an intruder, a Virgin and two kneeling figures. Abrupt dislocation assaulted her. Mike went into the porch.

"Here's your lamb," he said. "What a doorway! Look at these."

The columns at each side of the door had Norman zig-zags flanking them. Capping the top corners of the door were two fine stone heads, a king and a queen, staring inwards towards each other.

'Til Christmas falls on Candlemas, the King shall never kiss his lass. The words came into her head from nowhere in particular. She said them out loud, a hook for Mike to bite on, hoping he would know and explain but he just looked at her.

"You've been reading up about this place, haven't you?" he asked. "I wish you'd told me."

There was a tiny note of peevishness in his voice. He'd never accused her of secrecy before.

"No," she replied, stung by his tone but confused by that same dislocating sense of *déjà vu.*

She paused and played a deliberate game with herself as she followed Mike into the church, setting an image of the interior in her mind before they opened the door, just to see if there was a reliable memory lurking from her childhood subconscious, but she was disappointed. The dark oak pews in her mind's eye were lower, paler and more intricately carved in real life. The walls were plastered where they should have been whitewashed stone. She'd expected a gallery to her left and there was none. The whole interior of the nave seemed too high, too wide. She sighed, then took Mike's hand to lead him over to admire the Norman font, a square fluted bowl on a round pedestal, knowing he'd like it, seeking to repair the tiny gap between them.

Ferney saw them go inside the church as he came through the churchyard gate. His right hip and ankle were aching that morning, a painful reminder of his encounter with the truck. Down the lane beyond the gate he saw Barbara Nicholls walking back to her house, artificial hip joints swinging away. The Day of Judgement wouldn't be quite so dreadful if the skeletons came crawling up through the mouldering earth to the squeak of pivoting plastic.

The idea of Judgement Day had always made him laugh, to the fury of endless teachers and parsons. Religion in that form held no sway over Ferney, hadn't for goodness knows how long. His purpose today had nothing to do with God. Today he was after information and the churchyard was one of his sources. He walked carefully across the grass, found the stone he was after, knelt and began to rub at the lichen in the indentations to make the date he sought stand out more clearly.

It was in that position a few minutes later, lost in far-off thought, that he was brought back to himself by a man's voice. Him, the husband, out of the church now, standing by the tree, giving his opinions at the top of his voice to her, to Gally. Ferney levered himself up on the old gravestone, feeling it wobble under his hand like a loose tooth.

"Well, that too," the man was saying, looking up into the branches of the great tree, "but yews were always holy trees. Early Christians worshipped under them. They were thought to give immortality. People used to think the yews drew off the harmful vapours that came out of graves."

Ferney snorted to himself, louder than he meant, and the man turned, startled.

"What's all that, then?" Ferney said, "what you were saying?"

"Oh, hello," the man said stiffly. "I didn't see you. I was just telling Gally why yew trees were usually grown in churchyards."

"I heard," said Ferney. "But it's not right, what you said, not the main reason anyway."

The man let a smile slip out before he could catch it. "Oh no?" he said in a tone that irritated Ferney. "Why not?"

"They had to grow yews," Ferney answered. "Needed the wood to make bows. But yew berries, see, they're poisonous. Couldn't grow them just anywhere or the cows would eat them and die. Churchyard was the safest place. No cows in a churchyard."

"I've never heard that one before," said the man.

"You've heard it now," said Ferney, turning his head abruptly to Gally and fixing his eyes on her, his face softening.

"We're moving in today," she said. "Come and see us."

Ferney nodded. "I've got something for you. House-warming gift."

THE CARAVAN WAS on its last legs and an hour late, hauled in slowly by a tractor that sent most of its diesel fuel straight up to spatter the sky with a burnt black cloud. Gally thrilled to the sight of it, the guarantee that this night would really be their first within the boundaries of the space that was now theirs. The farmer took Mike's money with the air of one who'd lost an eyesore and gained an unexpected bonus and looked around with an expression that spoke volumes about the unfathomable ways of town folk in the country.

"You'll have your work cut out here, then," he commented.

"We don't mind," said Gally.

"I've got diggers and all that if you need them," he said, thinking of the wad of Mike's notes in his pocket.

"We might," said Mike. "There's some drainage to sort out."

"You know where to find me. I can send someone down," the farmer said, and soon the tractor's hubbub was fading down the lane.

They weren't left alone for long. Gally was pulling the musty cushions out of the truck to air them in the sun when a white pickup bounced in through the gate and rocked to a halt.

"Mr. and Mrs. Martin? Don Cotton. You phoned me, right?"

The builder. Standing there, adding up the evidence to feed into his estimate. Mike opened his mouth to speak in a deliberately roughened and slurred accent. It wouldn't have fooled the builder for a second, but in any case Gally's educated vowels cut the air before him and he swore to himself.

"Great," she said. "I'm so glad you're here. When can you start?"

The builder was a short man who addressed everything sideways; his body never faced the way he spoke. He had a big jaw and a flattened nose, the face of a man who would fight over imagined insults in his cups.

"In a hurry, are you?" he said.

"Yes," said Gally.

"No, not really," said Mike.

The builder looked first at the cracked and broken gable end of the house, making expensive sucking noises and shaking his head a lot. He picked an unnecessary amount of loose stone and mortar out of the biggest crack in the outer wall, then turned and went inside.

"You've got your own private river," he reported when he'd looked below the floorboards.

"What's the best thing to do?" said Mike.

"Put a pump in. Get it dried out and we'll see what we've got."

"Need more'n a pump," said a voice from the doorway. They looked up and Ferney, a brown felt hat in his hand, was standing there. His white hair was neatly brushed and there was a primrose in the buttonhole of his old tweed jacket.

"Well, you do keep popping up," said Mike, a shade sourly, thinking Ferney should have knocked until he remembered there was no knocker.

"Where else would I be?" said Ferney with a note of surprise.

"Now you're here, can we help you?"

"I can maybe help you," replied Ferney. "If you want. I came with my present."

Gally walked over to him. "That's lovely," she said. "Come and sit outside with me. It was nice of you to take the trouble."

Mike stayed with the builder as the man went on scratching and fiddling his way through the decay, noting large figures in his book which could have been lengths but were probably money, then curiosity got the better of him and he went to join them outside. As he walked into the dark hall, they were framed by the doorway, outside in the sun, warm and bright together. He paused as he realized they were unaware of him there. Gally had sat Ferney on a folding chair on the grass beyond the door and he was handing her a brown paper bag.

The object she drew from it was obscure, a mottled ring of horn perhaps, or some sort of soapstone. Mike couldn't tell. It seemed to have holes around its circumference and areas of latticework. From his position next to her, Ferney watched Gally closely. Mike watched them both from inside, excluded and puzzled. Gally held it in her hands and looked at it, very still, then turned it slowly. She lifted her eyes and she and Ferney stared at each other. Then she rose slowly to her feet, walked a few steps to the tangled grass inside the hedge and began to pick flowers, threading them one at a time into the holes in the ring.

Ferney clasped his hands together, then reached each arm right round and hugged himself as if holding something in. Gally picked faster and faster, laughing out loud, then twirled round and, lifting the ring, a garland now, set it on her head where it nestled, perfectly accenting her hair like a flower fairy in a children's book.

"There," she said, "is that right?"

Ferney nodded silently. Mike felt an oddly bitter pang of annoyance. Gally was always buying hats and hair bands and scarves to wind through her hair but she'd wear them once and put them aside in disappointment. He'd bought many of them himself and always somehow missed satisfying whatever itch drove her after them. Now someone else was basking in the reaction he had never had. He stepped into the sunlight which seemed suddenly less radiantly yellow now and looked closely at the flowers.

"Gally!" he said. "They're cowslips, for God's sake. You're not supposed to pick cowslips. They're endangered. You must have known that, surely?"

She stared at him, affronted, as if she didn't recognize him, and put a hand slowly to her head. He wished he could open his mouth and draw the words and their sting back in from the echoing air, then she looked at Ferney and Mike saw her eyes widen. With two quick steps, she crossed the space to where Ferney sat and Mike moved forward too, struck by the alarm on her face.

Tears were rolling down Ferney's cheeks.

"You knew, you knew," the old man said in a rusty, cracked voice full of acutely painful joy, then before they could do anything he was up and away through the gate as if it was all too much to bear.

"You didn't have to say that," Gally cried, turning to Mike in pain, and neither of them recognized her voice.

FERNEY'S HIP WAS hurting again as he sat down, but none of it mattered, not one bit. The sun came bursting out from behind a cloud, painting the hill bright green, a mirror of the exultant joy roaring and bubbling up through his chest. Everything had changed, years of loneliness—the longest years he could ever remember—

swept away. Hope had been restored. There was work ahead, it was true, and it might not be easy, but the house was going to live again and so was he. There'd been an agreement made.

Sitting on his stone right at the top of the hill, he looked out over a familiar landscape, south across all the flat lands to the old fortress hill of high Shaftesbury far away. A trace of mist rose from the fields below, thickest along the course of the river. From the main road, invisible down there, modern noise intruded in a drone of engines, rising and falling. He let his gaze wander across the landscape, changing, tuning as it went. The pylons in the valley flicked out and the cluster of new houses beyond them melted like butter. Ferney had a firm hold now and the road's noise no longer reached him. The woods writhed, grew ragged and stretched their boundaries; the fields divided themselves with old, forgotten walls and a hard, brash metal shed shrivelled back into a barn of sagging tile and stone.

He heard a girl's voice in his mind, conjured her singing a scrap of a favourite song, holding it there, using it to bleach out the upstart stains of the present and to paint in the true colours of the past. He slowly turned his head and there she was next to him on the bench, leaning weightless against him, her blond hair cascading over his neck, both arms round his shoulders. Sixty years slipped from him and he heard her voice properly, talking, not singing.

"We *can* do it," she said. "We can if we set our minds to it. No more of this hit-and-miss."

He'd needed no persuading. "It will be so much better," he told her. "There's never been joy with anyone else. It's only worth it when you're here."

"Are we agreed, then?" She'd lifted her head as her ghost, her memory, now did again, staring at him with a great, wide, joyful smile. "Shall we swear to it, swear we'll always, always do it whatever?"

"Yes." Then the problem struck him. "What if one of us forgets?"

"Then the other one has some reminding to do, that's all." She'd laughed as though that were the easiest thing in the world, laughed and tousled his hair.

"And if both of us forget?"

She stopped laughing then. "Well, maybe that will just have to be that if both of us forget." Then with renewed vigour, "But we won't, we mustn't. Other folks have God. We've only got *us*."

Ferney shook his head, amused at the old argument. "You don't know they've got God. You can't be sure. Could be we're luckier than them. They just stop, maybe."

They'd finished with talking then. He'd held her at arm's length, loving her, admiring her, drinking in the garland on her head set in the old hoop, feasting on the rich emotion of six decades earlier, a time when cowslips were plentiful, his dry old soul soaking it up like a parched plant under the watering can. He held the garland in the centre of his mind, thinking of today, of Gally now. Gally who, if she knew nothing else for sure, knew it for what it was and wove her garland without a questioning word.

The scene fluttered, shifted. Unthinking until it was too late, Ferney had kept the image of the garland on a dark head. The dark head was still there, a dark, loved head but not the same one.

It was the first time he'd given the garland hoop, the very first time, after he'd dug it from the pits. Just for confirmation he looked hard at the edge of the woodland, the straight, neatly trimmed edge—a landscape assaulted by geometry. From below the crest of the hill, old shouts crawled back to him across four long lifetimes. In his memory he walked down to them and saw a red, sweating zealot in a stained smock. Parson Mowbray, egging on his axe-men with crazed shouts as he peered down the line of his sighting sticks, glorying in the crash of timber.

"Not that one, damn you! Foil me with imperfections, would you? Hurry up down there. This is a race that we are running, Jonah, and unless you swing your axe the trees will beat us. They're growing faster than you can cut. That branch there, man, that and the one above it. They're spoiling my line. This is God's work, Jonah. The turmoil of nature is an insult to Him. We neglect the great gift He has given us if we let nature sprawl rampant across our inheritance."

All around, the landscape had taken on the geometric shapes that marked the silly fad of that temporary landscape. Queen Anne was dead and the foul-tempered German George had come from Hanover with his two mistresses. Every country conversation about the new king started with "He doesn't even speak English" and ended with "Well at least he's no Catholic." Some great daftness seized the country and raw nature became a threat to man's God-given right to dominate. The flailing Church, confusing nature with debauchery, saw threatening sexuality in every burgeoning hedge and went to work with sharpened steel to hack it back. Straight lines cut the countryside wherever you looked—fields, hedges, orchards, woods, all penned back to fantastic regularity in pursuit of some ideal of human domination, buttoned up into safe chastity.

Ferney smiled at the memory as he let it fade away—mad Mowbray,

the trees planted in intersecting rows, the squares, triangles and dia-
monds of woodland, a giant, hopeless, frightened child's picture of
the way the world should be. In the end he was left as he wanted to
be in the deep loving circle of this girl, whose face he could not quite
bring back, and a love which, even when diluted by memory, still had
the power to shake him.

3

UNACCUSTOMED EXHILARATION POURED through Gally the second she awoke. For once there was no sour-headed legacy of disturbed sleep. The scents and sounds of a fresh spring morning infused the caravan—beaming in, barely diminished by its thin walls and loose windows to where she lay on old foam and hardboard, curled against Mike's back in their zipped-together sleeping bags. She raised her head, but even that small movement sent a shiver through the trailer's flimsy joints. Hearing the change in Mike's breathing, she froze, unsure for a moment whether she was ready to share the pure experience of the first morning. He grunted, questioningly. She kissed the back of his neck.

"Morning, Micky. Stay there. I'll make the coffee."

A tee-shirt and shorts were enough and her bare feet met fresh dew as she stepped down from the cold ridged edge of the doorway. The house faced her, low and blurred by its green wrap of vegetation. Hers. Theirs. The edge of the sun was just crawling up over its roof and a magpie burst out of a dark top window with a clatter. One for sorrow, she thought, not believing it, but its mate followed. Two for joy. There was certainly joy to be found here. Now she did believe.

She stood there, gazing at it while the sun climbed fully into view. Keeping the greenness, that was what mattered. She wouldn't let it be raped, cleared away by builders who would only think of coercing the old walls into some dispirited forgery of a brand-new house. It had to be done, but it had to be done with care and love. She wanted it to stay just as it was now with only the grosser abuses of age set right. Almost just as it was, anyway. As she looked, straining to picture the perfect outcome, one detail kept imposing itself, something that was skewing it off-centre, not quite right.

Mike was shifting around as she boiled the kettle, but he didn't fully awake until she sat down carefully on the end of the bed and tried to find a place for his coffee mug among the ill-fitting foam cushions that filled the end of the caravan.

For a moment he thought of complaining at the early hour and the thinness of the mattress, but the joy radiating out of her snuffed out the negatives before they had a chance to form. There was a languorous ease in his limbs despite the bed, which brought home the fact that the night had been unbroken by the customary cycle of startled fright and calming words.

"You slept through," he said.

She nodded, smiling. "Oh Mike," she said, "it's so wonderful. Come on. I want to show you. Let's walk round the village before anyone else is up. We'll have breakfast when we come back. Everything's perfect. It's just what I've always wanted. We mustn't let the builders cut the vines down. Oh, and the front door's all wrong."

He put his hands over his ears and dived completely inside the sleeping bag. She smiled happily, threw his clothes at the lump where his head was and went back outside.

There were two ways to the village from the junction at the top of their lane. They took the long way, up to the right, the narrow road climbing between trees which opened out to small fields. Mike, infected by Gally's delight, felt the stirrings of his professional interest as they walked on and on past scattered knots of houses and came eventually to the church.

"It's really extraordinary," he said. "There's no centre to the village at all. We must have come at least a mile and there's still more of it. All these footpaths and little lanes. And look at the field boundaries too. It's still completely medieval."

"I love it," she said, leaning on the churchyard wall. "Can't you just feel it all? There's so little modern clutter to get in the way."

Mike looked at her, scraping the toe of his shoe in the road uncertainly. "The old man," he said abruptly. "Yesterday. What on earth was all that about?"

At that moment she didn't want to think about it, didn't want to speculate on something that had left her wondering herself.

"It was just a gift. I thought it was sweet of him."

"You don't usually like wearing . . ." The word escaped him. Hats? Head bands? ". . . that sort of thing."

"Oh nonsense, I'm always buying them."

Buying them, not wearing them, he wanted to say, but was reluctant to spoil the mood.

"When you put the flowers in it, he was crying."

She was silent, frowning a little, looking past him into the middle of nowhere.

"I think he was just happy."

"Well, I think he's a bit round the bend. I'm not sure we should encourage him."

For an illogical second, a passionate denial flared up inside Gally. The garland ring had touched her. She almost felt it had brought her the good luck of a good night's sleep and a perfect awakening.

"Mike," she said, keeping her tone to mild reproach. "There's no harm in him. Maybe I remind him of someone. Don't be horrid about him." She looked around, feeling a need to deflect the conversation. On the corner by the church was a wooden post topped by the village name in wooden letters, framed like an inn sign.

"Look," she said. "The sign spells it as two words. Pen Selwood."

"I noticed that when we drove in. The signs when we came into the village are the same," said Mike, "but it's joined up into one word on all our maps, Penselwood."

The church clock struck seven. From round the corner came an old woman, as wide as she was high. Although the morning promised nothing but sunshine, she wore a pink plastic hood knotted under her chin. White curls spilled out around it, framing a face so startlingly flat that it looked like a plate. Her cheeks seemed to stick out further than her tiny nose, and the mouth below, though outlined by generous lips, made little use of the acres of space available to it. Even from fifty feet she was twinkling at them and the twinkling grew with each step nearer. They stopped talking, frozen by the appearance of this force of nature.

"Morning, my muffeties," she said in a squeak laden with good humour. "I like to see early risers. Caravan all right, is it?"

This greeting seemed to short-circuit all the conventional possibilities for introducing themselves to someone they were both quite sure they'd never met. Mike shot Gally a startled look. "Yes, thanks," he said. "How did you know, I mean, have we, er . . . ?"

She stabbed him in the ribs with a playfully violent finger. "Get on with you. You're Mr. and Mrs. Martin. 'Course you are," as though they needed convincing of it. "I'm Mary Sparrow. Anything you want to know, don't ask me, cos I always get it wrong."

"You didn't get that wrong," said Gally. "We're just having a look round to get our bearings."

"That's right, my muffety," said Mary, beaming. "Looking's free. You do all the looking you like and if anyone says otherwise, you say I said it was all right." She pointed past the church. "Up there. That's where the battle was."

"Battle?" said Mike. "Peonnum, you mean?"

She cocked her head on one side and studied him. "You do what you like on 'em," she said, and shrieked with laughter. "More like drop rocks on 'em, I expect. Proper battle, my muffety," she went on when her laughter subsided. "Seven hundred dead, there were. Vikings. That's what I were always told, but then I expect I've got that wrong too." She looked past him. "Here's someone coming as might tell you better, though as often as not he don't have the time of day for strangers."

They looked round and Ferney, walking towards them with a touch of leftover stiffness, split the morning into Gally's delight and Mike's reserved mistrust.

"Knows everything there is to know, roundabouts," said Mary Sparrow in a stage whisper. "And so he should at his age. Eighty something, he is."

"Surely not," said Gally and looked again at him, moving at ease through his landscape, outlined in bright morning light. His eyes were fixed on her and held her gaze.

"Mr. Miller," called Mary. "Come and meet these two. They's new."

"I've met them already, Mrs. Sparrow, thank you."

He stopped in front of them, gave Mike an almost unnoticeable nod and addressed himself to Gally. "How are you this morning?" he asked and smiled.

"Very well indeed," said Gally emphatically, unaccountably glad to see him.

"Tell them about the battle," shrilled Mary Sparrow. "Don't be wasting their time with chat. They're busy."

"No we're not," said Gally. "Really."

"Go on. Tell 'em about Kenny Wilkins and the seven hundred dead."

Ferney turned on the old woman in mock rage. "Be off with you, Mary. You've got it all wrong. I'll tell them what I like. Go and bother someone else."

The old woman broke into gales of high-pitched laughter and stumped off. Ferney looked at each of them in turn. The eager kindness with which he gazed at Gally faded to a guarded, closed expression when he turned to Mike.

"We were just looking round the village," said Gally. "Trying to get to know it a bit." A flicker of expression seemed to pass over Ferney's face and she stopped. "Are you all right?"

"Yes, 'course I am," he said, rather abruptly. "What did that silly old woman tell you?"

"Just that there was a battle with the Vikings behind the church. Seven hundred dead, she said." Gally paused and looked round at Mike, inviting him into the conversation, but he kept his mouth shut so she went on. "Mike wanted to know if that was the famous battle. Peonnum or something."

"Well, it was a famous battle all right," said Ferney, "but not that one. Edmund Ironside and Canute's Danes, I suppose that was the one Mary meant. You want to know about Peonnum—that's a different business. You have to go up there a ways." He indicated the lane leading north.

Not on your life, Gally thought—then immediately, *how silly.*

A mile or more off, rising above the tops of the trees in the direction he indicated, was the summit of a tall tower.

"Is that it? Where that building is?" asked Gally, knowing only after she'd said it that it wasn't.

"That's Alfred's Tower." Ferney's tone was derisive. "It's just a modern bit of nonsense. Got nothing to do with Alfred at all. You don't go that far. Where you want is Kenny Wilkins' Camp." He was watching her closely and she again felt uncomfortable.

Mike wasn't interested in the tower or the old man's directions. "Peonnum probably didn't happen here," he said stiffly. "The battle was much further west. No one believes it was here anymore."

Gally's heart sank at the didactic superiority of his tone. That wasn't at all what he'd said before. Ferney's claim had clearly had a perverse effect, moving Mike to an opposing view on the matter.

Ferney looked at him mildly, "So I'm no one, am I?" he said. "And all the other people round here, they're no one?"

"What do you mean?" asked Mike cautiously.

"Everyone born here knows about the battles. Handed down from father to son. Old Kenny Wilkins and all that."

Until then Mike had been thinking that Kenny Wilkins' Camp was perhaps some caravan site. He was suddenly struck by a preposterous thought. "Kenny Wilkins? You don't mean Cenwalch?"

"Last few hundred years, they've called him Kenny Wilkins round here. Easier to remember."

"Look." Mike was almost at a loss for words. "Cenwalch fought

34   J A M E S   L O N G

the battle of Peonnum in 658. That's more than thirteen hundred years ago. Are you saying we should believe people here *remember* that?"

"You believe what you like," said the old man. "All I'm telling you is that's what people round here have told their children going back generations. They've called him Kenny Wilkins for donkey's years and they call that place his camp or sometimes his castle, depending on how the mood takes them."

"For, let's see now, sixty generations?" said Mike incredulously. "Cenwalch becomes Kenny Wilkins and that's supposed to be evidence?"

"So what's *your* evidence then?" asked Ferney, and he smiled at Gally. Gally immediately felt guilty, caught in a cross-fire, her loyalty challenged. She turned away and began to study the parish notice board.

Mike adopted a lofty tone. "There's evidence of West Saxon settlement around Exeter far too soon after 658 for the battle to have been here."

"What sort of evidence?" Ferney insisted.

Mike faltered. "Conclusive archaeological evidence," he said, and it sounded lame even to him.

Ferney just smiled. "You go down Exeter way then and you ask around there. See if they remember Kenny Wilkins." He waved dismissively at Mike, turned to go off in a direction that took him past Gally a few paces away, muttered something to her, then walked off without a backward glance.

In silence, they headed back towards the house. Finally Mike turned to Gally and said, "All right then. What have I done?"

"Well," she said judiciously, "you *were* a bit snotty."

"Snotty?" he repeated indignantly. "He comes up with all that nonsense and you call *me* snotty?"

"Who says it's nonsense? You should listen to people like that."

"Folk memories? If historians took folk memories seriously, there wouldn't be any history books and we'd all be making offerings to tree spirits."

"Double whammy," she said. "Both ways there'd be more trees left."

It was too good a morning to argue and she suddenly felt protective towards Mike, knowing intuitively but without being able to explain it that what he felt towards Ferney was partly jealousy.

"Come on, professor," she teased, "I'll make you some scrambled eggs and you can look through the history books and tell me how long ago they were laid."

They walked down the road with their arms round one another, peeping on tiptoe over the hedge as they approached the house to enjoy previously unseen views of their overgrown ruin, tucked under its hillside.

Over breakfast, his mouth full, Mike said, "We never did ask him about the Danes and the seven hundred dead. I wonder what that's all about."

"We'll ask him next time," said Gally cheerfully and refilled his mug.

"He keeps turning up, doesn't he?" said Mike morosely. "I suppose there's bound to be a next time."

"It is his village."

"Ours too. Anyway," he said, putting down his knife and fork, "what was he mumbling to you at the end there?"

She smiled at him. "He said, and I quote, 'Kenny Wilkins had red hair and a bloody bad temper but don't tell your husband because he'll never believe it.' "

JUST AS A job of work can be good, cheap or fast, but not more than two out of those three, so luxury and lightweight caravans don't go together except at a forbidding price. At the end of a long day spent measuring, planning, considering options and merely probing the masking undergrowth around the limits of their new home, Gally and Mike had been driven by a sudden, chill gust of rain into their flimsy box. They would both have liked a bath, but the plastic cupboard that doubled as washroom and chemical loo contained only brittle, discoloured remains of a shower system that looked unlikely to have worked even in the far-off days when it was new. Instead Gally heated soup on a gas ring, spreading a cloying warmth around the caravan, and dumped the dirty mugs into a sink that seemed to bow a little even under their minute weight.

Now she sat upright at the table, cramped into a constriction of right angles by the severe geometry of foam rubber and plywood. She was drawing plans, sheets of paper spread around with ideas for the house, lists of priorities. The main picture was the front of the house as she saw it in her mind's eye, the ghosts of former beauty restored, each window back in place. She kept trying to draw it to her satisfaction but the front door, and with it the symmetry of the house, stayed obstinately wrong.

She glanced over to where Mike was jammed onto the small seat next to the sink, deep in a book. It wasn't that they hadn't talked. Outside, they had batted their discoveries and their thoughts back and forth, with lots of "Look over heres" and "How abouts." Now, inside, she wanted a female exchange, her hopes and fears traded for his. It was what she needed to tidy up the debris of the day, especially on this day when, for once in her life, her hopes had a chance of outnumbering her fears.

Gally hated her own neuroses, the phobias that she had never been able to confront. She had a deep, abiding gratitude to Mike that he had patiently taken them on, that when nothing else worked, in the terrors of the night, the terrors of boilman and burnman, he would sit there holding her until she was calm again, never breathing a word of reproach, never showing except in his tired face the cost to himself of her nightmares. He had even found a side way into the village which he always took, never mentioning it, so they wouldn't have to pass the road construction in case it still retained the power to terrify her.

She looked at him for longer now, seeing that she was unobserved, fond and grateful but wishing suddenly that her connection to him was deeper and broader, and feeling guilty as soon as she did so. When they married she had believed that fullness would come in time. Here perhaps it would, but even as the thought came she was no longer sure. Mike was deep in his reading, his own sort of mental balm, and she knew he would be just slightly irritated if she forced him out of it. She studied him in silence. He was folded round the book like a collapsed music stand, all legs and elbows, frowning in concentration. A funny man for her—long, angular, direct, sharp as a knife, not at all the sort with whom she had ever thought she would be trying to build a life. She had thought he might be a key to the great locked room she could feel inside her. He could sometimes help her put the experience of *now* into the context of *then*, feeding fuel to the fire of her wish to know how the world had ticked its way to the present. Sometimes, but not always.

He looked up at her, sensing her gaze, and gave a little faraway smile. His hands, holding the book, moved slightly and she saw the word "Saxon" in the title. In the brief moment before he looked down again, she wrested his attention to her in the way most likely to succeed.

"Cenwalch," she said. "I want to know more about him. Do you know anything else?"

Mike smiled, yawned and stretched. "That's what I've been reading," he admitted. "I wasn't quite sure of my facts." He put the book down. "Actually I've just found something else as well. It was probably here that King Alfred rallied his supporters before he defeated the Danes."

That delighted her. "Aha. You mean folk memories might just have something?"

"Folk memories? Balls," he retorted. "Contemporary documented sources. Alfred's chum Bishop Asser wrote it down at the time. In the seventh week after Easter, Alfred gathered the surviving fighting men from the area at the Egbert Stone. Asser says it was somewhere he calls Brixton in the eastern part of Selwood Forest. There's a stone right here that they claim is the one."

She was delighted. "I see, Pen Selwood. What does Pen mean?"

"A clearing."

"So Mrs. Wotsit was right about her seven hundred dead?"

"Not that time. Alfred's battle happened in the early summer of 878 and it wasn't here. The Saxons marched off once he'd got his army together. The battle itself was nearly twenty miles away, somewhere round Warminster."

"Oh," she said, disappointed, "no seven hundred then," but he was in a generous mood.

"Well yes," he said smiling. "There were two battles a bit later on. The Danes came back in 1001 and apparently burnt the place to the ground, then fifteen years later Edmund Ironside thrashed them and that was definitely here. That one's the seven hundred dead."

"Old Ferney was right, then?"

"It's no great secret. Everyone agrees about it. It was a crucial battle—one of the steps on the way to uniting England." Mike was animated now, warming to it. "It's no accident, you see. This place was in one hell of a spot—a real bottleneck of key routes, one of the gateways to Wessex. Selwood Forest was one huge barricade right across the neck of the west and the tracks through it met here. Just imagine, miles and miles of it, all fallen trees and roots and brambles. Completely impenetrable unless you had loads of time and a sharp axe. If you wanted to take the quick route to get through it, you had to come this way and all these ridges and dips round here made it a great place to plan an ambush."

"What about Kenny Wilkins?"

"Umm," he said. "Well, I don't know. His name is usually given as Cenwalh, but sometimes there's a 'ch' on the end. You've got to see it all in context."

That was code for "Don't interrupt, this may take some time."

"Tell me," she said, because this was when she felt closest.

"Okay. The Romans had gone and what they'd left behind was pretty chaotic. Fat cats, merchants and bureaucrats still trying to live like nothing had changed. Now, I'm sure I've told you, the Romans had always hired German mercenaries to look after their turf round here, so the British chieftains thought they'd do the same."

She knew it, but she let him talk.

"Anyway, come the early sixth century the Scots and the Picts up north started threatening the south so the British chieftains hired a load more Saxons to help out. The trouble was the British didn't get round to feeding and paying them properly, which is not very sensible when you've got a well-armed cuckoo polishing its armour in the middle of your nest. The Saxons' homelands were getting very overcrowded, but the whole of Britain had less than a million inhabitants. It must have seemed like heaven, so they moved in and grabbed the south. Their mates the Angles came in and took over a bit further upcountry and after that the poor old Britons were easy pickings. There was only one thing that stopped the Saxons spreading west. Do you know what that was?"

She thought she did, but she shook her head.

"Selwood Forest," he said. "Coit Maur, the Britons called it, the Great Wood."

The name rang in her head, wild and thrilling.

"The Great Wood stopped the Saxons heading further west. So they settled in the lush river valleys round Salisbury and got a bit soft. The Britons from the Great Wood started fighting back and gave them a bit of a pasting, so the Mercians, who had moved into the Midlands, came down to help sort it out."

He saw the flush on her face and wondered, as he always did, that the dry dust of history had such direct, warm impact on her. "This is where your Kenny Wilkins comes in. The Mercian king was called Penda and he did a deal with your Kenny. Cenwalch was king of Wessex, you see, and he married Penda's sister to glue it all together. Anyway, something went wrong. Kenny didn't fancy Penda's sis, maybe, and he gave her the push, so Penda exiled him to East Anglia. Then Penda screwed up. He took a huge army up north and got himself killed by a tiny bunch of Oswy's Bernicians—Northumbrians, if you like. He must have been pretty incompetent."

"So Kenny was back on top?"

"Cenwalch came back from exile and took charge, but he had all these young bloods who were demanding land of their own and the best bet was to the west. Every other direction had seasoned armies blocking the way, but the west, beyond the Great Wood, was anyone's guess. So in 658, Kenny Wilkins and his men took on the Britons at Peonnum and that was pretty much that for the Britons—next stop Cornwall and I hope you like large lumps of granite in your farmland."

"Poor Britons," she murmured, and she really felt it, turning his words into a mental landscape of burning huts and people fleeing terror-struck into unfamiliar lands.

"I don't know. They've done quite well down in Cornwall. They've been ripping off the tourists ever since."

"So, it could easily have been here, couldn't it?"

"What?"

"The battle. Peonnum?"

"There's no direct evidence."

"Just a long tradition?"

"Just a long tradition."

She looked at him, transported, warm and open, and they both stood up. She nestled into his arms. "I love listening to you like that," she said.

"I know, but I still don't know why."

She kissed the side of his neck. "It all makes more sense. I feel . . . fuller maybe, as if there's more of me alive."

"Medieval history as an erogenous zone?" he said in tones of mock wonder.

"Do you have that effect on all your students?"

"I wish I did," he said and kissed her hard.

They swayed together towards the seat cushions, but the gap was too narrow and the folding table jammed in Mike's back.

"Oh God," he said. "The caravan as contraceptive."

There were a few seconds of silent hurried work as they collapsed the table into the gap and tried to remember the brain-teasing arrangement of the cushions that more or less added up to a mattress, then their clothes were on the floor and the caravan was creaking and complaining, semaphoring their lovemaking to the darkening world outside.

Gally swayed over Mike, leaning down to kiss him as she moved, seeing unbidden in her head a kaleidoscope of faces that would keep superimposing themselves over his, strangers' faces that seemed far from strange. At the moment when she should have been centred on the small compass of their own unity, she was seized instead by an overpowering, bewildering and wonderful feeling that the whole of her surroundings had reached in and drawn the envelope of her body outward so that she encompassed the trees, the stream, the walls and all the diffuse green life that made up the old farm. It was a wild, pagan moment and as she felt the accelerating stirrings of their movement she looked up and seemed to see straight through the trailer wall to the house beyond, where a phalanx of unknown friends were silently cheering. In the climax that immediately followed, the old plywood sagged under them, sliding them sideways against the base of the seat and she knew for absolutely certain in that same second that she was now with child.

4

IT WAS ONLY when he heard the racket of an unsilenced exhaust approaching down the lane that Mike remembered to tell Gally.

He poked his head in through the open doorway. "Hey! Here's the guy who's coming to do the digging. I never thought he'd arrive so early." He said it as if she should know about it.

Gally put down her coffee mug and went outside. "Digging?" she said.

"You know, to find where the water's coming from."

"No, I don't know. Who is he?"

He heard the storm warning in her voice, cursed himself for carelessness and sought refuge in evasion.

"He works for that farmer. Surely I told you."

A yellow bulldozer swayed in through the gate in a series of jerks accompanied by blasts of noise punched upwards in gouts of black smoke from its exhaust pipe.

"Hold on, Mike," Gally called after him as he went to meet it. "We haven't talked about this. Oh, hell!" she said, and went after him.

The driver was young, with a thin, indoors face. He turned off the motor, ignoring them completely, and began to fiddle with a newspaper and a sandwich box, shielded by the glass walls of his cab. Gally was appalled by the size and the brutality of the machine. The rusting, bent spikes along the front of its battered shovel spelt violent ruin. This wasn't the right tool for their first overture to the house, of that she was sure. This was a tank, a battering ram, a diesel rapist.

"Mike, we can't do it like this," she said. "It's going to make a terrible mess."

He looked harassed. "What did you expect, love? We can hardly do it with a trowel."

"You should have asked me. There must be another way. I can use a spade."

"I did say someone was coming to look at the water."

"Oh, come off it. That's like saying Genghis Khan was doing voluntary service overseas."

Mike looked at her, seeing the extent of her distress and how much further it might go. He was about to reply when the driver finally opened his door and climbed down, silencing them both. He nodded to them and scratched his chin. There was a lot of it to scratch. Some twist in his DNA had given him far more chin than forehead, giving the impression, confirmed as soon as he began to talk, that his mouth rather than his brain led the way.

"So what's it all about then?" he asked, looking around.

"We need to dig a channel," said Mike.

"We're just discussing it," said Gally simultaneously.

The driver looked at them and shrugged. Gally knew she hated him already.

"You discuss it all you like," he said. "The meter's running." Then to her amazement and indignation he walked over to the corner of the house, unzipped his fly without a second's hesitation and released a stream of steaming urine onto the corner of the stonework.

"Where the HELL did you find HIM?" Gally hissed.

"I told you. The farmer, wotsisname, Durrell. He works for him."

"We can't let him do it. He won't do it right."

"Look, Gally," Mike hissed as the man was zipping himself up, "you can't make an omelette without breaking eggs. There's no easy way of draining that water without making a mess. We've got to do it." He addressed himself to the driver. "Sorry, I didn't get your name."

"Slash."

"Sorry?"

"Slash. You know, like Guns 'n' Roses." He mimed playing an invisible guitar with a lot of unnecessary hip movement that went on for far longer than necessary. Gally looked at the corner of the house where steam was still rising. More likely to be from his personal habits, she thought.

"Right. Slash. Er, it's just that we need to be very careful not to do too much damage. We've got to find where the water's coming from, okay? Then we want to dig a channel to steer it away from the house."

Slash looked around and whistled for a bit. "Going to be a mess," he said eventually. "Can't help it, can you? I mean, water and dirt, what you got? You got a mess, right?"

"Well, surely, if we start at the house where it's coming in and just follow it backwards?" said Gally, fighting to be reasonable.

Slash laughed. "You ever seen it done? Scoop it out, the water comes in, don't it? Sodding hard to see where it's coming from. I'll have a go, but don't expect miracles."

"There must be some way of telling," said Mike. "Suppose we dug holes here and there to see which ones fill up?"

"Yeah," said Slash, "or get one of them meters the Water Board uses." For a moment, they thought he was being helpful but he soon dispelled that. "Only thing is, I'm here now, aren't I, so there's fifty quid on the clock for that and it'll be ticking up while you're messing about."

"What about a water diviner?" Gally said. Neither of the two men bothered to reply. She found her hands clenching at her sides. All the frustration she felt at the brutal arrogance of ignorant men was focused in her fists. Mike was wearing a hunted expression. She looked at him, then past him as a man walked slowly into view along the lane, a man who would help—Ferney.

She ran to the gate and Ferney stopped, his face lighting up with a degree of expectation that astonished her.

"Good morning," he said. "How is it with you?"

"Fine," she said. "Well, no. Not fine at all. We've got a problem. I just thought you might have an idea."

"Go on then."

"This horrible man's come to dig some drainage ditches and we don't know where the water's coming from and I'm absolutely certain he's going to ruin the whole place if we leave him to it and I just can't stand that happening and I thought, well, you knowing the place so well, you might . . . have some idea." She trailed off, thinking it sounded quite silly, but he smiled at her with an expression that stripped years from his age and brought a huge involuntary smile from her in exchange. She felt much better after that.

"I think I might," he said, and she opened the gate for him.

She followed him over to the other two. "Good morning, young Eric," said Ferney to the digger driver and the unmasked Slash looked a little sheepish.

" 'Morning, Mr. Miller," he said.

Ferney made a tiny nod to Mike and turned and surveyed the house, glancing back at Gally as if considering. He went to the right-hand end of the wall, thought for a bit and tapped at the ground with his stick.

"It started coming in about here," he said, and Gally pushed a broken piece of wood into the earth to mark the spot. He turned and stared toward the trees up the slight slope, parallel to the road. After a minute or two of concentration, he walked slowly past the caravan to the hedge about thirty yards from the house.

"Back here, I'd say," he called, pointing again. "A line from here to the house."

Gally, following him, pushed in another stick. "A straight line?" she asked.

"Near enough." He considered again. "Get young Eric to start at this end, in case I'm a bit off, and tell him to go gently."

Slash started up his machine, noncommittal. Mike, his face showing strong reservations, came to watch. The bulldozer crashed through the undergrowth, crushing a bush, and Gally winced. It rocked to a stop, pivoted, and the shovel came down for its first gouge of earth. It was on the third scoop that they heard, over the noise of the engine, a scraping sound. Looking into the hole, they saw that the bulldozer had uncovered the top of an earthenware pipe.

"Whoa, there! Stop!" Mike called urgently to Slash and pounded on the side of the cab with his fist as the shovel reared up again.

They looked into the hole.

"It's a drain, for God's sake," Mike said crossly. "A drain or a water main. Lucky it didn't break."

"Drains don't run uphill," Gally objected, "and you told me the main's water came straight in from the road."

They both looked at Ferney. "Well, whatever it's doing there, that's your answer," he said. "You follow that down and you'll see I'm right."

Mike wasn't happy but they did it anyway. Slash was bullied into exercising restraint, scooping the earth out in conservative steps until he scraped the pipe and piling it beside the trench as he went. It still made a mess, but at least it was a dry mess and within half an hour it was clear that the pipe did indeed run in a straight line towards the wall. They did the last bit with a spade while Slash ate his lunch. Ferney sat on a stone throughout, seemingly content to soak up the sunlight. When they got near the wall of the house, they found they were digging into dampness. The pipe ended just two inches short of the wall and they could see the slow stream of water emerging from the end of it, making its way through the gaps in the stone into the cellar beyond.

Mike and Gally looked at each other. "It's as if someone did it on purpose," said Mike. "What other reason could there be?"

"Perhaps someone tried to put in a water supply and they made a mess of it?"

Mike considered, scowling. "If it went through the wall and there was a tap or something, okay maybe, but it never even went through the wall, there's no hole. It's not the usual water pipe, is it? It's much bigger. Whatever, it should have been easy enough to put right. Someone just let it flood the house. Anyway, how did the old man know?"

"Ask him."

Mike looked uneasy. "You ask him. He just looks straight through me."

Gally went to Ferney and sat down next to him.

"That's good, then," he said. "You can fix it now. Put it back as it was."

"I suppose so," she said, "but what was it? Why did someone put the pipe there?"

"Some daft idea, I expect," he said, looking hard at her. "Someone probably had a good reason."

She knew that was all she was going to get out of him. "I suppose now we have to decide what to do with it."

He pointed with his stick past the end of the house. "Like I said, put it back where it was. It was a stream, you see, flowed under the ground as far as that tree, then came out and went down the valley."

She could see it in her mind's eye and in the mental picture it carried with it a measure of life missing in the decay around her now.

"Can you remember exactly how it was?"

"Every inch," he answered cheerfully, then looked at her with that same expectant, eager expression she had seen on his face before. "You could work it out if you put your mind to it, I expect."

"Could I?" It seemed unlikely. "Would you show us?"

So with little hesitation, except where the brambles were tangled, Ferney laid a trail of sticks through the undergrowth, down from the place where they'd uncovered the pipe, past the overgrown walls of what had once been a small barn to a point on the slope down into the valley where the leaf-covered earth still showed signs of a long-dry watercourse.

"I'll come back later," Ferney said. "See how you're going on."

At Gally's insistence they carefully cleared the undergrowth from the route Ferney had marked before setting Slash to work again. He'd dug about twenty feet of ditch when the shovel struck something with a great clang and instead of lifting into the air again, stayed embedded. The power of the rams pulled the nose of the bulldozer down so that its back wheels had daylight showing under them for a moment.

Slash tried again more cautiously and the same thing happened. He left the machine idling while he jumped down. They gathered round the hole.

"If that's buggered the hydraulics I wouldn't want to be paying your bill," he said sourly.

Gally stepped down into the ditch with a spade and stood for a second, suddenly delighted with the way the day had turned out despite its unpromising start. As she began to clear the earth away, a long white edge of stone emerged, its top lying only inches below the surface. She scraped and shovelled. "It's huge," she said.

"Looks like an old gatepost or a lintel or something," said Mike.

"Too big for that," said Slash. "What shall I do? Dig round it?"

"Yes," said Mike.

"No," said Gally and Mike sighed.

She put an arm round him. "Look, love, we're almost at the point where the stream would come up to the surface anyway. We could do the rest with spades," she said. *And put an end to the violence,* she thought. "Anyway," she whispered, "it'll save money."

Mike paid Slash far more than seemed reasonable and the bulldozer waddled off, belching smoke and spreading mud from its deep-cleated tyres all across the places it hadn't yet despoiled. Gally felt the house and the valley relaxing as the birds began to sing again. An hour's work with the spades saw the new channel completed. At the top, dry all the way up, it came to the point where the pipe leading to the house disappeared into the bank.

Now that Ferney had gone and the job was nearly done, Mike seemed in a better mood. He got the pickaxe out of the boot of the car and handed it to her with a smile. She weighed it carefully, took aim, then brought it firmly down on the end of the pipe. There was a loud crack and a gout of clear water spouted into the new ditch, soaking straight down into the gravelly substrata. Mike reached into the hole and pulled out broken earthenware.

"I don't think the pipe went any further. Now we just have to see whether the water goes where we want it to." He looked into the ditch. "It's completely disappeared."

"It's just running underground," Gally said confidently. "I'm sure it will reappear when it gets to the slope."

It did. It took a while to get there, but gradually, sluggishly, it began to course up the old waterway, welling up to wash a way through the leaf mould and the moss until it had, once more, a well-defined path of its own. The water level in the cellar began to fall immediately, so Mike and Gally began pulling up the line of old pipe.

"Not a bad day's work," said Mike.

Gally smiled at him and said nothing because at that moment there were no words for what she felt. It was as if they had pulled off a hazardous rescue. The house was safe. More than that, the valley was, with every passing second, returning to some previous state of balance and harmony. She felt momentarily immensely strong and full of life, an overdose of life, pulsing upwards.

Ferney reappeared while they were shovelling the dirt back into the ditch that the bulldozer had left.

Mike was inclined to be friendly now that Ferney's advice had achieved such a dramatic effect, but the latter didn't help much by once again ignoring him almost totally.

The old man addressed himself to Gally. "Did it work?"

"It certainly did. Thank you very much. Come and see."

He stayed where he was but looked over towards the new stream course beyond the caravan.

"Did you find anything?"

"No," said Gally, wondering what he meant, then she thought again. "Well, yes, I suppose we did. The bulldozer hit a huge slab of stone."

Ferney walked fast then, straight to the spot. In the bottom of the new trench, the gravel marking the sunken stream course was wet. It ran round the excavated shape of the stone, a seven-foot finger. He climbed down onto the stone, knelt awkwardly and brushed more of the earth off it.

"You've found it then," he said.

"Found it? What is it?"

He looked up at her as if she ought to know. "It's the Bag Stone, isn't it? Been fallen down a good many years. It has to be put up again."

"Why?" said Mike. "What for?"

This time Ferney did take brief notice of him. "Because that's how it belongs. It's been standing here for a lot longer than it's been lying down. House takes its name from it."

Mike looked around. "I suppose it might look nice over there, between the trees."

Ferney looked up at him with a fierce expression on his face. "It's got its own place—right here. It's always been here." He turned to Gally and softened. "You come down to my house. I'll show you. There's a picture." More quietly, but not so quietly that Mike couldn't hear, he said, "Just you."

5

MIKE HAD BEEN invisible somewhere inside the ruins of the biggest shed for much of the morning, old, splintered planks cartwheeling out of the door from time to time onto a growing pile outside.

He came out and headed for the caravan, brushing the flakes of rot from his sweater.

"Did you find my shirts?" he called over his shoulder. "There are none left at the flat."

"Hello, darling," Gally said. "Lovely to see you. I'm sure that's what you meant, so I'll say it for you. Just to save you time."

He held up his hands. "Sorry, sorry, but I really mustn't be late. The department's whole budget depends on the next two days."

"I know."

"You won't forget the oil tank's being delivered at four o'clock?"

"I won't forget."

"I hope . . . I hope you're going to be all right on your own."

"I sleep well here," she replied, suspecting it was the thought of leaving her to her nightmares that troubled him most. "We'll have to get used to living this way. I'll be all right."

"Are you sure?"

"Yes."

"I mean, you can't even call me. We must get a phone in."

"Go on. I'll be fine." She kissed him, waved goodbye and was glad when he didn't ask what else she had planned.

"See you Thursday," she called as he drove out onto the lane. "Drive carefully."

She felt a twinge of guilt for not telling him her intentions, but she knew he wouldn't like it and she wasn't going to change her mind. Ferney had invited her and despite Mike's underlying hostility, she wanted to go. There was an odd, illicit thrill about it which she knew was ridiculous. She knew there was no real reason to worry and it was better not to bother Mike.

She walked towards the village pondering that. Without any conscious thought process her feet took her towards Bleak Street, and by the junction she turned in and began to open the gate of the ivy-clad stone cottage on the corner. The sight of a blue BMW parked in the driveway stopped her in her tracks.

Gripping the gate tightly, she backed slowly out and latched it again as she stared over it at the car. It made no sense, but then the house made no sense either. An abrupt revelation came to her with the disorientating force of that moment in a dream when you realize you're walking down a crowded street with no clothes on. She didn't know where Ferney lived. She had set out without knowing and without it occurring to her that she didn't know and her feet had somehow brought her here. That was cause for concern. What new hole had opened in her mind?

The dislocation almost winded her, making her gasp at her own absurdity. What if she'd knocked on the door? Why on earth had she come here? She turned quickly away, aghast at herself. Someone had given her wrong directions. Ferney himself, maybe. No, not him. He'd never said where he lived. Perhaps she'd dreamed it? *Stupid, stupid, stupid,* she said to herself.

An old woman was walking a small dog and stopped, smiling, when she called to her.

"Mr. Miller? Yes, of course, he's down in the little close. Down there and right." She looked a shade doubtful. "Is he expecting you? He can be a bit short with visitors, I'm afraid."

"Yes, it's all right. He invited me."

"Well, that *is* something."

The back lane led to a cul-de-sac. It was, in a different way, equally bewildering, so much so that she thought she must have misunderstood the directions. It was a modern bungalow, set at the far end a little bit away from its neighbours, with the open hillside stretching up beyond it. Its white walls were topped by wavy red concrete roof tiles, but its huge picture windows looked out at a garden which was, in contrast, from an earlier age. There was no grass to be seen at the front, just wide flower beds with hollyhocks, lupins and marigolds. A miniature climbing rose was trained round the expanse of plate glass that made up the door.

She saw Ferney sitting in an armchair in the corner of the front room. He was watching television and didn't notice her. Through the glass she heard a line or two of dialogue in the clipped English tones of an old black-and-white film. "If you weren't there, how do you know you didn't do it?" said a voice. She knocked. The sound was immediately switched off and he called, "Who's that?"

"Ferney?" she called. "Mr. Miller? Hello? It's Gally. Gally Martin."

She wasn't sure how he'd react after the scene over the fallen stone, but whatever Ferney might feel about Mike, his reply showed it didn't extend to her. There was obvious pleasure in his voice.

"Gally?" he called. "The door's open. Just you come on in now."

The room beyond the hall was another surprise. The television set was enormous, flanked by shelves crammed with books and video cassettes. There was a state-of-the-art CD player with big speakers. The armchairs were modern and comfortable, but everything else was simply and beautifully furnished with old oak furniture. She wanted to take everything in slowly, but Ferney was watching her from his chair with an expression she couldn't read, demanding her attention. She saw with concern that he didn't look at all well. There was a touch of grey in his face and the marks of age seemed more prominent.

"I hope you don't mind," she said. "I took you literally. Tell me if you want me to go away."

"Oh no," he said, "never. Come and sit down by me. I'm sorry, I'm not feeling too good today. You found your way all right?"

"A woman I met had to tell me where you were." She found herself admitting, "I went to the wrong place. I can't think why, but I was quite sure you lived somewhere else."

"Where?"

"An old cottage down at the end of the road with a big box hedge."

He stared intently at her. "Lamberts Lea?"

She thought back to the name on the gate. "Yes, that's the one. I must have been dreaming. For some reason I thought you lived there."

His eyes seemed to be watering. "You remembered," he said.

"Remembered?"

"I did live there. With my wife. Not lately, though."

"Oh, I see. I don't think I knew," she replied uncertainly. "Unless you told . . ."

He coughed once, then twice, then uncontrollably, his body heaving as he scrabbled for a tissue from the box next to him. Gally darted forward, found one and put it in his hand, then crouched by him until it stopped.

"Have you seen a doctor?" she asked.

"I don't need one," he wheezed. "I know what's wrong. How's it going at your place?"

"The water's almost gone. The cellar's going to need quite a lot of work to put it right, but it's drying out really fast. I'm so grateful. The builders are coming to start fixing the end wall. The stream's running really well."

"And you?" he said. "Are you all right?"

"Why wouldn't I be?" In her own ears her voice sounded defensive.

"I just wondered. It's a bit of a strain, moving."

"No, it's . . . easier being here," she said.

He looked into her face for the space of three heartbeats and she was seized by his eyes. They had no trace of age in them. "And what about the stone?"

"Oh . . . Well, you know . . ."

"No, I don't," he said firmly. "You tell me."

"Well, Mike thinks it's silly. He says it would be a bit twee."

"What does he mean by that?" Ferney sounded younger, stronger, irritated.

"He means it's a bit self-conscious to put it up again. He says nobody even knows how it was exactly, so he thinks we should just let it lie there."

Ferney sat back and digested this in silence. Then he came to a decision. "You tell him I know exactly how it was. I told you. There's a picture."

"Yes, you said. Is it a photo?"

" 'Course it's not. That stone fell down long before photos came along. There's a painting."

"Can I see it?"

"Oh yes, of course you can. That's what I said."

"Where is it?"

He started to get out of his chair.

"No," she said. "Stay there. Tell me and I'll find it."

"The room right at the back. Go and see."

She went out into the hall. The bungalow was L-shaped and beyond the kitchen two doors opened off a short passage. The nearest door gave her a quick glimpse of shelves loaded with boxes and objects of all sorts. She had time to take in a row of clocks on the nearest shelf, all wrapped in clear plastic bags, before he called from the front room.

"The door at the end. Not the first one!"

She closed the door quietly and opened the other. It was a study or perhaps a tiny library, one wall lined with bookshelves, the other dominated by a great painting about four feet wide. The frame was battered, intricate gilt, and the picture itself was opaque dark brown, parts of it nearly black. At first glance, it looked heavy and indecipherable. She put the light on and peered closely at the surface, but that only made it harder to see the tiny variations in darkness that gave away the shape. Standing back again, she could make out the outline of a house surrounded by trees. A lighter, oblique patch indicated something tall and grey poking through the vegetation. She felt a thrill of recognition. Their house, undoubtedly. Their stone, the Bag Stone as it had once been. When? Oh, to see through the years of encrusted grime; but after looking for a while, letting her eyes stray where they would, she began to feel it was starting to reveal itself. Putting together her image of the house now with the faint, dark suggestions of the painting, she could make sense of the outlines, give it proportion, place the stone properly. Mike had to see this. Could he? Would she be able to bring him into Ferney's house? It puzzled her that such a problem could exist.

There was a gate at the front of the house and another lighter patch above it. She leaned closer then stood back, squinted, looked close again, trying to make sense of the dirty blurs of lighter paint. There was a figure standing by the gate. No. Something else. Two figures.

THE PLEASURE OF her company was intense, but in a perverse way he could enjoy it more in his memory now that she'd gone and the strain of possibly making a mistake had eased. Ferney could see the marks of the pain in her and he had to walk such a careful tightrope, watching the way her mind was working, telling her just enough and no more. That meant there was constant tension as well as enormous joy in having her there. Now that she'd gone he could relax and let the pleasure and the rest of it take over.

She'd wanted to know all about the picture. It came as a shock to find she couldn't see it quite the way he could. He knew its vivid colours well enough to see through the masking dirt of the years. She wanted to know how he had got it. He was vague. He'd had it for years was all he would say, but yes, it was the cottage and yes, it did show the stone standing—well, leaning anyway. Not all that accurately, there had been a lot of artist's licence taken with that picture, but the man who'd painted it had insisted on his right to take liberties with the landscape. Who were the figures? He just smiled. People who lived there long ago.

When was it painted, she'd asked, and he'd almost told her the date. Not just the year but the month as well, before he saw that would open up far too many questions. He could have told her 1823, that was the year, but all he'd said was, "Early last century some time, I expect."

If he'd been well he would have gone out when he was alone again and the house was quiet. The tight pain in his chest wouldn't let him go, so instead he dragged his armchair round to the other big window in the end wall and sat back to gaze up the hill beyond the garden where the field had barely changed.

He blanked out the present and almost instantly heard the mental echo of a roar of exhaust, saw the ghost of a blue tractor, tearing diagonally down the hill, much too fast, felt his ghost feet running as the machine slowly, inevitably, tipped outwards and tumbled. Horrible, vivid, recent. He pushed that one fiercely away, keeping his mind blank, scanning the ages.

A musical note came back to him across two hundred years, a note, then a bar, then a refrain. *"Fill up my loving cup, then you and me shall . . ."* No, not quite. *" . . . so thou and I shall sup. When the summer's come again . . ."* Then what?

To be dependent on the random dice-throw of the genes, that was the wild card, the delight and the horror of his lives. Once you've had the luck of a voice that could stop fights, silence politicians and make old ladies fall in love, it was hard to be saddled with a raven's croak next time round.

The last decade of the eighteenth century, just two and a half old men's lives ago—everyone scared by the bloodbath going on across the Channel, hearing the tales brought by the escapees, afraid that the anarchy might soon lap British shores. There was a burst of new songs to cloak the fearful French with derisive humour and the singers who spread them were the centres of attention. That one would have been a lonely life indeed but for his voice. His voice gave him the solace of instant acceptance, instant friendship as soon as he started to sing. Then he would be welcomed everywhere he went, loved momentarily by all who heard him. He was asked to sing whenever he stood still long enough, smiled at, embraced, toasted and encored every time.

His unsympathetic father forced his enlistment in the voracious navy so that death got him at the height of his powers and what a death—what a dreadful, confusing struggle back he faced in his next boyhood, born in the wrong place, cut off from all the familiar things that would have grounded him, led him gently to awareness. It was too much to expect anyone to go through that without madness twisting their path. He knew about nightmares. He knew the full horror that dislocation could bring and the overwhelming relief of finding the way back.

The first powerful memory that had crossed the bridge from dead man to live boy was the pure delight of soaring song which filled his head from the earliest conscious moment of that next time. But cruelly, it was only a memory.

That next time round he was a toddler as the nineteenth century dawned, adrift in a foreign land, adrift in mind as well as in body. He gurgled and cooed every second of the day but nature had failed to hand out the same rare bounty twice. There was nothing tuneful in this Ferney.

He'd come back to Penselwood from far away in a suspicious time, come back alone to sanity with no story to tell except that of a wanderer. The girl saved him from despair, as he stepped from no-where back into their life one day in his teens. She was barely fifteen, short and plain but beautiful to him from the second he saw her by Castle Orchard, and neither needing to know anything much of the other to be sure of what they'd found again. That straightened out the twists in him, but still from time to time he would open his throat and howl a semblance of a song, always to be disappointed. She would forgive him anything but that, so when he felt the need to give voice, he'd go alone up the hill.

It had been on such an occasion that he'd met the painter, a clear bright day with Napoleon two years safely buried at last and George the Fourth's poor Queen Caroline dying just three months later. Not surprising, the way George had treated her too. Nothing new, he thought, in royalty doing its best to drive a coach and horses through the sanctity of marriage.

He looked again out through the window and past the bushes, up the slope. It wasn't the same as being up there in person, but he could try to do it from here. He relaxed, focusing on the song, trying to pull the rest out of it. *"Fill up my loving cup . . ."* There wasn't quite enough. He saw an easel but he couldn't get it right. He tried for a face, but that was more elusive still. He sighed and let his head drop onto his chest in defeat. The instant he stopped trying, an unexpected, unbidden image arrived in full force and he half-laughed, half-gasped at the shock of it. He was onto it like a terrier before it could slip away.

Two legs, waving in the air—well-dressed gentleman's legs, with shiny black buckled shoes and yellow hose, somewhat darned and now grass-stained. He'd stopped singing, hadn't he? Yes. He'd been standing there talking to a horse. Horse-calming had always earned Ferney money when he needed it. There were many times, when he preferred the company of horses to men. Men followed stupid fashions, blocking off their chances to know the world better. Horses didn't change. They had one abiding driving force, whether pony, Arab or shire horse, and that was a monstrous, all-consuming curiosity.

All you had to do, however tricky the horse, was attract that curiosity and insist on playing the game your way. Stand there just talking quietly to yourself and gradually drop your voice as the animal came nearer. In the end, when you could barely hear yourself it would be right there next to you, bending its ears to pick up the faint whisper, standing there on your terms, so close it fooled itself into trusting you in its desperation to be in on the secret. Then you'd won. When it had been there, that close, that still, it forgot all about mistrust. For a man who had the knack, there was good money to be had from winning the trust of bad horses.

This time he was almost there, doing it just for fun, the horse circling him, five paces off, when it was distracted by something even more interesting. It led him to the hedge, attracted by another oddity it couldn't ignore. He looked over as it blew and stamped. There on the down-slope of the hill beyond lay an unidentifiable shape, a large white square flat in the grass. He climbed the gate to investigate, but before he reached it he could see it was a canvas, flanked by an artist's easel tipped on its side, paints strewn from a fallen palette. A painter? Outside? You never saw painters outside. They belonged inside in their studios far away in the towns, not up here on the hill. Then he heard a sound to his right that could have been a cry of joy or of pain and there, sticking up from the ditch, were the legs.

The man he helped up was perhaps twenty years older than him, in his late forties, tall and fine-looking, but with hair that had quite vanished from the top of his head, leaving only muttonchop whiskers and patches of greying curls over both ears. A keen pair of dark eyes fixed on him with a wild expression.

He remembered their conversation with unique clarity. It wasn't long ago, after all, but more than that, it was rare in those days to talk to a man of education, a man whose ideas were worth dwelling on, who could share his own thoughts with understanding. He'd thought through that conversation many times to keep it fresh, and if in doing so he had edited some of the words, he knew he still had the meaning right.

"Are you well, sir?" he had asked the stranger anxiously. He got another odd sound in return, a sound which started with a yelp and turned into a giggle.

"On a day like this? Why should I not be well? Look around you, man. Look at the beauties, the beauties all around you."

Ferney did as he was told, but the scene was as familiar as it could be, less wild than of old, more signs of man's incursions, but still a very fine view. "The sun's out, for sure," he agreed. "Did your painting displease you?"

"Painting is all my joy and all my sorrow," said the man, suddenly quieter. "It is the reason I laugh and the reason those around me weep."

He seemed suddenly to become properly aware of Ferney and looked at him with interest. Ferney knew this look, understood its roots in the effortless categorization of English class. He knew his accent was now an English countryman's accent, but he also knew his clothes showed him in an ambiguous light. They were not gentleman's outdoor clothes, not impracticably stylish. They were plainer though of good quality, the sort of thing for a quiet day in the garden. He had learned to appreciate good cut and stitching and he was not short of the means to buy it.

The man's damaged, distracted air had engaged Ferney's interest and he introduced himself. There was a silence while the other man, breathing heavily, looked up at the sky.

"I am called Ferney Tucker, sir." There was no response. "And you, if you don't mind my asking?" he pressed.

"Me, sir? You would know my name? Why, I am John Nobody. You may call me that. It is easier to tell you who I am not. I am not Mr. Landseer. Mr. Landseer paints PAINTINGS. He sets nature in its proper place. He CONTROLS it." The man invested the word with a curling sneer. "I am not Mr. Turner. Mr. Turner gets five hundred guineas for his . . . his yellow pea-soupers. The Academy likes them very much. The Academy does not like me. I am Mr. Nobody. No, better—call me Mr. Poorman, John Poorman, the bane of my poor parents' life."

He stopped and looked at Ferney closely for a moment.

"Do you know France, sir?" he asked.

"Most certainly I do," said Ferney.

"From the recent hostilities?"

"In a manner of speaking."

"Think what you will of them. It is only the French who have any time for me, sir. They wish to buy my paintings, sir, while my fellow countrymen seek only to search out the fault in them." He stopped, grunted and swept an arm around the horizon. "Just look, sir. All around us is the best part of England. Its very bones, its LAND-SCAPE. I would pass up all human company just to sit and contemplate a view like this if that were the choice."

Ferney, who often thought the same, nodded. The man shook his head fast, blowing out like a horse.

"The men at the Academy would like it if I would only paint more of their BROWN TREES, their fevered twistings of good English greenness into the knotted, dried relics of Italy or Africa. I am too green for them, altogether too green, but I paint what I see and I can do nothing else. Now they are building their National Gallery to fill with their portraits and their historical farragoes and their parched, foreign views. There will be no more worthwhile painting in England for thirty years, sir, mark my words. They hate colour. They wage war on colour. I must be drab to suit them and I will *not* be drab."

Ferney found himself almost unnecessary, an ear which barely needed a head attached to it, but he felt moved to say something.

"Well, paint then," he said, "paint as you see it. Paint as the view dictates."

The other man sighed. "I have four children, sir. Four children, a wife in poor health and another child to come. The purse commands me."

Ferney looked again at the painter. A gentleman did not usually talk of such things.

"Why were you in the ditch?" he asked bluntly.

"Ah. I was seized with a fury. I threw down my sketch and ran away from the foul thing. I did not see the damned ditch until it had me."

Ferney considered. "So what was it in your sketch that infuriated you?"

"You are a fierce examiner, sir!"

"You have told me something which intrigues me. Won't you tell me all of it?"

"I will *show* you."

The artist led him over to the wreckage of the easel, picked it up, jamming a broken leg in place with difficulty, and set the canvas straight upon it. It was rapid work, energetic and bold. A strong sky of writhing clouds drew the eye into the distance of the plain ahead.

"It is just a preliminary," he said. "Only the starting point for a work I shall make later."

Ferney looked at it with interest. "I see nothing there to infuriate," he said, turning to the man, who stood watching him with a frowning face.

The artist pointed into the distance. "Look, sir."

"Where?" asked Ferney, puzzled.

"To the south. Do you not see the blot?"

In the distance a thin wreath of smoke wound into the blue.

"You mean the chimney?"

"That is just what I mean. It is a foul encroachment."

"That smoke is from the new Boulton engine at the Gillingham brewery. Are you saying that steam power is an abomination?"

"In this pure landscape? Yes! And that is not all, sir. I have lately been sketching near that smoke at Parham's Mill. Do you know it?"

"This side of Gillingham?"

"Indeed. Do you know they plan to tear it down? That beautiful place. They will erect some monstrous modern factory there instead!"

Ferney turned back to the rough painting and studied it. For a man who appeared to demand great constancy from nature, the artist had taken some considerable licence. Two trees had been conjured from their deep-rooted homes and brought fully a hundred yards closer together to frame the view down to the plain. The border of the woodland stretched far further in the picture than it did in the reality before him. That caused him a moment of wonder. Except for the foreground trees, the view he had painted was just as it had once been before the shrinking of the forest.

He turned back to his companion. "You seem able to set right the damages of time quite well enough with your mind and your brushes. Surely one small speck of smoke cannot hurt?"

He was surprised by the strength of the despair in the man's reaction.

"It is not just the smoke! Do you not see? The whole of our land is changing. We are eating it up with our roadways and our vulgar new houses. Now the steam chimneys will stick their intrusions across all our horizontals." He began to dance in agitation. "Verticals! Precious verticals! On a day like this my painting is full of verticals. I know that God is in His heaven when I go all vertical. I DON'T WANT my verticals to be belching smoke. Do you understand me, sir?"

"No, I do not. You are unduly concerned. I believe you inflict unnecessary unhappiness on yourself."

"Unduly concerned!" said the other in an affronted tone.

"Try to let go of your fears. There is nothing fixed. The land does not stay still. Once maybe, but not at any time in the last ten hundred years at the least." Ferney pointed down the hill. "The wood you painted, down there, stretching across the first part of the plain, that was nibbled away. They started eating at it about . . . oh, shall we say, 1500? A hundred years it took. You see those fields? They came as the trees went, quickset hedges, hawthorns you would say if you're a townsman, grown and laid and knotted to divide them, but not all as you see them now, oh no. Over there," he pointed southeast with a flourish, "there were two fields fifty times the size. You see your green squares now. You might have found more variation for your palette then. They weren't like that. Ragged strips and open pasture. All the colours of all the different crops. Not for long though. Bang!" He turned on the startled artist. "The commissioners had them. Enclosure. A crime against the countryside and against the common interests of the countrymen. They threw off the little men, gave the wealth to those who already had the money, divided up their fields. Built their roads. You see down there?" He pointed.

"Where?"

"Where it is straight. That's the commissioners' road. Drawn on a map. Clapped across the land like a sword-cut through the brotherhood of man. Then after that it was houses. New farmhouses in the new fields. They all went mad about houses. About halfway through Elizabeth's time, it was. Let's see, when was that?"

"Elizabeth? Halfway?" said the other man. "My goodness, sir, you seem to be cracking along."

"History does not take long. Say 1570? Close enough. Houses

went out sideways and they went up. Privacy. All at once privacy was the thing. Wealth and privacy. More rooms to hide away in. Cleaner inside, too, so chimneys everywhere. Never mind your brewery chimney now, that was the time when the chimneys sprouted. Then there was the glass and how *that* changed things."

"Glass?" said the artist faintly, mesmerized. "Why?"

"The glitter of it. On a bright day. Something never seen before. No glass down here until they started to make it cheap, then suddenly a thousand mirrors flashing back the sunshine." He paused for a moment. "Now there's the gas coming. You see that house?" He pointed towards Milton.

"No."

"Beyond the copse, by the line of willows."

"I think I do."

"The first gas you can see from here. They set the pipes last year. I come up in the evenings sometimes and look out at that light. I imagine it as it will be when all the houses have those bright squares for their night-time windows. Heaven on earth. The sparkling firmament arrayed across our dark land."

The artist shuddered.

Ferney looked at him. "You do not like the possibility?"

"It is not MY England, and whether they like it or not, I must paint MY England. You threaten my picture, sir. How can you know? Are you an historian?" His tone sounded doubtful.

"You might say that."

"Well. I shall not argue then. In any case, you are an interesting man. I would like to talk more with you, but my gig will soon be waiting."

"Will you come back?"

"If circumstances allow. I feel almost as though we are friends, you and I. Do you know what I am saying?" The artist clasped Ferney's hand and looked at him anxiously.

"You feel yourself alone and that others understand less well?" Ferney hazarded.

"YES."

"Then I do know."

"I am not valued," said the other man quietly. "I lived on the generosity of my father until his death. He milled corn, he owned barges, he put the sweat of his brow into the canals and the locks they passed through. He wanted me to work them for him and he never understood that instead I had to paint them. Now I live off the stipend he left. I paint because I must, I absolutely must." His voice rose again, "There is nothing so grand as standing before a large canvas, stabbing and sweeping away to conjure nature out of the colours on your palette. But I must live and that is getting harder."

An idea came into Ferney's mind.

"There is a view near here that I like very much," he told the artist, "and I think it might appeal to you, too. I should be pleased if you would come down to see it with me on your way."

6

THE ALARM ON the Teasmaid woke Ferney from a dream of horses. He rolled over in bed to lift the steaming cup from the machine before the irritation in his lungs and chest got him and he slopped tea on the duvet as he fought to control the coughing.

It wasn't so bad now that he knew why he was ill. It was just the price to pay, that was all, but it told him that he had to take control. He was fully awake now, alert, thinking about priorities. The best way would be the slow and gentle way if he could afford the time, but he knew he couldn't, knew from the feeling deep in his gut that slow and gentle wasn't an option—knew, too, that he couldn't count on another opportunity to kick it off when the man Mike would be away. What to pick on? That was the question. He turned to the bedside table and the pile of books there.

Books were a boon. Learning to read and the mushroom growth of the paperback were two of the greatest blessings of the twentieth century as far as he was concerned. They ranked right up there with central heating and compact disc recordings of J. S. Bach and far above the motorcar for someone who had so much to lose by leaving home. It was history books almost always for him, history books and travel books. Novels mostly skated over the top of life, though he'd dip in and out of them, looking for signs that they might repay his interest. Just sometimes one would hit the mark, showing a wider understanding.

On rarer occasions, when a novel really made him think, he would get excited by what he found, detecting a degree of special wisdom in the writer. Once or twice a book had even made him wonder if the author could really have gained such insight in just one lifetime or if perhaps there were other people out there going through the same cycle as himself. Such writers were indeed worth reading, but you wasted so much time on the dross trying to find them. Not that history books were that much more reliable, but at least they helped fill in the gaps and string things out in the right order.

He found what he wanted and began to read. It was the seventeenth century seen through twentieth-century eyes so it wasn't quite right, but then how could it be? He'd seen this before in modern historians, so used to the telephone, the radio and rapid travel that the isolated, meandering mistakes of a peasant army trudging through rain and mud to total defeat in the wrong place at the wrong time seemed specially tragic, as if it could have been so easily avoided. It couldn't, of course. That was the way life had been for almost all of history, blundering in a limited compass inside an opaque outer ring where time and distance were so much less adjustable. He read quietly for an hour, then put the book down and began to think.

Ferney's memories, because there were so many, came in different bands of quality. At the lowest end, there were the fleeting shreds that would come back to him as little more than the gut feeling that something he knew was right. His dreams were full of bits and pieces like that and often he would lie in bed on waking trying to hang on to some tiny, slippery, wriggling end of an image so that he could drag it into the daylight.

If he succeeded that might take him to the second level, where he could use the visual tricks, go to the right spot and see what happened when he tuned the landscape.

Next up were the familiar big events, the ones he'd been over a thousand times, and they were like a painting to him, but a painting that was covered in layer after layer of old varnish, so that he had to take great care that what he could still see was the original and not the retouching of memory because every time he took them out to look he added another layer.

Right at the heart of him were the clear, core delights and catastrophes and they were more like flies in amber, every detail preserved by the power of emotion vested in them. The thread of his long love story ran through them and it was one of these that he had chosen for the day's work. He feared what was to come, but he knew it had to be done and hoped that she would, in the end, forgive him for it.

MIKE REALLY HADN'T been at all happy at the idea of leaving Gally for another two nights in the caravan by herself.

"Why don't you come to London?" he'd asked before they got up. "We might as well both use the flat if we're going to keep it on."

It was in his mind that she seemed a little better, but he didn't trust the reasons. He was sure that the only long-term answer was for her to continue to confront the horrors of her childhood with the help of caring experts. Finding solace in a house, a place and an old man's disquieting ways could be a dangerously wrong turning. Whatever route she took, he wanted them to take it together.

"London?" she'd said incredulously. "When I can be down here?"

"I don't know," he said unhappily. "The door doesn't even lock properly and it's in the middle of nowhere."

"No, no, it's really not. It's right in the middle of . . . somewhere."

It had sounded funny at the time and he had laughed, giving up the argument until later, but she'd meant it. Even waking once, by herself in the night as a pair of owls shrieked at each other, there were no imagined horrors lurking in the dark trees beyond the window. In her childhood, and often since then, she had been to places that seemed to reject her—where, when dark fell, she had to keep her mind free of imaginings in case the shreds of them should catch and cling together and start to form into something frightful. Here at the house she knew there would be no such fears, though down on the road and out along the ridge she knew there were less comfortable places. The house and its surroundings gave her a complex sense of security, a guard dog that had once been fierce before it knew her.

The morning was luxurious. She drank her coffee slowly, sitting on the doorstep in the sun. By the time the builders arrived to start un-derpinning the gable end, she had everything ready for them, an area—already desecrated by the digger—marked off for their mixers and their supplies. She had cut back those plants which might be in the way and lifted some of the smaller ones wholesale, bedding them carefully out of harm's reach and hoping they would survive.

Don Cotton's young foreman, Rick, was quite unlike his pugna-cious boss, cheerful, straightforward and prepared to listen to her pre-cise requirements about what should be touched and what should not.

Soon she had nothing to do but watch and think—and Ferney's painting was all she could think about. She wanted to see it again and talk to him some more. It was easier without Mike there and she wished there wasn't that unnecessary tension when the two men were together. Ferney seemed, in some way she couldn't yet pin down, completely integral with the house and Mike somehow wasn't. She suppressed the thought. Since finding the house there seemed an in-creasing number of thoughts she had to suppress.

In the middle of the afternoon there was nothing to do but watch the builders at work and she had already done enough of that. She wanted exercise and the hill beyond the road beckoned, exciting uplands from which to fix the surroundings in her head. She walked along the lane to the field gate, swinging the garland ring in her hand, looking for fresh flowers in the hedgerow to bring it to life again. The field had been grazed and she climbed the slope easily, turning from time to time to look back over her shoulder at the diminishing house. Shielded by a conspiracy of contours, it disappeared into the dip before she could get a really good view, but beyond it the flat land to the south was opening up in compensation. As she neared the top of the hill she could see the squat, straight-edged shape of an Ordnance Survey trig point. She came nearer. Just beyond it was a flat stone, a natural bench, and sitting on the stone, looking round at her with an intent expression on his face, was Ferney.

The only surprise was that there was no surprise. She had the sense for a moment of the man as a magnet, his field spreading down the hill to show some part of her where he was and perhaps draw her to his presence.

"Hello," she said. "You must be feeling better."

"I'll last the year out," he said. "I was coming down to see you, but I should have known you'd come up here."

"It's the first time I've been," she said, then, "Why do you laugh?"

"I've got a few things to tell you," he said. "Have you the time?"

"Mike's away. All the time in the world. There's some things I want to ask you, too."

"Go on then, sit down. You first."

Gally's way was the direct way. "You don't like Mike, do you? Why? I don't want you to dislike him. It makes things . . . harder."

Ferney seemed to withdraw a little into himself, looking away then back at her.

"I don't mind him. Just haven't got the time for folk, I suppose."

How could he explain it? Ordinary people could come and go but they only ever brushed past his life. It took a profoundly unusual character to pierce the barriers that time and experience had set around him.

"All folk or just him? You've got time for me."

"Most people you meet when you're . . . my age, you've heard it all before. There's nothing new in them. You're not like that."

"You hardly know me, Ferney."

"I hardly know you? Do you feel that?"

"Well no, I don't really," she said, groping for words, "but it sounds silly to say so."

"You *are* married to him, are you?"

"Yes, of course. Why do you ask?"

"You don't wear a ring."

"Oh. I don't like rings."

He nodded. "Do you know why?"

"No . . . well, they make me feel funny."

"What sort of funny?"

"Claustrophobia of the finger, Mike calls it. A bit panicky, I suppose. Why do you ask?"

"I know you," he said. "I know more about you than you think."

That nettled her a little and she looked at him defiantly.

"I know you're expecting," he said.

Time stopped. She stared. No one knew. Mike didn't know. She barely knew herself. It was just an odd little certainty scarcely two days old.

"That's more than I do," she said, but the words hung in the air, transparently false, and she wished she could take them back. She couldn't catch the sob that came.

"What is it?" he said, concerned.

"Nothing. I had a . . ."

He waited a long time, but she was staring into the ground, unable to find the words.

"You lost a baby?" he suggested gently.

She just nodded.

"You'll be all right this time," he said, and she looked at him as if he were mad but her eyes slowly dried.

He papered it over for them. "Do you like your house?" he said.

"I love it."

"Just as it is?"

"Just as it is. More or less."

"There's nothing fixed about old houses. Bits and pieces change."

"We've got to fix it one way or another. I think I'd like to fix it just the way it was in your picture. I wish I could see that a bit more clearly."

"The picture. Well, it was never quite like that. He changed it around a bit, you know. It was all right when he first did it, but that was just a rough sketch, he said. When it came back from his studio there were a lot of little fancies added in."

I couldn't see it that clearly, she thought. "What sort of fancies?"

"That little trickle of a stream was ten times the size for a start and he'd made the roof all tiled over and he didn't like the hill. Said it spoilt his composition, so he'd made it all flat. I ask you. This place. Flat."

"But for all that, it's the house."

"First picture of it. Still, that's just one moment in amongst a lot of others."

"Do you know how old the house is?"

"There's no real way of saying how old something like that is. You start with a hut, maybe, and if it's in a good spot people go on wanting to live there, so they build it a bit stronger when it falls down, first wood, then perhaps a stone wall or two. They might build more on it here or there. Who's to say what makes it that house? But your house has been around a good long time one way and another. The right-hand end, the cellar and the kitchen and the room above, that's new. Built the year Queen Victoria was crowned."

New, she thought? *That was 1837.*

"They put a new front door in then," he said. "Can't think why they did it, but I never got round to putting it right."

"You lived there?"

"Of course I did." Disappointment crossed his face. He paused and considered. "Well, on and off, you might say." Then he looked at her so that she had to meet his gaze. "You've got a feel for history, haven't you?"

"I love reading it," she said. "It's what I like most, I think. Mike's always very good for me, tells me the bits I don't know."

"I could tell you a story about that house."

"I want to know everything there is to know about it."

"All right, but you have to help me."

"What do you mean?"

This was it, he thought. Would she do it?

"You've got to try imagining it going on, the way I tell it to you. Try and get the pictures in your head, then maybe you can fill in the bits I can't tell too well. Can you do that?"

She smiled uncertainly. "I'm not sure I know quite what you mean, but I'll try."

"All right then," he said. "This happened three hundred years ago. You'll have heard of Jamie Scott?"

She shook her head.

"That's what people in these parts called him. The Duke of Monmouth, he was. Bastard son of King Charles."

"The Monmouth rebellion?"

"That's it," he nodded approvingly. "Good man, the Duke. He could be a bit of a twit, but he was good at heart. A lot of people backed him round here. Thought he had more right to the throne than the other one. James the Second. What do you know about him?"

She thought. "He landed at Lyme Regis, didn't he? Marched up towards Bristol and got beaten at Sedgemoor."

"Took a lot of men from these parts with him. Clothmaking was a big thing round here in those days and the weavers, they were Protestants, you know, almost to a man. It went with the trade. King James, now, he was trying to put the Catholics back on top. Cruel too, the way he was going about it, so all those weavers went off to join Monmouth as soon as the word spread that he'd arrived. Barely a weapon between them, so they took axes and scythes lashed onto long poles."

"Brave people."

He snorted. "It was pathetic. They were doing what they thought was right, sure enough, but really—Protestant, Catholic, what difference does it make? It's all mumbo-jumbo."

She wanted to find out why he'd said that, but she didn't want to stop the flow. "Go on."

"All right now," he said. "Now it's your turn. Imagine this. You're down at the house. The same house you've got now. It's thatched, not tiled. Just like in the picture. No kitchen on the end and the old stone's still there, leaning over a bit, but still there. Imagine it." He watched her and she closed her eyes. "Can you see it?"

"Yes." And she could, vividly.

"I can tell you the very date: July the seventh, 1685. A Tuesday. It's evening, twilight just coming on. Been a rotten month for rain, but it's gone away now. Puddles everywhere. You walk out of the house to watch for your man, then you decide to come up here, up the hill to meet him, because he often comes back this way. Just like you came up this time. He's here, sitting on this stone. Can you see him clear?"

Gally wasn't so sure but she played along with it. "Yes, I think so."

"What's he wearing?"

Needing something to say, she pulled an arbitrary image into her mind's eye. "Oh. A sort of waistcoat. A jerkin, is that it?"

"Ah! Yes, it is. What colour?"

"Light brown."

"What's he got underneath it?"

She frowned at what came to her but the image defied her attempt to change it. "Nothing," she said, puzzled. "You'd think he'd have a shirt on, wouldn't you? Just the waistcoat and trousers."

"And can you say what the trousers are made of?"

"Leather, it looks like. That must be hot in the summer."

"Leather for what he does. He's been breaking in a horse, a bad horse. Vicious. Leather for protection. The horse tried to bite him. Tore his shirt. The lady of the house has kept it to mend, see?"

Gally was pleased Ferney was playing along, making something of her off-the-cuff ideas. It stopped her feeling foolish.

"What's he look like?" asked Ferney.

"I can't see," she said. "Dark hair. Thickset, not too tall. Nice looking." She wanted to hold him.

"There's no news of all the men who went. No time for it yet," Ferney said. "Old Walter Bottle came home three days back, wounded in the arm. Swore he was sent home and hadn't deserted, but you can't tell with him. He said there's been a fight at Keynsham and there's no food and scores of men are leaving the duke. Anyway, the man and the woman—they're standing there talking when they hear a sound and they turn. There's horsemen coming towards them."

She made a little sound of slight alarm.

He paused, taking it in. "Horsemen are frightening, aren't they? Power. That's what horsemen have got if you're on foot. Height to cut at you from, speed and weight to run you down and these weren't just horsemen. These were army. Soldiers. Could have been anyone in that time, could have been ready to do anything. But there weren't many of them. How many are there? Quick."

Gally jumped. "Three," she said.

"Three men, dead in the saddle, swaying as they ride. Filthy with mud, blood and torn clothes. The horses are no better. One of them shies, rears, throws his rider. What happens?"

"You . . . the man goes to it. Says something. Very quiet. Calms it down."

"Yes," said Ferney. "Then what?"

"I don't know." She had her eyes screwed right up tight, trying hard, starting to be bothered by it. He saw that and eased the pressure.

"One of them spoke. A Dutchman or some such—Byser the Brandenburger, they called him. 'Who are you for?' he said. 'Monmouth or the king?' Well, you didn't answer questions like that, not if you wanted to live long, so the man said, 'Depends who is doing the asking.' 'I'll have an answer,' says the other and he draws a sword, but the man in the middle, a man who looks like he has seen the pits of hell, puts his arm out to stop him. 'No more of that,' he said. 'I've got enough deaths hanging round my neck already.' "

"He was Monmouth," breathed Gally.

There was a long silence. "He was. The other was Earl Grey," said Ferney, "and he told them that all was lost. They'd been slaughtered around him all because of a flooded ditch they couldn't cross and an enemy who heard them coming in the night. Now they were riding for their lives and they needed shelter. They still had armour on, not the right style if you want to go unnoticed, and they had a drum. Think about the drum."

She thought for a count of five.

"What colour do you see?"

"Blue," she said, "with a lion and unicorn in gold, but battered and cut."

"Yes," he said with excitement in his voice.

Her heart was beating fast and he put his face very close to hers. "What would you have done with men like that?"

"Taken them home. Fed them."

"Even if your man was against it?"

"I wouldn't respect a man that was against that."

"That's what she said." He clasped her hand and she felt an electric buzz go up her arm. "So they took them back to the house, careful that no one saw. Offered them a bed after they'd washed their wounds and given them food, but the men wouldn't take it. They thought they'd get a ship from Dorset if they were quick enough about it. The gates were closing. Then she said, 'Don't go like that. Go in old clothes. We have some smocks.' The Duke was all in, lost his spirit, but he almost laughed at that. 'On horseback?' he said. 'Shepherds on horseback?' 'No,' she said, 'ride like that in the dark if you must. Send the horses off before dawn. Walk after that.' "

"And what happened?" asked Gally in a voice that was trembling.

"They found a cousin, a friend to guide them through the night, Richard Madox, but they were caught in the morning. The Sussex militia had them even though they split up. That's what the books say now. Some soldier found him hiding in a ditch."

She imagined the glorious rebellion ending in a muddy ditch. "Ferney. The rest of that? Is that from a book?"

"Do you think it is?"

She looked down at the ground and her eyes were wet with tears. "No," she said and her voice broke. "No, damn it." He gave her space, just watching, and she looked at him in wonder. "I don't think this is a good idea," she said.

"It was your idea," he said gently.

"I don't know what you mean. You're muddling me up. I don't

think I want to play this game anymore." She stood up, wishing Mike was down at the house.

"One last bit," he said, and there was something in his voice she couldn't ignore. "They had to get rid of the drum, and the armour. They had to get them out of the way and they were glad they did when Jeffreys' men came to pry out the truth behind Madox's cover-up. No one found the stuff and that was just as well. But that wasn't all. Monmouth gave the girl something to keep for herself. What was it?"

"I don't know," she said. "I really, really don't know."

Ferney's voice was insistent, reaching into her head, almost shouting, and he rose to his feet, "His gold ring, that's what, and what did she do with it?"

"I DON'T KNOW."

"You do know. Just tell me."

"No, I don't."

"Just say the first thing that comes into your head, then that's it. The story's over."

Panic was rising in her at the thought of the ring, the terrible, deadly ring. "Oh please. I'm not enjoying it anymore."

"The first thing."

She closed her eyes, clenched her fists and could suddenly see only one thing. "Under the front door step," she wailed.

"Under the step," he repeated, nodding, and his voice was quiet and kind now. "That's the story. It's finished. It had to be done."

She turned without saying goodbye and stumbled down the hill, staring ahead of her, seeing in her mind's eye three tired horsemen riding down in front of her. Halfway down, mind racing, she looked at the house and it seemed smaller, thatch over slate like a double exposure. At the bottom, by the gate, she reached out for the wooden latch, but her hand met smooth, modern metal.

SHE SAW A blur of concerned builders looking at her as she walked in through the gate on uncertain feet, eyes red. She kept her face turned away from the house, not sure which house she would see. What she had just been through had drained all her strength, left her scoured out, limp and nervous.

"Are you okay, love?" Rick called, putting down his shovel.

Summoning up the strength to mumble something reassuring, she let herself into the caravan. She was so tired and it was much, much easier to give in to the tiredness than to face its cause. Lying down full-length on the thin seat she went immediately to sleep and the day went on without her.

She woke screaming in the quiet, sidelong, falling light of evening to the soft songs of birds finishing their business. She lay very still, whimpering, her heart thudding, as the boilman and the burnman crept back into the fringes of their loathsome hiding-place dragging their lumps of disfigured flesh. "I'm in the caravan," she said to herself. "I'm awake. It's all right." She wished Mike was there, keeping absolutely still, feeling any movement would commit her to some course of action, some relationship with her surroundings that might not be wise.

She breathed deliberately, deeply, like she'd learnt in the childbirth classes. It usually displaced fear by sorrow which was almost but not quite as awful. This time, instead of the memory of that draining birth that wasn't, she heard instead the calm assurance of Ferney's voice. "You'll be all right this time."

The speed of her pulse and the hollow tension in her stomach proved some of the fear was still there, and there was a swollen ache behind her eyes where the day's experiences had kicked bruises in her brain. By slow stages she regained control of her racing blood, using the breathing, and when she had the upper hand she was able to see that the fear wasn't coming from the memory of the dream anymore, but from herself. Nor was it fear of anything other than herself, not even fear of the unknown, but rather a fear of the immensity of the consequences of pushing open a closed door. The house was the source of it. There might be beasts waiting beyond the door but she knew there was love. It was the love that frightened her most.

She rubbed her hands hard over her face to squeeze out these irritating fancies. She stood up, opened the flimsy latch of the caravan door, looking down at the ground, then took a deep breath and lifted her gaze in deliberate challenge to the house.

It was just the house, nothing more. Fresh mortar gleamed bright in the revived stonework at the kitchen end. Boards, ladders and scaffolding poles enveloped it in the twentieth century. Fancies fled away, leaving her embarrassed and a little amused at herself. She stood still for a long time gazing at it, wondering how old Ferney could have filled her head so easily. What started as relief began to taste like disappointment in her throat.

A puff of wind carried a faint trace of a horse's whinny and reality fought with seventeenth-century stories. She walked slowly towards the front door, knelt by the stone step, knowing in half of her brain that there could be nothing there, no ring to bring nightmares in its train, but also knowing she needed to prove that fact to the other half. The step itself was heavy, worn into a subtle scoop by the friction of a million shoes. A long crowbar moved it after much struggle, then another five minutes of tugging and levering won the battle as inch by inch she slid it to one side. Hard-packed earth confronted her.

She had the run of the builders' tools. A pickaxe for the first assault, then a spade, and the crowbar again to prise out the larger stones. It got harder as the hole grew slowly deeper, and somewhere around the two-foot level she came to realize there was no remaining promise in what lay below. A clear victory for common sense, she knew, so why did it make her feel so sad?

There seemed far more earth than would fit back into the hole and when she had pounded and stamped it as flat as it would go, the step refused to bed neatly down and sat unsteadily, raised a little above the surrounding ground. The last of the sun gleamed on its edge and she wondered how long it had been since that part of the old stone had last been warmed by direct sunlight.

She went to bed early, tired out again—the caravan's flimsy water supply unable to rid her skin of all the grime from her digging. Sleeping with one hand curled up under her cheek, it might have been the faint smell or the touch of the drying traces of earth in the creases of her skin that prompted her dreams. A cavalcade of her day blended into them, love mingling with fear. She was straining again to lift the stone but it was easier. She was stronger and there were helping hands, powerful hands—the hands of a man who wore a jerkin and leather trousers, a man she loved with a painful depth. She was digging with a tiny spade, more like a blunt trowel, using it one-handed. Paralysing fear, dream-fear dragged at every movement. Hide it fast, her brain screamed, hide it before we're seen, caught, killed. Boilman and burnman were somewhere there, starting to harden in the shadows. Her hands were moving so slowly.

A motorcycle went up the lane in a sudden crescendo of high-pitched exhaust and Gally stirred in her sleep, rushing out of the wreckage of the dream in time to avoid the worst, groping towards waking. The sound faded and she plunged down into sleep again, spared the horror, trying to get back to the man.

He was there but he was different and only the love was the same. Smaller, dressed in cloth not leather, with marks of past hardship on his face. Then he grew smaller still and she knew she'd been tricked. He was just paint and you couldn't love paint. All that groaning love still in her and she was suddenly bereft, the tiny picture the only trace left of him. The whole picture spread out before her then and she saw it, bright and clean—an absurd, muddled dream mixture, a flat horizon behind, tiles where there should have been thatch on the roof and where there were now slates. The caravan and the digger were there in front painted in old oils. Through the still picture, a pair of magpies flew and landed on the thatch.

She sat bolt upright in the caravan somewhere between sleep and waking and groped for the curtains. Clean moonlight let her share its private view, painting the house with a narrow palette of solid blues and greys, bringing it closer. It was light to see unicorns by, but there was only the house. Shaking the clumsy sleep from her fingers, she reached for paper and pencil.

She wasn't aware of going back to sleep, didn't feel the paper slip from her fingers onto the floor. No more dreams troubled her and time jumped until the blast of Mike's radio alarm—always an uncertain timekeeper—woke her with the seven o'clock news, just too far into the headlines to make sense.

". . . ing Minister for the past two years is expected to resign as a result of the allegations."

Thanks, Mike, she thought. *Bloody thing.* She silenced it, stretched and listened. Birdsong and dappled sunlight washed across the caravan walls, filtered and directed by the trees' small movements. Barefoot, she opened the door and stepped down into dew-damp grass, breathing air that had not yet lost its crispness to the pollen fermentation of the coming warmth. The new mortar on the underpinned wall stood out from the stonework, warning her just how easily a ruin could lose its glamour to the process of repair. She walked to that end, looked closely, then—as if to reassure the house—pressed herself face-first to the corner, spreading her arms along the two walls. Closing her eyes, it felt to her that the house had dwindled to the narrow strips of stone that she could feel against her body, as if the only stone that existed was that reverse, hard woman-shadow defined by her touch. She opened her eyes and the rest of the house came back but then she tilted her head, looking up at the sky, and the clouds' slow passage made it seem that the sky was still and the house was slowly, powerfully, pushing her over. She stepped back, off balance, patted the wall and looked along it to where the remains of the latticework porch projected and at that point she remembered her dream.

It was a quick sketch that she'd drawn in the moonlight and she found it under the bunk where it had slipped in the night. The house was outlined in hard, decisive strokes. There was no Bag Stone standing in her picture, but otherwise the proportions of the house were much the same as in the painting. The yard in front was much larger, more realistic. What made her stare was the people. In her semi-sleep, she had drawn in the couple from the painting, rough and less defined than the house. The man stood the same height as the woman. He had side-whiskers and a twist to one marked cheek but that was all you could make out. The woman was just an outline.

Even that wasn't what kept Gally staring. The couple in her picture weren't standing at the gate as in the painting. The angle was different. They were standing outside the front door. She'd been drawing from life, though the pair of them must have stepped out of her dream. Something else had followed them from that dream. The front door was slap in the middle of the house, just as she wanted it to be, just as she knew it belonged, not off to the left where some interfering later builder had misplaced it when Victoria was newly crowned.

Ferney had told her. "They put a new front door in then," he'd said. "Don't know why they did it. I never got round to putting it right." She just hadn't listened to him well enough.

Walking eagerly back to the house, she searched through the ivy that covered that part of the wall, easing its stems apart and inspecting the stone behind. She was still there when the builders arrived.

Rick called a cheerful "Good morning" as he got out of the van. "What have you found?"

"You tell me," she said, pointing. "Could this have been the original doorway?"

He followed the line of the masonry. "I'd say so. Cut stone all the way down. Nice regular line both sides. That's what it is, all right."

"Could we put it back?"

"You might have to get planning permission, I suppose."

She thought of Mike's objections.

"Would it be expensive?"

"Don't reckon so. There's a stone lintel still there. Wouldn't need to cost much at all."

It was an odd sort of day, still full of the emotional hangover of the day before. Whenever Ferney popped into her mind, which was often, she pushed him away, feeling unready to face his complications. Instead she drew all day, first the house as it was now, then a careful study of it with the door put back as it should be and then finally, dredging up details from her memory of Ferney's picture and the clues left in the house's old fabric, of it standing as it did then, complete with the leaning stone in front of it. After that she drew a face, the face of a thin man with a scarred cheek and long sideburns, the face from her dream.

It was only when the builders left and the evening light duplicated the day before that she found herself thinking about doorsteps again and the obvious message that had been trying to claim her attention all day finally got through. If the door had been in the middle of the house, then the doorstep had been, too. She might have looked under the right step, but the step itself had been moved. She had been looking in the wrong place.

Another hole to dig? Her soul was reaching for the spade while her head recoiled. Then the logical side of her found a justification—a double check, the location of the door and the hidden golden ring—twin fancies that she could test at the same time. She knew it would be simpler if they were false.

There was no stone to lift this time, but the earth was very hard. An ivy root grew right in the middle of where she had to dig, promising to make life difficult, so she started to one side of it, realizing it was likely to be a long and awkward job. She had dug out only four small spadefuls when the edge of the blade snagged in something springy. Thinking it was the ivy root, she felt down into the earth with her fingers and touched the end of a thick fold of flaking, damp leather.

7

GALLY CLIMBED UP to the hilltop again in the last of the light. In her pocket was wrapped-up terror. The approaching darkness was her deadline. While daylight held she could just about control the eddies in her unquiet mind, but she knew when night came the new fears shaken into life by Ferney would reinforce the legions of familiar devils. She also knew that had not been his aim and hoped he had the power and the will to help.

Logic told her there was no reason for him to be there on the hill again, but something else that was off to one side of logic mumbled its disagreement. That uncertainty allowed her to go, otherwise the fear of definitely seeing him, of having to confront the situation, might have proved stronger than her need. The curve of the hill kept its secrets until she was fifty yards from the summit, then she stopped abruptly. The sun was gone, but its rearguard had left the western sky flat, clear and bright and Ferney's immobile shape was sharply outlined against it.

She stood and looked. His back was towards her and she turned to circle round below the top of the hill, wanting to come on him from the front so that they could move more gently into each other's full awareness. As soon as she came into his view, he lifted a hand in calm benediction and she had time, stepping nervously almost on tiptoe up the rise, to study him. It might have been the light, but she felt she could see signs in his face of a younger man and curiosity joined with her vast need to gain the upper hand over her hesitancy.

"I have to talk to you," she said when she came up to him.

He smiled, shuffled sideways and patted the stone next to him. She sat, aware that they were close together.

"Have you been sitting here long?"

"Since noon," he said. "Once up the hill's enough for me."

"You were waiting for me."

He just smiled again. There would be no unnecessary words from this man.

"That was quite a strange thing you did to me," she said. "It was very upsetting. I'm . . . well, I suppose I'm in a bit of a mess. I need to understand."

He nodded, then kept his silence for a while and she thought perhaps he was choosing a starting point.

"There's a lot you would understand already if you let yourself know it," he said eventually.

"I'm not sure what you mean."

"Are you not? Let your head try to tell you. You might find it's not all a complete surprise."

He turned his head and looked hard at her as he said it and abruptly she found it difficult to focus on his face.

"Mr. Miller," she said, trying to keep some distance between them, "turning it back on me like that doesn't help. I don't want to listen to that. I want you to tell me plainly and simply what you mean." She was pleased that she had managed to say it firmly, but in the next moment she let out an unexpected, partly suppressed sob and he made a gentle noise of sympathy.

"I'm not Mr. Miller," he said. "Not to you. Just Ferney. Surnames come and go, don't they? We should take it a bit at a time. It is for the best."

She found it impossible not to believe that simple statement.

"Ferney," she said. "Please. It's going to be dark soon. I think I would rather just hear whatever it is you've got to say straight out."

He turned away from her and she was glad to be relieved of the pressure of his disconcerting gaze.

"Well, I wonder if you would? I hope so," he said. "I know how the dark bothers you. That's one of the things you need to understand."

"The story you told . . . you made me tell. How did you do that? You were leading me, weren't you?"

"It's all about the past. Do you have any idea how much of you is tied to the past?"

She let her breath out in a sigh. "Everybody tells me that. I know it is. I've gone over and over things that . . . things that happened to me when I was little. They all keep saying it should help, but it doesn't."

"That's not what I mean by the past. That's recent. What about the real past? History?"

She looked at him, wondering. "I've often felt like there's a big bit of me inside I can't get at," she said. "Is that what you mean? I can't go anywhere without wondering what really happened there, what it was like. There's so much of history that's lost and just a few dried old tatters pressed out in books."

"History's much shorter than people think."

She laughed then, caught by the absurdity. "What?"

"You don't know what I mean? Well now, I was born in 1907," he said deliberately, scratching at the ground with the end of his walking stick as if to inscribe the date. "You stretch my life forward from there and you get to here. Thing is, though, to me it really doesn't feel like this life of mine has taken all that long. It's rushed by, really, that's how years are when you're living them. They don't use up much time at all." He looked hard at her. "You can do sums. You tell me what happens if you stretch my life back the other way."

She understood straightaway what he meant, worked it out in her head. "Eighty-three years back the other way? You get to 1824."

"Eighteen twenty-four. Go back again from there."

"Another eighty-three years? 1741."

"And once more."

"Makes 1658."

"That's right, 1658. Only four of my lifetimes back from here and there you are. Think about that. Oliver Cromwell died. The plague hadn't come yet. It would be another few years before they did the right thing and let London burn down." He looked at her keenly. "Do you know what I'm trying to say?"

It didn't seem to be an answer to the main question in her mind but it touched a deep feeling in her.

"Yes, I think I do. None of it was very long ago."

"Most people wouldn't see that," he said. "For most people, they think back to when they were babies and that's nothing, that's just like yesterday. Fifty years in your lifetime is hardly time to get your garden right. Ask them to go back just one year before they were born, though, and that's something else, that's ancient history, isn't it? Go back further beyond that, it's all pretty much the same, 1812, 1585, 1066. It doesn't make much odds. It's like you said, it's dry old stuff in a book. Dates are just page numbers."

A car horn down in the lane stopped him for a second. "You and I know it isn't like that. Henry the Eighth? Five old man's lives back. The Magna Carta and all that rubbish? Eight lives. It's nothing, is it?"

The idea caught her with such intensity that, for a moment, it pushed the other questions aside.

"That's what I try to tell Mike," she said. "He makes it sound as if it was all so long ago that evolution's had time to change people completely, as if we're different from people in history. I'm always trying to persuade him it's just the circumstances that change, that people stay pretty much the same."

"How could he know? He wouldn't understand that."

Ferney's tone was dismissive and Gally felt she had to be loyal. "He tries. He knows a lot more about it all than anybody else I know."

Ferney made a little sound of amusement. "Thinks he does, you mean. Doesn't know as much as you."

She felt on dangerous ground, tried to change the subject. "What do you mean by 'Magna Carta and all that rubbish'?"

"Makes me laugh, the Magna Carta, the way they teach it these days as if it set everyone free. D-Day for the peasants, that's the way they teach it in schools. Wasn't like that, was it? Just a private deal with the barons, nothing to do with ordinary folk. Ordinary folk didn't even know about it."

"Didn't they?"

"Well, did they? You tell me."

She started to feel he was pulling her back towards that mental cliff edge from which he'd conjured the Duke of Monmouth's shade.

"I don't know," she said, more emphatically than she had intended.

"You do, Gally. Just like you knew where the ring was."

All the fear flooded back.

"I don't know what I knew. I think you led me into saying it. Why did you do it? You knew I didn't like rings. It hurts and . . ." She stopped.

"Go on," he said gently.

"It scares me," she said quietly.

"I wouldn't *choose* to scare you for the world," he said. "What I'm trying to do is stop you being scared. I'm trying to show you the reason for it so you'll know there *is* no reason anymore. If I really scare you, you tell me so I know, so we can sort it out. You'll understand one day. But I didn't really lead you into saying anything. It came from you. Did you find it?"

She didn't want to answer but he waited her out and in the end she had to say something. "I don't know," she said in the end. "I found some old, curled-up leather."

Ferney nodded, "His glove, that would be. That's what it was in. You've brought it."

It wasn't a question. She put her hand in the deep side pocket of her jacket and, with enormous reluctance, brought out a plastic bag. In the fading light he took it, looked at it thoughtfully, then reached in and pulled out the twisted, earth-caked lump. As he forced it open, parts of it flaked and broke away and out of the middle he took an intricate round object. The thin band of the ring was obscured by dirt, but set in the top of it was a stone and when he rubbed it carefully back and forth against his sleeve, it caught the last of the evening light and hurled it back at their eyes in a white flash.

"Put it away," Gally said urgently, looking around the hill's dark margins in horror, then caught herself doing it and wondered why. Ferney put his hand out and patted her arm.

"No need for that now," he said. "That's what I want you to understand. Last time this saw the sun, it stood to kill those that hid it, just as the axeman killed the man who gave it to them. Not now. They've given up looking for *his* friends a long time back. You're free of that now, Gally. You must understand that. There's no need for fear."

A sudden gust of colder evening air made him cough. A bat wove dancing darkness round their heads. He held the ring out to her and she made no move to take it, but his hand stayed there, offering it across the air and in the end, with a great effort of will, she reached out, hesitated and then almost snatched it. As she felt the weight of it and all it had seen, she knew it was exactly what he said it was and in accepting that, the fear prompted by it stepped out of its blind box in her mind and came into the open to be recognized and weighed. She let out a deep sigh, looking at the ring, turning it over and over. For now, she felt no need to know more about it so she put it back in the glove again. Other questions were more pressing.

"Who do you think I am?" she said.

"You're Gally."

He said it as though that obvious answer spoke volumes. Gally had a sense that she had but to lean towards him, let him draw her into it and all that she now was would melt from her. She thought suddenly of Mike, stepped back from that abyss, held on to the picture of her husband and of her beside him.

"That's no more than a name," she said. "I've only just met you and you're not being fair. Either tell me what you mean or stop it."

"Just a name?" he said and laughed softly, "It's a name, but it's not *just* a name. Ferney and Gally, they're a bit more than just names.

You want me to tell you directly? Yes, I could tell you," he was speaking calmly and kindly, "but that would be just words and words like that fight their own meaning. You've got to tell yourself, really. Tell yourself how you found that ring for a start."

"Maybe you put it there in my mind," she said. "The way you were questioning me. Maybe you were forcing me to think what you wanted."

He shook his head. "Don't be so daft. That's just nonsense, whatever you call it, witchcraft, telepathy, whatever. I can't do that. Never met anyone who could. It's much simpler than that. It was you. You remembered it."

"No."

"You did, didn't you, and that's not all, is it? You dug it up, so you remembered where the door used to be."

She jumped to her feet, feeling the good being undone, knotting her hands together.

"Don't," she said. "Stop it. How can you say things like that? How can you say I *remembered* it? Something that happened three hundred years ago?"

"Only four lifetimes."

Now she felt uncomfortable towering over the old man, and in sitting down again the sudden belligerence went out of her.

"Go on then, tell me."

"Only if you agree to something."

"What?"

"That all you'll do is listen. For now at any rate. Just listen to me so it has a chance to sink in. Another time, when you're a bit more used to it, we'll talk it over."

She nodded and sitting there in full darkness he began, gently, obliquely.

"Supposing there was somebody, living in a place like this, a long time ago, and he comes to a pretty unfortunate end, you see. Violent times. Anyway, he dies and that ought to be the end of it. It's not, though, not the end of it. A bit later on, there's a young lad, oh maybe two years old, no more than that, and the lad starts remembering things here and there. He knows more than anyone his age ought to. Doesn't know exactly how he knows, but he does. So of course, he attracts a bit of attention, the way you'd expect, cos he's such a quick learner, better than all the rest of his age. He's talking before they've stopped crawling and as he grows up, he's better with tools, better at skinning meat, better at all the things that have to be learnt. Doesn't always pay, being better like that. Puts people against you and as I say it was violent times, so before he got much beyond his twenties maybe he said a bit too much and he got someone's knife between his ribs one night."

Ferney looked sideways at Gally, gave her a small, almost apologetic smile. "Next time round, see, he wouldn't make that mistake again."

His voice was tiny, stirring the cold atoms of air just enough to reach her next to him at the centre of a vast dome of night.

"Next time round?" she said and the thought that came to her in the silence grew and grew until it burst out in speech. "How many next times were there?"

"All the ones from then to now," he said. "A lot too many to count."

"Oh God."

"They weren't all lives you'd remember," he added. "No medicines. All that sickness. Plagues and that. Sometimes you'd barely get born then you'd be starting all over again."

"And that's you?" she said. "All of them?"

He didn't need to answer and nothing in her prompted her to challenge it.

"And what about me? You're saying *I* come into this?"

He drew a breath. "Can you imagine it?" he said. "I don't suppose you can. You get a bit demanding after a few lives. Too many people, down the years, all pretty much the same. No one else can understand, you see. They wouldn't believe you, anyway, not unless they'd been through it too and of course they haven't. Just all that long line of noisy, foolish people. You couldn't love them. They'd keep dying on you and you'd still have the memory next time round, still have to find another one to love—another one who wouldn't understand." He took her hand and his touch felt like the first electric touch of a suitor. "That would be impossible to bear, you know it would—but there was one thing that saved the day, saved *all* the days. There was *one* person who did understand."

"One person? The same one, all the time?" She couldn't help the sudden edge in her voice.

He didn't answer directly. "Suppose he was lucky enough, this man, right at the start there, not to be alone, so it wasn't just him who died but the two of them. That's how it chanced to be. It was never easy, though. Their timing didn't always work out. Some lives, they might not meet up at all, might be the wrong ages, but some lives they would, because it was always in the same place, you see? It was the place that held them."

She was shaking her head not out of denial but out of an unwillingness to hear it. "No, Ferney."

"Yes," he said and his voice was suddenly very firm. "Yes, Ferney and Gally, always. Right down through the years. And always here. You've come home, Gally."

"Home? No, you can't say that."

"It *is* your home, our home."

If she just moved towards him the slightest fraction, she knew his arms would open and part of her longed to know what that felt like. She recoiled from that thought, became abruptly aware of the time, of the darkness, of the pale shadow of Mike. She jumped up, calmness gone. "I must go. I'm sorry. This is too much."

"Gally," he called as she was walking quickly away. "I'm doing nothing we haven't both agreed to. You'll know that soon."

That made her run, stumbling in the gloom, anxious to be alone, hating going away from him, until suddenly she was down at the hedge, going through the gate as if it spelt safety. When she walked distraught into the yard she simply failed to register the car standing there, so that when Mike opened the door of the caravan, looking anxious and saying, "There you are at last," she looked back at him as if she'd never seen him before in her life.

8

MIKE'S ANGER NIPPED their best hope in the bud. If he hadn't been so upset she might have been able to lift the veil straightaway, to tell him a little bit about the huge truth that was flapping round inside her head—nothing like the whole of it because it was too close and too raw, but perhaps enough to have earthed some of the unsettling charge that had built up inside her. She spent a few moments searching for the right way to start, but the words weren't in her to do that lightly and then, after casting around, she realized that it just wasn't possible. The cramped caravan was beating with the anger smelted out of his alarm at her absence. She knew it was born out of love and only aimed at her for lack of an alternative target. She also knew that if she gave him half a chance he would immediately swing the full force of that anger onto Ferney, so she told something that was only half a truth short of a lie.

"I was sitting on top of the hill. I lost track of time. I'm so sorry."

"I was going out of my head," he said. "Couldn't think what had become of you. I was about to get a search party out."

"What sort of trip have you had?"

"Bloody tiring—then I get back to a cold, empty caravan and you're nowhere in sight and I'm bloody starving."

For a moment she couldn't push away the thought that he was smaller in spirit than she had realized, but then guilt overcame her. She saw that he couldn't bring himself to admit he was worried for her safety for fear it would sound demeaning. She poured him a whisky, suppressed the subversive clamour within her and talked to him of student numbers, faculty appointments, budget restrictions and traffic jams until he felt sufficiently loved.

"Have you been lonely?" he asked her in the end.

"No, not for a moment," she said, before it occurred to her that he wanted to hear the opposite.

"You can't have had anyone to talk to," he said. "Well, not unless you count the builders."

"I've hardly talked to them at all."

"Did you sleep well? No bad dreams?"

"I was fine."

He looked at her with an expression that said she was holding something back and from then on, through the remains of an unsatisfactory evening, there was a tiny unnatural edge to their conversation which disturbed them both.

In the morning, unusually, Gally woke after Mike and found him sitting on the caravan step in the sunshine holding her sketch in his hands and looking at the front of the house. It was Saturday, so they had the place to themselves.

"What's this all about?" he said.

"It's the way the house used to be. I found out that the front door's definitely been moved. Don't you think it would all work much better if we put it back in the middle again?"

He pursed his lips and squinted at her. "You found out? How did you find out? Did the old man tell you?"

"He's got a picture of the house. He let me go and see it. Then I looked at the stonework and it was really obvious. You can see the edges of the old doorway. The builders say it would hardly cost any extra to put it back there and . . ."

"You went to see the old man, wotsisname, Franny."

"Ferney. Yes I did." Why did it feel to both of them like a confession?

"You didn't tell me."

He looked extraordinarily hurt, as if he had some idea of the scale of the problem that Ferney claimed to pose. He couldn't know. She shrugged, tried to get him off the subject. "We'd need planning, but that wouldn't be difficult because we could easily show the planners there used to be a door . . ."

"You went to his house?"

"Well, yes. Just to see the picture. You don't mind that, surely."

Silence now from Mike and the tiny dislocation between them grew wider as three or four tense seconds crawled away.

"I don't like the idea of you rushing off to see him as soon as my back's turned," he said in the end.

"Don't be ridiculous," she said, nettled. "You make it sound like I'm having an affair. The poor old man's over eighty."

That made Mike seem absurd even to himself.

"It's nothing like that. I just find him rather rude. I think he's trying to get you on his side."

"What side? Why should there be sides?"

"I don't know, but there are and he's definitely playing on the other team," said Mike. He couldn't say what he really meant, that she was fragile, that he worried constantly about her, feared that she might easily be derailed, to go crashing off the track of sanity into the unrelenting swamp of madness.

Because he couldn't find the words they left it there and led a separate morning clearing weeds and saplings from opposite ends of the site. At lunchtime he put up the white flag, went down beyond the house to the valley where she was emptying the barrow and called to her.

"Let's go down to the Hunter's Lodge and get something to eat."

"Yes, all right."

He went to take the handles of the wheelbarrow from her and started in surprise at her hand.

"You're wearing your wedding ring."

She looked down at her hand as though she hadn't known. "Oh yes."

"I thought you didn't like the feeling . . ."

"It's okay here."

"Oh good." He smiled broadly and she gave him a hug.

It was fifteen minutes' walk down the lanes, talking mostly of plumbing, bathroom designs and central heating. They squeezed into a corner of a bar that was crowded with travellers breaking the trek to the west. At the end of the meal Mike picked up their folded jackets from the window seat next to them and the other ring, the old ring, rolled treacherously out of Gally's pocket and bounced onto the table.

Gally had forgotten it was there, tucked it away into a corner of her mind with all the other challenges of the previous day—too difficult to handle with Mike around—so that she froze as they both looked at it.

"Where did that come from?" he said in surprise.

"Oh, it's just something I found at the house," said Gally. "It's nothing much." She took it, too quickly, and made to put it back in her pocket.

"Hang on a second. Can I see it?" he said and she gave it to him reluctantly.

They went outside and he stood in front of the pub turning it over in his fingers.

"Nothing much?" he said. "You must be joking." He rubbed hard at it. "That's gold and there's a stone in it. It might even be a diamond."

"No, surely not. Do you really think so?" she said brightly. "I expect it's just glass. I was planning to clean it up and see."

She held out a hand, but he didn't want to give it back.

"It's got a bit of age to it," he said. "I think we should take it to a museum. It's incredible. Where was it?"

She could bear neither to lie nor to tell the truth. "Near the front door," she said, "in the earth."

He was sharper than she expected. "Which front door?"

"The one in the middle—where it used to be."

He stared at her. "I wish I knew what was going on here."

Back at the house he insisted that she should show him and it was obvious straightaway that she'd been digging through the earth.

"I wanted to see where the step used to be," she said lamely, hating the way circumstances were pushing her ever further from the path of pure truth, but Mike had his mind on other things.

"We should go deeper," he said. "There might be something else."

"It's difficult. The ivy roots are in the way."

"We can cut through them, pull it all up."

"But that'll kill the ivy."

"If you want the front door here, that ivy root's got to go anyway."

"So you agree we should have the door here?"

"Well, yes, maybe. We'll see."

It was the first moment at which Gally fully accepted the whole truth about the ring, that she had told the story herself, had been prompted but not manipulated by Ferney into saying what had been buried and where it could be found. Until then she'd kept that aspect of the story wrapped up in her mind as a dangerous curiosity—something it was more comfortable to ignore, to stay agnostic. Now, looking at the earth and the ivy root, she knew with complete certainty that she *had* known the ring was buried there and she now knew equally that there should be nothing else there. Recognizing

that knowledge, she also knew for certain that life was never going to
be quite the same again.

There was no convincing way that she could tell Mike he was
wasting his time, and what she had just learnt was claiming space in
her mind, so, preoccupied, she helped with the harmless game.

It was doubly bewildering therefore when she discovered she was
wrong. Mike had been working away with a trowel on the undisturbed surface just to the other side of the root for no more than two
or three minutes when they heard a pronounced "chink."

"There's something else," he said excitedly. "It sounds like glass."

He scratched around with the point of the trowel, then used his
fingers to shovel out the loosened earth.

"It's a bottle." He sounded triumphant.

It must be modern, she thought, but when he'd exposed two inches
of stubby neck, sealed with a hard earthy mass which seemed to
cover a decayed cork, he destroyed that thought.

"Brilliant," he said. "Look at this. Eighteenth century, I should
say." He went on delving and the shape that emerged with difficulty
from the packed earth had a conical neck, widening out into a squat
globule of black-looking glass. He eased it out of the hole. "It's an
onion bottle," he said. "What a find."

Gally stared at it, disconcerted. The ring had been the embodiment
of the faint shreds of a dream, only really surprising in its solidity
and weight. This thing in front of her was completely alien, unknown. It had no place there and that was wrong. Mike carried it
to the builder's standpipe, ran water over it carefully washing off
the dirt. It shone iridescent, dark green. A lump of earth came away
from the side of it and revealed a round glass seal, moulded onto
the neck.

"Onion?" she said faintly. "What have onions got to do with it?"

"Oh, that's just what they call this shape," said Mike. "It's an old
wine bottle. Look at this. It's got initials on the seal and a date. RW
1680. I think there's something inside it, too."

He held it up to the sun. A thick layer of paste an inch deep
covered the bottom and bulged under a jellied crust as he tilted it.

"Why would it have been there under the step?"

"I know why," he said suddenly. "It's a witch bottle. That makes
sense. They buried them under doorsteps to keep evil away."

No, she thought, there were no witch bottles. We didn't . . . Ferney
didn't believe in things like that.

"What would be in it?"

"A horrible mess, I should think. Blood and urine and bits of toenail. I seem to remember they used to burn their hair and put that in too. You wouldn't want to open it."

Gally hated the bottle and its uninvited intrusion into the faded archive of her memory, but Mike was as pleased as punch. It was his find, not hers and she knew it gave him back a proprietorial sense, put him back in the driver's seat.

"We could take it in next week," he said. "When I come home. Maybe we should try the Taunton Museum. I'm sure they've got people who would know. They could have a look at the ring, too. I shouldn't be surprised if they're worth quite a bit, those two."

"You're not saying we should sell them, surely?" she said.

"Well no, not the bottle. It would be nice to keep that, but the ring might bring in a few bob."

"I found the ring," she said. "It's nothing to do with you," and he just stared at her. "Anyway, what's this 'when I come home' business?"

"Oh, I was going to tell you—haven't had a chance. I'm afraid I've been lumbered with a conference because Tony Briggs can't go. Stafford or somewhere. It's only a couple of days or so."

What seemed to her to be more alarming than anything else was that she wanted him to go and had to cover her disappointment when he said he didn't have to leave until Monday afternoon. The ring had pulled her off balance, swung her violently towards another world that already felt more compelling. There were a score of questions she wanted to ask and that, she knew, was something she could only do in Mike's absence.

FERNEY WASN'T ON the hilltop on Monday. She went straight there as soon as she was by herself, letting all the enormous implications of his words out into her conscious mind immediately Mike had gone. She sat on the stone in Ferney's place, but everything was uncompromisingly twentieth century. Aircraft from Yeovilton and a tractor refolding the tired earth for the thousandth time dominated her sense of the scene before her. In any case she knew it was his hilltop, susceptible to his magic, not hers. Whatever was in her head seemed too big to think about, so that she kept bouncing off it into something approaching laughter. There was happiness there—a muddled hope that here at last lay the clues to the bits of her that fooled her, scared her, trapped her.

A more sensible voice questioned that. Where is all this going? she thought. Wouldn't it be wiser to stop now? To stay away from the old man and just remember it as his joke? But that wasn't possible.

Something inside her was pushing at the closed doors, determined to find its way back to freedom, and there were so many things she needed to ask. She recognized and felt shocked by the sudden knowledge that Mike's feelings were, for the moment, a side issue. That triggered a burst of guilt. Mike always put her first, she knew that. She owed him an immeasurable amount for the months he had spent beckoning her out from her tunnel, even if she had so far been unable to follow his coaxing. She owed him devotion and affection, but the rest, through nothing she could control, seemed in abeyance.

When she got to his house Ferney was up but sitting in his chair with a rug over his legs and she knew when she looked at him that in the three days since she'd seen him last he had lost a lot more than seventy-two hours from the dwindling store of his years. He wouldn't let her fuss over him, though he allowed her to make them both tea.

"Do you feel well enough to talk?"

"For a bit."

She felt tender towards him in his illness, wanting to tuck the rug in around his legs but she knew she couldn't, knew she was prevented by a sense of his dignity and the strength of his character.

He looked at her hand and she knew he too had noticed the wedding ring, but he didn't say a word about it.

"Did anything come back?" he asked suddenly. "After we talked before?"

"Something turned up," she said. "Something that surprised me a lot. I showed the ring to . . ." She was going to say "Mike" but the oncoming word brought with it an unexpected sense of betrayal and she choked it off. Betrayal of whom, she wondered. Of Mike? No, of Ferney.

". . . to my . . . my husband." That sounded worse. How could Mike be her husband?

Ferney gave a look of deep understanding which disconcerted her completely. "He insisted on digging where the step was. I couldn't stop him."

"Why should you want to?"

"Because I knew there wasn't anything else there."

He nodded, pleased. "So what did he turn up?"

"An old bottle. Very old, in fact. It says 1680 on it and it's sealed up. He says he thinks it was a witch bottle."

Ferney looked startled for a second, then he lifted his head in acknowledgement of dawning understanding and nodded. "That would be it. Daft idea. They thought it kept you safe from spells." He seemed to think some more. "Yes, I suppose that would definitely be it." He looked at her acutely. "It worries you."

It wasn't a question.

"Yes," she admitted, "it does."

"Why?"

"Because . . . because I didn't have the slightest idea that it would be there."

"And that was a surprise?"

"Yes." Another admission that called for an explanation for herself as much as for him. "Because since this all started none of it has really surprised me completely—but I didn't know that until I had something to compare it all to and the bottle was that something. I simply didn't know *anything* about it."

"Nor did I, but I can guess."

"Go on."

"You say it said 1680 on the bottle? Well, it wouldn't have happened in 1680. That was five years before the Duke of Monmouth came. The bottle wasn't put there then, I'm sure. It must have been, let's see now, a good twelve years, maybe even fifteen after that." He looked across at the shelves. "Pass me that book, would you, that big white one on the bottom shelf."

She went to the shelf and ran her finger along a line of history books. *"The Encyclopedia of Dates and Events?"*

"That's it." He coughed loudly, painfully, turning the pages. "Now, 1688. I thought so." He looked up at her searchingly. "You've got things that hurt inside your head. I know that. This might help."

"It does help. It has already," she said softly.

"What really frightens you?" he asked and she should have told him, should have said *boilman and burnman,* but you couldn't just bring them up into the open like that, not without a bit of time, and thinking he was helping her he moved in to fill the lengthening silence.

"I noticed before, you're not too happy about horses."

"How did you notice that?" she said, surprised.

"When we talked about Monmouth and the others, arriving on their horses."

She bit her lip. "It's not a big thing. I don't *hate* them at all, I'm just a bit nervous when they're around." That was only the half of it, she knew at a deeper level, but a childhood of horses, constantly afraid, constantly told not to be so babyish by her distant, horsy mother, had layered deep scar tissue over the first fear.

Ferney nodded and looked down at the book again. "Now, 1688. Prince William of Orange landed at Torbay. Call it come-uppance for what the king did to Monmouth, if you like." He smiled at her. "It shouldn't be like this. Me sitting here, telling you dry facts. It makes the words work much too hard."

"It doesn't feel like that. I get pictures in my head."

"Join in, then. Tell me. It helps me fill in the gaps."

This time she was a willing participant, waiting expectantly.

"We went to Wincanton. You still called it by the old name, said it was prettier," he looked at her, questioning, but she frowned and shook her head.

"Wyndcaleton," he said and the syllables chimed faintly somewhere. "Didn't know anything special was going on that day. We were going to sell something. Eggs I expect, a basket each. We came in the east end of town and walked straight into it. Soldiers everywhere— the Irish beast, Sarsfield and his mob, Irish Dragoons they called themselves. There must have been a hundred of them. King James's soldiers supposedly, but they were a bunch of ruffians really, barely a uniform amongst them that day, excepting Sarsfield himself and he was the most dangerous man you ever saw."

Nothing substantial came into her mind, which disappointed her.

"Are you all right?" he said, and she wondered why he was so solicitous.

"Yes."

"We didn't want to walk through them. You couldn't be sure what they'd do, except that it wouldn't be nice. We'd seen quite enough of Sarsfield and his louts in the area. Then we saw the other lot coming out of town."

A sudden piercing vision as if a powerful light had been switched on. In her mind's eye a small band of men were leading a string of horses down a track between hedges. There were low roofs beyond. She saw them stop, half of them turning back, leading the horses to safety. There was no doubting it, nor the acute fear it brought with it.

He saw her expression change. "You've got it."

"Yes, I think so . . . I don't like it."

"Take it easy on yourself, then. Let it go. Don't try to remember. Listen to me and I'll tell you."

He might as well have told her to turn off the sun.

"Who are the men with the horses?" She said it now, but in her mind it was her old voice speaking and all she did was repeat the words.

"Well, we didn't know, did we? Except that they had to be with the Prince of Orange and whatever they were like they had to be better than King James's Irish thugs."

Puffs of smoke erupted shockingly from the hedges in her memory. The sharp smell of black powder.

"They're firing at us!"

There was a quavering note of indignant distress in her voice. Ferney reached out for her arm and gripped it. "Not at us," he said urgently. "At each other. Stop now. It was all over a long time ago." She looked at him and he relaxed his hold. "I'll tell you the way the books tell it. They say it was the first skirmish of the rebellion. The Prince of Orange had landed down at Brixham in Devon. Dutchman or not, he had British soldiers with him, Mackay's regiment. By the time they got here they needed packhorses, so a young lad called Campbell took a few soldiers into town to get them and he met Sarsfield's hooligans on the way out. It was our bad luck we got mixed up with them."

That started her off again, pulled the curtains of her mind far enough apart to let in the hollow acid-wash of acute fear.

"It feels horrible, Ferney. What was it? What happened?"

"Nothing good." He weighed his words, gripped her arm tighter. "Not for you. Not for me. You . . . came to an ending there."

"I died?"

"Yes."

The simple statement reached into her head, connected and cauterized the raw stump of memory.

"The books don't say anything about *you*." His voice was quiet. "They say that Sarsfield and Campbell were both killed and thirteen of their men. They say that the townsfolk didn't like the Irish troops and they scared them off by telling them more of the prince's army was coming. Thing was, the military kept their records and counted their bodies, but there weren't any reporters coming round to write down what happened to you and me and our like, not in those days. No one noticed us when it came to writing history."

"I died?" Her voice quavered but her mind stopped searching. There would be nothing to find.

"Yes. Not right away. Not there. It was a horse that got you. I don't think you even knew. We were taking ourselves out of the way and I suppose it panicked. Bloody great thing came leaping over the hedge at us and knocked you for six."

"Go on," she said. "I think I'm all right now."

He looked suddenly distressed himself. "They wanted to take you into the houses. It was plain you were dying, but I didn't want you to die there, see? We're always afraid what might happen if either of us died too far from here."

That raised a tumult of questions in her head, but she pushed them aside for the present.

"I got three boys to help and we brought you all the way back here on a litter. I don't think you knew what was going on. I tried to do it all gently, but it was a long old way home. Then almost as soon as we'd set you down in the house I saw you'd gone." He sighed and his eyes turned obliquely away to the long slant of years.

"Did it matter?" she said and he swung his gaze back to her.

"I'm trying to understand," she said. "It's more than I can take in, but if you know that . . . the other person will always come back, doesn't that change things?"

"Do I have to explain that?" His voice filled with pain and disappointment."

"Yes, you do," she said, not as gently as she expected. "I'm not nearly as far along this road as you think."

"But you do know I'm telling you the truth?"

"I don't *know*, I *think*—that's all." It was a mild lie, born of the need to preserve herself, to withhold full acceptance until she was sure it was safe.

He shut his eyes for a long moment. "Do you hope that I am?"

Something in her didn't want to say even that, but the answer was undeniable. "Yes, I do."

He smiled then and she couldn't help herself doing the same.

"Death's touched you in this life, hasn't it?" he said.

"The baby."

"Not just the baby."

"No. My father too."

"It was very bad," he said and it was a statement.

"Yes."

"We'll talk about that when you want to."

"So what was it like for you when the thing with the horse happened?"

"I think maybe it's even worse for us when one of us dies," he said slowly. "For other people, I suppose it's a bit more simple. Maybe they meet someone else, maybe they don't—but if not, they haven't got too long to get through by themselves. Even if they're young, I mean thirty or forty years isn't that long." He started to cough again and it was a minute or two before he could talk. "For us, though, it makes you afraid. Chances are it'll be ten years before you know the other one's back—then they'll be far too young and other people always get suspicious when old men and young women get too friendly. Chances are you might not find each other at all that time or the next time or the time after that."

"But that doesn't mean you have to be alone, surely there are always other people?"

Ferney looked at her as though that remark was the true measure of how very much she still had to discover.

"What have other people ever been to us? You might get a bit of warmth from them, but you can't tell them, can you? Not so they really understand and if they did, all you'd get would be jealousy. You'd be asking them to take second best."

"So what are we to each other, Ferney?"

"The best, Gally, always the best. No one else ever comes near."

"You can't just tell me that and expect me to understand it. I don't know it's true." Her distress showed in her voice and blurred her vision. It was always so difficult to *see* him, she thought. The harder she looked the more he seemed to disappear, all except his eyes.

"It *is* true."

"But . . . it does happen? There have been other people for us?"

"Well you know the answer to that. There's you and that Mike." He stopped himself saying the rest—that it hardly ever happened and that Mike was the only other one she'd ever *married*.

"He's not 'that Mike.' He's just Mike and that's really not fair."

He started to cough again, bending painfully in his chair, and she wondered unworthily if he was using it to think up a response.

When he got it under control, he held up both hands in surrender. "I suppose it's different when you don't remember. Sometimes other people come into it when you do remember, when you've been left by yourself, but they never amount to anything."

"The bottle?" she asked, recognizing a certain slight jealousy in herself.

"Some woman. Can't even fix her name. Joan something? She tried latching onto me and I suppose I took a bit of comfort there, but not for long."

"How long?" she said, and thought herself immediately absurd for borrowing the tone of an angry lover.

"A year maybe."

"A year?" She thought about that. "So why the bottle?"

He let out his breath in a long whistle. "Well, you came back, didn't you? And then there was a whole lot of fuss about this and that."

Fuss? He started to cough and at the end, shaken and white, he looked so tired and ill that the need to care for him came suddenly before the questions. She did what she could, trying to persuade him to call a doctor, but he simply smiled and refused so firmly it left no room for discussion.

9

THE CURVING DEAD end of bungalows which culminated in Ferney's house was a machine-age comma stamped onto the gentler longhand of the overgrown rise of fields. Leaving the last of the bungalows behind her, Gally walked slowly into a trough of increasing doubt. It felt perverse. The houses behind her were new, brick—overwhelming evidence of the modern world. The lane ahead was ancient and leafy, and where buildings claimed their sporadic spaces their bones were of old stone whatever modern makeup they might wear. Walking from the new into the old should have made it easier to stay in Ferney's world, but it did not.

It's Ferney himself, she thought. *I'm moving out of his gravity. It's only when I'm near that he can make me think like him.* Every step took her further from his influence and ever-present guilt came oozing in to fill the gap. Ferney made her forget Mike, which surely was cause enough. That was what the guilt said, but a more insistent voice was still speaking and that voice, unforgivably, spoke a simple betrayal. Mike doesn't measure up to Ferney, it said, and she tried to shut its echoes out. She walked faster and that helped. She fixed Mike's face in her mind as an icon and wrestled with the lines when they tried to subvert her by blurring treacherously into a vague sketch of someone else.

Halfway home she was able to persuade herself that she had won. Mike had started to set solid again and she tried phrasing promises to herself. I'll keep my distance from Ferney, she thought, just for a bit. I'm letting myself be carried along and I owe Mike much more than that. Putting on a determined face, she strode on.

The halfway point was only the eye of the storm. As soon as she came in sight of the house it caught her unawares. She saw thatch again for just a moment where there were only slates, expected a warm greeting where there were only busy builders and was forced to accept that there were two sources of the power twisting her brain, not one. It felt more like a promise than a threat and as she came closer to the house so she became more aware of the tiny process of growth going on in her womb. It must be all right this time. This had to be the right place for her baby. She doubted she had the inner reserves to go again through that valley of pain into the tear-filled vacuum beyond. For the three remaining months after the miscarriage, when her body should have been swelling and ripening, she had been no more than a shadow, disrupted physically, mentally and chemically, always aware of the calendar of what should have been. This time it would be all right.

She faltered at the gate, but Don Cotton the builder was standing there talking to his foreman Rick and he hailed her. They were planning an assault on the roof and she was forced back across the divide into the present. It wasn't what she'd wanted to hear.

"You'd better tell your old man it's going to be cheaper in the end to strip this side off completely and start again," he said. "You'll get away with patching up the far side, but there's a lot of dodgy rafters in the middle there. If you leave them you'll just be storing up trouble for yourself in the long run."

She looked up at the roof, imagined it renewed, straightened out, with regular tiles, and knew it couldn't be. The house begged for slow, organic healing, not transplant surgery.

"No, that's not the way I want it," she said. "That's too brutal."

"Perhaps I'd better have a word with Mr. Martin when he comes back," said the builder unwisely. "I'm just worried about his chequebook."

"There's no need for that," she said stiffly. "You may treat *your* wife like that, Mr. Cotton, but I can promise you I speak for both of us." She saw Rick grin behind his boss's back. "I've told you right from the start that I don't want the house looking like some horrible modern conversion."

"Well, you're obviously the one calling the shots," he said irritatingly and looked round at the house. "Though I must say I don't know what you see in all the old stuff that makes it so worth keeping."

Far too much, thought Gally wearily, as a heavy ball of inaccessible information rolled around her skull.

She immersed herself in the garden for a few hours, working away on the far side of the house to clear the old borders and free the flower beds from the obscuring, harsh-stemmed invasion of weeds. I do this well, she thought. I don't ever have to wonder which the weeds are. Is that because I've done it so many, many times? Logic and intellect couldn't help her, but the calm, repetitive work gradually pushed out deliberate thought and she had time to be nothing but herself. In this meditative state the question still forced itself on her, but on a level that seemed to dwell slowly in her soul, not quickly in her intellect. She pulled up a weed with hands that had always been hers and yet all at once seemed not to be hers. Dropping the fractured stalk, she gazed for a long time at her fingers and thought they had become less real, less intrinsically part of her, nothing more than a soft, convenient, temporary machine—the latest in a long line. She liked her hands. They were graceful hands and the receptive, sensitive skin of her fingertips gave touch a high ranking in the order of her senses.

It came to her abruptly that they would not always have been like this. What if they had been malformed, damaged? What if chance genes had thickened the skin, dulled her ability to sense the world? Would that not have tilted the balance that made her what she was? It would certainly have changed her perception. The conviction grew in her then that she was not what she thought. If there was an enduring Gally, and now she was back at the house there was no longer anything inside her arguing against that with any conviction, then it would have had to sit inside a shell that had at least some temporary say in what that composite creature was.

She rocked back on her heels as the implication spread slowly through her, trying to imagine how different it would be if she were shorter, fatter, lame. She found herself feeling the shape of her own head with hands coated with parching earth-dust. If her brain were smaller, physically different, what then? Would she be a different mongrel Gally? If a different body held different glands would she be faster to anger, less able to reason?

For just a second she had a clear idea of the way past the blockage in her head—that if she let go of trying to find this modern version of herself in the past and could focus instead on the bit that was always there, she would have much more chance of breaking through. Trying to pursue that idea before it fled, a voice broke in to interrupt and sabotage her attempt, an old female voice rich with indignant affront.

"My goodness me, you've really let my garden go, haven't you?" and she looked up in shock to see Mrs. Mullard standing, bent acutely over a walking stick at the corner of the house.

"I didn't hear a car," she said, groping for meaning in the words.

"That's because I didn't come by car," said the old woman a bit more cheerfully. She prodded the earth with her stick. "You have to keep at it, you see, or the weeds get in. You young people think you can just sit back and say I'll do it next week. Still, I daresay you'll know better next time."

Gally nearly protested but she bit her lip and nodded instead.

"How long is it since you were here last?" she asked gently.

Mrs. Mullard peered round her for a minute before answering. "Oh, not very long," she said. "We had to stop coming because of the petrol rationing."

Gally took her round to the front of the house and introduced her to Rick and the builders. Mrs. Mullard wasn't inclined to let them off lightly either.

"You young men should be more careful," she said severely, pointing at the end wall. "There's no call to go bashing things around like that."

Gally sat her down in the caravan and made her a cup of tea.

"How did you get here?" she said as she arranged biscuits on a plate.

The old woman put four spoonfuls of sugar in her tea, stirred it with one hand and took a biscuit with the other. As she could not have weighed much more than six stone, it spoke of an extraordinary metabolism. Perhaps she stocks up when she can, Gally thought, remembering the bleak sparsity of her own home.

"On the bus," she said.

"Oh, I didn't know there was a bus."

"It wasn't the usual driver," said the old woman. "I think they've changed the route. He went a bit wrong so I walked the last stretch."

"Where from?"

"Oh down the way somewhere," she said vaguely and Gally suddenly wondered how many miles she had walked to get to this once familiar place.

"I'm being very careful about what they do to the house," Gally said. "It *had* suffered a bit since you left, you know."

"Nothing lasts, does it? But I suppose you've got lots of time to get it the way you want it."

Gally suddenly felt a need to confide, to share her secret with someone else, and by taking the risk, cement the certainty of it.

"Not that long, really. I'm going to have a baby so we'll want to get everything done in time for that."

Mrs. Mullard showed what seemed to be disbelief as she looked at Gally's slim body. "When are you due?"

Gally immediately wished she had never raised the subject. She could hardly say eight and a half months.

"Not for quite a while," she said lamely. "After the New Year."

Mrs. Mullard looked at her calculatingly. "You might not want to tell *him* that," she said.

"You mean Ferney?"

The old woman nodded, "He won't like it. He doesn't like children being born here."

"Why not?"

"Who knows? Who knows the half of what he does with his ways and his spade?" She looked hard at Gally. "It's why I came really—I thought it was only right to warn you."

"To warn me about Ferney?"

"Well, not so much Ferney, except for the baby. More about the tramp."

Gally poured her some more tea. The tramp? One thing at a time.

"What happened to you here?" she said quietly.

Mrs. Mullard dropped her voice. "I had to leave the house, you know. He made me. I was having a baby and he didn't like that. I was a bit younger than I am now."

"How did he make you leave?"

"He's a strange one, he is. He had a wife then. I got on well with her. She was . . ." Mrs. Mullard's voice trailed off and she looked momentarily confused. "Well, silly me. I was going to say she was called Gally but that's your name, isn't it, my dear?"

Gally's heart stepped sideways. "Where did they live?" she said.

"Down in the village. A nice cottage. Happy as clams they were."

"Lamberts Lea?"

"That was it. Peacocks."

"They had peacocks?"

"No, of course not. Whatever gave you that idea? Anyway, then I started with the baby."

"And that was a problem? Why did it matter?"

"You ask him. I don't know. He was always up round here. He'd behave like this was his house half the time, but I didn't mind because he used to do the drains and things like that for me, any odd jobs. He was good with the house. Until the baby."

"I don't understand what happened."

"He didn't want me to have the baby here, you see. He said it would be bad for it. Too damp or some nonsense like that. I had the other house from my aunt."

"The one you're in now?"

"Yes, that's it. I'm just there for a bit you know." Then her eyes clouded over as she looked out of the caravan window at the builders and gave a little shrug. Gally waited until she started again.

"He packed me off down there with some excuse—said the drains were blocking, though I hadn't noticed. Then I came back a bit later and you should have seen it. Water everywhere and the whole wall coming down. 'Course there wasn't any choice then. I had to go off to the other house and what with one thing and another . . ."

"Didn't *Mr.* Mullard have anything to say about it?" said Gally, greatly daring.

"Mr. Mullard, poor darling. My Johnny? He never came back from the war. His name's on a big stone at Vimy Ridge," she said with quiet pride. "He fought with the Canadians—all through Ypres and the Somme and then they got him."

Gally tried to work it out. That was the First World War, so the baby couldn't have been Johnny's. It was much later.

Mrs. Mullard helped her out. "I was married at sixteen, widowed at eighteen," she said. "Bessy, my girl, she wasn't Johnny's. It was the tramp."

She got up, leaning on her stick, awkward in the cramped aisle of the caravan, and slowly climbed down using its shaky step. Gally thought that was it, but the old lady turned and jerked her head to show she should follow. Gally walked next to her, matching her speed, wondering. Mrs. Mullard pushed gingerly through the still overgrown edges of the yard to the crumbling stub wall of a collapsed shed, now no more than two feet high, the remains of its tin roof lying aslant in the brambles.

"It's a good place for wood, this one," she said. "Nice and dry." She stopped and gazed at it, nodding, and when she started to speak again her voice had a rasp in it. "It was here." The pace of her words changed as if she were now speaking to herself. "I came to get the wood in and he was in here, you see, staying in out of the rain. A big man. I knew I'd seen him around once or twice up and down the road. He grabbed me tight so I didn't have a chance."

Gally, suddenly understanding where Bessy had sprung from, murmured sympathy, but Mrs. Mullard waved a hand. "He weren't a bad-looking man. I could tell he was an old soldier."

"Did he hurt you?"

"Hurt *me*? No, I hurt *him*. Kicked him as hard as I could you-know-where."

"Didn't that stop him?"

"Stop him? No, that was afterwards. That was because he hadn't been polite. I taught him. He was quite well trained by the time he left. I'd had three weeks to straighten him out by that time." She gave the remains of the shed another hard look. "Don't stack the wood right against the back wall. There's a bit of rain comes in there if the wind blows and if he's around don't come out here by yourself, because he might not be your sort." Fifty years had passed unnoticed in her mind.

"I won't," Gally promised.

"If I were you, I wouldn't tell Ferney about the baby. There's no telling what he might do."

"Do you know why?"

"It's a mystery to me."

"What happened to Ferney's wife?"

"Don't you know? I thought everybody knew."

Gally shook her head.

"She just went one day. No one knew where. Ferney wanted the whole hue and cry. Said someone had done away with her. There was no end of searching, but they never found anything. 'Course, I'd gone by that time, but that's the way I heard it. Never stopped searching for her, they say. Him and that spade of his."

THE NEXT DAY Gally got the message from the postman, not the usual way with a stamp, but in an envelope he'd found propped against Ferney's door with handwritten delivery instructions on it.

"He's never quite seen the point of the system," said the postman ruefully. "I don't know how many letters I've delivered for him over the years, all round the village. He gets ever so cross when I'm on holiday and the others won't do it. I dread to think what will happen if he's still around when I retire. I'll just have to buy him a big stock of stamps, I suppose."

The postman looked set for a good few years, but the note made Gally wonder if he'd ever have to buy the stamps. It was short.

> Gally, the doctor says my chest is too bad and I am going into hospital for a few days. Don't fuss about it. Don't think of coming to see me. It's better you don't. I will be back home soon.

His handwriting was so familiar and she felt a strong pang of loneliness that he should be miles away and barred from her.

Mike came back from his conference at lunchtime that day. He got out of the car with an expression that told Gally and the world that there was a triumph somewhere in the recent past. Gally would usually have to drag communication unwillingly out of him when he came home after a long drive, while she, being the opposite, would assault him with information he didn't want as soon as the wheels stopped turning. This time, she couldn't have held him back if she'd tried.

"My paper went down fantastically well," he said. "They loved it. Masses of questions. It went on and on."

"Great. That's brilliant. The builders have . . ."

"There was a man from Wagners, the publishers? He came up afterwards and said he thought there was a book in it."

"A book? Oh that's . . ."

"He took me out to dinner to talk about it. He's so keen. He's hoping to make an offer next week."

Gally knew she should be able to remember what the paper had been about, but it hadn't seemed like anything real when he'd told her. She also knew that Mike, though an academic to the core, had a secret dream of popular acclaim, of being catapulted onto the chat-show circuit by the force of his own ideas.

"What are you going to call it?" she said, hoping for the best.

"Maybe something like 'The Saxon Farming Revolution and Social Change.' I don't know, though, that could be a bit too long. It ought to be catchy, really."

"I want to hear all about it later on," she said then, fearing the builders might nobble him. "By the way, I've told Don Cotton to go easy on the roof. He wanted to strip it all off and start again. I said we wanted to keep all the sound bits."

Put that way, Mike saw it as a sensible money-saving argument.

"Of course. Do you know what else he said?"

"Who?"

"The publisher . . . about my paper?"

THEY SPENT THE afternoon the way she had come to love best, clearing away the wreckage and the tangled undergrowth, filling the latest in a long line of skips and heaping brambles onto the bonfire. With every load the old delineations of the house and its surroundings showed through more clearly. Mike was happy to go along with it, relaxed and cheerful. When the builders left, the sudden descent of peace drew them into the house. The stairs had rotted long ago and the builders had put ladders up to get at the underside of the roof. They climbed up on the clattering, insubstantial stiffness of mortar-coated aluminium and stood precariously where the remains of the floor planking crossed the beams. The walls dividing the old rooms were skeleton frames of dusty laths with patches of plaster sagging off in strings.

"It looks tiny," said Gally.

"That's only because you can look right through it from end to end," said Mike. "When they repair the walls you'll see there's plenty of room. Which one shall we have for our bedroom?"

"Oh, that end," she said, surprised that he should be in any doubt, and almost added, "where it's always been."

"Rick says they need to know where the bathroom's going because they'll be running the main pipes through the wall. I suppose next to the bedroom?"

"Well, I thought we ought to have a little nursery next to the bedroom," she said, and felt a bubble of horror enclose her as Mike turned a startled face towards her and she realized it was the first he'd heard of it.

She could hear the echo of her words, lighthearted, casual—not at all as though she was letting him in on a secret.

"You mean . . . you feel you're ready to try again? Are you really, love? We don't have to rush, you know."

"I think we might have rushed already," she said slowly. "I'm not quite sure yet," though she was.

"But when did you . . . how long . . . ?"

"It's just a thought I have," she said. "I'd put a big bet on it actually, but it's too early to know definitely."

My God, she was thinking. Two other people knew and Mike didn't. What am I doing to us? I've got to stop this.

It wasn't a good place for it. The need to balance kept them awkwardly apart, so he couldn't do all the things that absorbed culture told him to. He tried to put his arms round her, swaying alarmingly on the beam, and had to stop. They climbed down, with Mike taking exaggerated care that she shouldn't slip, and hugged in the dusty chaos of the ground floor, but a crucial handful of time had inserted itself to push the natural quality out of the space between the news and the reaction to it. He told her how excited he was and stroked her belly which was completely flat. He was unsettled by it.

"What's wrong?"

"Nothing."

"Yes, there is."

"Well, not much. I just wish we had the place all ready first."

"It's all right," she said. "The house won't take nearly as long as the baby."

"It's not just that, though. We don't know anyone here yet. Who's going to be around to help?"

"We didn't know that many people in Turnham Green. Not unless you counted awful Aggy and slimy Steve next door. I'll know people here, you'll see."

"Have you seen the old man?" he asked suddenly. It wasn't an accusation, just an interested question, and she wondered if it was his gift to her to fit the moment.

"He's been taken to hospital."

"Oh dear. Anything serious?"

"I don't know."

"Do you think we ought to ring up and find out?"

"That would be a nice thought."

There was a phone in the caravan now. Gally hadn't really wanted it, but Mike insisted he had to have one though it was really so he could reassure himself that she was all right in his absences. She couldn't wait to ring, but for the sake of prolonging the truce over Ferney which Mike seemed to be offering she hung on until they went in for a cup of tea.

"Was she a relation?" the hospital wanted to know. What a question. No, she wasn't and yes, she was more closely related to him than anyone in the history of relations. "No," she said, "just a friend."

The news was that he seemed a little better but they were keeping him in for observation. She put the phone down.

"It's a shame you two got off on the wrong foot," she said. "He's very interesting. He knows such a lot about the local history."

"He's an amateur," said Mike absently. "They're dangerous. They're always so sure they know more than they really do. Knowledge does change, you know. You've got to stay abreast of the latest thinking."

This is history, not nuclear physics, she thought, surely you know less as time passes, not more—but she kept it to herself.

"Tell me about the book," she said.

He looked suddenly enthusiastic. "I think it's being here gave me the idea," he said. "All these medieval field systems. It's so clear to see. I want to do something absolutely definitive about the way technology changed rural life. Plough designs had so much to do with it, you know—when they first used iron bands to edge the plough they could really start to get more out of the soil. A total revolution, and this place sits right on the borderline between two agricultural systems. You've got all the herds of sheep on the chalk uplands towards Salisbury Plain and down in the flatlands you've got heavy soil." He looked almost embarrassed. "I sometimes think the place is trying to speak to me."

"Great," she said, and thought, it's *shouting* at me.

THEY WERE GOING to Taunton the next day to look at bathrooms and as they were about to get in the car Mike said something Gally had been dreading.

"Let's go to the museum while we're there. I'll take the bottle and you can show them your ring."

There wasn't a way of saying no without having to explain and at least he had said "your ring." It was in her pocket anyway, where it always was.

They looked at baths that they thought were elegant but failed to convince. Georgian, Edwardian, Victorian plastic pastiches. All she wanted was a nice old rounded, cast-iron bath, but modern replicas with over-clever ball-and-claw feet were frighteningly expensive. They found what she wanted in a reclamation yard, chipped and scarred but real enough. Mike still complained about the price, but they arranged delivery and picked up a solid, simple lavatory there at a bargain price to make him happier. Then they headed into the town centre.

Arriving unannounced, they had to wait for someone to talk to.

"Shall we have a quick look round?" Mike said.

Gally was fascinated and reluctant at the same time. The display cases beckoned her like a family scrapbook, but she recognized the depth of the unknown contained in them and the danger that they might come out with a wider gulf between them if the fragments of old Somerset drew her in too far. In any case, however sensitively it had been laid out, the place smacked of Mike's analytical, intellectual approach and she feared it would feel like going to inspect the dissected labelled corpses of past friends.

The man who saw them was studious, friendly and at once interested in the bottle.

"That's right," he said. "If it was under the step, I'm sure it was a witch bottle." He tilted it against the light. "Mostly urine, I expect, plus all kinds of other unsavoury bits and pieces. Do you know what the idea was?"

"To protect you from witchcraft," said Mike.

"Well, clearly. But the main idea was to identify the witch. Boiling your urine stopped the witch being able to urinate. The only way she could free herself from the spell would be to come to your house to dig up the bottle."

"Then you scratched her," said Gally without conscious thought and the man nodded enthusiastically.

"Absolutely. You scratched her to draw blood and after that you were cured of the spell." He looked at her appreciatively. "You know your folklore."

Gally passed it off with a shrug as Mike raised his eyebrows. "When do you think it would have been put there?"

"The date on the bottle's a good clue," said the man. "Wine bottles were a pretty new idea. The landed gentry had them—that would be the owner's initials moulded into the neck seal—and they'd send them to be refilled at the wine merchant. This one was new in 1680, but they got out of date pretty quickly. The shape was developing very rapidly round about then. They got more like bottles and less like blobs and so I should think ones like this would have been thrown out by about 1690 at the latest—too old-fashioned, you see. There's a pretty good chance we could work out whose it was from those initials."

"There's something else, too," said Mike. "We found a ring under the step."

I found the ring, not we, Gally said to herself and with the greatest reluctance she brought it out of her pocket and held it out.

The man made an appreciative noise. "That's quite a find." He picked it up and looked at it carefully with a magnifying glass. "Stuart Crystal. It's certainly old. Seventeenth century obviously. Might I give it a quick clean?"

Gally nodded rather doubtfully and he left the room.

"They're from about the same time, then," said Mike. "That ring could be worth quite a lot."

"I wouldn't want to sell it."

She was thinking how close Ferney's woman, the questionable Joan, must have come to finding the glove herself when she buried the bottle. It was only six inches off to the side.

"Are you going to sell the bottle?"

"No," he said, hurt. "I want it. Anyway it wouldn't be worth nearly as much as the ring." Seeing her expression, he changed tack. "A ring like that ought to be in a museum, really."

They sat in silence for a while after that.

The museum man came back looking pleased with himself. "I've just given it a light clean, but I think a specialist needs to see this." He had it on a small plastic tray. "It's definitely gold. The hoop's enamelled black with some sort of scroll design on it, I think. Now the dirt's off the crystal, do you see?" He pointed with a pen. "Do you see the face on the bezel?"

Under the crystal was a light blue oval with, painted onto it, a man's head. It had long, dark hair and flowing moustaches. "Charles the First," he said.

"So it's a royal ring?" said Gally.

"No, no, no," said the man. "There were quite a lot of these. Certainly it would have belonged to a royalist, but I couldn't go further than that. It is very unusual, though." He pointed at the place where the bezel joined the hoop. "I'm pretty sure it's a swinging bezel. It's all seized up and I don't want to force anything, but it looks to me as though if you could swing the bezel round you would probably find the other side was a signet ring, and there's definitely an inscription around the inside of the hoop."

"So it could be valuable?" said Mike.

"It would certainly repay further investigation," said the man. "I'm trying to think what it could have been doing under the step. What's your house like?"

"Just an old farmhouse. A cottage really," said Gally.

"This isn't the sort of thing you find in folk medicine. More likely someone hid it for safekeeping. Where is this house of yours?"

"Penselwood," said Mike.

"Ah, a wonderful place."

"It's a house called Bagstone Farm."

The man looked suddenly thoughtful, scratched his head.

"Are you in a rush?" he said. "We could just pop over the way to the county archive. That does ring a vague sort of a bell."

Across the courtyard from the museum in the old castle building was a quiet, studious library, lined with books and box files. It was the sort of place Mike could lose himself in for hours and which Gally would previously have shunned as freeze-dried, tasteless history. Now she looked at it with new eyes, wondering if it might hold scraps of the right answers if only she knew the questions. The deputy archivist was a cheerful extrovert, oddly noisy in this silent place but the three scholars bending over their books at the tables seemed used to him.

"Penselwood?" he said. "Oh such a very rich place. Three Norman castles all inside a mile. How's that for a puzzle? Two major ancient highways. Four battles, Iron Age forts all over the place, the Pen Pits. You can't walk a step without stumbling over something. Still you don't want to hear me rabbiting on, do you?" He considered his colleague from the museum. "You've got a remarkable memory, Norman, or I wouldn't even bother to start looking."

He brought out a box file marked with the name of the village and started to shuffle through papers. Gally craned to see, fascinated by this evidence that part at least of the village's past had been recorded. She felt as an adopted child might feel, stumbling across its family tree.

Norman reached in. "I think I know where it would be. I was reading something one of the village people themselves wrote." He pulled out an old typescript. "This is it. Mary Harfield's local history. I remember. She quoted one of the older villagers saying her grandfather was re-roofing a house in Penselwood and he came across a drum, some armour and two swords from Monmouth's army, hidden right up under the old thatch." He thumbed through. "That's it. I'm right. Local tradition is that Monmouth himself passed through the village when he was escaping."

Three exhausted men drew their horses up in a phalanx across Gally's brain.

"Where does Bagstone Farm come in?" asked Mike.

"Well, that was the house," Norman said. "That's the point. They found Monmouth's equipment in your house."

GALLY WOULDN'T LET them keep the ring at the museum, against Mike's wishes and against their polite pressure. She promised to get in touch another time and arrange to take it to a specialist and then she made Mike drive her home. On the way she came to a decision, aided by her distance from the house. It went against the grain for her to have to tell half-truths, to be caught in some sort of crossfire between Mike and Ferney. There should be space enough for both, she felt. She should have no reason to feel guilt about her liking for an octogenarian, whatever strange history Ferney might insist they had. Equally, Ferney could hardly expect to overturn the present structure of her life.

"There's something I would very much like," she said.

"Anything," said Mike facetiously.

"I'm serious. I think you would find Ferney quite interesting if you gave him a chance. Would you have another go when he comes out of hospital?"

There was a silence. It was harder for Mike than she had realized. He knew how much it mattered to her and he was troubled by it.

"Well?"

"What is it about him?"

"I don't know for sure."

"Would you tell me if you did?"

She looked away.

"Gally, listen. I know what you've been through. I don't want you to be messed around by someone with weird ideas."

"You don't know him."

"And you do? In just a few weeks?"

He didn't understand her sudden smile and it sent him veering towards irritation, but he kept silent, breathed deeply and bounced back the other way.

"If it really matters, I'll give it a go."

He went very quiet after that, turning it over in his mind, but after what she'd just heard in the archives she was unable to leave the clamouring fragments of history and memory to their own devices, so she forced him to talk about it.

"What exactly happened to Monmouth?"

"Norman could be right. He certainly came through Selwood Forest. When they caught him at Horton he was in peasant's clothes. I think there was something like five thousand pounds reward out for him, an absolutely colossal sum, and they'd already caught the other two he'd been riding with."

A vivid picture of Lord Grey and the exhausted Dutchman, Byser, came into her head—offering them drink, dressing a wound on Byser's arm—all the stuff brought out of the depths of her mind by Ferney last time, lurking in some halfway house of memory that she hadn't suspected. Such pity.

"Some woman saw him from her cottage and sent the militia after him and they found him half-dead in a ditch."

Fear still clung to the memory like the smell that clings to burnt wood long after a fire.

"What would they have done to people who helped Monmouth?"

"Didn't you learn anything in school? After the Inquisition it was every schoolkid's favourite witch hunt."

"What?"

"Judge Jeffreys and the Bloody Assize."

She gasped and pulled back sharply.

"What is it?" Mike said, sounding alarmed.

"Nothing." In the dark of her mind, the monsters moved. The need to know became the urgent need to stop knowing. If the floodgates opened now, she knew she would be swept away by something unspeakably sad, unspeakably horrid. Now she knew exactly why the ring had been so carefully buried—an object which, if discovered, would have rushed them both straight to a tortured death. She reached a hand into her pocket and pushed the heavy weight of it down under a handkerchief as if it might still carry that danger with it. They hadn't died then, had they? Neither of them. She knew Ferney had still been with her three years later when she met her end at Wincanton under the hooves of the horse, but she wondered what had happened in between and greatly feared to find out because something was shrieking at her from behind the locked doors, something with echoes in the swirling flames of a burning car.

10

IN THE DARKNESS her feet were wet and she was walking in coarse, sodden clothing towards a fire that held no promise of comfort but only utter dread. The fire was all she could see through the rain, but she had been there so many times before that she knew exactly what she would find. The knowledge spared her nothing. The cauldron over the fire was as huge as ever and the face of the man who stirred it was as vile, and when she walked, had to walk, up to the edge of the fire and, obeying his pointing finger, rose on tiptoe to look into the cauldron, she saw there in the bubbling, steaming liquid the same grey-pink slabs of hacked bodies that were always there, and the head that bobbed and slowly revolved to show her its boiled eyes and burst, black lips was known to her so that she screamed with full horror, undiluted by familiarity.

Violent motion followed. The cauldron rocked and a man's arms pinioned her as she struggled to escape, still screaming. She hit out, hard, and the arms let go with a grunt. She hit out again and this time her fist hit wood and the pain stopped her and brought her out of her sleep into the remains of their bed, with Mike hunched over next to her and rain pattering on the caravan roof.

"Oh no," she said. "Was that you?"

"My nose," he said, indistinctly.

"I'm sorry. Are you all right?"

"Ummm. What about you?"

She gathered her wits, breathing hard. "Nightmare."

He seemed to be recovering, straightening up and putting an arm round her.

"I thought you didn't get them here."

"First one."

"Want to tell me?"

"It was the boilman."

"Oh, Gally," he murmured and he hugged her silently for a bit, then she said, "It's all right, he's gone now."

"Let's put the bed back together."

Their bedding was wet by their feet where a roof-seam was showing its age, but she didn't mind. She lay there in the dark with his arms around her as his breathing slowed into the rhythm of sleep and felt again that deep fondness which was compromised by the glimpse of how much more there might be. She drifted off to sleep and the pressure of his arms kept the boilman away. At breakfast time she could pretend it was all forgotten. A fine summer morning was evaporating the last sheen of night-damp and their bedclothes were drying out, draped over the car for want of a clothesline.

They drove down to Gillingham that morning to stock up with food and came back the long way by Zeals and Stourton because Mike wanted to check the opening times of the National Trust gardens at Stourhead for a future expedition. From the main road they caught glimpses of the colonnaded façade of the great house between its long wings, honey-warm in the sunshine, but from the moment she saw the first car park signs, the narrowing funnel shepherding glass-sided coach boxes of tourists to their heritage experience, shuddering with snorts of bass exhausts in the queue, she knew it wasn't something she had any wish to do.

The village, thick with camera-dangled visitors, was beautiful but unnatural in the sun. Mike made enthusiastic noises as they drove slowly through, looking at the lakes, the gatehouse, the obelisks carefully laid out to carry the eye through the sweeping spaces where man had taken a valley and carved it into a vista.

"Don't you like it?" said Mike, made curious by her silence.

"It's a bit contrived, isn't it?"

"Do you think so? I would have said it was one of the triumphs of the landscaper's art. It was revolutionary in its time—the first full-scale example of the new natural look after all those stuffy, formal gardens. It knocks spots off the rest."

Gally tried to put her finger on what she felt. "Imagine someone doing it now. There'd be complete outrage, wouldn't there? Suppose some billionaire City type bought a valley and built himself an ultra-modern mansion, then decided to play God with the landscape for miles around. He'd have English Heritage and the Department of the Environment down on his head in no time, wouldn't he?"

"But this isn't ultra-modern . . . Oh, I see what you mean."

Gally was laughing. "It was at the time, wasn't it? Okay, it was mock-classical but that was ultra-modern then, wasn't it?" She knew as she said it that this was only one layer of what she really thought.

"Don't you like it at all?"

"Oh, I quite like it, I suppose. I'd like to come in winter, though, not now with all these people getting in the way." She thought suddenly of Ferney's scale of time and recognized her true feelings. "It's not that old really though, is it?"

"Of course it is. It's seventeen-something."

"Three lifetimes, that's all. Modern really."

He looked at her without understanding.

"It's a funny thought, isn't it, that barring natural disasters, they'll never let it fall down now, will they?" she said.

"I hope not."

"Not for a hundred years? Five hundred years? Five thousand years?"

"Well, that's a pretty long time."

"No, but do you see what I mean? Unless something happens to the world, that place and all the other historic buildings are going to be there forever effectively."

"What would you prefer, that we knock them down?" said Mike with a touch of sarcasm.

"Don't be difficult. Now they're starting to list 1960s office blocks as historic. If we go on doing that sort of thing *and* making sure all the old buildings stay up too, there'll come a time when the whole surface of Britain is covered with listed buildings."

"I'm sure we'll manage to destroy enough of them somehow," said Mike. "What is this, a complaint?"

They drove slowly out of the village through a fantasy rustic arch of jagged rock.

"They could make a start on that," said Gally and he laughed.

"I like it," he said defiantly. "Stourhead, I mean, not just the arch. It's one of the architectural wonders of the southwest."

"It's not that I don't like it," she said vaguely, but her spirits began to lift as she looked ahead at the long wooded spine of Pen Ridge, looking forward to this fresh approach to their new home. They were out of the tourist danger zone now, leaving the last of the Stourhead lakes behind as the narrow road took them through the stone cottages of Gasper on a long detour north, climbing up the side of the ridge. The cedars above them supported their high green copy of the hill's contour on trunks that offered inviting summer shade, broken here and there by logging tracks and the timber corpse piles awaiting collection. Gally looked at the logs as they passed, at the saw-cut cross-section of their ringed history, and momentarily envied them the certainty of that physical record.

At the top, in a dip in the long spine of the ridge, the road hair-pinned sharp left to follow the summit southward. Instead of following it round, Mike turned into a track entrance, braked abruptly and switched off.

"Do you fancy a quick walk?" he said. "If you think Stourhead's too modern, there's something just up here you'll like."

"What?"

"If I remember the map, Kenny Wilkins' Castle is only a hundred yards up here. Let's have a look."

An unexpected reluctance took Gally by surprise. "Do we have to go now?" she said. "I want to get back."

"That's not like you. There's lots of time."

There was, but that wasn't the point. She didn't like it, but she got out anyway. They walked on warm tarmac up the slight rise through the woods towards Penselwood. There was birdsong in the darting green sunshade of the high canopy and occasional scuffling in the dry disorder of woodland sediment covering the toes of the trees. Even under that disguise, there was no mistaking it. As they reached the top and the road leaped suddenly ahead, a slot through the wood that marked the long spine of the ridge, an ancient barrier loomed out of the undergrowth to each side, a massive, domed earth rampart fronted by a ditch that was still deep despite the efforts of the ages to fill it in.

Mike moved into friendly lecture mode. "It's an Iron Age hill fort," he said. "Seven acres of it, apparently. Two hundred yards across. I looked it up in the books. There's a tradition that the Roman general Vespasian captured it with the Second Legion on his march west."

That stirred nothing in her. The Romans had always seemed a sterile subject. He picked his way through the undergrowth, climbing up on the rampart. "It's in incredibly good nick, really," he said, looking round.

They picked their way along the right-hand parapet of the rampart which dominated the steep slope down the western side of the ridge. To their left inside the camp, between them and the road, were scrubby beech trees and brambles. To the right, down the sharply angled side of the ridge, soaring conifers allowed glimpses of a vast landscape opening out below with no clear sight of the bottom.

"These trees wouldn't have been here then," Mike said. "It wouldn't have been any use without a proper view."

"So would they have felled them?"

"The climate was different. They wouldn't have gone to all that trouble. I'm sure it was a bare hill."

They walked on round until they came to the far gateway where the road passed through, bisecting the long oval. This side of the camp was thick with cedars and the rampart was higher still, but the trees blotted out almost all the view to the east.

"Cenwalch now, your funny friend's Kenny Wilkins, he was an interesting character."

Gally was not at all sure she wanted to hear about Cenwalch, not here, but the price of stopping him telling her, of breaking the main spell that had always brought them together, seemed too high.

"Old Bede, who had a pretty good idea about most things, said Cenwalch was a truly second-rate commander, that he had a habit of messing up things and losing large chunks of his kingdom to his enemies. That's probably why he started looking for more land to the southwest."

This was fine, she thought, whatever the disquiet was that she felt, she seemed to be holding it at bay.

"Anyway he won a battle at Bradford-on-Avon in 652 and after that he controlled the land all down the side of Selwood Forest, so he'd probably been sitting down there looking up at the Britons holding the ridge on and off for six years. Of course this was six hundred years after Vespasian."

"The trees would have grown by then, would they?" she asked, wondering why it mattered.

"I shouldn't think so. Defending a fortress in a wood would have been a quick route to suicide."

The memory of skylight stampeded through the trees so their trunks became glass in her mind and the horizon to the east chopped across them. A door in her mind, carelessly left unguarded, was unlocked. For a wild, reeling, disorienting moment, she looked out across an ancient valley to the outline of the other great fort on the chalk heights of Whitesheet Hill. The ditch below her feet was clear, the rampart refreshed into sharp-profiled earth, stone and timber and she was frightened, frightened for her life. Mike spoke again and she staggered physically off-balance as the trees thickened abruptly around her in rescue. There was no pleasure here.

"Let's walk on," he said. "They think the fort always straddled the road like this."

She wanted to go back to the car and drive away, but if they had to walk, the road at least was a modern-day bitumen anchor to her imagination.

She thought Mike hadn't noticed anything, but she was wrong.

"What upset you?" he said when they'd gone a short way leaving the fort behind them, a vague threat she would have to face again when they went back for the car.

"I don't know. I just didn't like it there."

"I thought you liked everything about Penselwood."

She sighed, shrugged. "Maybe it's just the trees or the shade or something."

"It's not old Ferney, is it? I have a feeling he's getting at you in some way. Has he put some idea in your head?"

She was walking along keeping her eyes firmly on the ground, unwilling to take another risk with the shifting trees, and she answered more vehemently than she intended. "No, he hasn't. He's not like that at all. Anyway you said you'd be nice to him. You know he's ill. For all we know, he might never come out of hospital."

"He's a tough old bugger, I should think. I'll bet you a fiver he's up and about inside a week."

"I'm not taking any bets on his health," she said firmly.

"That's a pity."

"Why?"

"Because that would have been the fastest five pounds I ever made."

She looked up and saw an old man in a tweed jacket walking slowly along the road towards them from the direction of the village and she knew straightaway that it was indeed Ferney.

She was amazed to see him up and walking and it filled her with a sudden, ecstatic pleasure, but she knew without looking that Mike was studying her for a reaction and that she had roughly a hundred yards to decide how to greet Ferney and how to handle the encounter between him and Mike in a way that would start them off in the new direction Mike had promised.

"Oh, good," she said. "He looks fine."

"He certainly does."

"Will you . . . will you be friendly, Mike?"

"If he's friendly to me."

The distance was down to fifty yards and Ferney lifted a hand in greeting to them. They weren't completely alone. From behind them she heard horse's hooves and, looking round, saw a middle-aged woman riding a chestnut mare trot out of a track into the woods and turn onto the road in their direction. Once on the road the horse stopped, the woman swung herself out of the saddle holding the reins and picked up one of its forelegs to examine the hoof. As she did so, there was a shrill, rising blast of noise and an open-top Ford Escort in loud metallic blue with a louder exhaust and music blaring came rocketing down from the village as if the country lane was a race-track. The young driver braked hard when he saw the horse, but it was too late. As the car swerved past it to disappear round the bend through the old camp, the animal reared up, overcome with terror, jerked its reins from the woman's hand and, ears flattened back and eyes rolling, bolted down the road towards them.

Gally, who would previously have turned tail, instead stepped into its path and held out her arms to stop it, but Mike caught her hand and hauled her roughly onto the verge as it tore past. She shook herself free and turned to run after it, taking in the sight of the old man standing stock-still in its way.

Ferney didn't even try to get clear. He was calling out to the horse as it careered, terrified, towards him and Gally, running behind it with Mike coming along in her wake, was sure he would be knocked flat by it. The horse, however, lifted its ears when it was twenty yards from him, slowed to a brief trot, then to a walk and circled round him with its ears pricked up and its head on one side. Gally reached him with Mike and the woman rider not far behind. Ferney nodded at her, but motioned the other two back with a sweep of his arm. "Whor," he was saying softly, "whoot, whoot," then as the horse, panting, put its head nearer, "hutta, hutta, hutta." He stroked the horse's flank. Gally found herself murmuring unfamiliar sounds: "Prut, prut, prut." They went on making the noises together until the horse gave a great shuddering exhalation and seemed to relax. They continued stroking it for a minute or two, then Ferney handed the reins to the rider, who thanked him effusively.

As the horse walked off they turned their attention to the old man.

"That was brave," said Mike.

"You had me really worried," said Gally sternly. "It could have knocked you flying."

"I know how to stop a horse," said the old man defiantly. "I've stopped enough in my time. You did pretty well." He lurched slightly and leaned heavily on his stick.

"You've overdone it, haven't you? When did they let you out of hospital?"

"This morning."

"This morning? And you're dashing round the countryside stopping runaway horses? Come on, we'll take you home."

"You stay here," Mike suggested, "and I'll go back and get the car." He jogged off back towards the camp.

"What was wrong with you?" asked Gally quietly.

"Just fading a bit."

"Are you better now?"

"There's better and better. I'll go on fading, sometimes faster, sometimes slower. You get used to it, you know."

"I don't want you to fade," she said simply.

He sighed. "Ah . . . well, there's ways, you know." He nodded in the general direction of her tummy. "He's waxing, I'm waning, that's all."

That seemed so sad that she had to divert down a different turning. "Those sounds," she said. "The sounds you were making to the horse."

"Yes?"

"I knew them."

"You did. You had them right yourself."

"What were they?"

"Just old horse sounds. The sort of words horses understand. From way back."

"How far back?" she said. "From Kenny Wilkins' time?"

He chuckled but swayed again, so that she found herself watching carefully in case he needed catching. "You walked through the camp, then?"

"Yes."

"You didn't like it much." A statement, not a question.

"It was all right, then the trees sort of . . . went away."

He nodded. "I'll tell you about that. Not now. When we've got time."

"The horse words. You didn't say."

"They're old, right enough. They were old words then, but I couldn't say about things that happened before that."

"Why not?"

He found that genuinely amusing. "Well, I wasn't there, was I? Anyway, seems you're not scared of horses anymore. He'll be a bit surprised, your Mike."

"I don't think he ever knew I didn't like them. You don't get many horses in London."

Their car came into sight soon and they put Ferney in the front passenger seat.

"Shall we take you home?"

"Come back and have a cup of tea," he said, "both of you."

It was only three minutes to Ferney's bungalow and he let Gally make the tea. Mike did what he always did in a strange house and made for the bookshelves, bridging the gap between himself and the stranger by tossing titles across the divide. It was no charade. Ferney's shelves were packed with history and Mike was startled by the depth of what he found.

"You've got the Gimpel book."

"I got two of them. Which one are you looking at?"

The Medieval Machine.

"Oh, yes. Interesting as far as it goes."

"Whitelock, Thomson, Draper, Underdown," Mike breathed a litany of sources.

"They scratch the surface."

Mike was nettled, "They do a bit more than that, surely?"

Ferney pointed at the coffee table where that morning's *Independent* was neatly folded. "You look at that. That's history. It may be only what happened yesterday, but it's history. You find me anyone who was involved with any of those stories in there and they'd all have a bone to pick with it somewhere. They'd all have seen it a different way."

"Fair enough, but that's journalists for you."

"So what's a historian then, if he isn't a journalist who doesn't have to talk to anybody?"

Gally came in with the tea. "You know Mike's a historian, don't you?" she said.

"Do you write books?" said Ferney. His tone was mild, but in the context of what he'd already said, Mike sounded defensive when he replied.

"I'm a lecturer mostly, but I have been asked to write a book."

"What's it about?"

"It's about how agriculture changed in the ninth and tenth centuries."

"Oh yes?"

"Well, you see, I think you can trace the improvements in plough design through to the fact that they started growing various sorts of beans and that improved the diet enormously. I don't think it's any coincidence that you got this sudden outburst of creativity. It was the dietary effect of the legumes, the amino acids combined with the grains, you see. It really made people able to get up and go."

"They were full of beans, you mean." Ferney said it drily, but there was a twinkle in his eye. Mike looked startled for a moment, then laughed.

"I suppose you could say that."

"It's what it means, isn't it?"

"Perhaps that's what you should call it," Gally put in, passing the cups around.

"Not very academic," said Mike.

"All the better."

Ferney was shaking his head. "That might be a bit of it," he said, "but there's another point that you might just be missing, you know."

Mike paused with his cup raised almost to his lips and peered at Ferney over the top. His tone of voice was indulgent. "Come again?"

"It was horses, really."

"In what sense?"

"Changed everything, did horses. You go back to those days and all there were to pull your ploughs were oxen."

"And?"

"Well," said Ferney as though it should be obvious, "have you ever tried to get oxen to go far?"

"No, actually."

"They take a long time over it. They might be strong, but they're slow, are oxen. So back in those days, if you had fields to plough you had to live right there on top of them, otherwise it would take you all day just to get the oxen to the field."

Mike thought about it, flashed a conspiratorial wink at Gally that she hoped Ferney hadn't seen and said, "Right," with the slow down and up emphasis of obvious doubt in it.

Ferney's tone grew sharper and Gally tightened her hands into anxious fists.

"It meant everyone lived apart in the country, see? In scattered little hamlets because they had no choice, not until oats came along."

"Oats?"

"Couldn't keep horses over the winter until there were oats, you see. Everyone thought they were just a weed to start with, then they heard that over in other countries they grew them for fodder and it was good for the soil, so they started planting three crops a year not two and after that they had enough oats to feed the horses through the winter."

Mike drained his tea, thinking, then put the cup down. "So you're saying the horses were better than the oxen?" He was sounding interested despite himself.

" 'Course they were. Your horse could go much further to the fields, see? That meant the farmers could move together into villages to live and still get there and back without taking all day over it."

Mike was shaking his head. "I don't see what that's got to do with tenth-century creativity?"

Ferney hooted with laughter. "Sex," he said. "What else? Out there in the little hamlets, they might not see anyone all year except their sister or their first cousin if they were lucky. The old what's it called, the old gene pool didn't get much of a stir. Half daft, most of them, except the ones that were completely daft. Then oats came along, so they all moved into villages and they had a much wider choice, see? It was one hell of a social life after what they'd been used to. Those genes started whizzing around all over the place. That's your tenth century for you. They probably needed the beans to keep their pecker up, but it's the horse you've got to thank."

Mike looked stunned. "Where did you read this?" he said, seeing an unsuspected gulf opening up in his carefully plotted path to publication.

"I'm not sure I did. It's just something I know," said Ferney, and Gally knew that wouldn't do for Mike.

He got up and went to the bookshelves again, scanning through them as though searching for an alien book, a title he didn't recognize that might contain in it the bibliography and pedigree of Ferney's theory of horses. Ferney watched him.

"Of course, I might be wrong," he said with an unhelpful attempt at diplomacy.

Mike wouldn't leave it at that. "It's not the sort of thing you just dream up out of the blue," he insisted. "If that's in one of these books, I'd really like to know about it."

"No, it's definitely not in the books. Folk memory, you could call it. Common sense, I'd call it." He watched Mike, who was still scanning the shelves, with a touch of amusement. "You're on a bit of a hiding to nothing, aren't you? If it's already in a book, there's no mileage in you writing it. If it's not, you won't believe it. Go on, call it my free gift to you—a countryman's gift."

Mike looked at his watch. "Come on, Gally, time to get back if we're going to get anything else done today."

"Before we go," she said, "can I just show you the picture—if that's all right?" she added, turning to Ferney who nodded assent.

It seemed to mean little to Mike. He was unable to see behind the layer of dark, dirty varnish and accepted her explanation of the dim outlines of the cottage and the stone with a doubtful expression. He was impressed by the frame, though. "This must have cost someone a bit," was all he said.

They went back and thanked Ferney for the tea.

"I'm glad you're feeling better," Gally said.

"I'll pop down and see you tomorrow maybe." He looked at Mike. "You think about what I said, now."

In the car Mike surprised her. "I'll give him his due. Assuming he's gone through all that stuff on his shelves, he's incredibly well-read for an amateur."

"So you think he knows what he's talking about?"

"That's what worries me. I still think he must have read all that horse business somewhere. I'd better find out about it. If not, then I suppose he must have made it up—like Kenny Wilkins and his red hair."

"Kenny Wilkins *did* have red hair," she said, stung, and immediately regretted it.

"Oh, ha ha," he said and the moment passed.

She believes him more than me, he thought. I'm the one who's studied. He's just read this and that in books and half-remembered old stories. Why does she believe him? On the other hand, at least he has read the books. Mike had found it easier to deal with the reality of Ferney than the idea. Somehow the idea, the frightening idea that sat in his head when he started to worry, was of an ageless, powerful Ferney, a true threat. The physical reality was an old man, fresh from hospital, and all Mike's upbringing said you had to be polite and caring towards people like that.

"By the way," he said, "you were pretty good with that horse, too. I didn't know you knew about horses. Where did all that prut prut stuff come from?"

11

THE NEXT DAY was the clearest of days. From the top of the hill
Glastonbury Tor stood out pin sharp, almost within reach, the way it
used to look so much more often. It was reassuring for Ferney, who
had wondered in recent years if his eyes were getting weaker because
such days of crystal air seemed to have gone. Some rare trick of the
Atlantic wind had swept man's burnt fuel fog away and on this day
he felt that if the earth didn't curve away under him he could see clear
across the kingdom.

When his eyes were sated with the view, Ferney sat brooding on
the recent past. This last lifetime held more mystery than any he
could remember. He wondered how old Gally was. Somewhere in her
late twenties certainly, which meant there was a gap of thirty years
unaccounted for. That gap mattered to Ferney because it held the clue
to the stone and the stream, to exactly how the whole thing worked,
to what had gone wrong before and might well go wrong again. He
had to accept that Gally's return meant he might have made some
wrong assumptions. It no longer all seemed quite so certain. His
mind going round in circles, he fell to thinking of how it had been before, of the roadworks, of Cochrane's smithy and of the search that
now seemed so much less urgent.

That train of thought brought him to Billy and the overwhelming
mystery of that poor young man's actions. Billy Bunter, they'd called
him when he first came into the village. Got himself taken on as a
farmhand in about 1952 or '53, was it? He was a big, simple lad who
could hardly get a single word out without it tripping over his
tongue. There was a touch of what they used to call the Mongol look
in his flat face, but the village people were mostly kind to him in a

limited way. He'd liked to be with people. He'd just come and knock
at the door, make his noise and point at one of the empty chairs as his
way of asking. A lot of people drew the line at having him inside their
house like that, but Ferney didn't mind and they'd spent hours sitting
across the fireplace from each other in mutual peace.

It was one of the great regrets of Ferney's life that he hadn't seen
it all coming. It was common knowledge that Cochrane, too old
and drunk now to pick fights with capable men, had turned his
spite on the big, slow farmhand. He bullied him, ridiculed him,
tripped him and tormented him. Ferney knew Billy hated and feared
Cochrane but he also knew there were times when Billy, perversely,
sought Cochrane out, becoming so tongue-tied by emotion in his
presence that he would stand there gibbering and spitting at him until
Cochrane drove him away by force. Ferney was never there at the
right time to do anything about it because Cochrane stayed clear of
him in those days, fearing his wrath. The smith would turn a different way if he saw Ferney coming in time. It was 1959 when Cochrane
pushed Billy once too often and met his death, to his complete surprise, face down in a cattle trough at the hands of the simple lad who
could wield such strength if he chose to. They took Billy away and
Ferney never saw him again. Sometimes, if the wind played tricks, he
would still start up at a noise at the door, hoping Billy Bunter had
come back, wondering what it was that finally goaded the poor boy
into so extreme an action.

He brought himself back from that diversion to think about the
Bag Stone again, knowing he had to reach a conclusion before he
went down to the house. It would do no harm to play it safe, to put
things back as they should be, if only the man would listen to him.

When he reached the house, finding them hard at work, Ferney found that Mike's attitude to him had gone through a subtle
and positive change. After a few hours spent thinking about it,
Ferney's horse theory had altered him in Mike's eyes, made him suddenly much more real, a man who was dealing in a currency he
understood—the weighing of historical argument. Until Mike could
establish its parentage and intellectual viability to his own satisfaction, Ferney's theory would ensure its owner a position inside the circle of Mike's mental limelight.

It showed in the way Mike greeted him when he first appeared at
the gate. Gally knew perfectly well that previously he would have
pretended not to see the old man, let Gally do the greeting and ac-
knowledged him in his own time in a way that made it clear he was
busy. Now, though, Mike hailed him, cleared garden tools off the

bench outside the caravan to give him somewhere to sit and lit the gas under the kettle. Gally, putting down her spade and walking towards them from the far corner of the yard, had a momentary profound sense of their different tidal pull on her—Ferney as the sun, far off, massive and central, the core of her system, Mike as the moon, nearer, affecting her daily tides. Seeing them talking politely made it so much easier—the two forces in temporary conjunction.

Ferney understood perfectly well what had brought about the change in Mike's approach. He even had some sympathy for it. He knew all about the feeling that there were too many people who were too ordinary to bother about, the same simple types repeating again and again and again, though he felt Mike had less excuse in his short life to feel that need to be selective. Time was when everyone you were likely to come across mattered to you somehow; either you depended on them or they depended on you. Their skill or their strength or their hunger made a direct difference to whether your belly stayed full. Their anger or their madness decided your safety. Now they had grocery stores instead of fields and flocks, Match of the Day instead of the doubtful justice of one-on-one combat. You never saw the whites of anyone's eyes anymore. He only bothered with the tiny handful who were special these days, who stood above the grey ranks. Who was he to argue if Mike chose to do the same?

He decided to press home the advantage and Mike himself provided the opening.

"I keep thinking about that horse," he said to Ferney. "You calmed it so well."

"I've always had a bit of a way with horses," the old man said. "People mistake them, think they're stupid, but they're not. They don't have much knowledge like a pig does and they're not calculating like a cat, but they'd like to make sense of it all if they could. They take in so much, see? A horse is just a great big machine for asking questions without knowing what the answers mean, so it gets frightened very easily." He could read the slight wandering in Mike's expression, knew there wasn't enough bait on the hook. " 'Course, you go back a while and people said horses didn't have brains at all."

"What, literally?"

Gally joined them and sat down on the grass, apex to their triangle.

"Back in the 1600s there were men who said they'd cut open horses' skulls and when they looked inside they found nothing. Suited their book, didn't it? If you said animals like that were just machines of some sort, then it didn't matter how you treated them."

It rang bells for Mike. He nodded and Ferney, encouraged, went on.

"It was all about religion, wasn't it? It's always had a lot to answer for. They seemed to forget everything they'd ever known in those days. Priests said you shouldn't dress up like animals. No hobby-horse dances or anything like that. Anything bestial was evil. You shouldn't have pets, shouldn't even have them living under the same roof. That's when farmers started moving them out into barns so they'd be separate, you see?"

Mike, who would think to his dying day, despite all the evidence, that the universe ran to the laws of logic, spotted a flaw. "How could they say animals had no brains and say they were evil at the same time?"

"They'd say what suited them, wouldn't they? Always been the same problem with religion—priests making up God's rules to suit the system."

"Where did you learn all this?"

"Here and there."

"What you were saying about oats and horses, yesterday—you haven't remembered where you read that yet, have you?"

"I'll think about it," said Ferney and decided the moment to strike had come. "But I had something I wanted to ask you."

It was entirely between him and Mike. Gally just listened.

"You saw my old picture?"

"I did. I thought it would be very nice to have it cleaned."

Ferney gestured as if to say it would make no difference. "I wondered whether you'd thought of putting the stone back up, now you've seen it."

"I couldn't really see it that well."

"It shows it clear enough. I can tell you just how it would be, the end of it's still lying in the right place. Stones like that one, they don't go far."

"Well . . . I don't see why not." There was a warm silence in which Ferney and Gally smiled in unison.

Ferney offered a reward. "When you write your book," he said, "don't forget the difference between the chalk and the cheese."

Mike's eyebrows rose involuntarily.

"You see them both from here," said Ferney. "Both sorts of people." He waved a hand southwards. "Down there where the soil's heavier, they've always had cows. All that milk they drink takes its toll of a man. They used to say it cooled the brain too much, turns them into a slower, paler, puffy sort of people." He turned his head and looked east towards Whitesheet Hill and the edges of Salisbury

Plain. "Chalk's always been different. The sheep country on the uplands, that's where you get the lighter-spirited folk. Everything's different up there, the water, the work, the wind, the food. You'll never
understand the history of the country people unless you know the
difference between chalk and cheese."

He glanced up at the sun and rose stiffly from the bench. "You've
got things to do. I mustn't take up your day."

"Do you want a ride back?" said Mike.

"A ride?" said Ferney blankly. "Oh, in the car. No, no, I'll be fine."
He looked at Gally. "Unless you fancy strolling back with me? Be my
companion today?"

It sounded like a quotation, the deliberate way he said it, and
Gally found ready words springing to complete it. "Thou art the end
and the beginning. Thou carriest me. Thou art the way and the journey's end. Even so, God, be my companion today." She spoke the
words out loud, loving the sound of them.

Mike's face had tightened when Ferney asked Gally to come with
him. He now frowned as if straining to understand the odd litany
that had just bypassed him. "What is that?" he said.

Ferney looked at Gally for the answer, but she shook her head and
he made a little face. "King Alfred's prayer," he said.

She looked quickly at Mike and he shrugged. "Go on if you want
to," he said, but his face showed he wished she hadn't asked and she
knew part of the bridge Ferney had built to him had just wobbled.

She and Ferney walked slowly along the lane. A rabbit bounded
down the bank, froze, then kangarooed off into a field entrance.

"Thank you for being nice to Mike."

"He was nice to me."

"Was that prayer really King Alfred's?"

"Tidied up a bit, but that's what they've always called it." He gave
her a now familiar look and she knew what he was on the verge of
saying.

"I know. You were going to say I didn't really have to ask. I keep
telling you, I *do* have to." She cast around for the words. "It's not
like getting rid of a blockage so everything suddenly flows freely. It's
more like every little bit has to be teased out."

"That's all right," he said, but his eyes showed it wasn't.

"I have so many questions to ask you. You don't know what it's
like. I have to go on behaving like everything's . . . normal, so I don't
upset Mike, and all the time I'm going over and over it all in my mind
and I feel like you've just let me glimpse a tiny corner of it all."

"We've got a bit of time before us."

She looked at him as though there was a dark meaning in his words. "Did the hospital decide what was wrong with you?"

"No, 'course not. Hospitals aren't any good unless you want something sliced off. You go to a hospital, it's like going to a shop, isn't it? Chances are you'll come out with more than you went in with. They've got the lot there, haven't they? Everything you don't want, bugs of all sorts. If you want to get ill it's a great place to go." He stopped by a stile. "Let's take the old path," he said.

"But you're completely better?"

"Some things are on the mend, but you can't stop the days dwindling," he said without any hint of sadness. "Nor should you. That way there's nothing but trouble."

A vague connection asserted itself. "Mrs. Mullard came over the other day."

He looked at her sharply. "Did she?"

"She said I shouldn't tell you about the baby. But I didn't. I mean I didn't need to tell you, did I?"

He shook his head.

"She also said, more or less, that she had to leave the house because of you. I think she meant that you flooded it on purpose."

He looked away from her.

"Well, someone did, didn't they?" she said. "We found that pipe."

"I had to get her out."

"Why? Because . . . because of me?"

"Yes, of course. Because of you. We were having the best time ever, you and me. Then she and that . . . man, right on top of the stone. It was killing me, her baby. I was going to die if she had it there. You must know." His voice was urgent, pleading.

"I *don't* know. I can't remember. I've told you. You mean because she was pregnant, there, by the stone, it was killing you?"

He nodded.

"Let me get this straight," she said in anger that seemed less directed at him than the blue dome of the sky and all the countless atoms of the ever-moving world. "It's the stone. Is that it? That's what keeps you coming back?"

"Us."

Us. The running question behind everything about them. Was it one person's fantasy or two people's truth?

"Okay, us. The baby growing there meant one of us would . . . start to die?"

"It draws out the life," he said like a tired teacher explaining for the twentieth time that one plus one is always two. "You can feel it. Draws it out so you know it, you just know you'll be that baby."

"Then, God almighty. You being ill now. That's because of me? Because of my baby? *I'm* killing you?"

"It's all right this time," he said. "The stream's back. You're back. There's ways of making it come out well for us."

"What ways?" she demanded. "What's the stream got to do with it?"

"Not now."

"Yes, Ferney. Now."

"No. There's months yet. It's the start that's worst for me, then it gets better for a long while. I won't go on being ill all the time, not until you get near your time."

There was deep love in the old eyes that locked on to hers. As so often when she was talking to him, she had the sense of an abyss into which she might easily fall. She had to concentrate on the twentieth-century noises around her—the sound of distant cars, a helpful aircraft. If she let that slip, the lines of age on his face began to fade to an earlier familiarity and she feared where that might lead.

"Just trust me," he said. "There's a time to talk about these things."

She was suddenly glad to leave the subject.

"That prayer, Alfred's prayer. I don't remember ever learning it. Maybe I heard it at school or something."

He knew what question she was asking. "It was always a favourite of yours."

"Did Alfred really write it?"

Ferney considered. "He wrote it down. Who's to say if he heard it somewhere first? I reckon it sounds like him, though. It always meant more to you than me."

"Why?"

"Because you've always believed in something and I haven't."

"Don't you believe in *anything*?"

"I believe in life everlasting," he said simply. "Would you have me believe in Heaven?"

"Maybe not for you . . . us," she said, "but what about all the others?"

"That's what you've always said."

"Don't be so frustrating. I don't know whether I've always said it. Just try to behave as if you've never heard it before, please?"

"I don't know if we should be talking about what happens when we die. Not yet."

"I don't see why not."

"No, that's right. You don't."

She looked at the set of his face and tried a different tack. "Is it all religions you're against?"

"I don't know that much about the rest," he said. "I've read a bit but I don't *know* them."

"What about Buddhists? They believe in reincarnation."

"*Believe* in it? You and me, we don't just *believe* in it, we live it. It's like saying you believe in toothpaste—you couldn't make a religion out of that. Seems to me you can only call it a religion when it's about faith. If you know something for absolutely certain, it sort of spoils it, doesn't it?"

"What's so wrong with being a Christian?"

He made an expansive gesture that took in half of the horizon. "That's what's wrong with it."

"What?"

"The effects. I've got no problem with loving your neighbour, though some of my neighbours have been pretty tiresome. Christianity's all right for people. It's the poor old world that's suffered. You go back to pagan times, even the bloody Danes, they knew about nature. If you cut down a forest, you had the forest spirits to reckon with. It was all about keeping a good balance with the world."

They walked on close together and she found it easy to match his step, sensing when he would slow down or turn to look around.

"Surely Christianity doesn't . . ."

"Christianity doesn't give a toss," he said loudly. "First time round it wasn't so bad. Those Irishmen at Glastonbury, they didn't have any inclination to possess the world, but dear oh dear, when the Saxons got converted, do you know what the message was then?" He put on a pompous voice and Gally wondered if he was aping some long-dead bishop. " 'God has put all this here on earth for you, my children. Use it as you will.' That's what Christian teaching's always been about. God made the world for us so we can do what we want with it—animals too." He snorted. "We've been paying the price of that ever since. It's no good you looking shocked. You know it's true really. If I had to be anything, I'd be a Hindu. At least they believe the world has a spirit too."

The path had taken them to the corner of Coombe Street, where houses dotted the old Roman lane and Penselwood's intricate contours opened up a long valley down to the east below them, speckled with sheep. A Fleet Air Arm Harrier from Yeovilton cut the sky with a roaring sword of noise which rose to a shriek as it slowed to a hover in a violent battle with gravity. It hung in the sky, driving out all thought of anything except itself before banking away and battering them with the departing earthquake vibration of its jet pipes.

It was like a jug of cold water over Gally's head, bringing her blinking back to an awareness of the overwhelming strangeness of all the man at her side had to say. "So what about Alfred's prayer, then?" she said rather tartly. "Why do I bother with that?"

"I always said it was because you liked Alfred."

"Huh? I liked King Alfred?"

"You had a lot to say about him."

"Are you pulling my leg?"

He stopped, looked round to see no one was close and pointed down the valley. "What's down there?"

She couldn't and wouldn't play that game. "Sheep."

"I mean down at the bottom."

"Some sort of old factory from the look of it." A mile off, down the far end of the combe at the back of Bourton, was a hotch-potch of old stone mill buildings with modern corrugated iron mingled in.

"That's the Egbert Stone, down there," he said with dignity and she suppressed what might have been a tiny guilty flash of recognition. "It stands at the three counties boundary, just by the edge of the river. That's where he came."

"Why?"

"To raise the troops against the Danes."

"Why there?"

"They reckoned it was a good, hidden spot. I reckon it was because he didn't have much cash. You didn't have to pay soldiers, you see, not until they had to leave their county. He got away cheaply that way. Three counties' worth of men for nothing until they marched off. You said he was the finest man you ever saw."

"So you're saying we saw King Alfred?" she said and the sound of the words made it seem completely absurd.

"No, I didn't. It was just you that saw him."

"Why?"

He looked wistful. "You were eighteen," he said. "I was only four. My mother wouldn't let me go."

The Harrier's air-rending reverberations were gone and so was its effect. He spoke with the utter clarity of simple truth and disbelief was no longer an option.

IN THE NEXT few days a test confirmed to Mike the pregnancy that Gally had not doubted for a second.

"How do you feel about it?" he asked her as they sat, wearily, in the caravan one evening.

"It's okay. I think it will be fine."

"You must take it easy."

"Mike, the doctors last time said it wasn't anything I did. It was just one of those things that happen. I'm not some delicate Victorian who has to go to bed for nine months."

"I know you're not." He meant it. There was a sea-change going on in Gally that mixed hope and doubt together in him. She was still wearing his ring with no further signs of any of the irrational, fretting discomfort that had pierced him to the quick before. He used to feel, despite everything she said, that it was a rejection of him in some degree rather than just a physical phobia. It comforted him greatly that she could now wear it with ease, but he knew the old man was intricately tied up in all of this and that was where the doubt came in. He didn't know where Ferney's true aims lay, but he was aware that they were focused entirely on Gally. While they were doing some sort of good he was trying not to interrupt, although it was something that called for a very close watch.

"I suppose it's all right for you to fly?" he said as they packed.

"Of course it is. You think I'm going to miss three weeks in Greece for a mild attack of pregnancy, then you've got another think coming. It's fine."

The holiday had been planned for a long time and though Gally felt some regrets at entrusting the house entirely to the builders for so long, even she was looking forward to a break from the caravan's cramped environment.

Mike was still wondering about Ferney's horse theory. As it was the summer vacation, most of the researchers to whom he had access were off enjoying themselves. One of his Ph.D. students, a solitary, pallid person who liked spending his summer months in library gloom researching pre-Black Death epidemics in Anglo-Saxon England, had agreed over the phone to check the databases for any mentions. His letter arrived, enclosing a few photocopied sheets, the morning they were due to go, and Mike was delighted.

"That must be where he got it from," he said. "The Lynn White book, *Medieval Technology and Social Change*. I remember it. It's very good." He was sitting at the caravan table as Gally sat on the step in the sunlight. The builders worked away carefully repointing the front wall around the new doorway and she was keeping a close eye on them.

After he'd been silent for some time she prompted him. "What does it say?"

He sounded doubtful. "It's not exactly the same. It says it happened in the eleventh century. I'm sure he said it was the tenth. Maybe he just got it wrong. It talks about the move into bigger villages, but there's only one line which supports his gene pool idea and that's something about farmers finding it easier to get suitors for their daughters."

"Same thing, surely?"

"Maybe," Mike looked doubtful. "It's just it doesn't go nearly as far. Anyway it's all useful material if I can get a better line on it. It's a bit difficult, but you have to admit he might have something. All that 'full of beans' and 'chalk and cheese' stuff. How am I meant to tell if it's just homespun or if it's the real thing?"

"Surely homespun *is* the real thing."

THEY COULD HAVE gone off quietly on their holiday if Gally hadn't remembered, just before they left the caravan, about the Stuart ring.

"Wait a minute," she said and opened the cupboard where she'd left it. There was no sign of it. "It's gone," she said, "the ring's gone."

"No it hasn't," he said calmly. "I put it in my money belt. I thought it was safer to take it with us." He unzipped the pouch and showed her.

"What did you do with the glove?" she said, looking around.

"Glove? That crusty old bit of leather? Was that a glove? I threw it away. Surely you didn't want it?"

"Monmouth's glove? You threw away Monmouth's glove?"

The words were out, shaking in the air between them, and he looked at her in utter astonishment.

12

EVERY WORD THEY spoke in the car to Gatwick, waiting in the departure lounge and squashed in the ungenerous seats of the Boeing charter flight to the Aegean was brittle and unsuccessful. They'd passed an ugly accident near Andover, paramedics and police working on someone trapped in the front seat of a Lotus sports car wedged and foreshortened under the back of a petrol tanker. Usually Mike would have distracted Gally, got her to turn away, but in this conversational desert his words would have stood out like oak trees, so he watched her wrestle with her horror, sneaking glances at the scene, tensing up, looking away then always turning back. He accelerated hard as soon as he could to leave it behind. Still bewildered by the alien passion of her fruitless search of the dustbin and the skip, he then tried unwisely to engage her in artificially cheerful speculation about the Greek tower-house they had arranged to rent. It all sounded wrong to his ears as soon as it left his mouth and it only added to the blockage in their communication. His words slid off Gally, generating only monosyllabic shards, dredged up from some distant place, conversational returns into the net. She wasn't angry, she was dreadfully sad, so sad that even the sight of the accident only disturbed her briefly, and he couldn't understand. Even she wasn't all that clear. The ring itself was a strong witness to a previous time, but gold is too unchanging to measure the years well. The glove's decay was something she had been keeping for a quiet moment, an organic cross-reference, rich in finite age. Its loss left her bereft.

It was the worst moment for Mike since they had first come to the village and met the old man. He felt more than ever out of his depth in this new shadow world where so much went on that he could not see for himself. He knew that his whole life would be impoverished and desiccated if he were to lose Gally and yet he seemed to be blundering further and further in that direction. It had been bothering him that she didn't seem to want to talk about the baby and, thinking it might be the fear of another miscarriage that stopped her, he hadn't been pushing her. He had high hopes of this holiday—a chance to get away from new influences and to take stock—but now he seemed to have wrecked it in advance by a single act whose consequences he had not for a moment considered.

In the silent separation of the car, anger at Ferney fermented in him. By the time they reached the airport Mike was determined that he would have this out, not with Gally but with the old man himself, and if Ferney had been there in the crowd by the check-in desk Mike would have overcome all his scruples about age, infirmity and politeness and pushed the matter to a conclusion. He was prepared to fight not just for his own sake but for Gally too, because he didn't understand what was being done to her and he didn't want to believe it might be good for her.

This new Gally who wore his ring, who woke far less often—though still too often—from the burnman's horrors, whose burden of guilt and fear was noticeably lighter than it had formerly been, disturbed him. He had come to know and almost to rely on her terrors, to feel that he had a role in helping her fight them off. Unable to face the fact that the source of his concern might be his replacement in that role, he preferred to think of Gally as a dupe of some strange influence that would let her down when her need was greatest. He forgot for the moment Ferney the book-lover, Ferney the theorist, the Ferney to whom he could relate, and branded him instead unbalanced and intrusive, a danger to the careful nurture of his damaged woman.

Ferney of course was not there at the check-in desk and the confrontation could happen only in Mike's mind. Tension ebbed a little in the no-man's-land of the plane and they both read books. He knew the holiday was not after all lost as soon as the aircraft door opened on the ground in Greece and the English machine-air was washed from the plane by a warm flood of thyme and pine resin. It was air that had boisterously enveloped and sidelined a million modern intrusions and it blew away the remaining links to the direct source of Gally's distress and Mike's concern so that, quite suddenly, everything seemed fine.

They collected their hire car at Kalamata and wound their way

down the Gulf of Messenia into the old wild land of the Mani
with the Taygetus Mountains rising to their left. It was the first
time Gally had been more than fifteen miles from Penselwood since
they had bought the house. A more familiar Gally came out from
inside the taciturn stranger and enfolded it, to Mike's enormous
relief.

Afternoon was turning into evening as they came to their first,
startling sight of the village—a miniature, primitive Manhattan sky-
line of medieval stone skyscrapers. In the plane, accepting his rebuff,
Mike had sunk into Patrick Leigh Fermor's *Mani,* greatest of all
the English books on Greece, and now he began to regurgitate its
contents.

"They're from the days of the Maniot blood feuds," he said. "The
families would spend literally years trying to destroy rival families in
the same village."

"Vendettas?"

"Not like the Italians, not over women or insults or anything like
that. It was all about power and influence, being boss. One family
would see another one getting too big for its boots and decide to have
a crack at it. They'd ship in cannon from Venice or maybe from London, haul them up to the top of the towers and just batter each other
to pieces."

Gally looked at the tall towers ahead and tried unsuccessfully to
picture it. "How did they get them in if they were fighting?"

"They did harder things than that. Some of the towers were built
completely under fire from beginning to end. The builders would do
it at night. Can you imagine? Levering the blocks up, one at a time in
dead silence in case a sniper across the street hears you—always trying to make your tower higher than your neighbour's so your cannon
would have the advantage."

Gally had no insight into it, could glean no sense of this incompre-
hensible history from looking at the towers. They were clustered so
closely together. She tried to assemble the imaginary scene, relentless
men crouched round hot iron guns, their cannonballs bludgeoning
each other, stone chips flying in crashing clouds of powder smoke.
The towers were men-of-war in close combat, ships that could
never move apart on the wind or the tide. It was impossible to picture, sterile—but, perversely, as the landscape failed to respond to
her, it gave her a strong momentary sense of the contrast with Penselwood, where faint electric stirrings of shared history prickled with
promise from every view.

"How could they live like that?"

"They'd have a general truce in the planting season or when they had to bring in a harvest—all the warring families working silently in the fields side by side and the ones who stayed behind quietly restocking their arsenals." Mike had the academic's gift of taking ownership of other people's information as if the process of reading made it his own.

Arriving at the house they saw how German and Swiss money had fleshed the angry bones of the surviving towers with the soft pleasures required by peaceful invaders, fitted kitchens displacing the tough ghosts. Windows had been set into the upper stories where, when the towers were new, the smallest chink would have been an invitation to sharp-eyed death. They climbed straight to the roof and found there the one part of it where little had changed except the chances of survival. It put them at the centre of a hemisphere of visual drama—more than a hemisphere, because below them the olive-bearded slopes fell steeply away so that they were poised above the whole world.

It was a stone landscape, shaped and unshaped. In their immediate surroundings the geometrical masonry of the other towers rose in stumpy crystal growths from their rougher bedrock. Gally exhaled the recent past into the warm dusk air as she looked down the hill to the splayed fingers of steep headlands that split the immense, gentled, evening sea.

"Shall we go to the taverna?" said Mike, putting his arms round her and when she covered his hands with hers, he thought everything would now be fine.

The holiday was a respite from Gally's secret and from Mike's disquiet. For the next eighteen days they swam and sunbathed every day until he got restless, then explored monasteries, chapels and assorted remains until evening folded the shadowed mountains in towards them and tavernas called them with bulb festoons between the trees and laughter from unsteady metal tables. Gally and Mike became again what they had been, a happy, close couple feeding off the opposites in each other. Gally tried not to think of Penselwood and Ferney because, on the frequent occasions when such thoughts came creeping into her mind, it brought sharply home to her that a large wedge had been driven into her life. Here, with only Mike, it was much easier to be what she had previously been. However much she loved the cottage, however strong her confusing feelings for Ferney insisted on being, it was easier and simpler to be here, back in the old ways.

From the second or third day in Greece, she had started to look towards their return to England with the dread of a schoolgirl on the first day of the holidays knowing that inevitable, irreversible time will slide the calendar to that sudden point where she would be looking back, not forward, at the pleasure. It wasn't the escape from Ferney she was enjoying, it was the relief from her all-pervading sense of guilt.

Time moved unfairly past until there was just one more full day left, a day that could not shoulder the burden of all the possible choices. They tossed a coin to decide what to do and Mike won, but in a generous mood he chose a lazy day by the sea and she knew he had done it for her. In the evening they went to their favourite taverna for the last time. The waiter produced a bottle of wine and Mike moved to pour Gally a glass but she held up a hand.

"No thanks, I don't think I want any."

"Are you okay?"

"Oh yes. More than okay. I feel great. I think the baby's telling me not to."

"The baby. Do you realize that's the first time you've mentioned it since we've been here?"

"You too, come to that. It doesn't mean I haven't been *thinking* about him."

"Him?" Mike looked astonished. "What's with this *him*?"

"Oh, just a feeling, I suppose. Anyway, have you been thinking about it?"

"Of course I have. It just feels a bit risky to talk about it." He poured her a glass of water instead.

"What sort of risk?"

"Bad memories. Sadness. Things that might spoil the holiday."

"We have to look forward now," she said gently.

"Oh, it's so great to hear you say that. I hated watching you suffer. You seem to have suddenly got so much stronger."

"There's no point in dwelling on that. I suppose after last time I thought maybe I was . . . defective? That all the other women in the world were having babies and it was like it was my fault that I wasn't and it seemed so very sad that we should just, I don't know, stop short I suppose."

"And that's gone now?"

She nodded. "I think so."

"How?"

"Maybe getting out of London."

It hit her only then, while she was talking, that she knew precisely what had changed, that it wasn't just the sense of powerful magic contained in Ferney's assurance that the baby, this baby that would drain him of his vitality, would come to its full term, but there was more. She would continue regardless. Life would not stop here. More than that, if she had lived so very many times, then presumably she *had* borne children. In fact for all she knew they might even be alive now. Whose children? Ferney's? From the 1930s? She wondered if that was possible. They'd be in their late fifties now. Wouldn't he have said? The thought was so strong that she feared for a moment that she might have spoken it and she had to check Mike's face to make sure that she hadn't. Suppose it were true? Amazing that she hadn't thought of that before.

"What are you thinking about?" asked Mike, watching her.

"Nothing I can explain." She shook her head, smiled to chase away the unwanted thoughts and looked around for something to fill the void and keep them out. There was something she had been wanting to know. Over the door into the taverna was a painted sign, bleached blue paint, highlighted in yellow, neatly arched in a long curve. The way it was written suggested a quotation because under its end, in smaller letters, were two words that seemed to be a name and a date, 1803–1869. She spoke little Greek and had idly wondered several times what it said, but after nearly three weeks she did now at least understand the Greek alphabet. Deciphering the letters of the name aloud, she discovered that it wasn't, as she had supposed, some local poet or author of whom she would never have heard. It spelt out the name "Hector Berlioz." The composer did not seem an obvious source for a quotation.

"Can you read that?" she asked Mike and he looked at the words for a while.

" 'Kronos' is time, isn't it?" he said. "I don't know the rest."

The waiter came to take their order.

"Dolmades for Gally, the ones without the meat? I'll have the souvlakia, please, and a big salad and while you're here, could you translate that quotation for us?"

The man smiled and didn't need to look. " 'Time is a great teacher,' " he said, " 'but unfortunately it kills all its pupils.' "

Mike gave a sharp laugh. "God, that's good. Look at all my students. They'd understand so much more if they were sixty not twenty, but then they wouldn't have time to use the knowledge. So many things are wasted on the young, aren't they? Education, beauty.

Wouldn't it be good if you could learn all the lessons, then start all over again with a young body?"

He said it with no guile, as if it were the most natural thought in the world, and her heart missed a beat. She wondered for a moment if he had guessed something and seized the chance to bring it up. For whatever reason, he had created a sudden opportunity for her to open up and try to describe the tug-of-war facing her back home. She stood on the edge of the precipice, groped for an opening phrase and was fatally interrupted by the arrival of the salad.

"There aren't many olives in it tonight," Mike complained, and the waiter promised to bring him an extra dish.

"Mike," she said as the man left. "That's an interesting thought you . . ."

He held up a restraining hand and stopped her in mid-flow. "I'm sorry," he said. "Don't forget what you were going to say, but you must look behind you."

Over the headland, the full moon was rising, painting the heave of the night sea with a band of skittering silver. Mike's the moon, she thought again and he's waxed while we've been here. He's big now. I hope he stays that way. Mike himself destroyed the thought before it had time to set.

"Haven't you ever thought it was odd," he said, "that the sun and the moon look as though they're the same size?"

"Why should that be odd?" she said quietly, and what made you settle on my metaphor, she thought.

"Because the sun's infinitely bigger and more important, after all. It's pure coincidence that the moon subtends the same angle." Mike used words like "subtend" without thinking. "It's a thousand-to-one chance against it working out like that." Still gazing up at it, he added, fatally, "It's given us its best for the holiday. It's on the wane from tomorrow," and shot her a startled look as she let out a single great sob.

She clamped down to stem the salt sea that threatened to follow it and closed her eyes tightly until she was sure she had choked them off.

"What is it?" he kept saying. "What's the matter?"

She shook her head.

"The end of the holiday? Is that what's wrong?"

A nod, because in a sense, that was true.

"Don't you want to go back? Surely you want to get back to the cottage?"

She just shook her head, but now she could open her eyes and blink and see that nobody at the other tables was looking, just Mike with fright in his eyes—fright and kindness.

Then with extraordinary and unlikely insight, he said, "Is it about the glove? Monmouth's glove?"

"Why do you say that?"

"I've wanted to ask you right through the holiday, but I thought I might . . . spoil things, I suppose. Is it?"

"In a way, I suppose."

"You think the ring and the glove belonged to Monmouth so you're sad that I threw the glove away?"

She nodded.

"That's a big assumption you're making, love. Just because the man at the museum told us about the drum and the armour, that doesn't prove anything about the ring."

She turned and looked away because the decision she had to make was not to be influenced by the pleading in his eyes. She looked up at the moon and spoke to it as much as to him.

"It was his. I *know* it was, you see."

"Well, we'll see what the experts say, but you can't *know* that, can you? You can only guess."

"Mike," she said very deliberately, "I'm not guessing. I knew the ring was there before I looked."

His mouth moved but he didn't say anything. The waiter brought the souvlakia and they were both grateful for the respite before his departure rang the bell for the next round.

"How could you know that?" he said and his voice was nervous.

She had to go on.

"There are things I find that I know about Penselwood. Look, Mike, I have to tell you because it's really hurting me. This is about Ferney."

His look broke her heart. She was astonished by the pain in it. It was as if she had said she was leaving him.

"I knew it would be."

"How did you know?"

"Because . . . because he likes you and he doesn't like me and ever since he first showed up you've changed a bit. I know it's good, a lot of it's good, but I sometimes feel like you've gone sort of slanting away from me."

She reached across the table to take his hand but cutlery got in the way and took the softness out of it.

"This is very difficult," she said, "and I know you'll say it's all nonsense, but please, please will you just let me say it all?"

"Yes."

"And . . . do you also promise not to say anything about this to anyone unless I say you can?"

"Yes."

"Especially to Ferney?"

He frowned then nodded. "Yes."

"Ferney says—believes—he's lived many times before. Always around Penselwood."

Mike snorted, saw an instantly guarded look start to close Gally's face and held up both hands, palms forward, to try to nullify the snort. "Sorry, I'm listening. You mean, he told you the ring was under the step."

"No, he didn't. He made me remember it myself."

There was a short silence while the implications of this sank in and then he gave a small groan. "You mean, he's trying to say you've . . . lived before, too?"

"Yes."

"And you *believe* him?"

"Mike. He starts describing something and I get this amazing, clear picture of it, like a memory, not like imagination."

"How do you know the difference?"

"Oh, lots of ways. It's never a complete surprise, that's one thing. And when I imagine things, everything shifts around. This doesn't. I see it like you really see things, from one point of view."

"Gally, he's persuading you, that's all. He reads all those books and he dreams up ideas and he hooks you with them, don't you see? How on earth would he know it was the same you who lived three hundred years ago? It's ridiculous, surely you can see that?"

"He's not saying it just happened once," said Gally, surprised that Mike should think that. "He's saying it happens over and over again. It's always been like that, him and me."

"Oh, what?" Mike sat in silence then looked wildly all around, his mouth moving, before he swung back to her. "I get it. You mean he's telling you that the two of you have always been a couple?"

"No, not *always*, but often." It was like breaking bad news. She could have said "usually," but "often" seemed kinder.

Mike started to sound angry. "You must be able to see what he's doing, surely? He's just a lonely old man and he fancies you something rotten so he's spinning you a yarn. You can't be taken in by that?"

"You promised you'd listen."

"I am listening, but it's just nonsense."

She sighed. "It's not nonsense." She looked around at the Greek trees, the Greek sand, the hushed wavebreaks of the Greek sea and distance undermined her. "At least, I don't think it is."

He was smart enough not to trumpet the small victory. "Eat your food," he said softly. The fat was congealing white on his pieces of lamb and she picked at the salad. There was so much more she had wanted to say.

"How do you feel about him?" Mike asked.

That was the hardest question to answer because she had shied away from answering it to herself, let alone to him.

"I'm very fond of him," she said. "I do feel like I've known him for a long time."

"Should I be jealous?" He said it as a joke but it was far from that.

"Don't be silly," she said, "he's over eighty," but she knew that wasn't the point. When, before coming here, she thought of Ferney it wasn't the ageing, present envelope that came to her mind, it was the living essence of the man—an essence that had always joined with her own fiercely, brightly, fully. Being here, she found herself looking at the memory of that emotion rather than the emotion itself and that made it easier to pass the question off.

"I don't know what to make of this," Mike said unhappily. "Do you think, maybe, it would be a good idea if you stayed away from him when we get back?"

"Mike, he's very old and he hasn't been well and I think he's going to die quite soon. Surely it can't hurt if he takes a little comfort from talking to me?"

"It can hurt. You've shown it can hurt."

"It does me good, too. He makes me feel much more, well, calm, I suppose."

Mike nodded, unable to deny the truth of that.

"I'm sorry," Gally said and meant it. "I didn't mean to do this at all. This holiday is so precious. I don't want to ruin it. Let's just stop talking about it for now."

"Can you do that?"

"Yes," she said firmly, aware that there was so much more they hadn't even touched on—the baby for a start and all that might imply. "Eat up and let's go for a walk along the beach. I want to share it with you."

Each managed to pretend that their sadness was simply the sadness of the holiday ending. They papered over the cracks with a walk along the shore, then drove back to the village for glasses of ouzo on the roof of the tower as the night whispered past. In bed, with wide-open windows failing to stir the room's stored daytime heat, they made love like gentle strangers, both feeling it was expected of them.

The morning jumped on them with demands of travel and timing that, for Gally, made the leave-taking an unsatisfactory and rushed affair of stolen backward glances as the last reality of the village was wiped away by a bend in the road. Slow steps of readjustment took them through the airport check-in, the departure lounge and on to the plane, but even then there was the sight of Greece beyond the window to anchor her. The final residue of the holiday was only rinsed away when London appeared below the wings and Mike said, "I wonder how the builders have been getting on?"

It was better to have told him something than nothing, she thought as they drove down the A303, and it was probably better to have told him something than everything. In his own time he would get round to asking more questions. She just hoped she would know what answers to give.

They usually turned off to avoid the roadworks, but when they got close they could see something was going on ahead.

"What's all that?" said Mike, slowing.

"I don't know."

It might be another accident, he thought. That would be a bad way to arrive, but whatever it was seemed to be happening off the road. The traffic was slowing to look but there was no blockage. In any case he feared the place still had the power to worry her. He glanced at her, but if any emotion showed in her face it seemed to be mild, curious excitement.

"You want to see?"

"Yes, let's."

"Something's definitely happened. There's two police cars there."

A small knot of people clustered by a digger and Mike pulled onto the verge when he'd turned off the main road and switched off the engine.

"Come on," he said, "let's see what's going on."

Gally found she still didn't like the place, but she followed him with an increased pulse rate and slight shortness of breath.

A section of the great excavation had been cordoned off with incident tape and in the bottom of the trench a man in overalls was busy. A sudden burst of irrational fear stopped Gally in her tracks. Mike hailed their postman who was standing on the fringes of the group of men. As she saw Ferney, talking to a policeman on the far side of the ditch, he lifted his face and stared at her and she heard the postman say, "It's a body. Bones, I should say. The digger uncovered them a couple of hours ago. Coroner's men have been down and some of these forensic people, they say."

13

FERNEY HAD FIRST heard about the plan for the roadworks almost a year earlier, and from the moment the surveyors began to peg out the line of the excavation along the A303 it had been the focus of his existence. It seemed to him then that it was the main un-finished business of his final life and he believed the diggers must suc-ceed where his spade had failed. The focus and much besides had shifted with Gally's unexpected reappearance. He no longer found it so pressing to keep a close eye on the hole when it suddenly became clear to him that, against the odds, the story hadn't ended there after all. Since then he spent his time instead keeping an eye on what was happening at Bagstone Farm and had more or less forgotten about the excavation, so when Michael Garrett's grandson stopped his raucous, shuddering tractor in the lane by Pear Ash and told him the diggers down there had turned up human bones, it took two heartbeats before the meaning of the news sank in. When it did a strong emotion seized him, part anger, part sorrow and finally part exhilaration at being near at last to the final proof of his long-held suspicion, and he began to walk with greater speed than his legs could gracefully accommodate down the hill in the direction of the main road.

All the work had stopped when he got there and he saw at first glance that the police had already started the process of protecting the public from any accidental exposure to the evidence of death. Flapping plastic sheeting strung between poles shielded one side of the excavation from direct view by the passing traffic and three sides of white tape, forbidding entry with thin authority, completed a square. He got round that easily enough by crossing the road further

down and coming up along the far side of the hedge. It was a route he
hadn't taken for a long time and he noted with momentary surprise
that there was no longer any sign at all of the old path to the forge.
Screened by the undergrowth, the policemen by the great trench
couldn't see him, but equally he couldn't get a clear view down to the
bottom of it, so cautiously he squeezed through between a tree trunk
and a bush and found himself looking straight down onto a scene
that took his breath away in sharp sorrow and old anger.

A man in official, freshly laundered overalls crouched in the broad
bottom of the ditch, maybe fifteen feet below ground level. The long
side of the ditch showed a narrow, vertical mark. It was darker than
the surrounding earth to either side, packed with looser material
where the diggers' long slice had cut a cross-section through Cochrane's old pit, and sticking out from the side towards the base of that
mark, where the man was scraping and brushing at the earth with archaeological care, was a pincushion of stained ivory. Letting himself
feel the sorrow for the sake of all those years, Ferney looked at the
earth surrounding the bones as if for signs of the soft, sweet flesh that
had rotted away into it. There was nothing to see but the bones themselves and they seemed haphazard.

It was no burial. Her limbs had not been laid out with care. She
had been tipped into the hole, head first from the look of it, if that
was indeed her skull down at the bottom where the man was taking
such trouble. It was the thought of that casual act of savagery and the
succession of bleak years that had followed that brought Ferney too
far into view. In his mind's eye the old smithy had regrouped its dis-
persed stones to take shape before him, the little storehouse behind it
blocking his direct view of the pit, so that he moved out into the open
to see round it, down through the double-vision, ghost earth to the
bones. The policemen on the other side noticed him then.

"Excuse me, sir. Do you mind moving away from there, please?
This is a closed area."

They were insubstantial, less real than the smithy, their voices
thinned by his retreat from their time so that he paid them no heed
and they, out of concern for his agitated state more than displeasure
at his attitude, came round to him and jarred him back to the present,
not by words but, when those failed, by the touch of their hands.

He heard one of them say, "Is there anything wrong?"

Confused, he replied, "That's my wife down there," before he
came fully back to the present and caution rushed in to warn him.

They sat him in the back of the car then, half official, half solicitous, and a sergeant came to occupy the front, an intelligent man

with quick, observant eyes and a twist to his face that gave him an accidental smile on the side that faced Ferney.

"What makes you think that's your wife?" said the sergeant. Ferney recognized one of the constables outside the car, but he didn't know this man at all, a man with a voice from somewhere else.

"I shouldn't have said that."

The sergeant nodded. "But you did say it, so I do have to ask you."

Ferney nodded but stayed silent and the sergeant considered him. "Something made you say it."

They weren't going to let him just shrug it off, that was clear. "My wife disappeared, you see?" he said. "I suddenly thought that might be her down there."

"When would this have been?" asked the sergeant gently.

"July the tenth, 1933," said Ferney immediately.

The sergeant raised his eyebrows, reached for his notebook.

"I'd better write this down," he said. "Could I start with your name?"

"Ferney Miller," he said. "That is, William Miller, number twelve, Castle Orchard Close in Penselwood."

"And what was your wife's name?"

Ferney had to think about that for a moment. "Jennifer."

"And when you say she disappeared . . . ?"

"That's what she did. She went out one day and she didn't come back."

"Did you tell anybody?"

"Of course I did. I told everyone. We went out looking for her for weeks on end."

"But did you tell anyone official? The police, I mean."

Ferney thought back. "Yes, I did. It wasn't like today, you know. I sent a boy with a message to Wincanton and someone came out on a bicycle in the end. Didn't do any good."

The sergeant thought a minute, unclipped the microphone and called his headquarters.

"I have a gentleman here," he said, "thinks these remains they've uncovered might be his wife. He says he reported her disappearance. Can you do a check for me? Over."

He knew what their reply was going to be and looked as though he was savouring it. The voice on the speaker was businesslike. "Is there a date on that? Over."

"Yes, 1933, July the tenth. Name of Miller."

There was a short silence. "Confirm 1933. That is three three? Over."

"I say again one nine three three, over."

The voice became a little less formal. "Sarge, where do you suggest we start looking for that?"

"I haven't a clue. Try the archives. They must keep the files somewhere."

He signed off, turned back to Ferney with a quizzical look, but before he could continue a PC came to the car and knocked on the window. He excused himself and got out to talk.

The window wasn't completely shut, but the policemen clearly didn't expect someone as old as Ferney to have keen hearing. He could just about follow their conversation.

"The foreman says the old boy was always coming down, looking in the hole. Wouldn't say why," said the constable. "A bit barmy, he reckoned. Nearly got himself run over by a truck once. Oh, and chummy down the hole says the skeleton's female, probably a woman in her twenties."

That was it. The confirmation that he didn't really need.

"Any idea how long it's been down there yet?"

"He said more than ten years, less than a hundred. He'll need a lab test to get nearer than that."

"No idea of the cause of death, I don't suppose?"

"Nothing obvious. The skull's intact."

Ferney thought about that. All that really mattered now was whether she had suffered.

The sergeant got back in the car and his attitude showed he was taking it more seriously now. "Look, Mr. Miller," he said, "if there's anything in this, we'll have to go through the protocol later and get it all down, but just to cut corners, would you mind telling me the story first?"

"I don't really know what else to say. She went out in the morning saying she was going to see her aunt in Chaffeymoor and she didn't come back at lunchtime like she was going to, so I went down to find her and her aunt said she'd never even got there."

"How long had you been married at the time?"

"Nine years. Got married when we were seventeen. Known each other all our lives."

"And had you had a row or anything like that?"

"Did I kill her, you mean?" Ferney snorted. "We never had a row about anything."

"No, I didn't mean that at all. I just meant, was there any reason why she might have decided to leave?"

"She wouldn't have left me," said Ferney simply.

The sergeant thought about the foreman's words—he was always coming down, looking in the hole. Caution told him to keep them to himself, just in case this calm, pleasant old man should turn out to be the least likely of murderers, but that still left an obvious question.

"What made you think this might be her?"

Ferney was starting to fret at the cramped confines of the car. "Can I show you how it was?" he asked. "Out in the fresh air?"

They got out and he led the sergeant a few yards down the verge next to the excavation. "There was a blacksmith's shop here," he said. "Been a smithy here for a hundred and fifty years since the turnpike came. Tatty old place, it was, just about on its last legs by that time. Trade was dying out with the cars." He looked round and hacked a heel into the ground. "The door would have been just about here. It was a long, low, tumbledown sort of a place. The forge was at the other end. He gave up on the blacksmith work in 1935—turned it into a petrol garage instead. He put a shed on the end, all timber and iron and great signs all over it."

"You wouldn't know there'd ever been a garage here," said the sergeant, looking along the verge.

"Didn't last long. No sign of it now. Anyway the smith, he'd dug this ruddy great hole at the back. Said it was going to be his toilet, you see, but he never finished it off. Left it like that for months—but then he filled it in again."

"Where was that exactly?"

Ferney gestured down towards the excavation. "Just there. You can see the marks of it all the way down the side of the trench, right where they found her."

"So why should your wife's remains be here, Mr. Miller?"

"The blacksmith was called Cochrane," said Ferney slowly. "It wouldn't be fair to blame him entirely, I've come to think. He had a bad time in the war, the Great War, that is. He was a stoker in a ship that was hit at Gallipoli. Shell-shocked. He was on the rum." He turned his eyes on the sergeant. "But he wanted my girl, you see? Wanted her so badly it made no difference that she was married to me. He went right on pestering her and bothering her for years."

"You're saying this Cochrane killed your wife and put her body down the hole?"

"That's what he did," said Ferney, nodding. "I've thought that for years and now here's the proof. He filled in the hole that day, you see?"

"Didn't you tell people that?"

"Oh yes, I told everybody. I wanted them all to help find her. We even dug down in the hole but they wouldn't believe me when I told them how deep it had been and they gave up too soon." He nodded towards the figure in the trench. "You can see for yourself. Who'd have thought she would be down so far?"

The sergeant was a Londoner, but he'd transferred to a more rural force because he had one great weakness as a policeman—a vivid imagination which all too often compelled him to put himself in the position of those he had to deal with in everyday life. It occurred to him that the old boy didn't seem quite as upset as he might have done, but then, he told himself, he'd had not far off sixty years to get over it.

The PC by the car shouted for him and he asked Ferney to wait. There was a photographer working down in the trench now and Ferney saw the flashes, subliminal reinforcements of the afternoon sun. On the road, cars were slowing down as they passed the scene, unsure what to make of the police cars and the tapes. Ferney wondered for a minute at his own detachment. Six months earlier he would have been distraught. During that terrible time when the men first started digging out the hole for the road junction, he had been in a constant ferment of anxiety, unable to stay away from the hole in case he should miss the evidence he had sought for such a long time. Now he took advantage of the sergeant's absence to walk back to the edge of the hole and look in. No one bothered him. The photographer was packing his gear away and the man in the overalls was picking the bones out of the earth and putting them, one at a time, into a bag. It meant nothing now, just tidying up some old rubbish, the remains of a suit of clothes.

She had come back, that was the point. By coming back she had chased away the demon that had sat on his back for fifty-seven years. That demon was guilt because every day of every month of every one of those years, Ferney had wondered where he had condemned her spirit to go, so alone, when he sent the water flowing in to wash out Effie Mullard and in doing so broke their long life-line. Terrible visions of limbo had troubled him all that time, much more than the death itself. It was the first time he had felt truly bereaved, but now her tenacious spirit was back by some miracle he did not yet understand and those bones down there brought no tears, only regrets and the vestiges of tired anger.

The sergeant came back to him. "Well, Mr. Miller," he said, "there's some people down in our cellar with dusty clothes thanks to you."

"Did you find it?"

"Yes, we found it. Lucky the mice hadn't got it. Just as you said except it doesn't list your wife's name as Jennifer."

"Did it say Gally?"

"Yes."

"That was what you might call a pet name. She was born Jennifer."

"Now, identification's going to be a bit difficult, but you'd better tell me whatever you can about this man Cochrane."

"I don't know that much. I had a set-to with him and he stayed away from me after that. I tried to have it out with him, but he'd run for it every time he saw me. A big man he was, much bigger than me."

"He was older than you?"

"Oh yes, ten years older, I'd say."

"So, he'd be how old now?"

"I'm eighty-three so he'd be ninety-three."

"The chances are he's no longer with us," said the sergeant.

"Oh no, he's not. He's been dead for years."

"Ah, right," said the sergeant in relief. "You know that for certain, do you?"

"Yes, I do. He died in 'fifty-nine."

"Do you know where?"

"Here. Up in the village." Ferney might have left it at that but he wanted to explain that Cochrane was a man of violence. "Someone killed him, see?"

"This man Cochrane was murdered?"

The sergeant sounded incredulous.

"Well, killed. Self-defence more like. Seemed fair enough to me. He was half-Danish. They're a violent lot. I've always had trouble with the Danes."

The sergeant frowned. "Did they catch the man?"

"Didn't have to. He didn't try to run anywhere. Lad called Billy. We used to call him Billy Bunter. Wasn't his fault. Cochrane was always attacking him."

"I'll find all this in the records, will I?"

"Should do."

"We'd better leave it there for now," the sergeant said, scratching his head. "I can't say I've come across one quite like this before. I suppose we'll have to look through the old files and get back to you." He stood there in silence for a minute, clearly feeling there was something more he ought to say.

Ferney looked again at the ditch and the scatter of old bones. The man in overalls tugged a femur out of the side of the hole and Ferney tried unsuccessfully to see a connection between the bone and the memory of the living woman. Instead he only felt a vague worry about the present Gally. They must be due back. He'd been missing her.

The sergeant came to what he wanted to say. "We'll have to be in touch again when the lab reports come through." He paused. "I'm very sorry," he said, "if it is your wife, I mean."

"It was a long time ago," said Ferney vaguely.

"It must have been lonely for you."

"Oh yes," said Ferney, then he looked up and saw Gally and her spidery husband walking up to the other side of the pit, joining the crowd. Gally looked golden brown and beautiful and the life came pouring out from her and drove the last possible sadness away from the spare parts down there in the hole. He was tempted to go straight to her, but he needed a bit more time. He felt that a sad chapter had been finally closed and knew that he'd been given a warning—a warning that they must both stick to the old plan and together make sure that what now followed was far, far better.

14

GALLY CLOSED HER eyes as they drove in through the gate. Three weeks away, three weeks of stored-up surprises. The healing of the house, previously robbed of dramatic impact by her constant presence, should by now have leapt ahead. She wanted to gain the fullest effect by keeping her eyes shut until after the car stopped so that she could take it all in at once, but she didn't get the chance. She felt the car sway diagonally into the uneven yard then start the swing round to face the house. That was when Mike uttered an exclamation of astonishment and she couldn't help opening her eyes to see what had prompted it.

At first she looked in the wrong direction. The house basked in the evening sun, looking even better than she had hoped it would. The roof and the front wall were finished, so that for the first time it gave an illusion of completion and yes, the builders had listened to all that she'd said about the need to be sympathetic to the structure. White primer shone where two new window frames had been set in to replace terminally rotten originals, but apart from that everything was harmonious and once they were painted she knew they too would blend in perfectly with the weathered appearance of the rest of it. She took in all of that in the briefest of glances, checking rapidly for the source of Mike's displeasure, then she realized he wasn't looking at the house at all, but off to the side towards the Bag Stone. Even then it took her a second to work out why he was surprised. The stone was in its usual place, leaning at a gentle angle from the edge of the stream towards the valley beyond the house just as it had always been.

"Who did that?" said Mike incredulously and then she was

equally astonished at the sudden realization that it shouldn't be there at all. When they left it had still been lying flat, partly buried by a long accumulation of earth and leaf mould.

"The builders must have done it."

"But why? We didn't tell them to."

"Well, no, I suppose we didn't . . . but we did say we were going to do it some time, didn't we?"

"Some time, maybe, but not now. I told them exactly what we wanted them to do while we were away. I gave them a list, damn it."

"Perhaps they did it all."

"Perhaps they did, but they didn't even ask us where we wanted the bloody thing."

"It's all right, love, it's in the right place. That's where . . ." She was about to say "where it's always been," but changed it in time. "That's where it is in the picture." It wasn't quite, but she knew with some inner certainty that was only due to artist's licence.

"He's behind this, isn't he?" said Mike grimly. "He's been in and somehow he's persuaded them to do it."

It seemed likely, though she didn't want to admit it.

"Let's go and see what's been going on in the house," she said quickly.

She went inside, hoping he would follow, hurt and sorrowful that all the conflict they had left behind had stayed here to come leaping out of the shadows and chase away the holiday calm. If it was Ferney's idea, it was hardly diplomatic. She hoped the builders had simply taken it into their heads to do it as some sort of a surprise, but she knew that if they had it would be different, standing there the wrong way round or at the wrong angle, not just perfectly so. The change inside was startling enough to provide a diversion. The upstairs floor was in place, new boards on the old beams, and they'd started making good the damaged sections of plasterwork in the downstairs walls. The new staircase was in and now that they could walk freely upstairs across defined, reliable floors it had begun to feel like a habitable house again. She found herself longing for it to be finished, to be able to sit down in a comfortable chair in her parlour and look out at the sunshine.

Mike had followed her and came up the stairs behind her. "Not bad," he said grudgingly.

"It's better than that," she said. "I think they've got on really well."

"I'm glad they didn't spend *all* their time putting stones up."

"Don't go on about that. What's wrong with you?" she said, not as gently as usual. "They've done much more than I expected and anyway I think it's really great to have the stone back there. You should be pleased."

He looked slightly ashamed of himself. "I would be. It's just that it's *our* house and I want things done the way *we* want."

"Well, I'm half of the *our* and the *we* and my half likes it. Come and look at it with me."

She took his hand, dry and long-fingered with brittle papyrus sun-burn circles crumbling fragments of skin into her palm, and led him out to the stone. The geometry of the house felt complete and satis-factory to her as though the stone that faced them focused it all. When Mike had argued against putting it up again he'd said it might look fake and fanciful, but it could never look either of those things. It held mystery and gravity and it was not to be approached lightly.

"I don't know about this," said Mike as they walked slowly to-wards it. "It's not very . . ." he searched for a word ". . . cosy."

"You wouldn't want it to be, would you?"

"Don't you feel it? It's sort of . . . severe, I suppose."

"I don't mind that. It's what it is."

They stopped short of it and the stone loomed above them, a little taller than Mike at its oblique tip. Gally wanted to touch it, perhaps even to press herself against it to welcome it back, but Mike's doubt-ful presence inhibited her.

"Good evening," said Ferney's voice behind them. "Did it give you a surprise?"

He must have seen us down on the road, she thought, delighted to hear his voice, completing the satisfaction of the stone's return, but at the same time she wished he hadn't come at that precise moment and knew that it would set Mike in his opposition. Ferney was standing by the open gate, one hand resting on it, on the edge of their prop-erty, perhaps unsure about intruding.

"Yes, it certainly did," she said. "Hello, how are you?" and speak-ing over the top of her, Mike said, "Yes, it did. Was it something to do with you?"

"I'd have to say it was, I suppose. You did agree you wanted to put it up, so I talked to the builders. They had to get a little crane in from Wincanton to lift it, but they've done a good job bedding it back in. It took them an hour or two to get it just right, mind."

That was too much for Mike. "I have to say I'm not entirely happy about it, Mr. Miller." Gally thought that was just the way he would sound when he was handing back an unsatisfactory essay to one of his students. "The thing is, I didn't really want them to do it right now. There were other jobs that were a bit more important."

Ferney looked evenly at him with an air of resigned patience. "I'm sorry to hear that. I made sure to ask them to do it after they knocked off at the end of the day, you see, as overtime. I thought it would be a nice surprise when you came home."

Mike's voice rose. "Overtime? They did it on overtime?" He turned wordlessly to Gally, then back to Ferney. "That really is a bit much. We have a tight budget to get this house done and I don't really think it's up to someone else to come butting in ordering cranes and telling builders what to do in overtime that I'm paying for."

His words were all about facts, costs, bills, but the feelings that fuelled them were more visceral—intrusion, resentment, fear.

Ferney screwed up his face as if trying to make sense of this. "You didn't pay for it," he said in a tone that said it should be obvious. "Not any of it. I paid them, of course. Wasn't going to make anything of it, but if that's why you're getting upset I'd better set you right."

"You paid them?" said Mike stupidly. "With your own money?"

"Well, I wouldn't use anybody else's." Ferney frowned. "I expect you've had a long journey. I'll be off." He looked hard at Mike and turned away.

Gally had hung back. This was between them and anything she said would seem disloyal to one or the other. The new closeness of the holiday had been shredded up and blown away by the conflict and she felt torn in two by it. She made a half gesture of waving goodbye to Ferney's departing back and went to Mike who was standing there with his hand to his mouth.

"Oh God," he said. "I've really put my foot in it."

"You could go after him."

"No, I couldn't."

"Why not?"

Mike looked around at the house and the stone. "The money's not the only thing. Okay, I was wrong about that but he's still messing about without asking us. The money thing just makes me sound as though I'm being horrible, that's the trouble."

"He did it to be kind to us."

"Did he? If he wanted it back up it wasn't for us. He does things for his own reasons, that man."

"Which are?"

"Oh, I don't know." Mike laughed ruefully. "Maybe he's planning to sacrifice me on it." He ruffled her hair.

"You deserve it."

"Maybe. I'm sorry we walked straight back into all this. We never asked him about the business down the road with the bones. Will you go and see him in the morning, take my apologies along?"

"Coward."

"Yes, I know."

They went to bed early, tired by the travelling, still on Greek time. Mike fell asleep immediately, but Gally found her mind returning to the crater by the main road, the crater that stirred up draughts of nervous unease in the pit of her stomach, wondering about the bones. She lay there for a long time, staring through the gap between the curtains out at the spangled sky beyond the trees, groping without success for a meaning. Mike was breathing evenly in deep sleep and after an hour she sat up carefully, switched on her table light and read history for a while. When her eyelids finally started to droop she put the book down, reached to turn off the light and saw, just as it went out, Monmouth's ring where she had put it when they unpacked, on the ledge that served as a bedside table.

The dream didn't start for a while.

Gally slept soundly until the nadir of the night, close to four o'clock when the spirit seems at its lowest ebb and whatever warmth was left in the caravan had drained into night-black. Then, groping out of vague comfort into a dream-pit, fear overwhelmed her. She said "no" for the tenth time, shouting in dream silence, and the man, excited in his cruelty, waved an abrupt hand to the soldiers who pinioned her arms, forced her stumbling through the archway where the rank swirl of hot pitch-smoke gagged in her throat.

And there stood the burnman.

"Just doing my job," he said in his slow, cracked lilt. "Just a job."

"Show her your work," said the doom-voice behind her, "so she learns to say yes," and though she'd seen it so many times before, she still retched in horror as he pulled the half-cooked grey forearm, curled hand stiff at the end, from the pile on the ground and plunged it, turning, into the tar. The cauldron was a car, burning, and she could not move towards it, could not help—then it was a cauldron again. Her scream came up inside her then, but not until he pulled it out, the hot tar dripping, cooling to dull black, and thrust the claw into her face did it cross the barrier of sleep to ring out through the night and shock Mike awake.

When his own racing heart quietened, he calmed her as he was so used to doing in London.

"What was it?" he said as he felt her start to relax.

"Them."

"Both of them?"

"No."

"Are you all right now?"

"I think so."

She wasn't. Twisting acid guilt had her. She'd killed him, killed him by not fighting free. The therapist had told her to say to herself, you were injured, you were far too young, you could not have helped, and she repeated that mantra over and over until it built a frail wall between her and the receding dream. She kept silent.

For all that, Mike sensed it and lay quietly alert, breathing deeply as if he were sleeping until he was sure she was completely asleep again and only then did he let himself follow her.

FERNEY TOOK MIKE'S secondhand apology in his long, country stride when she met him in the lane on the way towards each other in the morning. It always seemed so easy to run into Ferney, as if they could each sense the other's intention. She'd woken very early again, while Mike was still snoring gently, and had gone straight to the stone to experience its return in the clarity of a Sunday morning liquid with far birdsong. The nightmare-scare had robbed her sleep of some of its benefit, leaving a sourness in her head, but on an impulse she stood against the stone as she had once stood against the corner of the house and it magnified the pulse of the blood in her, the pulse of two hearts not one, so that she became clearly aware of the baby growing inside her.

Who are you? she asked it, but there was no discernible answer, just the microscopic tickle of cells dividing. The stone's slant seemed at odds with its mass, denying its weight. The builders had done their job cleverly. She ran her hands up its surface almost to the top and the tiny channels, facets and craters of the stone's ancient division from its mother rock were no strangers to her touch. It strengthened her.

She walked slowly away, looking back at the stone every few paces, feeling some tangible force in the currents of her blood that was more potent than before. Mike's loud snores came through the walls of the caravan like warnings of battle. The discord of the previous evening seemed worse with time and he had after all asked her to apologize on his behalf. Ferney might well be up and she decided there was no harm in walking over to check the bungalow for signs of life. She'd gone less than a hundred yards, startling a small crowd of rabbits that fled into holes in the high bank, when she saw him ahead in the lane and he waved his stick in greeting.

He seemed cheerful enough. "It came as a bit of a shock, I expect," was all he said when she gave Mike's apologies. "No need to worry. I probably shouldn't have done it. He still doesn't like me much, does he?"

She was suddenly embarrassed, hesitant. "I told him a little bit while we were on holiday, about you and about me."

He shot her an appalled look. "You didn't. What made you do that? I don't think that was a very good idea."

"He'd sort of guessed a bit of it. About the ring. It was a long way away from here."

That seemed to make more sense to him than to her. "It's always different when you're away," he said, nodding, and gave her a considering look. "You don't look too great considering you've had a holiday."

"I'm okay, I just didn't sleep as well as I might have done last night."

"Bad dreams?"

"Did I tell you that?"

He shrugged it off. "Have you got time to come and sit down for a minute?"

"I've left Mike asleep," she said. "I suppose I shouldn't be too long."

He nodded at the gateway to the field that sloped up from the house. "Let's go through here, then. You can see down to your place, so you'll know when he comes out."

They sat side by side on the grass looking south. The roof of the house poked out of its little clump of trees below and the caravan showed no signs of life. The Bag Stone was foreshortened from this angle and Gally could see clearly how the little depression and the green line of vegetation that marked the course of the buried stream brushed past its heel.

"Do we have to talk about the dreams?"

"Only if you want to. It might help, though."

"It's past now," she said, "for the time being."

He nodded down at the caravan. "I wouldn't want to get halfway. Best save that for when there's lots of time."

"And for when I'm feeling brave. I've got a lot of other questions to ask, though."

"Tell me what they are and I'll tell you which ones we've got time for."

"There's the stone. I'm glad to see it up again. I know that's how it belongs, but it's got another side to it. Mike says it's not cosy. I know what he means. Oh, and we both wanted to ask you about the bones, down at the road yesterday. They said you'd been talking to the police about them for a long time. What's that all about? That's if you don't mind."

"How could I mind? It's you as much as me. The bones and the stone. The end and the beginning, you might say. It's quite a lot to ask. Was that all?"

"No, it wasn't. There's lots more, like why shouldn't I have talked to Mike?"

"And?"

"There's one really big thing."

"What is it?"

Would it sound silly? She didn't care. "Have I got any children?"

"Oh, well now." He blinked. "Shall we do that one first? I don't really know because I don't know where you've been lately, you see."

"Mrs. Mullard told me your wife was called Gally and she disappeared."

"Well, she's right enough about that."

"So . . . that was me."

"Of course it was."

"There's no 'of course' about it. I don't know anything about her, about your wife, I mean, about me."

"You would if I helped you. Anyway, you did know something about her. You went to our old house, didn't you? That first time. Only time we ever lived there was that time, you and me."

At that moment, beset by so much uncertainty, she felt more like a daughter than a wife.

"Anyway, I went away. Is that right?"

"You've never ever gone away from me by choice, nor have I ever done that to you," he said with force.

"So it wasn't by choice."

"That's right. I had some ideas but I couldn't tell for certain. I knew you must be dead."

Gally flinched. "How did you know?"

"How wouldn't I know? I couldn't feel you anywhere. It had to be, didn't it? I'd messed things around down there, you see," he waved an arm down at the cottage and the stone. "Stupid of me after all those years."

"I don't understand."

"Have I got to spell it out?"

"Yes, you'd better."

"Some things were obvious, I suppose. We always knew it was the stone that did it, that brought us back. The night it fell down, we feared that might be the end of it. We even had a go at putting it back up again. Couldn't do it, but anyway we both knew pretty soon that nothing had changed. It was only later, after you were gone, I first got the idea that it might be the water that mattered too. I thought it was the combination, you see, the water going past the stone. I'd changed the course of the water, you see, to get *her* out of the house and then you went missing and suddenly it all felt . . . dead, you might say—like things had changed forever."

She was struggling to understand, reluctant to interrupt.

He gave a great sigh. "Oh, do you know how I looked for you? I went to see every baby for miles. Had to find an excuse to go knocking on their doors, so I bought a great pile of baby clothes, saying I had no use for them anymore now you'd gone so I was giving them away. People must have thought I was mad. I went on looking for months, but I couldn't find you anywhere."

"Would you have known?"

"Oh yes. I think I would. I always hoped you'd turn up one day—just come walking in—but you didn't, not until now anyway."

Babies, death, water and stones were whirling in Gally's head.

"I'm not sure I really understand, Ferney. Just go through it slowly for me. What went wrong?"

"I'd only done the business of the water down there for us. You do understand that, don't you?" He spoke like a lover begging forgiveness for some current lapse.

"Not completely. At least not up here." She tapped her forehead, "Not where I can get hold of it."

He sighed and started again, speaking slowly, punctuating each sentence with an emphatic chopping movement of both hands.

"Effie Mullard was having her baby, right? It was killing me—growing in her, down there right by the stone. Do you remember? It wasn't giving us a chance. We had such a good life, you and me, and because of her and that tramp I was getting more and more ill the bigger she got. I knew it was going to be me when it was born, so it was clear enough that I was going to die and there was only one thing to do, you see? I had to get Effie right away from the house before it was born, then maybe it wouldn't be me. You knew. We talked about it. You knew what I was doing. You didn't like it but you knew it had to be done. I used the water to do it, I flooded her out."

"Wait, I don't know about this. You're saying that if Effie Mullard had stayed here, you would have died when her baby was born?"

"That's right."

"I see."

He was getting a little agitated, but now he took a moment to draw breath and started again in a calmer voice. "The house was empty. She was safely away and I got better and we had a good time again, but then it was all for nothing because you vanished and it seemed to me you'd gone forever because of what I'd done. Fifty-seven years, Gally, do you have any idea what it's felt like? But then you came back again. It's the in-between I don't know about. What year were you born—1965?"

" 'Sixty-three."

"Where were you born?"

"Bath."

He looked surprised as though that was the wrong answer. "Bath? How could that be? Was that where your parents were living?"

"Yes, they'd been there about six months, I think."

"So where were they before that?"

"London."

He shook his head. "Somewhere else."

"No, I don't think so. They used to spend the weekends with my granny."

"Where was that?"

"Amesbury."

"That would be it. That's where it must have happened, you see? There's the big stone circle there. It grabbed you. That still leaves thirty-odd years in between to work out. Last time you were here was 1933. You were Jennifer on your birth certificate, Jennifer Moldrum before we married."

"Ferney, you're talking all around it. I . . . Jennifer disappeared. You say she must have died. Come on. Tell me what happened in 1933?"

"Someone did you harm." He looked at her soberly. "Doesn't matter now, but my guess is someone must have been passing by when you died who was getting near their time. Could have been in a car even, so you were born way off somewhere else. That's the trouble with cars and all this fast transport."

"It's as easy as that?"

"Travel's always been dangerous for us. It's worse now."

She added it up. "So I must have been born again in 1933, and then that person . . . I . . . died in 1963 when I was only thirty?"

"Sounds right."

"So I could have had children?"

"Children? What's that got to do with it? You could have. You didn't have any the time before." He sounded casual and saw her frown. "You shouldn't get too bothered about it," he went on. "There's always been children. When you count the grandchildren and the great-grandchildren and the rest, we must be related to most everybody that's lived round these parts. Doesn't mean that much. You come back and the ones that were your kids are so much older than you are and they don't know you, so it's difficult to feel the link. What I'm telling you, this isn't about children, it's about you and me."

As with so much that he said she felt a vast array of questions open up before her and had to hold firmly on to her train of thought. "The stone's right at the start of all this, isn't it? Will you tell me about the stone?"

"Not now. We'll need some time for that, time when we're not going to be interrupted."

"Tomorrow," she said. "I'm by myself tomorrow. Mike's got a faculty meeting." It sounded a little like treachery.

"All right. If you're sure."

"What did you mean when you said the bones and the stone were the end and the beginning?" The explanation of the other part of it came to her as she spoke and she shivered. "The bones down at the roadworks. Who were they?"

"I'll tell you tomorrow."

"They were me, weren't they? That's what happened to me in 1933. That's what you meant, wasn't it?"

He looked hard at her and nodded slowly.

"And that's why I didn't like it down there. When we first came, I got all panicky in the car."

He knew for her sake he should tread very carefully. "Could be. There was a man you didn't like, used to live down there."

"Who was he?"

"Wouldn't you rather wait until tomorrow?"

"I've got to know a bit more."

"Well, then, I'll try a name on you. Carl Cochrane. Does that mean anything to you?"

The faintest tingle of unease. "Not really," she said. "Nothing I can put my finger on."

FERNEY 169

"Good," he said. "Then that one's best left for now. All you need to know is he did for you. I'll tell you the rest very soon. It doesn't matter anymore."

Fifty-seven years ago, she thought, and pity seized her. "I left you to fend for yourself for all that time?"

"It wasn't your choice," he said, then, seeing her eyes, "Dry your tears."

"It's so sad to think of it," she said, wiping the wetness away with the back of her hand. "You being on your own all that time." At that moment she felt closer to Ferney than she could ever remember feeling to anyone. Mike belonged to some distant planet where loyalty was not an issue. She put her arms round him and held him to her, surprised both by the fragility of his old shoulders and by the strength of a feeling that was far more disturbing than pity and that paid no heed to his physical age. She let go, shocked.

"We don't have to go through that again," he said. "A separation like that. Not ever again if we don't want to."

"How?"

Before he could reply there was a faint squeak of old hinges and down below them they saw the caravan door swing open and Mike's head peer out. His voice came faintly up the hill: "Gally?"

"I'd better go," she said. "Oh dear. We've hardly got started."

"Telling other people has never been a very good idea," he said urgently. "Don't tell him any more, not until we've had more of a chance to talk."

"It's so difficult," she said, "me between the two of you. I can't just leave him out in the cold."

"It doesn't help if you tell people. It's never helped. What you and me are, that's been counted a heresy often as not. You won't remember what they've done to heretics."

"Who?"

"Christians for a start."

Mike's voice came again. "Gally?"

"Go on," he said. "He's looking for you. You'd best be off. I'll see you tomorrow morning, shall I?"

"Yes. Nine o'clock?"

He nodded. "Come and meet me. If we're going to talk about the start of it, we'd better meet where it began."

She waited and he looked at her for a long, expectant moment then gave in.

"Kenny Wilkins' Castle," he said, and saw her shiver. "I'll see you there. You'll be all right with me."

·   ·   ·

" 'MORNING, LOVE," SHE said when Mike, hearing her footsteps, stuck his head out of the caravan door again.

"Not a very romantic start to the day," he grumbled. "Waking up with only a pillow to hug."

She suppressed all she'd just heard for his sake. "It was a beautiful morning. I thought I'd let you sleep. I was sitting up there in the field so I could tell when you woke up."

He'd made a pot of coffee and he poured her a cup.

"I keep thinking about the old man," he said. "He probably thinks I'm a complete shit after last night."

"I've already seen him. He was in the lane. He said it was fine."

"You've seen him?" Mike frowned. "That was quick."

"He just happened to be walking along."

"Pure coincidence?"

"Yes," she said, nettled.

"What did you talk about?"

"I gave your apologies. He accepted them."

She hoped he would leave it at that and he did.

15

ALFRED'S TOWER ROSE above the distant trees, marking Gally's direction as she set off northward along the ridge, a magician's castle bursting through the smooth green humps of Nutwood in the Rupert books of her childhood. She wondered why the sight of the tower made her want to laugh. There was nothing laughable in what lay between. Her rendezvous was well short of the tower and the contours soon hid it. She half expected to see Ferney on the road ahead of her—for both of them it was the only route out of the village—but there was no sign of him as she left the houses behind, no sign of him as she reached the start of the trees to the left of the road and still no sign of him when the woodland spread to both sides and the outer banks of Kenny Wilkins' Castle loomed green across her path between their trunks.

She stopped and looked at the ancient ramparts, disturbed by the immediate unease she felt. Nothing less than his unequivocal demand would have made her come here. When she was little she'd had recurrent dreams of a wood like this, tricky light slanting down through a black canopy bewildering her eyes as she watched, terrified, for the witch hiding behind the trunks, the witch she thought she'd seen way over there at the edge of her vision, but who would suddenly step shockingly from behind the nearest tree and rush at her. She wondered at herself, recognizing the old fear, and then made the mistake of thinking it must be that dream that had led to her unease. Without conscious thought she got rid of the wood, blotted it crudely out of the picture, handling the old tool clumsily, savagely, through long disuse.

It was the wrong thing to do.

In an instant, the scene changed dizzyingly as the sky burst through to dissolve the trees. She stood on a wet track, on a bare hill facing ramparts that were still old but had a palisade of fresh-cut pale stakes around their summit and storm clouds behind them. Men, or rather the threatening sense of men, swarmed through the gateway towards her. Gaping, rooted, horrified, she heard a horn-blast sound behind her and swung round to face this new enemy. She could see nothing. The track led straight back along the top of the ridge. The horn sounded again and asserted for a moment an alien shape, square and yellow, that flickered before her. Again it sounded and this time the shape filled out, bringing back with it the tarmac and tree trunks, and she stepped out of the way of the slowing van whose driver made a questioning, insulting gesture at her as he passed.

Drawing a shuddering breath she turned back to confront the fort, and the high trees once again had it under their roots. She walked on, senses alert and bristling, through the gate where she had just seen the timber towers that once rose out of the rounded earth shoulders. The van's engine note had faded round the downhill bend towards Stourton and in the complete silence under the leaf canopy, Ferney's voice said, "Was he hooting at you?"

He was sitting on the parapet up to her left, perfectly disguised by his brown tweeds in the dappled light, a wood spirit in a Dunn & Co. jacket.

"I'm afraid he was," she said. "I forgot where I was."

"You mean 'when I was,' don't you?"

She nodded.

"Come and sit down," he said. "I expect it scared you a bit."

He lifted an arm and she slipped naturally in against his shoulder and felt better. "There was a wooden fence and towers."

"That's the first time you've done it by yourself, without me pushing it along."

"Oh. Yes, I suppose it was."

"You'll get better at it."

"I'm not sure I want to. Actually, it wasn't really the first time. I saw the house in the middle of the night, with the old front door in the right place."

"You wanted to know about the beginning. Do you still?"

"I think I have to. It's not really a question of what I want."

"You're right there," he said. "All the things that twist you and pull you, the dreams and the black dogs that stalk you—there's only one way to get rid of them and that's to call them out into the daylight and look at them, see where they came from. When you see they come from real things that happened, well, you'll get the better of them."

"But my nightmares don't come from those old times. They come from things that happened this time. I know what they were. I just can't seem to do anything about them."

He considered her for a moment. "What did happen this time?"

"I . . . We had a crash, when I was little."

"Were you hurt?"

"I broke my arm. My mother hit her head. That didn't matter."

"What did, then?"

"They got us out, but there was petrol everywhere and my father was trapped in the car. It burned."

"You saw it?"

She spoke through tears. "I tried to get back to it. I knew I could get him out, but they wouldn't let me."

"And now you dream about it?"

"It keeps coming in. It's a strange dream. It's not directly about it."

"Go on then, tell me what it *is* about."

She found she couldn't name them directly. "Boiling and . . . burning." That was as near as she could get. The beasts in her head rattled their bars.

And then he amazed her. "The Boilman and the Burnman, is it?"

"You couldn't know that," she said in indignation. "How could you?"

"I know it well. Gally, it's not about what you think it is. It's something older. I can help you with it."

She shivered. "Not here."

"No, not here. This place is bad enough already, isn't it? And you need to know the whys and the whens of that first, but we will get to it, and soon." His calmness touched her. The beasts were stilled.

She looked somberly at the trees. "I have a feeling that whatever happened here is going to be a pretty scary thing to remember, but I suppose it won't go away by itself. None of this will go away."

"Not unless *you* go away."

"I don't think I can."She shivered.

"You've never liked it here in the camp, but it's better to face it."

"Go on. I want to get it over with. Just tell me and I'll listen."

"Will you?" he said, smiling. "Well, it might sound funny, but I can't tell you all that much, not from me at any rate. There's bits of it that come back, but it's always been you who remembered it much better than I did. You knew the place, you see? I'd only just come here, so it sort of didn't stick the same way. Mostly I can only tell you what you've told me."

A rook wheeled down through the trees, cawing raucously, and settled on a tree stump across the road.

"There is a limit to what you can remember," he said. "I read a book the other day about those people who remember everything. They call them idiot savants. Have you heard of them?"

"Yes."

"They can memorize whole telephone directories. Some of them can take one look at a building and go away and draw it perfectly, brick for brick, but it gets in the way of their thinking, you see? Makes them mad because there's no order to it. It's very easy to go like that. I did it once."

"What happened?"

"Oh, it's not very interesting. I was born rich. Hasn't often happened round here. We're mostly peasants, but I was the son of one of the cuckoo lords and I didn't have that much to do with my time."

"Who were the cuckoo lords?"

"The four big landowners back in the 1700s? Doesn't that ring any bells?"

She shook her head.

"Two earls, Ilchester and Egremont, plus the Bigings and the Hoares. They owned all the land round here then. Turfed a few people out of their nests to get it too. The Hoares were the best of them. I was a Hoare."

"Where was I, then?"

"Down in the village. Older than me. They barred me from seeing you when they found out. I was kept in the house for two years and I wasn't really in control that time round. I tried to remember it all, everything, and it did for me. Blew a gasket." He made a face. "Anyway, that wasn't what I wanted to tell you. I was just explaining you can't remember everything, you shouldn't even try. You have to be a bit selective. I suppose it's all in there somewhere, but if you bring too much of it out into the wrong bit of your head it gets in the way, see?"

"The beginning, then." She was so tense that her hands had begun to shake and Ferney, feeling it, patted her arm.

"The first time round for both of us, I'm sure. Like I said, it's your words really, not mine. You hadn't lived here for that long. You used to say you'd come into the forest with your family from over there beyond Whitesheet after a battle." He pointed to the east. "Probably six years before, because that's when the books say the Saxons started moving in, so I suppose you could say you were refugees. Now, this ridge we're on was all bare then. It stuck up out of the forest. The true forest, Coit Maur, ran off to the north and the west, but there were still thick woods on the other side, too, and the tracks came this way. You used to complain about how hard you'd been made to work, all of you, making the old camp good again, cutting the stakes, clearing away the scrub, knowing the Saxons would come one day."

"Watching the horizon."

Ferney looked at her. Had she forgotten already that she was just going to listen? Which way was better?

He nodded. "Watching the east, knowing one day we'd be coming over the hill."

"We?"

"I was one of *them*. One of the Saxons. I don't know anything from before that. I've tried many times, but it's just not there. I wasn't very old, I know that much for sure, and I don't think I'd ever fought before. From what I've read recently, the chances are I would have come from round Salisbury way. The Saxons settled all round there in the valleys, but then they ran out of space. You had fields further down the ridge." He indicated the direction of Penselwood. "The plan was that when we came, all of you would get in here as fast as you could, because the old fort had always been a good place to fight from."

"But . . . it didn't work?"

"No water here, you said. Everything to eat, everything to drink had to be lugged all the way along the ridge. You couldn't keep everyone here like that, so there was a message bonfire going all the time and horns to blow, then everyone was meant to come running."

"A pile of dry and a pile of green." Her inner voice was becoming stronger. "A small fire always burning, even in the rain, and always a pile of dry wood next to it, then green for the smoke. Oh, that was hard, keeping it dry."

"Everyone took turns at the watch, lining the walls every thirty paces," he said. "You were a girl, just old enough for babies, and you were one of the watch when we finally came."

"It wasn't my fault," she said absently. "It was the storm. I could hardly see across to Whitesheet in the rain. I was so cold. The rain was driving at me and there was hail too and my head was aching with it. Nobody could have seen them. I wasn't the only one charged with looking that way. I'm not even sure they ever came over the hill.

I think they came round the edge and up the valley." She stopped speaking and stared east as if trying to make up for a past failing.

Ferney let the silence go on until she relaxed a little. "I can't remember which way we came," he said, "or what the plan was, except I don't think it would have been Kenny Wilkins' idea. It's always been in my mind that there was a smart lad called Cuthbert or Cuthred who did his best thinking for him. The books don't say, except that he did have a nephew with a name like that so it could have been him. Old Cenwalch, I've read what they say about him. He was the dangerous sort. He'd gone a bit glorious by that time. He was doing Christianity for the second time round, building himself a cathedral at Winchester even, but he was a pagan at heart. You couldn't tell with him. No real beliefs except that he had a guaranteed seat at the right hand of any god on offer."

"One moment it was our place," she breathed, looking around at the northern entrance anxiously, "our safe place—the next they were appearing out of the rain from nowhere. The fire wasn't any good, was it? Even if we'd had time, you wouldn't have seen the smoke in that rain. The horn was the only chance. I grabbed it and ran and I was trying to blow it and scream and breathe and run all at once."

The words were marsh gas bubbles rising from muddy depths and at first her voice was just the place where they burst on the surface then the increasing stream of words brought with them solid gouts of the source mud itself so she hardly knew when she stopped talking and started being.

Trying to run and blow, lacking any control of breath to make a sound louder than a thin, nightmare squeak. The rain stopped and she looked back at the fort on the bare ridge against the storm clouds and saw men, Saxon men, running out after her. Terror tipped her right over into dreadful bravery so that she stopped running, stood still breathing hard, in and out, in and out to get her breath, watching the men coming for her, then raised the horn to her lips and sounded one long clear blast into the wet air before hands grabbed her and tore it from her.

She was slim, fair-skinned and healthy and when they pulled her by her arms and her hair back towards the fort, instead of using the knives in their belts, she had a pretty fair idea why. They lashed her to a stake in the camp and mercifully she couldn't see past the ramparts to the fight that followed, the fight that moved rapidly down the track as the surprised, straggling Britons rushing up from the village to meet the threat were forced back in a spray of blood to the southernmost summit of the ridge. For the first few minutes she could hear the yells, but those dwindled into the distance leaving behind just one voice, screaming over and over again in terminal agony until someone sliced through the throat that was issuing it.

She hadn't been left alone. A dozen of the oldest and the youngest Saxon soldiers had been left to guard them and the camp. The one who came nearest to her was barely more than a boy—about her own age, a thin creature with huge blue eyes and matted, fair hair. He was nervous, jumping at every noise, straining to see down the slope into the trees as if a hundred fierce Britons might rush him at any moment. She could have told him there weren't a hundred fierce Britons left. The screams had established that. She wondered what had happened to her father, her sister and her three uncles and knew by now they were either dead or running for their lives far away from her. She sniffled a bit then and the Saxon boy turned, ducking his head to see, and giving her an unexpected little hint of a smile before he snapped back on watch, worried someone might have noticed. She hadn't expected humanity.

That awful day went on and on as the chill rain kept returning, washing away her strength and will to live. The Saxon boy looked at her from time to time but she avoided his eyes until, greatly daring when the older men, bored with their task, gave chase to a deer, he came to her and thrust small pieces of hard, flat bread into her mouth, followed by a rancid swill of water from his skin bottle. Some time later there were shouts and calls and she lifted her head to see the brutal ranks of tall Saxon men walking back into the fort. In their midst, yoked wrist to wrist with rope, was a sad, stumbling gaggle of women. She did a quick count: fourteen of them and she recognized every one. The face she most hoped and feared to see, her sister Fanwy, was not there.

If Cenwalch was a true Christian he gave little sign of it that night. The men were called together in a half circle while the red-haired chief, standing up on the rampart, gave a guttural invocation that sounded alien beyond belief to her ear, so unlike the music of her own tongue. Then he gave out the day's prizes. He pointed into the crowd and called out names which were greeted by shouts of derision and envy and each man named came swaggering out to claim his due. She was the very first to be chosen by a huge pig of a man with a running sore covering half his cheek, and fetid breath that whistled between broken stumps of teeth. He grabbed her by the wrist and reached to cut her ties and she was preparing to fight but a sharp word from the chief up on the rampart stopped him. He let her go with ill-concealed disappointment and chose the shapely Magan instead, who sobbed and screamed as he pulled her into the trees. She'd never liked Magan but, for all that, pity tinged her relief. As the next man chose, she looked up and met the chief's eye. He nodded down once to her and pointed at himself. She looked away and saw the Saxon boy staring in obvious horror at this transaction from the far edge of the crowd.

Cenwalch had other business that came before her and she was left tied to her stake while the men strung a tight-woven cloth from branch to branch as cover against the sporadic rain and built him a bed platform of woven sticks. In among this, at a moment when no one was close to her and the darkness had come down to shield them, the boy crept across to her and, against all likelihood, cut quickly through her ties and led her, astonished at this ally from the ranks of the enemy, to the rampart. They were over it like cats and she slipped from him, down the slope into cover, intending to make her escape by herself. Then, briefly, she looked back and saw him still standing in the gloom outside the palisade. Moonlight caught the angle of his face and the lonely terror stamped on it twisted something inside her. Wondering why she was taking the risk, she whistled softly from her cover and in doing so changed everything forever.

His face lit up and he rushed to join her, making far too much noise in the night wood. She led him down the slope to the lower pathway, the hunting path that followed the contour of the ridge halfway down, running fleet-footed to the south. They ran for ten minutes without stopping, skirting the dome of the southern rise, and she stopped her ears against the groans that came from a man's shuddering form which lay facedown across their path. The rain started again and exhaustion overcame caution. She took him to her family hut, moving fearfully towards it, afraid of who might and who might not be there. It was intact but empty down under the far swell of the hill and they lay together listening with animal intensity to the noises of the night, fearing the sound of the chase.

He held her, stroked her to calm himself and her in the dripping hut. Looking into her wide eyes he let her know his name. "Ferney," he said, patting his chest with the flat of his hand. "Gally," she said, putting her trust in him.

They slept just like that, wrapped tight around each other for warmth and comfort and she jarred awake in the first grey light to find him already alert, head arched back, listening. They should have gone on before dawn. There were footsteps and voices, Saxon voices. A jar crashed to the ground in the next hut and there was coarse laughter. Ferney crouched by the entrance, risked a quick look and stiffened. She slipped to his side, saw two Saxons walking towards them and another four behind them, probing the undergrowth with their long spears.

"Come," she whispered, but he looked at her without understanding, so she took his hand and tugging him along behind, ran for her life through the doorway to an explosion of Saxon shouts.

Down the path they raced together with the one thought in her mind that if they could get into the thick forest they could never be found, but Saxon horns were calling and Saxon voices were giving tongue and, cutting them off from both sides ahead, came leaping men. She swerved left and Ferney followed, battered through the hedge and down the rough pastures where pigs, her father's pigs, still rooted. Over the hedge at the bottom and nearly into the trees, more Saxons came from the left and she ran with no clear intention for the Beagh Stone beyond the track, the life stone, the stone that could sometimes bring health back to the dying. A slice of fire stole her balance as a hurled spear cut open the muscle of her calf and she heard a despairing cry from the boy behind her as she stumbled and slid down on one knee. He pulled her up, half hoisted her on his thin shoulder and on they went, but their speed was half what it had been and as they reached the stone, another spear took him in the back. He stopped, swaying, let her slide down against the leaning stone and held her in his arms, his blood running down and mingling with the blood from her leg in a moment of unexpected peace before a third spear, hurled with heavy-muscled power, burst right through his thin chest to pin him to her. His face was forced forward onto hers so that their lips met abruptly in an involuntary, fatal kiss.

Sound went away, fading to hissing silence. Sight narrowed, bleached out so nothing was left to be seen save a narrowing circle of his face then just his eyes, burning into hers. There was a last sense of his arms round her, slackening in death then seemingly growing stronger again to hold her and shake her gently.

"Enough now, stop there," he said and she wondered how she could understand the Saxon words. "Don't go further, Gally," he said.

The shocking intrusion of the fierce spear inside her was worse than its direct pain. It had spawned a point of bright light in her head that was growing, cutting off the feeling of the spear, stilling all the restless questions so that she started to quieten, to be content inside the light, feeling it grow. A shouting voice wouldn't let her. It grew irritatingly louder and with every shouted syllable the light pulsed, weakened again. The voice kept hammering her name at her and she was forced reluctantly to let go of the last of the glow of it, the wonderful, loving glow, surrendering to the long, elastic tug of the far future.

"Oh, do shut up," she said wearily and opened her eyes to an unknown place and an unknown man holding her. The spear-thrust tunnel through her had filled, the beautiful light had all gone and this old, worried stranger in his impossible, tidy construction of cloth slowly re-formed into Ferney and his tweeds with his arms round her.

"Oh, my dear," he said. "Don't do that to me. I thought you'd gone."

She shook her head mutely, pushed him away from her. A dull drone pulled her eyes skyward, fearing what might be above the leaf canopy, but twentieth-century information, pouring back in, labelled it as mere machinery before the incipient panic had a chance to take hold.

"That was awful," she said uncertainly.

"I've seen it once before—when you were going back over it. It was easier to stop you that time. You mustn't ever get into that when I'm not here. Will you remember that?"

"What would happen?"

"I haven't a clue."

"Was that . . . death?"

"I expect so," he said in a matter-of-fact voice. "Was it very white?"

"Yes, bright and growing."

"That was death then."

She had to know more. "What happens next? After that, I mean?"

"I don't know what would have happened this time. I mean I don't think you were *dying*, you were just remembering it, but I think it would have been extremely upsetting going through the next bit."

"Tell me how it is." She saw he looked doubtful. "I won't be able to stop thinking about it. I'd rather know. Is it always the same?"

"Just about. You're a passenger. The light takes you—makes you feel safe. You're very happy. Then the next thing, I suppose, is you get this strong feeling that you're going somewhere and there's something marvellous waiting for you at the other end."

"That's just the way people describe near-death experiences."

"I've read all about that. It's pretty much the same until there, but from then on it's different for us. From that first time, the stone had us. It gives us a great tug off to one side. We never get there."

"Just us? Other people do get there?"

Ferney looked suddenly wary. "How would we know?"

She was fascinated. "But for other people there might be some-thing, Heaven, whatever?"

"Don't let's start on that."

She recognized the missing word "again" in his tone of voice.

"Have I said that before?"

He laughed. "Before and before and before. It's the thing we never agree on."

"Why?"

"No, that means me telling you what you think and that always annoys you."

She snorted. "Don't tell me what always . . ." and trailed off.

"You see?"

"So I have to work it out for myself? Well, I suppose what I feel is that if we weren't pulled sideways like that, we'd get somewhere else and perhaps it would be somewhere nice, so perhaps all those people who believe in God and Heaven aren't wrong."

He nodded. "That's your view," and she wondered how many times he had heard it. "I always say there's no point in wondering. We can't ever get there, so who knows? Some of these new books say it's just a trick your mind plays on you, the tunnel and the light, to make dying a bit easier."

"Ferney," she said gently. "If I hadn't come back this time? If we hadn't put the stream back as it was—and the stone—you would have finally found out. Wouldn't that have been better, maybe?"

A car, the first since they'd started talking, drove past on the road and he waited for it to pass before he answered.

"Oh, now that's the big one. That's the question. You know when I flushed Effie out of the house with the water, it just crossed my mind that if I moved the stream away from the stone that might change it. It wasn't much of an idea, just the tiniest suspicion, but even if I'd really felt it strongly, I might just have done it anyway, you know. We were so happy, you and me. It was the most perfect of times. If that had been our last time, if we'd gone on and died together and not come back, I thought I wouldn't mind, that it couldn't ever be any better."

"Did you ask me?"

He looked slightly ashamed. "No, I kept it to myself. Like I say, as thoughts go, it didn't add up to much."

"Even so, that wasn't very fair."

"Maybe not. Anyway, I was wrong, wasn't I?" He shifted his posi-tion, sat up a bit straighter. "Maybe I wasn't entirely wrong. I think the stone's stronger up than down, and stronger with the water than without it, but it's never powerless. It's worked fine lying flat for the last hundred-odd years, but it belongs upright and there's no harm in being sure. Anyway when Effie moved out, that made everything feel different. I got better and we were so happy then and I didn't think about it again until after you'd . . . gone . . . and I couldn't find you anywhere." Then he smiled at her with the smile of a younger man, a sweet, sad smile that stirred an emotion so deep it dwarfed everything else she could ever remember feeling.

"I shouldn't have to explain this," he said, "but when it's gone badly that's because we haven't had each other for one reason or another and then I've wanted to find you so much I sometimes haven't been able to wait to start it all over again. All the times we've been together, well . . . we'd never want that to end. When you're old, like me, it's quite exciting thinking you'll be young and strong again."

That wasn't the half of it, he thought, looking at her and trying to hide the sudden hunger. That wasn't the half of it, but just as well to hide it. If she had an inkling of what was in his mind it would scare her. He remembered keenly what she had forgotten—the depth of satisfaction in being together, each in the full glory of their memory, knowing how far back they went and how deeply they ran together, but then something much more. When age had brought its slow taming of physical love, there was that other fierce excitement—the excitement of the knowledge that soon they would again be young, and if they could just contrive it they would be young together. All that old love to fuel the fierce delights of their renewed, perfect, powerful virgin flesh.

He remembered a time so perfect that every detail except the date was etched into his mind. It was long, long ago in the time soon after the French came, when the seeds of abortive revolt were in the air and the castles were going up. They'd been inseparable youngsters until he was four and she was six, then she'd gone away with her aunt and no one told him where. It was only a middling walk, really, to a smallholding at the back of Gasper, but it might as well have been the moon. Certainly it had been far enough to put her out of the range of his immediate knowledge and it was only ten years later when he'd been sent to bring back a pig from that way that he had chanced to see her, climbing out of the stream where she'd been washing, her thin clothes wet and partly sticking to her like the wisps of bark on a peeled willow twig.

His heart turned over and in his certainty, he cried out "Gally" and she, to his great joy, looked up, shading her eyes, called "Ferney" on a rising note of ecstasy and ran, alive, young and perfect into his arms.

The present Gally, watching him, knew he was away somewhere and, guessing that some previous Gally was there with him, gave him some time then gently asked, "Why didn't I know this time? Why does it go wrong?"

He shook his head. "Now you're really asking. Death's a pretty rough ride. It's not like you can sit there hanging on to every detail, you know. It's more like being sucked down the plughole. You don't wind up as a baby thinking, 'Now what was I saying?' It's more like you slowly, slowly come out from under the anaesthetic, but all you get to start with is little scraps of feeling and your brain's not used to straightening it all out and your voice doesn't work so there's nothing you could do with the words anyway. Whatever, sometimes I think you just miss the chance to hang on to it all. Sometimes it's simpler to give up on who you were and just take the easy way and then it all gets covered up with what happens next."

"Being away makes it different, too, doesn't it?"

"If you're born away from here it's always much harder to remember. I'm sure that's the way it was for you and the one before you." He thought of saying the rest, that madness could lie that way, but he thought better of it.

They were both silent, both thinking of the missing Gally, the Gally of the 1930s, the one they knew nothing at all about.

"It's dangerous times for us, then," said Gally after a while.

"Aeroplanes and cars. People rushing about. Anything could happen these days. It frightens me, like when you went to Greece. I kept listening to the radio in case they said there'd been a plane crash."

"How would I ever get back if that happened?"

"I've done it once."

"Tell me?"

"Not now. There's been a lot too much for one day already. Let's go back." Something nagged at her as they walked slowly back down the lane. It was an uncomfortable thought, so obvious that she let it hang there in her mind for a while, unable to put it into words, but Gally was, in the end, a direct person and the moment came when she could not avoid saying it.

"Ferney. When you die do you come back right away?"

"Get born again, you mean? Near enough. It's not like there's a fixed rule. Depends what's around, I suppose. As far as we've ever been able to tell, sometimes it's like it's fairly instant, sometimes you maybe spend a month or two tucked up inside before the baby's born."

"This time," she said, "when you die, you're going to come back as a baby and I'll be much older than you."

"That's right," he agreed affably.

It was dawning on her that they had it easy right now. Apart from Mike's feelings, who would find it odd that a young woman and an old man should be fond of each other?

"It's going to be dreadful then, isn't it?" she said uncertainly. "How can we be . . . close like that? I mean, no parents are going to want some strange woman making friends with their child, not these days. They'll be suspicious as anything."

"That's certainly a problem."

"Well, let's hope it doesn't happen for years," she said firmly.

"Oh, but it's going to," he said in a tone of slight surprise.

She stopped and faced him. "What do you mean? When?"

"About six months," he said, as though it should be obvious.

"Six months?" She was horrified. "Why? Did they tell you something in the hospital? Why didn't you say?"

"No," he said, puzzled. "It's nothing to do with anything they said. They didn't know anything, did they? Haven't you understood? I thought you'd realized by now. I'm so sorry, I should have made it plainer."

He was looking surprised.

"What? What should you have made plainer?"

He seemed tongue-tied.

"Tell me."

"It's like Effie Mullard," he said softly, his eyes on her. "You know the story."

"Like her?" said Gally. "You mean I'm like her? She was having a baby by the stone, you said, and it was going to be . . ."

"Me," he said for her.

16

THOUGH RELIGION WAS a locked door to Ferney, the church was the one building whose doors were never locked—indeed, the only familiar building in Penselwood where, as the years passed, a sudden change of ownership would never bar his entry. It was only as an empty building that he liked it. Caught up in a long conflict with those who had used it to preach unattainable heaven and meaningless hell, he had fallen foul of some of them across the years—the narrow churchmen of the authoritarian times who had used their pulpit power to fetter the community with fierce, unloving ideas. There had been dangerous times when it simply didn't pay to let them mark you as a nonconformist, when the tides of Puritan rebellion had turned every pew into a political hot seat. During those years Ferney had been content to play a defensive role, compelled to take his Sunday place and think his own thoughts under a show of attention, garnering some pleasure from the stones around him and the sound of the music, but none at all from the words of the service.

He nodded to the stone heads above the door as he pushed it open and walked in, knowing just exactly how his footsteps on the flagstones would sound, echoing like drips in a well. Few sounds had stayed constant, but this was one. Birdsong was another, he thought, but even the cows and the sheep had changed their voices as centuries of breeding layered meat on their widening frames. True, he had leather on his soles now, not wood, but he favoured hard leather, valuing materials around him that did not quickly erode, and the sound it made was pretty much the same as the old sound of the wood. In here, above all, it was possible to get away from the constant recent background noise of petrol being burnt in a hundred ways which upset him not so much for the noise itself as for the squandering short-sightedness of it.

An enthusiast for most modern conveniences, Ferney generally excluded the car from that. Walking through your surrounding landscape strengthened your responsibility towards it. Enclosed speed, he had soon decided as the post-war years brought cars doubling and redoubling, steel algae infesting the world, removed that responsibility and provided the illusion that like a malignant comet, you could always travel away from the debris in your wake.

The sounds barely touched him in the church. Here it was easier for him to abandon the structure of laborious, ordered, maintained memory and slip instead between the times in a reverie of peace. It had changed, of course. They'd mucked around with the proportions and the details a fair bit with their restorations and their rebuildings, but it still consisted of most of the same old stones and it still sat squarely on the same patch of ground, and through all the changes it still preserved the same quality of cool, high silence inside that made your thoughts louder. Above all it had its records written in stone and Ferney liked to ground himself from time to time through the contemplation of the engraved evidence of who he had been. He had come now to exercise his memory and blow the dust from what had nearly been a final sidetrack off the main course of his life.

He was on a mission of mercy. Ferney would never have admitted it, but he was shocked by the state Gally was in. Knowing her as she usually was, he could see how deeply she was currently undermined by being out of touch with her past. Whatever different aspects were dictated in different lives by time, circumstance and body chemistry, those were just overlays to the strong serenity that always marked her out. The Gally he knew so well was a smiling haven of calm, a wise and loving beacon. In this life he still had a sense of that, but in front, obscuring the real woman, was a damaged façade of fright and phobia. There was, he thought, only one option and that was to carry carefully on, locating the pain and filling in the gaps for her, but he needed to know her pain more closely.

Once before and only once he had felt the same pain and had come close to losing Gally forever. The life that started with the glory of his singing had led to a lethal exile. In the recent aching years, believing this time he was truly alone, he had found it too painful to consider what had followed then. Now, still slightly aghast at the proposal he would soon have to make, he knew it had the power to stiffen his resolve. It was not easy. In this joint heartland of theirs, the constant ridge of Penselwood, there was always an echo to call up the memories, but this one was rooted in a foreign landscape, a disconcerting world where there had been nothing the slightest bit familiar to serve as a crutch to a young, struggling mind—a world in which that mind had been bent to madness by the discord of unfamiliarity.

He had to get there the long way round, via the death that came before the birth, because the suppression of all that was Ferney in the young man who died had, he was sure, made the youth who came after him all the more vulnerable to alien insanity.

"James Cumberlidge. Born the first day of October 1777," said the small marble tablet set low in the wall. "First Lieutenant in the Royal Navy of his Britannic Majesty, King George the Third. Gave his life most gloriously in the service of his country at Quiberon, France, in the fight against the enemies of our sovereign, the twentieth day of July in the year of our Lord 1795."

He sat sideways in the nearest pew and stared down at the inscription. It must have cost William Cumberlidge a great deal, he thought. William Cumberlidge, just one from the long line of his fathers, the men whose genes had dictated the varied bodies his constant mind would enter. He could pull individuals out of the muddled ranks—the brutes and the friends, the kind men and the autocrats—but William Cumberlidge was as distant as the arctic, a pompous bully who had passed on the family's recognizable barrel-chested build but had never for a moment come to understand his son's mind. He read the words again, thinking it so typical of that man to exaggerate the rank, deriving more satisfaction from the boast of his son's death than he ever had from his life. That father had lost patience with his only son at a very early stage.

"You're James," he would say when he came back to the big house on the edge of Bourton from his merchant's office in Mere. "Stop this Ferney nonsense. I named you James after the apostle and James you will stay," then he would turn away and stride into the house as the boy who knew as yet only that he was Ferney watched the grooms unharness the fine chestnut horses from the landau.

So James suppressed the dawning Ferney in him, to turn away from confrontation and trouble, and became for most of the time an outwardly cheerful little boy despite his father's harsh formality. His mother made up for the shortage of love, and though he was kept away from villagers who were deemed unsuitable playmates for a merchant's son and denied the company of the local aristocracy through their similar view of him, he was superficially content with his limited world within the garden walls. On the day before his fifth birthday, at the very end of a warm September, he was taken in the landau with his mother and father to visit his grandmother at the old house in Penselwood where he had been born and that was where the dam of memory broke.

They had taken the long way round through Chaffeymoor because the track from the east past the jute factory was for horses only and the encroaching brambles might scratch the varnished bottle green flanks of the new carriage. The horses had to trot up the hill towards the village, though the ruts and bumps made the ride uncomfortable. Mr. Cumberlidge thought distance was a trick designed to cheat him of time and time was on an hourly rate that ticked in his head. James, allowed to stand on the floor of the carriage so long as he kept a good firm hold on the top of the door, looked out and saw a slender woman of perhaps twenty-five standing in a cottage garden, a woman in a brown smock, stacking firewood for the coming winter. A sharp dart of adult anguish flew into a corner of his heart and, leaning far out over the side so that his mother, fearful he would fall under the back wheels, made a grab for him, he called out, "Gally, Gally" as they went by.

His mother chuckled. "Who's Gally?" she said. "You don't know that woman. Who did you think she was?"

"Don't you try and talk to people like that," said his father more fiercely. "They'll take it all wrong and think the less of you."

He sat on his mother's knee, silent, muddled and heartbroken that the woman, who must have seen him, had shown no response to his call and for the rest of that day he was disconsolate. His mother put it down to the greengages he had eaten at breakfast: she could hardly be expected to recognize the sickness of lost love in a five-year-old, just as he could hardly be expected to know that infection, in the brief years since he had last shared her life, had robbed his Gally of her hearing.

His grandmother died the next year, bringing an end to the expeditions that would always have him craning, intent on that cottage and on every woman they passed in the village. His voice, his peerless singing voice, developed during that time, but it was another six years before he was held to be old enough to leave the house by himself on occasional country rambles and though he haunted the lane into Penselwood with obsessive determination at every opportunity, she was gone—carried off, he came to think, by one of the illnesses which scythed through the unprotected poor and which would have his mother closing windows and stoking fires as if to beat them back by the sweltering heat.

Cut off from his background, in touch only with an acute but formless sorrow and scared to allow himself his proper identity, he diminished into a shadow world. Looking back, Ferney found even those memories so insubstantial that he seemed only half present in this unhappy boy. There had been other times when the part of him that carried the long memory of his identity had been forced to play second fiddle to an overwhelming physical presence. Overactive glands could occasionally produce a monstrous body for the uneasy soul to inhabit, where floods of manly aggression could swamp the rational messages of the quiet mind. In those lives he was only ever partly the true Ferney and the memories were always confusing, warped by the strength of the parasitic body, but such lives, thankfully, were few and far between. This hadn't, he thought, been one of those occasions. From the wisps of feelings he could trawl back, this had been a boy so disabled by that tragic moment of recognition that he had recoiled from the other messengers from the past, pushing them away at the expense of the balance and strength of his character, so that only the singing was allowed to matter.

His father thought him mostly worthless, a dim-witted milksop whose one acceptable gift was his voice. It was James's sole solace, that perfect heaven's flute of a voice which survived puberty to re-emerge deeper but equally spell-binding. Singing was his true pleasure and even his father tolerated it so long as the songs he sang for him were manly and patriotic. He was twelve when the Bastille fell and word of the great terror that followed came winging to England brought by those of the ruling classes who escaped across the Channel. He was much in demand to sing the patriotic songs that could chase away the fear of the ogre across the water. His father, safe in his own advanced years, was all for a family offering to be sent into the reek of blood and he lost patience with his son's soft life. Believing he needed a tough regime and male company to put him to rights, and that patriotic duty called, old William enrolled young James into the navy. If James survived he would be a man. If James died then the family would have their very own hero. The old man kept those thoughts to himself as he defended his decision against a surprisingly bold attack from his wife.

FERNEY FOUND HIMSELF in a dream, still standing by the memorial tablet on tired legs, and turned to lower himself onto the end of a pew, pushing a heavy crocheted kneeler out of the way. There would have been little time for introspection in that regimented naval world and here again, reflection on this Cumberlidge

mongrel character made him wonder how it must have been. It
hadn't taken many lifetimes for Ferney to learn a few unchanging
rules for survival and happiness. The first golden rule was don't work
for others, or at least not for long. There was no freedom if you did.
It always led to a choice, either to hide your light under a bushel and
have to obey the commands of fools, or to let your ability show
through and that was usually a bad idea. Don't show your wisdom
was, therefore, the second rule. Let others catch sight of the wide-
ranging skills that came with such long experience of every human
foible and they would elevate you, put you in charge to get the most
out of you, milk you dry, contest your decisions, bring you down and
finally grind you in the dust. That was the way of power and the
usual reward for ability, in his experience.

Cumberlidge must have been content to submerge himself in naval
discipline, though Ferney could just touch on the absent moods that
would still capture him and get him into trouble. Only his voice made
him popular with his fellows on board and though he hated the
coarse tunes they wanted him to sing, those tunes were the price of
his being left alone the rest of the time.

Sitting there undisturbed as the church clock ticked the day past
him, Ferney could catch snatches of it—a wildly unsuitable life for
this young man. Under "Black Dick" Howe, he served in the flagship
Queen Charlotte in the lackadaisical blockade of the French Channel
ports, rolling around at anchor in Torbay for much of the time. He
fought in the battle that was finally joined with the demoralized navy
of Villaret de Joyeuse. Ferney knew far more from the history books
he'd read since then than he ever discovered by delving into the
memories of this shadow creature. Cumberlidge's perceptions had
been dim at the best of times. The books said that the French officer
corps had been decimated by the guillotine. Villaret de Joyeuse himself was a stripling lieutenant, promoted to admiral because he was
one of the few to survive the purges. His response to his unskilled,
poorly led crews in their ill-prepared ships was to have the decks
painted red, bloodred, so that the inevitable carnage they would face
in battle would show up less clearly. By this he hoped to avoid rapid
demoralization.

In 1794 young James showed himself in his true useless colours.
Large parts of France were in danger of starvation in the unruly after-
math of the Revolution and the French fleet was trying to bring a
convoy of American grain through Howe's blockade. Ferney could
just recall disguising the fear in partly hysterical excitement on
28 May, when billowing sails first hardened through the early morn-

ing haze to show that they were closing on the French ships. They
traded a few shots only, then darkness and bad weather stopped
them. In a fully remembered life, Ferney would have been scared in a
wholly different way, he thought, terrified at the prospect of death
there, burial at sea far from any retaining, restoring stone—death
with no prospect except slow dissolution in the dark bottom mud of
the cold Atlantic. As it was that hardly seemed to matter to this youth
who had no great interest in whether he lived or where he died.

The first of June was a calm, clear day and Black Dick chose his
moment for battle. The *Queen Charlotte* was one of the few ships
that succeeded in following his order to cut through the French line,
but even though the tactics went awry the battle was won. James
Cumberlidge, typically, could claim no associated glory from his
part, spending the last half of the battle below decks with a broken
arm when, suddenly dreaming even at the height of danger, he was
hit a glancing blow by the shattered debris of French cannon fire.

It was just the sort of contribution his commanding officer expected of him and it was received by him in just the same vacant way
that drove his superior officers to despair. It was therefore the main
reason why, a year later, he was detailed off for a hazardous return to
the coast of France, being regarded as entirely expendable, and here
Ferney's memory was much more certain because the extremity of
danger had forced even James Cumberlidge to a degree of awareness.

As plans go that had been a truly ridiculous idea. Ferney had
searched through the books to confirm it really had been the way he
remembered it. The accounts were only sketchy but they all agreed
that the "Screech Owls" were real. Breton smugglers were fed up
with the results of the French Revolution because they had no one to
chase them anymore. The upheavals had destroyed the French cus-
toms service. With no danger of being caught, any amateur could be
a smuggler in such anarchic times and the bottom dropped out of the
business. The smugglers formed themselves into a paramilitary rab-
ble, named themselves the "Screech Owls" and decided they wanted
the old order restored. They were to join a small army of exiled roy-
alists who had persuaded the English that if they could be landed on
the Breton coast the people would flock to them. No military strate-
gist would have given a fig for their chances of success but, despite
that, the Royal Navy was given the job of landing the motley force.

Young James Cumberlidge went into the operation in the same fa-
talistic, half-aware trance in which he did everything else. It took him
a moment or two to realize that the frigate's captain really was ordering him to take command of the ship's pulling boat.

"There's a group cut off just round the point, Cumberlidge. They've signalled for help. You're to take this powder and tell them to hold out. Come straight back here to report."

"Sir."

"Repeat my orders."

How well his captain knew him. How well, too, his captain had assessed the situation as probably hopeless. The defence force was too strong. Cumberlidge was dimly aware that his boat's crew were the ship's shirkers, but it took Ferney, riding piggy-back on those memories later on, to understand the cynical significance of that. It was always likely to be a one-way ticket and the boy made certain of that by reading the sea wrong, steering too far south, failing to spot the danger of the swirling current that carried the boat, against the frantic, uncoordinated efforts of the seamen manning the sweeps, in under the headland and into the enfilading fire of the skilled marksmen of Louis Lazare Hoche's defending force. Everyone in the boat was killed in seconds, excepting only young James himself, who, clipped across the temple by the first bullet, fell into the bottom of the boat unconscious and was missed by the volleys that followed.

He woke to the reek of blood, stiff and frozen in the evening light in a boat holed and half filled with a nightmare soup of red seawater and dead flesh. It lay, rolling in the slight swell, drifting towards a beach and he sat up, blinking blood-encrusted eyes to see avenues of grey stones beckoning to him from the shore. The boat, inert and disregarded, had drifted down the length of the Quiberon peninsula into the bay of Carnac. The great, grey, innumerable stones in their ordered lines called him and it seemed to him that there, standing between them, holding a bundle of firewood in her arms, staring towards him with the love that was all he had wanted in his short, cold life, was the girl in the brown smock. He slipped over the gunwale of the boat, trying to walk to her as he sank through the surprising water and drowned in one deep liquid breath.

FERNEY GROANED ALOUD at the sudden and vivid memory of surrendering his lungs to the heavy, choking water and a voice from a long way away said something insistent.

"Are you all right? I said, are you all right, Mr. Miller? Mr. Miller?"

He came back to the church in the here and now and the vicar, who was standing over him with an expression somewhere between concern and exasperation. Caught out, he stumbled for words and said too much.

"I was thinking about war."

"War? I thought you might be ill. I don't often see you in the church."

"I'm all right. I like to sit here quietly sometimes."

"You should try our services. Were you in the war?"

"Everyone was in the war."

"I meant, were you in the services?"

Ferney looked up at him. "Funny that, isn't it?" he said. "The same word twice in a row. Services. Like they're something to do with each other. Killing and God."

The vicar looked slightly affronted. "That's just words. I expect we'll see you on Remembrance Day at least?"

Ferney could just have left it there, but he looked down again at the marble tablet which so completely failed to tell anything of the reality of that death and felt a question rising.

"What do you tell them about war?"

"On Armistice Day?" The vicar was too young to have known even the Second World War. "I tell them we have to remember and give thanks for the sacrifices made in a just war. I say a prayer for the United Nations and for the wisdom not to fight again."

"There have always been people you couldn't trust with a sword," said Ferney, suddenly vehement, "so there's always been a call for a few people around you *could* trust, with sharper swords. Then it was cannons and machine guns. Now it's jet planes and missiles. It's the same people, you know. You still can't trust them, so you just end up putting tighter and tighter controls round them and they still keep busting out—and every time they do, the mess gets bigger."

"My goodness," said the vicar, startled, "that's a gloomy way of looking at it. We do try to teach people something about morality."

"You'll have to try a lot harder. You can't change people," said Ferney, dissatisfied with the argument and feeling a sudden yearning for Gally's company. Annoyed that his journey had been interrupted before he reached the crucial part, he flapped a hand in farewell and made for the porch's tunnel of sunlight leaving the vicar relieved to be alone.

17

MIKE ASKED GALLY to come for a walk that morning and it was clear he had something to say. Mike was not a natural wanderer and his walks, unlike hers, always needed to have a destination in mind.

"Let's go to the Pen Pits," he said.

"If you want to." He'd mentioned them before, but the name held no great interest for her. "What are they?"

"They're one of those wonderful red herrings that gave people daft ideas in the old days. I'll show you."

The walk took them up the eastern side of the scattered village with Mike in one of his lecturing moods. "You know this is called Bleak Street?" he asked. Of course she knew. "It's not exactly a street, is it? More of a lane, but 'street' usually shows there's a Roman origin."

His voice got between her and her surroundings so that they all seemed unknown to her. They came to a meeting of two lanes where the left fork would have led them to the church and then past it up the long ridge to Kenny Wilkins' Castle. He took the smaller right fork.

"They used to be all over the place, these pits," he said. "They're still there in the woods, but the ones in the fields got ploughed up. Thousands and thousands of them. Back in the last century there was one of those strange crazes about them. Every antiquarian under the sun had a theory. A gigantic prehistoric village was the favourite for a long time, then they decided it was a necropolis, some massive burial centre. Completely potty, of course."

She guessed that he'd been going through the library at the faculty to find bits and pieces to interest her, but it brought nothing to her and she wondered at the deadness of her response. If Ferney had been telling her, would she have found some echo of personal memory within her? Was it that Ferney's voice could reach into layers of her that Mike's simply never reached? She felt instant, deep disquiet at that thought and as if he could smell it, Mike twisted the knife.

"I wanted to talk to you about something," he said.

"Good. What about?"

"A few things, really."

His voice showed it was difficult.

"All right."

"You've started having the nightmares again."

"Not often."

He sighed, "I thought . . . I sort of hoped they'd stopped since we came down here."

"I think they'll be all right soon."

"Why?" His voice showed sharp surprise.

What could she say? Because Ferney's told me he can explain them? That would be twisting the knife.

"I think I can cope more down here. I'll be able to deal with them."

"Gally, the best therapist we could find couldn't make the tiniest bit of difference to them."

"I know, Mike, but that was before we came here. Everything feels more hopeful now."

"I can feel the difference," he said miserably, "but I can't get anywhere near understanding it. There always seems to be something you're not saying."

"Maybe it's the baby," she offered, dwelling on the weasel word "maybe" to stop short of a lie.

There was a longer silence and Gally knew Mike was searching for a way to get to the main point. He scratched the back of his neck and spoke abruptly, as though the words had been piling up behind a blockage. "About the old man."

"Go on, then."

"I know you like him a lot."

"Yes, I do."

"I'm just not sure he's good for you."

How much better it would have been if he'd said anything else—"I'm jealous," perhaps, or "I want you to myself," or even "I'm frightened." Instead he tried to take control of her feelings, her decisions, and by doing so took a further step in the wrong direction.

"I can think for myself, Mike."

"He seems to be thinking for you."

"What do you mean?"

"He's using you for some reason. He's got you chasing all kinds of ridiculous ideas. I'm starting to wish we'd never come down here. When we were in Greece and it was just us it felt great, then he pops up as soon as we get back and it all goes weird again."

She said nothing because there was too much to say and he took that for an invitation to go on. "It's absurd, really, when you think about it. I mean, it was random chance that we ever came here. You have to admit it's a pretty stupid idea that there should be some sort of special connection."

Why couldn't he sense her dilemma? Why couldn't he give a little space to the tearing, testing, thrilling process she was going through?

"It wasn't random chance," she said shortly. "Whatever you might think. I wanted to come here."

"You've wanted to go to a lot of other places. There could have been a crazy old man in every one of them."

Mike fell silent because a woman, with a small terrier on an unnecessary lead, came round the next bend towards them and Mike could never bear any semblance of hanging out his dirty washing in public. Gally, recognizing it as unfair even as she did it, took the opportunity to press her point. Her only concession was to make sure her voice was even and reasonable.

"It's something I have to get through and I'd like you to help me if you can. It's not craziness, you know. There *is* something to it. I'm not nearly so impressionable as you seem to think. I'm sorry if it's difficult for you, but it would be much easier if I felt you were on my side."

Mike didn't answer for a moment. He nodded a distracted acknowledgement instead to the woman as she passed. She was fiftyish, with tight town clothes and makeup that spoke of a tremendous need to fortify herself against even these natural surroundings. Either that or she was on her way to deliver a university lecture. He let five more seconds elapse then could restrain himself no more.

"He wants you to himself. He'd like me out of the way and he's spinning you some stupid line to justify it. I don't see how you can let him do it. You're encouraging him. It's completely daft."

"Maybe it is. Maybe it's not. Can't you see I need to find out?"

"You need to remember we're married." She just looked at him and he couldn't restrain himself. "All right, I *am* bloody jealous, but *you're* making me jealous." It was much, much louder than he intended and he looked back to see the woman with the terrier had stopped and was staring back at them. He flushed, pulled his head down into his shoulders and speeded up his pace.

"I'm sorry," she said. "You hate that, don't you?"

"Right through my childhood," he said miserably, "my parents would have fights in public. They'd get so carried away they wouldn't notice everyone looking, but I did. I always did."

She felt keenly sorry for him then, took his arm and hugged it to her. "Come on, love. We'll talk about it another time. I'm here and I'm staying here. You don't need to worry."

"Of course I need to worry. You're always thinking about him and I'm cut out of it."

"No, you're not. What about the oats business?"

"A crumb from his table. He decided to take just enough notice to keep me in line. Look, I know he's doing you some good. I'm not blind, I can see that. You seem less . . . less bothered." He looked at her bare hand. "Though I see you've stopped wearing my ring again."

"I just didn't put it on this morning, that's all." Was that somehow linked to the return of the burnman nightmare? She wasn't sure. Forgetfulness was an easy answer.

"There is something else, though—something I really have to tell you. Will you promise to listen?"

"It depends what it is."

"I'm not just being fanciful. I was talking to one of the builders, John, the one with the headband?"

"I know John."

"His father's a policeman in Wincanton. You know when we were coming back and we saw all that business going on down at the roadworks? Well, he says Ferney told the police that was his wife buried down there. They're taking it very seriously. She was reported missing years ago, apparently."

Gally felt helpless. What could she say? Yes, he's told me—that was me? "Poor man," was all she could find to say.

"Supposing it's not 'poor man' at all? Maybe he did away with her. I don't know what to make of it all."

"Oh come off it, he'd hardly go and tell the police then, would he? Surely you don't really think he's a murderer?"

"He may not seem like one to you, but he's after you and it bothers me."

" 'After me'? What does that mean? Mike, I hear what you say but he does mean well, I promise." She sighed and used the argument she hated to use. "He's not very well. He won't be a problem soon, you know. If I can help him for just a while, surely that's not so bad?" He gave no answer. "Come on," she said, "forget it. Tell me about the pits."

They turned right at Pear Ash and the woodland lay ahead.

"They were just stone quarries really," he said without much enthusiasm. "For grindstones or something like that, back from when they couldn't really dig deep shafts. They'd just make a hole, get out what they could then dig another one next to it."

The track through the wood brought them abruptly into a twisted and unlikely landscape. The trees to their right took precarious root on the narrow ridges between the pits where ferns and brambles half-filled the innumerable hollows. It was familiar in several different, conflicting ways.

"It's like the trenches," she said, and realized that was a new type of recognition, overlaying a dimly felt, much older one. "The First World War without the mud." Something else nagged her. "Pen Pits, of course. There's a Paul Nash painting, isn't there? I didn't realize it was here." She looked at Mike. "Why are you smiling?"

"Oh . . . It's just nice when you remember things in ways I can understand," he said ruefully. "We could go on a bit. There's a Norman castle at the end of the track, or perhaps you knew that already?"

She ignored the crack. "Is there much of it left?"

"The mound of course and a few stones where the keep was. It *is* odd though, just like the man at the museum said, there were three castles built here, all about the same time, quite soon after the conquest, all within about a mile of each other. I don't know anywhere else like it for that."

Fear came suddenly snaking through the trees to her and she had to hide it from him.

"You go on," she said and looked down through the trees into the open grassy valley below, the valley where the water meadows had once been and where the Frenchmen had . . . What Frenchmen? Had done what? No answer came and she felt a strong need to be by herself. "I'd like to sit in the sun for a bit." She patted her tummy as though that explained it and he instantly gave in to the unchallengeable mystery of pregnancy.

"Are you sure? I won't be long." She knew he wouldn't mind the excuse to lose himself in some ruins for a while. "Where shall I see you?"

She pointed down into the valley. "At the far side, where the path goes. It'll be in the sun."

Mike looked, couldn't see a path but chose not to mention it. Gally picked her way through the foliage down the slope of the hill and he carried on along the ridge. He had gone perhaps two hundred yards when he saw a movement in the undergrowth ahead to his right, where the tree trunks crowded more thickly between the pits. He stopped. Too large for a rabbit or a fox. It was behind a tree. A deer maybe? More movement revealed a man, back towards him, stooping down. Mike kept quite still—sure, for no good reason that he could name except perhaps the look of the man's tweed jacket, that it was Ferney prowling about in the pits. Seized by the idea this might be the chance to get to the bottom of some of the old man's peculiarities, he began to move very softly closer.

FERNEY HAD TO count from the big tree, stooping stiffly under the branches, to make sure he was in the right hollow. He had always kept maps, but there were times when they were apt to go astray, so mostly he tried to remember. He got down into the crater, looked around carefully for a few seconds and then began to probe with his trowel through the roots and leaf mould down at the bottom to find the stone. It was harder to lift than he remembered.

Richard Wellesley-Cave had been the first to come up here with his hired diggers, brought every day by carriage from Mere to stand there muttering over the little bits of this and that they were unearthing, making unshakably wrong pronouncements over every tiny find to suit his set ideas. Every lump of accidentally flaked stone was a domestic tool. Every rabbit leg bone was a skeletal sign of ancient man. It was eighteenth-century mumbo-jumbo and if Wellesley-Cave had suddenly declared the latest bones to be Adam's rib, Ferney would not have been at all surprised. The one time Ferney had taken him something recognizable, a broken antler pick from the Bronze Age digging, he had flung it off into the undergrowth in scornful rejection. After that, when Ferney unearthed the garland stone and recognized the age in it, he kept it to himself with few qualms. Still, Wellesley-Cave had paid good money for their scrabblings as had so many after him. The pits were ancient and mostly deserted even in Ferney's earliest memories back in the old times of his first lives. Even the marks of the Romans were still fresh in comparison—the stones of their high road still more or less in place, being forced slowly apart by the extraordinary undeniability of each spring's new vegetation. In that time the walls of a villa still stood on the flat land down to the west of the ridge, shunned by people who invested the lost sophistication of its structure with unearthly powers. The mosaic floor, half covered in the heavy shattered curves of broken roof tiles, revealed part of a bearded, helmeted head and, on the other side of the fallen roofbeams that heaped up in its centre, a fist holding lightning bolts. The braver children would go to look at it as a rite of manhood then rush away in terror of the devils who were said to haunt the sad, silent place.

The pits, though, held no such mystery for Ferney. Though their heyday was well past there'd usually been someone there, down through the first centuries of his ages, scraping a precarious living digging between the old workings to get to the broken, plundered layer of green sandstone that could be hacked out, shaped and sold for grinding. None of the antiquarians who brought successive new ideas to the site believed his simple explanation. There was no glamour in grindstones and, anyway, he never pressed it hard enough to interfere with the employment it brought. It did give him an idea, though, an idea he had used ever since.

Crouched there, he had a sudden memory of Billy Bunter. The boyman had been much in his mind lately since they'd found the bones. It was a matter of grief to him that they'd taken Billy so far away to serve his sentence and that Ferney had failed to do his duty by him, the one who had visited on Cochrane his deserved, secondhand vengeance. Billy had found him up here more than once and he'd had to sit, humouring the big, loving fool, knowing he couldn't risk digging with such a curious audience on hand.

He worked the trowel in, levered the stone up with it and scraped around underneath until he struck a metallic edge. The box he pulled out was wrapped in the remains of a piece of oilcloth. Its seams were soldered shut all the way round and he inspected it carefully for damage before he put it in his bag. Then he drew out another box—this time a food container in white Tupperware with a snap-on lid. It was wrapped round with heavy duty adhesive tape. He scraped away enough earth to fit it into the hollow under the stone and carefully pushed and pressed the earth back in place until there was little sign of his handiwork. He rose to his feet, looked around again, failing to see Mike behind a tree trunk thirty yards away, and made his own way back to the path. Behind him, Mike moved carefully forward, marking the spot and, using his fingers, began to dig into the crumbling, loose earth.

Buzzing in Ferney's mind still was the Cumberlidge life and what had followed because it was important to him that, despite the vicar's interruption, he should get back to remembering the bit that mattered, the bit that came after. He took the slope down into Coombe Bottom and headed south across the rough grazing, between the cows, towards Pen Mill. It was here, under the hedge on the far side, that all had come good, when—his impossible journey almost completed—all his wishes had come true and his mind had righted itself. He had limped across the field, fearful of having to try out his newly rediscovered English, twisted by a French tongue, on any stranger in this time of war. He had failed to see the girl sitting under the hedge until he was almost on her, then she, as if she had been waiting for him for years, rose with slender grace and said, "Hello? Who are you? Are you Ferney? You are, aren't you?" and he had replied, *"Bien sûr, c'est moi,"* then seeing the astonishment on her face, had begun again with difficulty, "Yes . . . truly, it is me."

The girl in his mind's eye came together with the girl who now rose out of the same place ahead of him. "Ferney? Why are you speaking French?"

"Well now. How did you come to be standing here?"

She looked as though she had to think about that one, then frowned a little. "Oh. It's Mike. I said I'd meet him here. He was going to look at the castle. Have you seen him?"

"No, but it is very right that you should be here."

They sat down on the grass, against the fence.

"I was thinking about the time when we came closest to losing each other forever," said Ferney.

Gally stopped him. "I don't know if this is the moment to talk. I've had a problem with Mike this morning."

"A problem about me?"

"Yes."

He needed no explanation. "It's always a problem when you tell anything to other people. We don't fit into that world."

"I don't know how to deal with it. Has this kind of thing happened before?"

He didn't want to tell her the truth, that it had never happened—that though they had been separated, never before had the grip loosened so much that they could make any significant commitment to someone else, even, so far as it was possible to know, in the forgetful times. He doubted that she could take the consequences of that at this moment.

"You don't like driving, do you?" he asked.

He could see her instantly start to ponder the possibilities behind the question.

"I did," she said. "I'm not so sure I do now, since I came here. I think I might get a bicycle. Why?"

"People don't have so much time for the detail now," he said, giving her the less vital of the two answers. "You don't have to take so much responsibility for something you can rush through, do you? You don't drop litter on your own doorstep—at least some do, but there was never any hope for that sort. When everybody walked everywhere, most places seemed like your doorstep. You looked after it because four miles an hour wasn't very quick and anything ugly, anything broken was in your sight for long enough to rankle. Now it's all whizz and gone. People chuck packets out of the window. They dump stuff beside the road. What does it matter so long as they can go off at sixty miles an hour to somewhere else?"

"And?"

"What do you mean, 'and'?"

"I know your tone of voice. That question wasn't about litter, it was about you and me."

He snorted with laughter and took her hand and the warmth of his skin sent the two halves of her in opposite directions, her rational mind creasing, appalled, and her heart soaring in recognition of the love that poured through her.

"It was." He was content to look at her for a long moment and all she could see was the essence of him shining in his eyes, dizzying. "It's like I said before. Cars can take us apart just like that now. The way it used to be, when either one of us died then the nearest woman carrying—expecting I mean—would be bound to live quite close. Even if it was some grand lady passing in a carriage, chances were she wouldn't come from that far off. Now people race around all over. You could be carried off anywhere, with anyone passing by down on the road who's got a baby growing. It's a lottery."

"Yes, I know. There's nothing to be done about it, is there?" she said. "And this time, I mean, I did come back, didn't I?"

"You did and I'm glad you did, but here you are and I'm the age I am and you're the age you are."

"It doesn't matter."

"Oh yes it does," he said firmly, "it matters a lot. This old crock of a body of mine has no pleasure in it for you. You've got your other man. How long could I stand that for, do you think? We need to be of an age, you and me, and together. That time before, when we were so far apart—that was terrible." He looked around. "I was so far away that I had no idea what all the memories meant. In the place I was, they just came out as madness. My responses were all wrong, you see? People marked me down as mad and I started to believe them—pictures in my head, words that didn't mean anything, fears and dreams and all that."

"Like me, you mean?"

"This was where we sorted it out. It was right here we met up again when I finally got back."

"You were in France."

"You know that?"

"You were speaking French just now."

"I was. I was in France. There was a sea and a war between us. I thought that was the end of us. Killed in France and then born in France, all because my father sent me to fight. My memory came to me one day, as clear as you like. That's what got me back."

"You got back from France in a war. The First World War?"

"No, no," he said with a touch of the schoolteacher chiding a child for not trying hard enough. "This was 1810. Napoleon."

"How did you do it?"

"You dragged me back. There came a time when all I could think about was you and I could suddenly hear the English voices in my head."

"How old were you?"

"Thirteen maybe. Thirteen when I sort of woke up. Before that it was different. The two who were my parents that time—they weren't happy together at all. He was quite an old man—over forty. He had a fishing boat and when the weather was too bad he worked leather—a bit of cobbling, a bit of saddlery, all sorts. She was a Gascon, almost a Spaniard, always on at him, always on at me, too, for being so daft. If I wanted peace I had to go down to the stones in the evening. I'd been drowned there you know, at Carnac. In the navy. Have you heard of Carnac?" She nodded. "Great avenues of them, the most amazing sight you ever saw—all cut by hand and set in their right place. The people round there, they wouldn't go near when it got dark. They were frightened, superstitious folk. All round those parts, the farmers would leave one corner of a field bare on every farm. That was for the devil to use so he wouldn't spoil the rest of their land."

Gally smiled but Ferney, looking at her, shook his head. "It may sound silly now, but they believed it then. There's something about that sort of belief. You let it in and it's like the first little stick that might catch in a rock on its way down a river. That stick catches another two and they catch ten more, then a log and before you know it the whole river's blocked. It doesn't do to start fearing nothing in case it brings something that's worth fearing. Anyway that sort of superstition played its part. The father—his hands got too stiff to work and we were all short of food and the woman had had enough of starvation and sea fogs. She was a shrewish sort. She heard there was a chapel at Tréguier where women went to pray for the deaths of their husbands—'Our Lady of Hate' it was called—so she took herself off there thinking that if the Lady heard her prayer then she was still young enough to marry again. Only thing was . . ." Ferney paused for effect and looked again at Gally ". . . it did for both of them. When she came back to Carnac, he was laid out as stiff as a board and I was howling and screaming by him, from seeing him die. She thought she'd head south right away and leave us both behind, but the villagers got wind of where she'd been and they didn't let her. They took her down to the stone rows and left her there, bound tight, hand and foot, lashed to one of the stones so she couldn't move. Two nights she was there and I'd creep in and out of them looking at her—a bit torn, I suppose, and certainly confused. I hated her for what she'd done to my father, but I knew she was all I had."

"What happened to you?" Gally said softly, thinking this felt all new to her as though he'd never told her the full story before.

"Two men came and took me away back to the houses, where they made me eat. I crept out later for another look but there was no sign of her—just cut ropes with a mark or two of blood on them. The next morning I went away. It was the first time I'd ever left the area round the stones and there wasn't a clear thought in my head, just all the usual jumble of nonsense words and pictures. I headed off east to start with, I think. Then as soon as I got an hour or two away, something seemed to clear just a little in my head. Whatever it was, it started calling me north. I was lucky. I had a ride from a carter, I remember, and I slept under his cart that night and shared his food. He didn't seem to mind my ways. When I woke up my head was full of words, as usual, words that had never made any sense, but now I was starting to know what they meant."

"You realized you were English?"

"It wasn't like that at all. I didn't know what they were then, but I saw you. Not your face, you know how it is, but *you*. I could feel you like a magnet, away to the north. I knew I could find you if I went there and I started asking what was to the north. Brest, Morlaix, people would say, Saint-Pol de Léon, places like that—but they didn't mean anything to me." He pronounced the place names as a French-man would.

"How did you get here?"

"I just walked. I didn't have any food, but even then, when there'd been so much to fear, the country people would share with you if they saw you were harmless, particularly if you were simple. I walked for three more days. I didn't have to work out my way, I shut my eyes when I wasn't sure and I could see glimpses of you and the hill with the village on it, like following a compass. All the memories started pouring back, properly this time, making sense. It was too much to take in to start with, so I was walking like I was in a dream. I suppose it could have been more than a young boy could bear but the *me* part came back too, the older part, confident and strong, so that I was in charge of it and in fact all my fears and worries started easing away. I could feel myself getting stronger and stronger and knowing more and more. The further north I got, the clearer it was. I couldn't sort out where I was, though. I knew I'd never been in this place before, but I didn't seem to have the right knowledge to make sense of it—then one evening I came over a hill and there in front of me was the sea. Oh, that was a shock. You were still pulling me that way and there was nothing but the grey waves. Then for the first time, I really understood how it was and that undid me for a bit."

"You thought you'd find me and instead you found the sea?"

"I suppose I knew, really, but if I'd let myself believe that, I might never have started. There was a watch on the coast. Soldiers every-where, boats patrolling, all the harbours controlled. I asked everyone about England and they all said the same—bloodthirsty pirates, who'd skin you as soon as look at you."

"But you got here?"

"I had to find a boat that wasn't guarded. I remember I just walked and walked along the coast. I found a place, east of Saint-Pol, where there were mussels everywhere on the rocks so I stopped there and gorged on them for a day or two. Oh, it was a strange place, that—the seashore was slate, all up on edge, slanting, and in the middle of it there was a great lump, heaved up like a cathedral. I was standing there staring out to sea. I even wondered about swimming, I was a good swimmer—had to be at Carnac with the boats—but I didn't know how far I'd have to go and it was just as well I didn't try. The second night there I had a bit of luck. A small warship sailed into the bay and dropped anchor. It lowered a boat and sent an officer ashore and I watched when it sailed back again. They didn't hoist it back on board—just set it riding on a line from the stern, so when it was dark I swam out and climbed in. I had to be very quiet because I was pretty sure there'd be a watch up on deck so I slipped the line and let it drift off on the tide until I judged I was a good long way away before I dared risk trying to get the sails sorted out."

"How did you know where to go?"

"Simple. Easiest sailing I ever did. The wind was behind me all the way and I just headed for you. The nearer I got, the more the English came back to me. 'Course I didn't dare land, not in the boat—not with all that was going on—so I chose a bit of a beach with no houses and I jumped off and swam in."

"Do you know where it was?"

"You couldn't mistake it. Never been there again, but I've heard it described and I've seen all the maps and the photographs now. It was the Chesil Beach by Portland Bill and I know I walked through Dorchester not daring to talk to a soul in case they spotted I was French. They would have strung me up in no time."

"And we met here?"

"We did. Right here."

"There's a bit of me that doesn't like this place but it's not all bad, not like Kenny Wilkins' Castle."

"Does Kenny Wilkins' Castle still feel bad?"

"No," she said in surprise. "Not since we talked it through."

"Nor will this place when you know what happened here. Anyway, it has joy in it too. We were together every day from then and I had nothing to fear because you told everyone I was from Wales and they'd never heard a Welshman's voice. In any case in only a few weeks I was speaking just like you. We married as soon as we could, you know—as soon as we were old enough—and we put it all behind us."

"And the lesson of all that is?" She asked because she knew there was a purpose to it.

"That we have to be careful not to risk anything like that again."

"How? It's outside our control."

"That's what I mean, about the cars and everything. We have to be much more deliberate than we used to."

A stranger appeared out of the wood opposite, a stranger who took the path towards them, a stranger who turned into Mike but remained disconcertingly a stranger. He wasn't looking in their direction and Ferney pulled himself up to his feet. "I'll be off. I'd better not intrude."

She didn't try to stop him, needing time to readjust. When Mike reached the far side of the meadow and stood for a moment, unde-cided which way to go, she got to her feet as well and waved. He walked up to her, stared at her and spoke softly.

"I've seen something very odd," he said. "I don't know what's going on but I'm frightened for you . . . for us. I think something ter-rible could be coming."

"No," she said with certainty, but in that she was wrong and he was almost right.

18

"HE DUG UP something."

"What sort of something?"

"It looked like a box—wrapped in some sort of thick cloth. He took it away."

"Where were you then?"

Mike looked uncomfortable. "I happened to see him so I watched."

"And he didn't see you?"

"No."

"So you were hiding."

"Look, I saw him doing something funny and I just stood and watched, that's all. It would have been very embarrassing if he'd seen me, wouldn't it? I didn't go out of my way to advertise myself."

"Okay, so he dug up a box. What does that prove?"

They had been walking, but the argument had taken over even the automatic movements so they were now standing in the pathway, facing each other.

"Well, don't *you* think it's a bit odd? It can't be anything aboveboard—not if he's sneaking about in the woods like that."

"Sneaking? How can you say that? You were sneaking too, weren't you?"

"For Christ's sake, Gally, listen to me. They've been talking to him about a murder down at the road and now he's up here digging where he thought no one could see him. Don't go for me like that. Use your brain. It's not normal behaviour, is it?"

He was using his hands in agitation and she reached out abruptly, caught him by one wrist and stared at his fingers. Earth was lined darkly into the creases of their joints and under his nails. "What have you been doing? You've been digging with your hands, haven't you?"

"I had to find out what was going on."

"After he'd gone?"

"Yes."

"But you said he took the box away."

"You sound like a policeman. Lighten up. I'm on your side, remember?"

"I'm not sure what that means. Why were *you* digging, Mike?"

Mike looked up and down the track and sighed. "He buried something, too. I had to find out what it was. Don't look at me like that. I really need to sort out what's going on here."

"Well? What was it?"

"Just a plastic box. That's all."

"Come on. You didn't go to all that trouble then not open it."

"No, of course I opened it."

"And?"

"There wasn't much in it." She just stared at him until he was forced to go uncomfortably on. "Just some . . . some crazy stuff."

"What exactly?"

He looked a little uncomfortable. "All kinds of things."

"Such as?"

"Well . . . not the sort of things a normal person would bury, a whole lot of old phone cards and stamps and stuff like that."

Like a waking dreamer, Gally had the form and feeling of an idea but not its substance. "Was that all?"

"No that wasn't all." Mike would sometimes lean his bony form forward when he was getting cross, as if to inspect his opponent more closely. Gally had seen him do it to others, but this was the first time he'd ever done it to her. It was a shock, not just because it revealed the depth of his disquiet but also because it showed her how little she had been aware of him physically in the recent weeks—as if, until this moment, he had been little more than a name and an idea.

"If you must know there were also a couple of toy cars, about a dozen plastic carrier bags, a whole lot of china ornaments and a small carriage clock."

Gally couldn't help laughing and it only reinforced his discomfort.

"Well, Sherlock," she said, "not exactly a revolver or a bottle of cyanide, is it?"

It had come, in her relief, as humour but, already feeling misunderstood and unfairly treated, he took it for sarcasm and flushed. In her suddenly heightened perception of him she noticed how tight the skin was over his cheeks so that the cheekbones made white crescents across the pink.

"Look, Gally. It's a sign that the man's deranged. No one who was right in the head would go around burying stuff like that."

"People bury time capsules all the time."

"Schoolchildren bury time capsules. Schoolchildren and lady mayoresses laying foundations, and they put in notes saying 'this is a letter from the past' or some crap like that. This was not a time capsule." He considered. "There's something else. Something I didn't say earlier."

"What?"

"John—the builder—he told me something else."

"Well?"

"We're not supposed to know this."

"Okay, don't tell me then."

There was a short silence.

"I think I'd better," Mike said.

Gally said nothing.

"John's dad told him when they got out the old files about Ferney's wife. You know, after they found the bones?"

Still silence.

"They found a bit more. A query later on. Sometime in the fifties there was another killing. A blacksmith. Ferney blamed him for his wife's death, then someone killed the blacksmith, some local simpleton. They thought maybe Ferney had put him up to it."

She'd been looking away. Now she snapped round, glaring.

"What the *hell* gives you the right to start poking into things like that?"

"Everything, I'd say. I'm trying to look after you and you're not helping." His voice was rising. "You may be the founder member of the Ferney fan club but I think he's got some big problems and I don't want him polluting you with all his mad ideas."

"All because of some ancient gossip?"

"It's more than gossip," he said defensively, "it matters."

"Does it? Have they done anything about it?"

"There wasn't any proof."

"So it was just rumour, right?"

"Who knows?"

"Well, you don't for one."

They walked on then in a renewed and noisy silence of teeming minds until they came to a crossroads that was both mental and physical. Ahead lay the lane back towards the cottage. To the right was the way to Ferney's house. There was a decision waiting there for Gally. Her nature was always to tackle grievances, to get them out into the open air before they began to fester. One way, the way home, led to compromise, to papering it over. The other way led to something much less safe. It was a way that she knew Ferney would not want her to take at this moment, with this man, in this mood, but she couldn't help it.

"All right, Mike, come with me. We'll go and sort it out now. Let's go and see him."

"Oh, what? How can I do that? You want me to breeze in and say I saw him in the wood?"

"More or less. I certainly can't go on like this." She began to walk away.

"Just stop a minute," he said and when she showed no sign of listening he caught her by the arm. It brought her up short, jerked her shoulder painfully. It was the only time he had ever treated her roughly and the shock of it took her breath away, but, perhaps in the need to justify his force, it gave Mike the chance to say what was in his mind. Usually he was succinct, clipped. Now the words tumbled out.

"You can bloody well listen to me first," he said, forgetting to look round to see if they were alone. "We came down here because *I* wanted to make *you* happy. I know how hard it was to lose the baby. I lost it too, you know. I've gone along with it all the way you wanted. I never thought you'd bury yourself down here. Do you think I'm going to like being up in London by myself? We were going to do all this together. If you think for a moment I'm going to let some crazy old bugger take you away from me and fill your head with complete crap, you can think again. I've had it up to here and it's time it stopped, right now."

"He's not crazy."

"He is or I am, or . . ." he was going to say ". . . or maybe you are," but that was something he had never said in all Gally's agonies because it was too close to his fears.

"There'll be an explanation." She was breathing hard, spitting the words.

"I'd like to hear it."

"Good, let's go then."

She towed him in her wake to Ferney's house, caution overruled by the pressing need to be out of the jaws of this human nutcracker. Mike followed because there was nothing else for him to do. Her mind seethed with warnings of dangerous outcomes, but they could

not overcome her visceral resolve. It never occurred to her that Ferney might not be home, that he might have gone somewhere else. She
knew he was there. On the way to the front door Mike's anger was
barely enough to overcome his enormous reluctance. For a second he
lagged behind her, but he felt conspicuous standing out in the gaze of
the blank windows of the other bungalows and, caught between two
evils, came slowly to join her at the door. There was just a moment as
Ferney's indistinct shape, broken into impressionistic strips by the
front door's fluted glass, moved to undo the latch when she knew
that what she was doing was probably a huge mistake, then it was
too late. The door was open and he was standing there looking at her
and past her to Mike with an expression that passed through surprise
and apprehension to finish in a calmness that touched Gally and quietened her too.

"Come in," was all he said, and they followed him into the front
room. Mike took refuge in looking at the books again. Ferney walked
slowly to the fireplace, half-turned to look quizzically at Mike, then
back at Gally with a raised eyebrow. She was quite sure she knew
what that look meant. Why are you taking this risk? Why can't we
keep it all separate?

"I think we should all talk," she said by way of reply to the silent
questions. "We *have* to talk. Mike is very concerned, aren't you,
Mike?"

Mike looked embarrassed, but was forced to turn away from the
books. "Well, in a way."

He seemed so childlike, eclipsed by Ferney. I can fit them both in,
she thought—surely that can't be so wrong.

"Mike happened to see you in the woods just now, digging up a
box," she said, speaking in a calm, paced way that showed she was
just an intermediary, that there was no accusation from her. "He
heard that the police had been talking to you down by the road and
he's worried for my sake."

Mike looked as if he wanted to disappear into the carpet.

"He thinks you might be dangerous in some way to me, Ferney. I
know you're not, but we all know I've told him what you've said
about you and me and the past," to her acute surprise her voice
started to choke on her, "and I've just got . . . got to the point where I
can't keep on . . . pretending everything's . . ."

Both the men took a step towards her and each man, seeing the
other move, instantly stopped so that they were frozen in a triangle,
watching her as she breathed heavily and struggled for control. Mike

stayed where he was, but Ferney took another step and touched her gently on the shoulder. She got her balance back.

"What do we do?" she said.

"We all sit down," said Ferney calmly, "at least you two do, and I'll make a pot of tea."

Mike looked glumly at the carpet after he'd gone out and Gally looked at Mike with a sudden depth of understanding.

"I'm sorry to be putting you through this," she said quietly, but he looked blankly up at her then down again.

Ferney came back with a tray and put it down on the table. "How do you like it?" he said to Mike.

"Just milk . . . please."

Ferney passed it to him, put milk and one sugar in Gally's without asking and gave it to her. That was not lost on Mike. Gally, super-sensitive to all that passed, almost said, "You've got a good memory," but realized how absurd that would sound, so she just took it and smiled.

"Now tell me," said Ferney. "What exactly did you think you saw?"

"I wasn't following you or anything—but I was walking along and I saw you dig up some sort of box. I stopped and then it all got a bit difficult because I didn't want you to think I was spying so I had to sort of keep still after that."

Ferney just waited for him to go on and Mike, hanging on the hook of silence, had no real choice. "Look, it was only because of the police." He took a deep breath. "I saw you bury another box, so after you went I dug it up and had a look."

Ferney nodded, considering, then held up a placating hand. "All right. I understand. I know you've got Gally to think of. I'll tell you about the boxes. I'm sure you'll keep it to yourself?"

Mike nodded.

"I put things aside—stuff that's of no account now and likely to be worth a bit later. It's a bit of fun, you could say. I just dug up an old one to have a look and maybe to sell a thing or two and I put another one in its place. I do quite a lot of that."

Mike wrestled with that. "But that stuff in it. I saw it . . ."

"I hope you put it back properly."

"Phone cards? What's the point of that?"

"I suppose you undid the tape? I'd better get it up again and seal it, otherwise the damp gets in."

"The phone cards?"

"I chose them carefully. People leave them in the boxes when they've run out. They've got all sorts of designs on some of them. They'll be collected when their times come."

"Yes, but not in your lifeti . . ." Mike choked himself off. "Sorry, but you know what I mean. They'll just be so much rubbish for years, surely."

There it was, brought out into the open, the central issue flying under the false colours of a bunch of phone cards. The three of them all focused their gaze on the carpet at the centre of their triangle for a long, silent moment.

"Well, she's told you, hasn't she?" said Ferney in the end. "I wasn't planning on digging them up this time round."

"Oh so *that's* it. It's that business again, is it? These lives of yours."

"I can't hope that you can understand and it's better just kept to those who can."

"Meaning you and Gally. That does shut me out a bit, doesn't it? I mean if it's always been the two of you, as you say."

"That's just the way it is," said Ferney slowly. "We didn't choose for it to be that way, but until now that *is* the way it's always been."

Gally was watching them both, letting Mike go on, aware that she'd started something that had to run its course. Mike looked hard at Ferney. "How far back are you saying you go?"

"A fair old bit."

"More than five hundred years?"

Ferney shrugged a vague nod.

"More than a thousand?"

"Maybe a bit more."

Mike looked around the room. "I'm a logical person," he said, "I have to test things. Do you understand that?"

"If that's your way," said Ferney.

"I'm a historian. You say you're, well, history itself, I suppose. Maybe I could ask you some questions."

"You could, but it wouldn't help."

"Why not?"

"Everything you know came from a book, right?"

"That's putting it a bit too simply."

"It came from someone else's knowledge. Doesn't really matter if they wrote it down or they told you. You didn't invent it."

"Your point is?"

"You could ask me a question and if I give you the answer you want then you'd just think I'd read it too. Chances are, though, I wouldn't give you the answer you want. I've pretty much always been a countryman, mostly round here. A few times history came marching right through here, through the forest tracks. A lot of blood got spilt here. Sometimes it was mine. Mostly, though, we only saw the small stuff of history. No one told us much. We heard rumours. People told tales. Maybe they were right, maybe they were wrong. When they were right maybe that's not the way history wrote it down, because we both know that depends on who's telling the story. But that's not the main point. Even if you asked me a hundred questions and I gave you all the right answers it wouldn't make any difference."

"Why do you say that?"

"Because you *can't* believe. You don't *want* to believe. It's not in your *interests* to believe."

"You're right, I don't believe this, I really don't. You believe it if you want, but I need evidence."

"Mike," said Gally, "calm down."

"No, leave him be," said Ferney. "I can see how it must feel." He pondered. "You don't want evidence. You'd just want more and more and if you ever did believe it would be worse for you."

"I'm sorry," Mike said, "I know you're by yourself. I'm sure all this makes you feel better, but it's not all right by me, not at all. It's messing us around and you've got no right to do that."

"I'm not messing anyone around," said Ferney firmly. "I'm just saying what's got to be said. You came here because she brought you here and you can't turn the clock back so it's best you understand it. Anyway, she needs it. You must want her to be happy."

"Of course I do."

"Was she happy before she came here?"

"That's . . . that's our business."

Ferney snorted. "I know about nightmares. I know what lies at their roots. Now, come with me, I've got something to show you."

"What?" said Mike, but Ferney just walked past him out of the room. Gally beckoned. "Come on," she said.

Mike turned on her. "Why do you do that? You're just encouraging it."

"No, I'm not," she said, startled. "But surely you're not going to stay here?"

"Whatever he's going to show us now," said Mike emphatically, "it won't prove a damned thing."

Ferney went in front of them down the corridor to the room of books at the end where the painting hung and pointed at it. "Have another look at that for a minute," he said. "Painted by a good painter, that was."

He left them standing in front of it, Mike peering again at the dark, grimy surface.

"Stand back," suggested Gally. "It's easier." She could see that this time he was picking up the shapes and knew at least there would be no more argument about the stone now that he'd seen a historical source of the sort he could understand. The picture's importance came to her, direct and personal. It was the first proper image, the first time there had been something to pass on down the years, the first window on their past that was more than memory. She tried to stare through the dirt at the dim outline of the couple by the door. It was too hard for her in Mike's presence and she could feel nothing. She thought perhaps that was all Ferney had brought them to see, but it was only meant to serve as a waiting room. He came back in through the door clutching a large cylindrical object shrouded in a piece of sheet and laid it carefully on the table.

"You've got the ring still," he said to Gally, and she nodded. "I want you to have this, to look after it. Keep it to yourselves or there'll be never-ending questions. I've got nowhere for it to go for safety after I die." He looked at Mike. "Do you promise?" Mike shrugged. "Do you?" insisted Ferney and Mike nodded curtly.

Ferney looked at Gally. "You described the drum, Monmouth's drum. Do you remember?"

"I think so." She shivered.

"Don't worry. I think I know what the rest of your fear is now. I can help you. Describe it again, just the way you see it in your head."

"Blue, dirty and damaged with a gold lion and a unicorn."

He pulled the sheet off and what was revealed had age encrusted on it in undeniable witness. It was a drum, once dark blue or black perhaps, with a red, yellow and gold crest, cut across, grimy and partly worn away on one side. The skin on top was cracked and flaking and the hoops and clamps were tarnished silver, but the gold was recognizably royal: a rearing lion, a shield surmounted by a crown and most of a unicorn, reduced by time's damage to a mere horse, a dark, rubbed dent across where its horn had been.

It scared the hell out of Gally.

"It's Monmouth's drum," Ferney said and Mike, instead of scoffing, gently put out a hand to it, recognizing a pedigree that would not allow disbelief.

"How did you find it?" he said.

"I hid it in the first place. Gally and I. We put it up under the thatch."

"What thatch?"

"The thatch that used to be on your house. Two hundred years ago. His Dutchman, the gun man, had been carrying it. They left it."

"The museum told us it was found there. They said there was armour too."

"The thatcher came when I wasn't expecting him. I'd meant to move it first but he found it and I had to make out I hadn't known it was there. I got it back in the end."

"When was this?"

"I don't know quite. Gladstone had just quit being prime minister."

"Eighteen ninety-four," said Mike.

"If you say so."

"A hundred and six years ago?"

Ferney nodded. Mike sighed. "Just explain, will you? You must have . . . well . . . died after that?"

"In 1907. I was halfway through a book, *Kipps* it was, by H. G. Wells. I've never got round to finishing it."

"So what did you do with the drum?"

"Put it back in my roof again."

"It was *your* house then?"

"We've usually contrived to have it one way or another."

"So why isn't it still yours?"

"Lawyers. It all went a bit wrong. Next time round someone else was in it."

"How did you get the drum back?"

"I got it out when I heard Effie Mullard was having it all slated. I went in when she wasn't there."

"And now you want us to look after it and keep it quiet?"

Ferney's look said it was Gally he'd had in mind but he just nodded.

"Historians should be able to see this," said Mike forcefully. "I'm sure it's unique. I don't think it should be tucked away."

"One thing I've learnt," said Ferney. "You say too much and people start asking so many questions. There's no end to them. If there's something big at stake, money or whatever, they'll never leave it until they've unravelled you. Best to keep quiet. Mind you, I don't listen to my own advice. If I'd kept quiet down at the road when they found Gally's bones, you wouldn't . . ."

"Gally's bones?" Mike jackknifed forward.

There was a sudden profound silence. "I didn't tell Mike that bit," said Gally quietly to Ferney and the old man shook his head at Mike. "What else did you think?"

"You're saying it was *Gally* who was murdered?"

"Well of course it was. Do you think I would have married anyone else?"

"You'd better tell me all about it," said Mike grimly.

"It was a long time before *you* were born," said Ferney. "She just disappeared one day. We'd been very happy, never apart, then one day she just vanished." He looked down and sighed. "I think I knew straightaway what had happened. There was a blacksmith, you see, a man called Cochrane. He was a violent man and he always had his eye on her from when he first arrived here. He was wrong in the head when he drank and he thought for a long time that he could get her to come away with him." He looked at Gally. "She would never have done that. She was never interested in anyone but me." To Gally, tension flickered between them then, but Mike seemed unaware.

"He killed her, I'm sure. That place where they've dug the hole, that was where his forge was. He just tipped her into the pit. The police say they accept that's what happened. Anyway there's no proving it now. They asked me all about Cochrane, but he's long dead, I told them."

He looked round the room. "You can see her if you like." He went to a shelf. There was a small framed photograph on it and he picked it up and looked at it for a long moment in silence then, seeming to reach a decision, he turned round and thrust it out to Mike.

"This isn't evidence but it's what it's all about. That's us. That's Gally and me last time we were together."

It hadn't occurred to Gally that there might be a photograph. More than that, it seemed inconceivable. She had accepted the significance of the painting immediately, but the photograph seemed entirely foreign. It was almost an affront that there should be this small, square, precise witness to the memories she couldn't find. As Mike took it and stared at it, Ferney seemed to read her thoughts.

"First one," he said. "Only one. We didn't run to cameras."

She longed to take it from Mike, but he just stood there, looking at it and shaking his head. "It's not in the least bit like Gally," he said, completely missing the point.

"Not to look at," said Ferney patiently. "That's all you can tell from a photograph. It's not like children. There's no genes carrying on. But it is Gally. A month or two after our wedding, that one was."

Mike put it down on the table and Gally stared towards it with hunger.

"Can I see it?"

"What?" he said absently. "Oh, if you must."

He held it out reluctantly. "I'm sorry about your wife," he said, "I can see it must be very odd for you—but I'm quite sure it's just a co-incidence that she had the same nickname as Gally."

Ferney was looking at Gally and Gally was looking at the photo. The sepia-tinted, plain-faced girl in the photo was a disappointment. Where Mike had failed to find a genetic trace, she could find no echo of the consciousness. I can't see myself there, she thought. It is after all just silver salts and paper. The girl was short, fair-haired, dressed simply in a skirt and blouse. The background was a wall, but what wall she could not tell. Then she looked at the man next to the woman and saw Ferney in the fresh morning of his adulthood and warmth flooded from the centre of her soul's gravity to every extremity of her body. This was so entirely familiar. This was the way, she knew, that she felt Ferney's shape in her mind when he wasn't there. She stared hard and long at the picture and teased out a wisp of memory, a faint trace of a day, far away, with a scent of lily of the valley in the air. The memory took boisterous and unexpected form round a cheerful, fat photographer with brilliantined hair and she frowned, trying to hold on to that and to fill it out but raised voices blew it away.

"I want to know," Mike was repeating. "I have a right to know. How did Cochrane die?"

"If you don't believe all this, what does it matter?"

"You can't just say that." Mike was flushing red again. "This is something that happened in this lifetime. I don't have to believe the rest of it. You come careering through our lives saying stupid things like that and . . ."

Ferney's voice was rising too. "It's not stupid. It's the way it was. Always just the two of us. Who did you think it was? Like I said, I wouldn't have married someone else."

"Well *she* did. She married me, so why should I believe you? What right have you got to screw us around? I've heard quite enough of this. Stay out of our life from now on, right?"

"It's not just your life."

"It bloody well is and I don't trust you."

"I've done nothing to deserve mistrust."

"Oh no? How did this man Cochrane die, then? Why were the police interested? You had a hand in it, didn't you?"

He could not have chosen a more painful accusation.

"No, I did not. It was a lad, a simple lad. Billy. You don't under-stand, you don't . . . you . . ." Ferney's voice trailed off and he stood there, reaching a hand out to the table for support, missing it and sliding down onto it on buckling knees as his eyes rolled up in his head. His arm swept the drum to the floor with a crash and then he followed it to slump down onto the carpet.

19

THERE WAS A second when neither of them did anything, then another second when they both tried to get through the same gap at the corner of the table at the same time, and each of those seconds felt like minutes to Gally. Ferney lay twisted on the red carpet and some abstracted, irrelevant part of her brain registered the slight pattern in its weave. Then she was on the floor, kneeling by his head, searching for signs in his face and finding nothing but slack absence.

Mike was crouched next to her, his head on Ferney's chest.

"He's stopped breathing," he said, his voice fast and high. "I'm not sure there's a heartbeat."

"Oh God. What do we do?"

"We don't panic. We . . . er . . ."

Sketchy diagrams of mouth to mouth and heart massage offered themselves in imperfect images to Gally, half-remembered posters she had glanced at in doctors' waiting rooms and had never needed to remember before.

"Help me straighten him out," said Mike and they untwisted him. He was surprisingly heavy. Gally put her hands together on his chest and pressed down abruptly. It felt horribly dangerous, as though she might crack his ribcage.

"That's right," said Mike encouragingly. "It's got to be hard. It's three times, isn't it? Then you do the mouth to mouth."

She bent her head to his face, held his nose, put her mouth over his and blew into him. Mike watched for a moment then stood up. "I'll phone for an ambulance. I'll be back in a minute, love. Keep going."

It took him more than a minute. She heard him talking urgently on the phone, trying to describe the way to the bungalow and realized he didn't know the address. She kept going rhythmically, breathing her air into the still body, then pumping his chest, then breathing again and suddenly had a shocking sense that instead of forcing life into him, she was drawing it out. Every time she put her mouth over his, she began to feel a stronger and stronger sensation that something electric was trying to find its way towards her from him. *He is dying,* she thought. *I am not helping him live, I am helping him die and this is too soon.* She sat up in distress, but he was still not breathing and death lay that way too. She bent to him again, trapped, and in the distance she heard Mike sorting out the problem, putting the phone down and crossing the hall. She guessed he was looking for an envelope from the morning's post.

"Twelve, Castle Orchard Close," he said when he got back to the phone. "How long will you be? . . . Okay."

He came back in quickly and she looked up in relief. "Mike, please, will you do this? I think I'm doing it all wrong."

"Me? No, it's okay, you're doing fine."

"I'm not. You've got to do it. If he dies . . ."

Was she going to say ". . . it will be your fault"? He looked at her face and didn't argue anymore. There was a moment of hesitation when he bent to Ferney's mouth, but then he steeled himself and blew in the first breath.

She stood and watched, horrified, and she had a sense that she was still too close.

"I'll find a blanket," she said and ran down the corridor in search of Ferney's bedroom, feeling with each step she took that she was leaving the threat behind. The first door she tried was the bathroom. The second was indeed his bedroom, but there was only a duvet on the bed and she rejected that as too bulky. Against one wall was a heavy chest of drawers and she pulled the drawers open in turn. The bottom one yielded a green tartan rug and as she bent to take it out, her line of sight crossed the piles of books and magazines on top of the chest and lighted on a white envelope, propped up against a table lamp. She saw her name on it.

She hurried back and spread the soft, heavy rug over Ferney, working round Mike, but again she found herself inside the old man's tidal pull and knew she was reversing Mike's gains.

"Are you all right?" she said to Mike and as he stopped the mouth to mouth and started to pump Ferney's chest once more, he nodded.

"I . . . can't stay in here," she said. "I'll go and make sure the ambulance knows where to come."

"It won't get here for a while yet," he said in a voice that wanted her to stay, but then he bent to blow again and she backed out of the room. Ferney doesn't want me to leave, she thought. This is the moment of passage for him. He wants my baby close to him. Somewhere deep inside her she knew he was wrong in this. It's too early, she thought. This tiny thing growing in me is nowhere near ready for invasion. It couldn't take it.

She went to the front door, heard an engine, but it turned into a blue and yellow truck that passed the end of the entrance to the close and went on its way. It was hard to stay there, leaving it all to Mike, wondering what was happening on that carpet battlefield inside, fearing he would be feeling deserted. A stronger instinct kept her outside—an instinct that said she had to protect both Ferney and her baby.

Her heart jumped when another approaching engine note slowed and a white vehicle crawled round the corner into the close, but it was just a van. It stopped almost opposite and a man in a white coat climbed out with a plastic basket of bread. She had a sudden urge to tell him. Surely he should know that there was a man dying in here? Surely he shouldn't just go on his baker's way not knowing? He left his bread on the doorstep of the bungalow next door, nodded to her and left. No one else was about in the neighbouring houses. Time crawled fretfully by and then across the distance there was a far off two-tone siren, blowing like the wonderful bugles of a rescuing force rushing to lift her siege. She hurried inside to the study doorway. "They're coming," she said. Mike waved an acknowledging hand in the air and kept at it.

The ambulance swung into the close and drove straight to where she stood waving. A man and a woman jumped out, capable-looking. The woman came straight inside with her and the man brought a large pack of equipment in behind them. Mike, drained and pale, surrendered his place to them.

They bent to examine Ferney in silence. "You've done well," said the woman. "Go and have a sit-down."

Gally hugged Mike and started to lead him away but Mike turned back, picked the drum up off the table and brought it with him. She fought down an urge to shy away from it.

"We'd better not leave it there," he whispered and she took that for a sign that he believed at least one small part of Ferney's story.

"Bring it through here," she said, and led the way to the bedroom. He tucked it out of sight behind a chair and she closed the door firmly on it. They went into the front room, away from Ferney's danger zone, where they looked at each other and she knew that the last

ten minutes of desperate activity had given Mike a shared interest in
Ferney's survival.

"What have I done?" he said miserably.

"You've saved him."

"I caused it. I brought it on."

"You couldn't have known and you've kept him alive. Thank
you," she said.

She could feel the change in him. All the pain he'd felt, all the raw
anger and all the sense of betrayal was buried under a mountain of
concern and responsibility. They sat together on the sofa, holding
hands in silent tension, listening to the activity down the corridor.
The man went to the ambulance and brought back a stretcher. Mike
jumped to his feet.

"Can I help?"

"It's okay. We've got him stabilized for now. He's breathing."

Mike did help, for all that, moving furniture out of the way while
they carried Ferney on his stretcher out through the hall. An oxygen
mask was over his face and a monitor was strapped to him.

"You go with him in the ambulance," suggested Mike.

"No . . . I don't want to. Would you mind going to get the car? I'll
lock up here."

"It'll take me five minutes," he said, puzzled.

She just nodded.

The ambulance went on its urgent way and now there were people
in the close. Mike told them briefly what was going on as he passed
and Gally looked up to see the broad figure of Mary Sparrow stumping down the path.

"Hello, my muffety," she said. "Here's a business, then."

"He just fell down," said Gally.

"He's still kicking, though. It's a blessing you were here."

It wouldn't have happened if we hadn't been, thought Gally miserably. "I was just going to close the house up," she said.

"He won't want anyone in here," said Mary, looking round the
hall. "There's the key, see? Why don't you take it and look after it for
him?"

Gally nodded and picked up the key. "I'd better just make sure
everything's switched off," she said and walked quickly down the
corridor, checking each room. She came to the bedroom, crossed the
room to the chest of drawers, picked up the envelope and put it in her
pocket. She longed to know what was in it, but this was not the time
to look.

She was halfway back to Bagstone Farm when Mike appeared in the car. He was gentle with her on the way to the hospital.

"Did you find it too upsetting?" he asked.

"It wasn't that. I felt . . . I felt I was killing him. I don't know."

Is it her guilt again, he wondered, her ever-present guilt that she didn't save her father? Is that what froze her into inaction? It wasn't, but anyway he didn't press the point.

They waited a long time at the hospital sipping plastic-tasting coffee out of soft, floppy mugs. It was an hour before there was news and the news was that Ferney had suffered a major heart attack, but that, thanks to Mike's first aid, he was still alive and was now in intensive care. A young female doctor told them he was likely to be in hospital for some time because there were some indications of other problems, too, and that they should phone later to see if he was well enough for a visit. Gally knew that visiting was the last thing she should do.

On the way back to Penselwood, Gally expected more questions, but Mike was in no mood for them. He was obviously worried.

"It was my fault," he said.

"Because you were angry?"

"It must have been the tension. That was what triggered it."

"Don't keep saying that. If it was anyone's fault then it was mine," she said softly. "It was me that made you go there."

"But if I hadn't watched him in the wood, none of this would have happened."

"Look, Mike, I know you were only doing what you thought was the right thing."

"Where does this leave you?" he said, turning his head to look at her for much longer than she felt was safe on the winding country road.

"About as confused as ever."

"If he doesn't make it . . . that leaves a lot of things unresolved."

She knew he wanted reassurance, but the letter, hot in her back pocket, held a promise of resolution and she knew it was unlikely to be in a form that would reassure him. It was clear to her that she must read it alone.

"I'm sorry if it's made you unhappy, Mike, I really am. It hasn't been fair to you."

"Thank you," he said and they each felt closer than they had been for weeks.

Back at the caravan it was harder. The house pulled bits of her

away from him. Time passed in their separate bubbles of distur-
bance. After a long period of vacancy, Mike pulled a folder out of
his case.

"I forgot," he said in a weary voice. "I haven't done my notes for
tomorrow."

She knew what that meant. He needed to spread himself out,
undisturbed, across the caravan table and that could be the best
thing. "I might go for a walk," she said.

The top of the hill was the right and only place to go and it was an
unexpectedly poignant moment when she saw the stone seat was
empty. She sat down on it and did nothing for a long time except
to stare out over the landscape. Glastonbury Tor was clear on the
horizon twenty miles away. The letter felt like a turning point, as
though she would be forced after reading it to divide her life up into
before the letter and after the letter. A letter was not something
Ferney would ever write lightly. In the end, as a compromise, she
pulled it from her pocket and spent a long time looking at the envelope. His handwriting spelt out PRIVATE across the top left-hand corner and then

Please Deliver To: Gally, Bagstone Farm, Penselwood

as though he couldn't bring himself to write "Martin" down as her
surname. Maybe he couldn't remember it, she thought. Surnames
couldn't mean much to a man who had accumulated so many.

She held it in her hand for perhaps five minutes before carefully
opening the flap and even then it was another minute or so, holding
the letter still folded, before she started to read.

My Dear Gally,

If you are reading this then it must be presumed that the next
stage of our journey has begun. I am writing this letter because,
thus far, I have not found the moment to tell you something of
great importance to us both. It is my dearest wish that this letter
will never reach you—that I will have done this task with my
voice, not my pen, and then perhaps I shall be writing quite another letter.

I have tried to talk to you about the dangers we face in this
modern world which will, all the time, do its best to separate us.
The old stone wasn't put there in a time when such dangers
could be imagined. I know very clearly how painful it is to be
separated by accident of birth from this place of ours and from

you. I cannot judge whether we would always be able to find each other again as we have done these few times but I fear that will not be the case.

Now I must come to the point and you may be cross with me if I tell you that this was your idea and it is at your insistence that I tell you this. About sixty years ago, before Cochrane took you so brutally away from me, you and I were sitting up on top of the hill, where I am quite sure you are sitting now to read this.

A shiver passed through her and she looked around as if someone might be watching. There was no one and she read on.

You told me then that we could only be happy if we made quite, quite sure that we would be born close to each other both in time and space—that the only lives worth having were the ones when we could be young together and grow old together. We both know that the end of a life is not so dreadful. What is dreadful is beginning a life in the growing knowledge that the other is not there.

You made me solemnly swear on that day that we would agree on a course of action from that moment on and that if one of us was to forget then the other would have to remind them. Your idea, to which we agreed solemnly and jointly, was that when in the future one of us were to die—the other would rapidly choose to follow by whatever kind means were at hand.

Rapidly choose to follow. Gally groaned and looked up at a dizzying sky full of rolling cumulus. The letter went on.

On this occasion, you will be aware that there is a big difference. When I die, I am quite sure that I will be born again as your coming child. It must therefore be after the birth is complete that you follow me. Do not think this would be cruel to your new child. It would be a greater kindness.

There was a break in the letter where a slightly darker ink took over and Gally guessed that time had elapsed in the writing.

You have a husband, I know, and that will make it very hard for you. That was not anticipated. I cannot guide you in that. All I can do is to repeat your words. Better still, as a letter is no powerful witness, you may perhaps be able to hear your own words.

I recall exactly what you said on that day and perhaps if you repeat it right, you will hear yourself say it and know that it is true.
If it helps you remember, I was wearing a brown jacket. You
were in a cotton dress, pale blue with pink rosebuds in the pattern and in that time you had long fair hair. You said, "We can
do it. We can if we set our minds to it. No more of this hit-and-
miss," and then you said, "If both of us forget, maybe that will
just have to be that—but we won't, we mustn't. Other folks have
God. We've only got us." Try to remember that, Gally, because
you would be your own best witness.

20

A WEEK OF broken, screaming sleep brought Gally and Mike to the brink of a joint precipice. For Gally it was the worst it had ever been. Every day she did her duty by walking up to Ferney's house, checking the post and making sure all was well, then came back home without lingering there. Although there should have been nothing in the least frightening about his clean, light bungalow, she used the stratagems of a child walking through a dark wood, refusing to look around her, concentrating on the moment when she would be out of it. It wasn't the house, it was the drum lurking behind the chair in the bedroom. She wouldn't even go far into that room, simply opening the door for a quick glance, just enough to see that all was well, and even then she wouldn't look towards the chair for fear that the drum might have the power to make her nightmares into flesh and bring the monsters racing at her from the shadows.

She lived in a state of hidden tumult for every moment of that week, constantly surprised by how fast or how slow time was passing in equal measure, feeling afraid of everything and personally responsible for every part of the mess that surrounded her. Mike, unsettled by his own matching guilt, seemed hardly to notice except when he was shocked awake twice or three times every night by her repeated nightmares. When they talked he continued to blame himself for Ferney's collapse so that she praised him constantly for saving him and tried to camouflage her own off-key responses to everything around her in the ripples of his unease.

At first the news from Yeovil Hospital was minimal and not encouraging. Ferney was in intensive care and no one was making predictions. Visiting was out of the question for any except direct family

and there was of course nobody who fitted that conventional defini-
tion. Gally was inwardly grateful on two counts. She had a strong
idea that she should avoid Ferney's immediate physical presence
while his life teetered on the edge in case she tipped the balance, and
she was still quite sure that it was too early for the stability of the
new life growing in her. There was something else. She was angry
with Ferney, angry that he held all the cards, crushing her into a corner with the heavy words of his letter. His claim that it was her idea,
that he was only following her own instructions, made that worse,
not better. At times it almost seemed to stop her breathing when she
thought about it. It gave her no space.

She knew, but did not wish to recognize, that he had anticipated
she would feel this pressure and that in giving her the clues to take
her mind back and live through it for herself, he meant to pass the responsibility over to her, but at the moment it wasn't a responsibility
she was prepared to take. For a brief minute at the top of the hill,
with the letter in her hand, she had tried repeating the words he had
given her in her head, but her recoiling mind was racing with adrenaline and there was no silent space available to let the words take root.
Then she had lied to herself, choosing to take that as a sign that he
was wrong, crumpling the letter in her hand in a childish wish to pretend it didn't exist. Later, though, she had straightened it out, unable
to throw it away but aware that it held all the dangers of an unex-
ploded bomb and that she must make quite sure Mike would not find
it accidentally. The caravan was too small and the house was too exposed with busy builders to provide a hiding place and after long indecision she found a hollow tree down in the thickness of the valley
at the end of the sloping garden and tucked it away out of sight, inside the trunk, wrapped in a plastic bag.

Underneath it all she knew she needed to see Ferney. He held the
knowledge that would untie the knot of the boilman, the burnman,
Monmouth and the burning car. She wished he had explained the
dreams to her when the question first arose and every night she paid
the penalty for that omission.

Mike was coming near the time when he would have to go back to
the faculty and start preparing for the approaching term. At the end
of ten days, during which the work on the house seemed to have made
enormous strides, the phone rang and it was Gally who answered.

"Mrs. Martin?" said a brisk female voice. "It's Yeovil District
Hospital here."

For a second her heart turned over. Was Ferney dead? Wouldn't
she have known?

"Yes, hello," was all she could manage.

"You asked to be kept informed about visiting?"

"Oh . . . yes?"

"Well, Mr. Miller *is* quite a bit better and he's moving to a general ward tomorrow, so visiting *is* now possible."

"He's better," she found herself repeating.

"I couldn't say he's better, but he's a lot better than he was. I'm afraid he *is* likely to require a long period for *full* recovery at his age."

"Yes, of course, but we can come to see him?"

"From tomorrow—just for short visits."

The caravan creaked as Mike stepped up into it with a screwdriver in his hand. "I never want to see another flat-pack kitchen unit," he said. "If you get killed in a kitchen collapse, just remember I'm an academic. I'm not meant to be practical. Who was that?"

"Yeovil Hospital." She saw his immediate look of alarm. "He's okay. In fact they say we can go and visit tomorrow."

"Really?" He considered. "Maybe you should go by yourself. We don't want to overpower him."

"Coward," she said and tried to smile. "I'm sure he won't blame you. In fact, I'm sure he'll be very grateful that you saved his life." Will he, though, asked an inner voice? Isn't he looking for the quickest way out? No, he'll want to know for certain that I've read the letter and he'll want to know I agree.

"Well, let's see."

He went out with the car early the next morning to collect more of the rolls, the packs and the boxes whose contents were quickly turning the simple walls of the finished kitchen into a complex marshalling yard for pots, pans, plates and gadgets. Gally, trying to hang on to the simplicity, had little enthusiasm for this, apart from a feeling that if Mike really needed digital egg timers and suction wine-bottle sealers it was better that there were drawers to hide them away in. She was too weary to argue. As he drove off she knew she had a brief opportunity and a decision to make. It was already quite clear he would do anything to get out of the hospital visit and it was also clear that if Ferney was well enough to talk he would ask her about the letter.

What were her choices? Refusing to discuss it, she knew, would not be an option once those all-seeing eyes of his were fixed on her. It came down to a simple choice. Either she would try piloting herself back along the trail left for her to some lost Northwest Passage of memory and deal with the consequences of what happened, or she

could refuse. That was her right. She could make a deliberate choice
to tread the safe path and live in the present. That way was fairer for
Mike, better by any normal assessment, and yet she found she could
not take it, not while sitting there on the caravan step as living summit to the triangle whose rooted bases were the Bag Stone and the
house. She went down to the tree, making sure none of the builders
were watching, and took the letter out.

It was a form of residual cowardice, however, that steered her
away from the hilltop. She dressed it up to herself as something else,
a simple precaution against manipulation that this should happen in
the place of *her* choice, not Ferney's. She walked northwards through
the straggling cottages looking for a quiet place to sit until she came
to the church and found herself, without any awareness that it had
always been her destination, walking up the pathway towards it. The
two old heads, facing each other across the corners of the inner
porch, welcomed her. Just as on that earlier visit, she was struck by a
sense of disappointment that the inside of the church was not as she
expected, but now at least she had some ideas why. She took a blue
leaflet from a pile on the table. "St. Michael's Pen Selwood," it said,
"Church History." The pew ends were carved in 1927. A gallery
across the west end of the nave was removed in recent times. That,
she thought, was what felt wrong. Going back into the porch with
the leaflet in her hand, she looked at the ancient carving of the Virgin
over the outer door. It felt old but unimportant. Cross-checking herself, she looked through the leaflet. It *was* old, nearly six hundred
years old, but it had been brought back from Italy around 1850. The
two crowned heads were another thing altogether—deeply familiar.
"As yet unidentified" said the leaflet. "Believed by some to be King
Alfred and King Guthrum." Guthrum? The Viking leader beaten and
converted by Alfred's scratch army? She gave a derisory laugh. This
was a woman, anyone could see that, though the head was certainly
more weather-beaten than she expected.

Somewhere at the back of her mind there was a suspicion that if
she could just hold on to it she could draw out a fleeting tag of
memory with names on it—a name for the king and for the queen.
She tried, failed and was saddened for a long moment, then Ferney's
letter asserted itself in her pocket and now she decided was the time
to face it. She stepped back into the nave, where her light steps
echoed softly from cool stone edges and went unknowingly to the
same pew in the far aisle where Ferney had sat to conjure up the sad
life of James Cumberlidge. Holding the letter in the quiet, high light,

she read the words deliberately to herself, with a measure of fore-
boding. "We can if we set our minds to it. No more of this hit-
and-miss." They ran through her mind even after she had stopped
consciously reading them, but it was her own modern voice that
spoke them and nothing came.

How long had she got? She looked at her watch and could make
little sense of it. What time had Mike gone? What time had he said
he'd be back? Mike had worked it all out—the journey time to
Yeovil, the visiting hours, and she had retained none of it.

She closed her eyes then and tried to quieten her breathing, to
smother the present with a blanket of silence. Irrelevant thoughts
kept pushing their way in. Had they got any mustard? Should she
take Ferney flowers? Every time she wrestled to blank her mind
again, saying a mantra to herself: "No more of this hit-and-miss, no
more of this hit-and-miss, no more of this hit-and-miss." The pew,
the church and the sense of here and now left her and her heartbeat
became very loud in her ears. An eager, young face turned to her and
she loved it with a bubbling, physical rush which took her breath
away. Ferney, maybe thirty, beautiful Ferney, listening as she told him
her terrible, wonderful idea. At the start, there was just the face, inside the church with her then a sense of the walls opening up and the
vast sky around them.

How much time did she still have? In the present world, up in its
tower above her head, the church clock clicked around and with an
admonitory whirr sent its powerful message of the hour clanging out
across the village on the ridge. The first bronze stroke sent a flicker
through the forming features of his face, bringing her sharp anticipation of loss. The second stroke changed them and by the third they
were re-forming. This face was broader, middle-aged, darker-skinned,
the nose broken and the chin larger, but the eyes were still Ferney's
eyes and the love was still there though it was older and calmer.

The fourth stroke of the bell sounded and they were both looking
up, hand in hand in the crowd. Gally's legs were tired from climbing
Shaftesbury's hill and she was thirsty. It was the first warm day in a
foul, wet year and the coarse kersey cloth chafed her shoulder under
the strap of the leather bag. They'd buy ale when they could, but the
first thing was to see the machine, the reason they'd come all this
way. The word had reached them yesterday, spreading fast through
the countryside, that a machine to count the hours had come to
Shaftesbury to be put in the church and anyone could go to see it.
Most of the village had been straggling out along the muddy road as

they left, but Ferney and Gally, preferring to walk alone, had out-
paced the rest of them. It took them half the morning to get there and
for the last quarter of the journey they could hear a bell, growing
steadily stronger, ringing first once, then after they had gone perhaps
another mile twice more, then three times as they approached.

It was set up on a wooden frame outside the Abbey, on display
waiting to be lifted up to the platform now being built inside the
tower. They were patient, using the slow rearrangements of the growing crowd to work their way ever nearer to the machine until they
could see the sun and the moon, the weights on their chains and the
shining wheels with their pegs and teeth turning the ornate iron
hands. They each stood staring up at it, both fascinated by the precise, organized look of the thing. Delicate metal was unfamiliar except as jewellery or church ornaments. Delicate metal that turned
and shone and fitted, part by part, into other turning, shining pieces
was unsuspected, entirely new.

There was a man up on the gantry, fussing around it, a man in a
gown that marked him out as leading an easy, looked-after life. He
was watching the mechanism intently and all at once he turned to
the crowd and held up both hands as if to make an announcement.
The buzz of speculation rose sharply then stopped, so that all there
was to hear was the hushing spreading out to noisy latecomers, the
whisper of the turning wheels and the clatter of jackdaws around
the tower above. Then came a click, a whirr and a great clang from
the bell hanging from its wooden scaffold beside the machine. A gasp
and a murmur went up from the crowd, but the man with the cloak
held up his hands again with an impatient frown. Another clang and
another and another rolled out from the hilltop across a land that
had only heard the ringing of bells as summons, celebration, warning
or mourning, never before as measurement.

"It is ten hours in the morning," shouted the man, "by the precise
authority of the clock," and a burst of cheering went up. Ferney suddenly turned away.

"Let's leave," he said, "I'm thirsty." He sounded unhappy.

They bought mugs of ale at the street corner. Gally wished it were
water but Ferney never trusted water away from their own spring.
She wondered at his sudden downcast mood and regretted it. She
would have liked to spend the morning in the town. They very rarely
gave up a day to come this far, but he clearly had no wish to stay.

"What is it?" she said as they left.

The bell behind them gave one single clang.

"It's that," he said.

"Why?"

"I'll show you," he said and turned down the steep slope of the lane towards the flatlands and the way north.

They walked on in silence at a steady pace on the sticky, puddled track. In places, where there were banks, there was no choice but to wade through the mud. In others, travellers had beaten new paths, widening the track in their search for firmer ground, but mostly just spreading out the mud so that it ran to forty paces wide or more. Gally, taking her mind off her wet feet, thought of all the wheels with their tiny teeth and wondered what tools were used to forge them. Shaping metal, she knew, was hard and that was not the sort of work done with a furnace and a hammer. After a fair while, there came a distant double clang behind them and Ferney stopped and wheeled round.

"So tell me what's bothering you," she said.

"How far have we come?" he said. She measured the distance back to the ridge with her eye. "Six furlongs," she said, "maybe seven. Why?"

"When we came this morning," he said, "we moved in eternity at our own best pace and we arrived when we arrived. Do you see how it's changed?"

"I don't think I do."

"They'll have those everywhere soon. That won't be the only one. Can you really not see what the difference is? We're going back and we are no longer moving in eternity. Now we are moving in measured time. The machine is measuring us. While we walked it rattled and it turned and it spat out one fourth part of the hour."

"That doesn't hurt," she said cheerfully.

He gave her a tight smile. "It sounds four times every hour. Can't you feel it drawing us into its cogs? People never measure without a price coming into it. A pint of ale, a pound of corn, a yard of cloth."

"How can time have a price on it?"

"They'll find a way," he said. "They'll not pay working men by the year, not with this thing about in the world. They'll measure off the hours they work and they'll measure off the hours they don't work. This machine we've seen . . . this will serve to fuel the preying dreams of merchants and rich men." He looked back down the road. "Do you think we've walked fast enough?"

"We've walked, that's all—walked at our speed."

"But we've got time walking with us now and one day someone

will say you're not fast enough, you haven't gone far enough or maybe they'll say that job took too long—the clock says so and it will no longer be enough that it was done well."

"Ferney," she said, sad to find the joy of the day evaporating around them, "time's not new. There's been time always."

"Water clocks," he said, "candle clocks, sand glasses. You've never taken them seriously. Short hours in winter, long hours in summer. Guesswork—not authority." He nodded back up the road. "That thing back there isn't going to be our slave, it's going to be telling us what to do before we know it."

"Let's break it, then," she said and a door opened noisily in the middle of this open countryside and blew her thoughts away.

She blinked, wondering why there were walls around her, and stared blankly at the figure bending apologetically in the bright light of the doorway, one hand on the door handle.

"So sorry," said a man's voice. "Did I disturb you?"

"No," she said, rubbing her head and standing up. "I was miles away." He had, though, and she resented his arrival.

The man wore a dog collar. "I do apologize," he said. "Were you at prayer?"

"No, I was thinking."

"Comes to the same thing, sometimes." He was boyish, young, with curly fair hair and an embarrassed grin. "I'm just a stand-in, you know—for a few weeks." She didn't say anything and he looked even more embarrassed. "That's why I don't know my flock yet, you see. I'm Roger Wigglesworth."

"Gally Martin," she said slowly. "But I'm not part of your flock, I'm afraid."

"Still," he said, "jolly good to see someone using the place." Then he thought. "Gally Martin. Are you down in a caravan somewhere?"

"That's right."

"Oh, in that case it was you and your husband who saved poor Mr. Miller?"

"My husband more than me."

"Jolly well done. How is he?"

"Off the danger list, I gather."

"Jolly good show. He must be quite tough."

"Do you know Mr. Miller?" she said curiously.

"Oh no, but I really think I must go and see him in hospital. He's the first of my flock to fall, if you like."

Ferney will want that like a hole in the head, thought Gally. "I'm fairly certain he's not one of your flock either," she said carefully.

"Well, any sheep in need," he said. "Who knows, I might be able to help in some way. Or perhaps he's of some other church?"

"No, I don't think so."

"Oh well, do go on with your thinking or whatever, I'd hate to stop you."

"I must go, actually. I've done enough thinking, thank you all the same."

He stayed in the church when she left and she stopped as soon as she was out of sight. The letter, unresolved, crouched in her pocket, a paper Judas waiting to give the kiss. Mike must not see it, yet she could not bring herself to throw it away.

That was a giant step in there, she thought. I can do it by myself without Ferney leading me. It is there. In the same breath she doubted it. The vicar had shattered the chain too abruptly, driven it all too far away, so that with every second it was harder to be sure what it had been, daydream or memory? It had felt real and detailed and she had to hang on to that, but now it was receding from her too fast to be sure.

She took a deep breath. Time to be practical, she thought and looked at her watch. Seven minutes to the hour. Mike had said he'd be back by eleven. Gally wondered if she could get home in seven minutes. She walked fast, but the clock struck the hour long before she came in sight of the cottage and she hated its tyranny. If time wasn't measured, lateness wouldn't hurt. She wanted more time to herself but there was a car pulling into the gateway as she arrived, and it wasn't Mike.

21

ALL THE WAY to Yeovil, Gally was in the wrong century, driving as if the whole process were new to her, sawing at the steering wheel, reacting too fiercely and too late in delayed recognition of what other cars were doing. She wasn't in the right frame of mind to drive a car at all. The whole alien business of controlling this lump of intricate steel was for once almost beyond her, but Mike had found all kinds of reasons to stay behind.

The woman who had arrived in her elegant metallic grey Lancia just as Gally got back to the house had a delicacy about her that had made Gally feel clumpy and ill at ease as she showed her into what she suddenly saw to be an extremely shabby caravan. The woman was brittlely polite with an on-off smile. Fortyish, bird-boned and perfectly made-up, she wore immaculate tight clothes that must have hung, amongst many others, in individual plastic protectors.

"I'm so sorry just to drop in," said the woman, "I didn't have a phone number. I hope I'm not interrupting you. My name is Victoria Melhuish and Geoffrey Pringle asked me to get in touch with you."

"Geoffrey Pringle?"

"At the museum?"

Gally still looked blank.

"Taunton Museum? You called on him recently."

"Oh yes . . . sorry."

"I'm the jewellery specialist, Stuart jewellery. Geoffrey asked me to take a look at the ring you showed him."

Gally, raw through and through from abrasive history, found with irritation that she was too polite to refuse, though that was her strong inclination. She opened the plywood door with the one surviving hinge on the cupboard under the caravan seat and got out the leather box in which the ring now lived. Victoria Melhuish bent over, watching as she opened the box, drawn to it, and she lost just a little of her poise as she saw the ring. She pounced on it, holding it up to the window, then produced from her bag a magnifier in a grey silk pouch and bent to study it.

"Do sit down," said Gally, deriving a guilty shred of unworthy satisfaction from the difficulty the woman faced sliding into the narrow gap between the stained cushions and the splintery edge of the table without hazarding her clothes.

Victoria Melhuish turned the ring over and over, staring through the eyepiece, then spoke without looking up. "This is very interesting," she said. "Would you mind if I did a little more cleaning? Not too much, of course—just enough to see what we're dealing with?"

"Go ahead," said Gally. "I just need to go and see how the builders are getting on." She didn't want to stand awkwardly by, marginalized, while her ring was put through this process.

Rick called to her from upstairs as she went into the house and she climbed the stairs in time to see him nailing the last sheet of plasterboard into place on the wooden framework of a wall. The rooms were delineated again, boxed off.

"It looks a bit modern," she said, looking at the straight edges and the matte grey texture of the plasterboard.

"It won't when the plastering's been done, I promise," he said. "Mark's already at it down in the end room there. I've told him everything you said, don't worry—wobbly edges and not too regular. I think it goes against the grain a bit. He's not used to doing it badly on purpose."

"Thanks, Rick. I'd hate it to look like new."

"I'll take my hammer to it then, shall I? A few holes here and there?"

"No need to go that far."

She went downstairs and sat on the doorstep. The builders' radio was playing Radio 3, which meant old Andrew must have been the last one to get at the tuning dial. The next one past would have it back on a pop channel, she knew. Someone was sawing upstairs and the house was loud with their footsteps and their hammering. Through the window of the caravan, framed by dirty orange curtains, she could see the jewellery specialist's head bent over the table, working away, groping indirectly nearer to a truth that she knew she could reach by a much straighter path. She imagined the ring as it would look when clean and the noises around her faded away as her mind went somewhere else, stepping straight into a deep puddle of memory for the second time that day.

The caravan went and the trees shuffled around. Monmouth, long hair tied roughly back, was standing in the lane, far too proud for the smock they'd put him in. They wanted him gone, out of the way, now he was fed and changed. Madox, risking his neck to guide them, was waiting impatiently for Grey and Byser to follow and old, wasted Mother Mogg, the last person they wanted to see, the woman with the biggest mouth in Penselwood, hobbled into view around the corner with her eyes widening at the unexpected sight of strangers. Then the Duke, taking in the old woman's scrofulous swollen neck, instead of turning his back and hurrying away, was advancing towards her like the Lord God with hands spread out to touch her on the neck and Mother Mogg was recoiling and staring at him in wonder as he blessed her in tones that belied the smock.

Grey had pulled him away, back into the yard, as Mother Mogg had gone off at her best speed, looking constantly back.

"Do NOT do that, sir."

"She has the King's Evil. I have the touch. I *am* the rightful king. I must cure when I can and that will be one of the signs."

"It's *your* neck you must save now," Grey said, then looked back at Ferney and Gally with a grim face. "Hide all well. Do not be found with traces of us or it will go badly for you," and then Madox had urged them away.

In a space in the middle of the yard, a woman's face appeared, hanging in the air and said, "I say, do come and look." The caravan slowly developed around it as Gally fought her way back. Victoria Melhuish was staring at her. "Do come and see," she repeated. "It's come up well."

The ring lay on a square of cloth on the table. There was an astringent smell in the air and a small array of plastic bottles was ranged next to it.

"Thank you so much for letting me see it," the woman said. "I think you've made quite an important find here." She picked the ring up carefully. "Do you see the cypher?"

Under the crystal, below the king's enamelled head was a device of two intersecting semicircles.

"The double C," she said. "Charles the Second, done in gold wire. Now that doesn't by itself mean it was a royal ring but it *is* present on the rings that we know Charles gave to special favourites, and there are some other rather special things about this ring. Look at the hoop for one thing."

The outside of the hoop was decorated with damaged enamel in an intricate pattern, gold showing through the black. Inside, Gally could see lettering.

"Use this." Victoria Melhuish held out the magnifier.

" 'Prepared be to follow me,' " read Gally.

"Now," said the other woman, "I've freed the bezel, though we have to be careful. It swings round, you see. There's the crystal and the portrait on the front and there's the signet ring on the back." She took the ring and gently turned the bezel round. Gally used the magnifier again and found herself looking at an indented shield.

"It's the Stuart royal arms," the woman said, "and do you see the initials? They're reversed too, of course."

"JC?" said Gally.

"That's right. Now this might be a coincidence but there is a record of a royal ring given to the Duke of Monmouth and those initials would fit."

"I thought he was Jamie Scott."

Victoria Melhuish raised an eyebrow in appreciation. "That was the country name for him, I think, but in all the court references he was known as James Crofts."

"JC."

"Well, we mustn't jump to conclusions, but it certainly needs further study and the inscription is rather interesting."

" 'Prepared be to follow me.' You think that was Monmouth's call to arms?"

"Oh no, not for a moment. I should think Charles might have had that engraved as a gentle reminder to his natural son that he owed his loyalty to his father. The question is really, how did this come to be under your step?"

"Yes, that is the question, isn't it?"

"Of course with what happened after Sedgemoor, anything identifying Monmouth's supporters was better off buried."

A tickle of unease.

"Because it was dangerous?"

"George Jeffreys and the Bloody Assize? I should say so. I think they executed a hundred and fifty in Taunton alone, didn't they?"

They'd come in the night looking for friends of Richard Madox. The knowledge hit Gally like a punch. She flinched and the woman looked at her, surprised, but mistook it for an invitation to carry on.

"Well, King James didn't want any more plots so he made quite sure everybody got the message. There's a horrific royal warrant telling them how to do it." Victoria Melhuish had an odd enthusiasm about her that suggested her tight elegance restrained something darker. "They had to hang some of them, then quarter them, boil the bits and coat them in tar. Then they displayed . . ."

"No, stop. That's enough." Gally lurched out of the caravan and was loudly sick into the nettles.

"Oh my goodness. I am so sorry," said the woman, appearing at the caravan doorway behind her with a concerned look. "Was it what I said?"

"Not your fault," said Gally weakly. "I'm pregnant."

Boilman and Burnman. The names rang in her head. Boilman and Burnman.

"Are you all right now?"

Gally nodded.

"It's a question of what happens to the ring now, you see. I wondered whether it would be best if I took it to the museum for proper conservation. It should be catalogued."

There was no strength left in her for argument.

"Oh . . . I suppose . . ."

Mike drove blessedly in at that moment, the car's roofrack loaded with sagging rolls of matting, interrupting them. Gally introduced them.

"I was just asking your wife if it would be all right to take the ring to the museum." She smiled at Mike brightly.

Mike had the sense to defer to Gally and the brief pause had let her catch her breath. She felt a sharp sense of anxiety. "How long would you need it?"

Victoria Melhuish pondered her words. "Well, the important thing is that the law has to be observed, of course. You've done exactly the right thing by informing the museum and of course there'll have to be a coroner's enquiry."

"About what?" said Gally, startled.

"Ah. Perhaps you don't know the system. It would probably be classed as treasure trove, you see."

"Would it?"

"Any gold or silver object found hidden with its ownership unknown belongs to the crown. Something like this, of historical importance, would usually go to the museum. You would be compensated for its value, of course."

I don't want compensation, Gally thought wildly. What does she

FERNEY — 243

mean, "ownership unknown"? It was given to me. She opened her mouth to say so and in a confusion of doubt stopped herself in time. Mike, watching her closely, seemed to pick up on her distress.

"I'm sure compensation's not the issue," he said. "Perhaps we can discuss it then bring it over in the next few days."

The woman raised an eyebrow and looked doubtful and Mike plunged on. "Not, of course, that we doubt what you say, but we've never met you before . . ."

The woman looked rather shocked as if her honesty was being impugned. "Oh, I see. Well, you could always ring the museum if you're in doubt."

"Yes, we will," said Mike, ushering her towards her car.

"You will put the ring somewhere safe, won't you?" she said as she got in reluctantly. "It must have quite a considerable commercial value."

When she'd gone, Gally gave Mike a hug. "Thank you. I thought she was planning to go off with it right there."

"Poor you."

"They'll have to have it, though—won't they?"

"Do you feel bad about that?"

She looked at the ring. Boilman and Burnman and tarred joints of quartered humans hung on hooks to scare the people out of ever massing against their king again. She shuddered. "No, perhaps not."

SHE PARKED AT Yeovil Hospital and made her way, despite misdirection, to Ferney's ward. She was nervous. The sister told her where to go.

"He's doing all right," she said. "He keeps us in stitches with the funny things he says."

"What sort of funny things?"

"Oh, it's the medication, I expect, but he does have some odd ideas. When Dr. Barraclough asked him if it was his first heart attack, he said he'd had lots."

Ferney was propped up in bed, very pale, and she couldn't at first see anything but the old man's body around him. He saw her immediately and gave a small smile.

"How are you?"

"Still here," he said.

"What have you been saying? The sister's asking questions."

Ferney made a face. "I'm not quite myself sometimes and they keep giving me these chemicals." He shrugged it off. "Did you read my letter?"

"Look, Ferney, before we get to that, I wasn't sure if I should come—in case it was bad for you. It does feel different now, though. At your house, I felt I was killing you by being too close. Does that make sense?"

"Killing? No. Helping me die, maybe."

"I don't feel that now."

"They've propped me up with chemicals and that. Life's hung its hat up again. It'll be that way for a while. I want an answer, Gally. Did you read my letter?"

"Yes."

"It shocked you."

"Of course it shocked me."

"Have you . . . have you been able to check it?"

"Well, not really. Not yet. Other things came instead."

He watched her closely and she forgot his frailty in those time-less eyes.

"Do you remember seeing your first clock?" she said.

He looked puzzled, then thought about it and nodded. "We both saw it."

"Well, tell me then," she said. "You and me—we went to see it. Where was it?"

"Shaston, I think. Yes, I'm sure."

Shaston. It was just a daydream then. Shaston, not Shaftesbury. Shaston?

"Where is Shaston?" she said slowly.

"Shaftesbury now, isn't it? They called it Sophonia for some silly reason for a while, way back when, but it was Shaston for a long time—oh, right up to recently."

She surprised herself by feeling pleased.

"You remembered that by yourself," he said and his eyes gleamed.

"Yes," and she couldn't restrain her smile.

He gripped her hand. "What did you remember about it?"

"You—on the way back, saying it was the end of eternity and all our time would have a price on it from then on."

"Huh. I was right, too, wasn't I?"

"You were."

"Do you remember what it was like before?"

"Tell me."

"There was that daft man. Some lord or other, I forget. Anyway he had the old manor for a time and he saw what the monks did over at

Stavordale—they had this great water clock they filled up every day and every night for their services, so he had to have one too. That was the way—that and candles. But there wasn't such a thing as a regular hour, you see. They just divided up the daytime in twelve and the nighttime into another twelve. It meant an hour on a summer day was twice as long as it was in winter. Do you remember that?"

She shook her head. "So was that better or worse?"

"Neither of them was any damn good, but the Church liked the new clocks. The Church was all about keeping the poor in their place, always was. The merchants with their special pews, they saw the possibilities of the clocks right off. Poor old eternity never stood a chance." He looked out of the window for a moment. "Oh, that was a real time of change. They tell you about the Industrial Revolution at school, this recent one, like it was the only one. That was the real revolution, though, back then. All kinds of things, cranks, cams, springs, gears—all coming one after the other. That's what really changed life. Sometimes for the better, too, I have to admit."

"When was that?" she asked, thinking, how far back did I get?

"The clock? I wish I'd remembered exactly, but I've tried to work it out since. As near as I can get I reckon it was 1348."

That was a date that rang horrible bells and he saw it dawning on her. "Funny isn't it?" he said. "Maybe just exactly then, when you and I were listening to that clock chiming, there was some seaman getting off his little sailing ship just down on the coast there at Melcombe, wondering why he didn't feel so good. I don't know what month it was but the Black Death came in on its ship in August, the books say. You could probably remember it yourself if you try. You've cracked it now, I reckon. If you just work at it, you'll get anything you want back."

"I don't feel in control. I really need to talk to you about the bad bits."

"The nightmares."

"Yes."

"I knew they might be a problem. I've been lying here worrying. When I gave you the drum it was meant to be the start of the explanation. I never thought I'd have a silly turn like this."

"A silly turn? You mean a heart attack."

"Whatever. Anyway I realized it probably made it all worse. These nightmares of yours—they'll be about what came after Monmouth. That man Jeffreys."

She took a deep breath. "Boilman and Burnman. They've been in my head for years. I thought it was my father dying, you see? I thought it was because he'd burned up, but I was wrong, wasn't I? It was Jeffreys and the Bloody Assize and that's why the drum frightens me, the ring and the drum. This woman came from the museum to look at the ring and she told me a bit."

"Don't dwell on that," he said. "It wasn't a good time."

"I need to know. You know I do. It's the only way I can get rid of it. You said as much yourself. Those two, they've been my nightmares ever since I was old enough to remember." Ever since well before the car crash, she suddenly realized for the first time.

"They would be. You see, all those cloth workers round our way that marched with the Duke, they came looking for them afterwards. Everyone accusing everyone else. Jeffreys, he was a true sadist. They grabbed me, took me in. Do you remember that?"

She shook her head.

"We'd buried the ring, but we only had time to tuck the other things, the swords and the armour, away in the roof. There was an old woman saw Monmouth with us."

"Mother Mogg."

"You remember that?"

"Just a bit of it."

"Well, well. She must have said something. They came searching for Madox and for me. They would have searched the roof, only you thought up some clever trick and distracted them, but like I say, they took me away."

"And?"

"You know what they did with the bodies of the people they killed?"

She nodded. "I think I do."

"The man who boiled up the bits for Jeffreys—they called him Tom Boilman ever after. He was struck by lightning in the end. Burnman, his real name was Raphael. He provided the wood for the fires, tended them carefully, helped Boilman pour the tar. Nobody would ever talk to him from then on. He wasted away."

An image of butchered, blackened flesh kept trying to creep out into the open and she pushed it away. The guilt she always felt, the guilt that had always seemed to belong, in defiance of logic, to the car crash. Was that because she'd let him down? Was she somehow responsible for his death?

"What did they do to me?" she said in a voice that shook.

"Scared you and threatened you. Took you to the boiling. Told you I'd be next into the pot in pieces if you didn't save my life by admitting everything."

"And did I?" she said fearfully.

"No, of course you didn't. You had far too much sense. You knew the best chance for both of us was if you said nothing. All that time, knowing the drum was up in our roof and the ring was under the step, you held out and in the end you fooled them. A lot of people came to an end then, but not you and not me because you were brave."

She breathed again. It might not spell the immediate end for the nightmares but she knew at that moment she would be able to set them in their place, that—given time—she could now think them through. A huge burden had been lifted, but there remained a part of it that the story hadn't touched.

"No one died because of me, because of something I did?"

"No one," he said, puzzled. "Is something troubling you?"

She shook her head. It must be her father then. That at least would still dog her even if the nightmares went.

"It was such a cruel time," he said. "You and I, we've seen all sorts of cruelty. Most cruelty is fear, really. People do it to you in case you're going to do it to them. The more afraid they are inside, the crueller they are. Cruelty gives them the feeling it will always happen to someone else, not to them. It's different for us. We've been through enough pain to know we won't ever take any pleasure in it."

"Is this a better time to be alive?"

"Better than some," he said. "Better than the plague times. We didn't get to stop long then. Proper revolving door that was, either busy being born or busy dying."

She smiled. "Isn't that a line from a song?"

"I must have heard it somewhere. Not that the Death was all bad. Lots of land to go round afterwards and it got rid of a lot of priests."

Gally looked up to see a recently familiar face heading for Ferney's bed, a face above a dog collar.

"Here's one it didn't get rid of," she said quietly.

"I don't want to see him," said Ferney aghast.

"I can hardly stop him," Gally hissed.

"Tell him I've got the Black Death," said Ferney far too loudly.

The man wheeled to an uncoordinated halt beside the bed. "Mr. Miller? Oh hello again, Mrs. Martin. How nice to see you here. Always nice when the younger ones take the trouble. I'm Roger Wigglesworth, the stand-in vicar. Heard you were laid up, Mr. Miller, so I thought I'd pop in. Did I hear you were talking about the Black Death?"

"I'd better tell you I'm not a Christian," said Ferney bluntly. "If you've got others who are waiting on your visit, you'd better not be wasting your time on me."

"Oh gosh. That makes me sound a bit like the RAC, stopping to help someone who isn't a member," said the vicar, simpering slightly. "The fourth emergency service, what? Rushing to the emergency after the ambulance. That's rather good. I might use that."

"They'd sack an RAC man if he went round doing that," said Ferney but the vicar took no notice, pulled up a chair and sat down. Ferney glared at him. "That's what they did in the Black Death," he said. "Except there weren't any ambulances."

"Jolly brave, those priests, going in to minister, don't you think?"

"Jolly dead most of them. Bloody fools thought it was all fore-doomed, thought only the sinners would die. Didn't do 'em much good."

Wigglesworth gave a vague smile that turned into a frown. "You can't hold *that* against them, surely?"

"Maybe not, but there's a lot of other things."

"Oh dear. Are we so very bad? A lot of people have gained a lot of support from the . . . you know . . . the *unchanging* Church."

"Unchanging? *Unchanging?*" said Ferney incredulously. "It changes every time you take your eye off it."

Gally saw a slightly manic look come across his face and wondered if she should try to shut him up.

The vicar kept trying to find his smile again. "What *do* you mean, Mr. Miller?"

"Well all those miracles and saints and things when everyone was stupid enough to believe in rubbish like that. Then Protestants and Catholics and Protestants again and Puritans. Not being *allowed* to play games, then *having* to. Burning the maypoles and making new ones."

The vicar was trying his best. "This is, er . . . the Reformation you're referring to?"

"Of course it is. A new religion every ten minutes and onto the fire with anyone who disagrees. What's God got to do with that?"

"Well, that was rather a long time ago . . ."

"No it wasn't. Then there's class, that's another thing. Pews you weren't allowed to sit in because they were for the smart set and I even remember one vicar who served different communion wine. Expensive stuff for the nobs and rubbish for the rest of us."

"Dear me. I'd never do that in my church." He had no idea that Ferney, adrenaline reacting with his medication, was in free fall back through time and he grabbed for a straw. "So you were a churchgoer once, Mr. Miller?"

"Only when they passed the laws forcing you to go."

"But surely there's never been a law that says . . ."

Gally broke in. "I think perhaps this is a bit much for him, Mr. Wigglesworth. Maybe it's time we left him alone to get some rest."

"Oh yes," said the vicar hastily. "I'm sure you're right. Goodbye then, Mr. Miller, I hope you're up and about again soon."

"I'll have time for religion when it has time for me," Ferney said to his retreating back, "and when it takes account of all the other planets out there and when it stops telling people they can ruin the earth in any way they please because it was put there for our convenience."

The vicar had gone.

"He came a long way to see you," Gally said with a hint of reproach.

"I wish he hadn't."

"Just because he's . . ."

". . . a vicar it doesn't mean he's not a good person," Ferney finished for her.

Gally clenched her fists. "Look, let me say it by myself. I may have said it a million times before, but don't do that to me." There was a silence in which Ferney turned his face away. "Have I said it a million times before?" she asked more gently.

"A few times," he said.

"Am I wrong?"

"No, you're not wrong." He turned back towards her. "They call it a rock, their Church, like granite. Always there, always the same, but we've seen it twisting and turning. Okay, there have been plenty of good people in it, but it's been part of the government much too often for me, part of the whole setup for persuading all the poor, suffering people that the entire unfair business was for the best. Oh and the blood that's been spilt. Henry and Bloody Mary and Elizabeth, ducking and weaving and changing the rules and having people killed who said their prayers the wrong way. It made people forget to think for themselves, you see." He grabbed her wrist and held it tightly. "Follow the sovereign, they always said, it's the sovereign's duty to choose. We do what he says and God won't be cross. Crap. The Church helped invent the class system. It gave all the land-grabbers the best pews. It told us to obey them. Don't ask *me* to respect that."

"Well, that puts the last two thousand years in their place," said Gally faintly.

"Hey, don't you forget, we've been around well over half of that. We're entitled to a view."

The sister arrived, took Ferney's pulse and tutted. "Are you getting worked up, Mr. Miller? And after that nice man came all this way?" She looked at Gally. "Mrs. Martin, the doctor said could he have a quick word. In my office?"

"I'll be back," said Gally, pressing Ferney's hand as he lay back on the pillow looking suddenly exhausted.

The doctor was middle-aged and looked depressed. In a hospital full of youngsters fresh to medicine or older, rich consultants, he was clearly neither.

"Mrs. Martin, Sister told me you were here. I just wanted to have a word about Mr. Miller."

"Yes?" she said, surprised.

"I'm afraid we have found some signs of another possible problem with him. It requires a bit of further exploration, but it may be that he has a growth on his intestine."

"Stomach cancer?"

"Well, it's only a possibility. We're not certain, of course. It's a question of whether we should tell him or not."

"Why are you asking me?"

"You are his granddaughter, are you not?"

"No, I'm not."

The doctor looked at his file in confusion. "Oh, I am so sorry—but he's put you down here as next-of-kin so I assumed . . ."

"I see." That was a poser. "Well, it's certainly true that he doesn't have any closer relatives. I think you should tell him everything."

"You know him well, do you?"

"I've known him for a very long time."

"It's just that there have been occasions when he's said some odd things and we weren't entirely sure that the balance of his mind was holding up. He told Sister yesterday that he wanted nothing but raw onions and marjoram. He said he'd been eating it for the last five hundred years and he wasn't going to stop now. Then there's this business of the heart attacks."

"Don't worry. Just ignore that sort of thing. He's very sane really."

"I'm glad you think so."

She went back into the ward again and sat by Ferney who looked a slightly better colour. "What did you say to the sister yesterday about your food? The doctor thinks you're bonkers."

Ferney looked blankly at her. "Food? Nothing."

"Something about marjoram."

"Nothing wrong with that."

"You told her you'd been eating it for the last five hundred years."

He looked abashed. "It's this stuff they give me. I can't always remember what I'm not supposed to say. You're still a vegetarian, aren't you?"

"Still?" Oh, good heavens, she thought, and I believed it was my own moral, rational decision. This me, not some me from way back. "That is irritating," she said.

He understood. "We know what's good for us, you and me—vegetables, milk and fruit. We know all the other things to steer clear of. What do you make of supermarkets?"

The question felt rather fierce.

"They . . . they worry me."

"Why?"

"All that distance things have to travel, I think. From halfway round the world, most of them, just so we can find we've let the fresh mangoes go rotten in February."

"I'm glad you realize. We've always been in touch with the seasons. Our bodies' needs change with the seasons. You shouldn't live the same right through the year. Spring and summer, that's when you need the quick sugar. Winter's for the slow-burning foods. Now it's all muddled up—it's not surprising people don't know whether they're coming or going. I think all this youth crime has something to do with that, though I must say, I suppose it's been worse in the past."

"Is there anything you want?"

"I was serious about the marjoram. Next time you come, can you bring me some and maybe a bit of lavender and either onions or some garlic. It's good for this." He rubbed his heart. "If I've got to go on a bit longer, I'd rather do it with my own stuff than their chemicals."

"Speaking of going," she said, "I must get back. Mike needs the car. He's going to be taking it with him, so I may not be able to get here except at weekends."

Mention of Mike made his eyes cloud. "You stay away from cars," he said, looking at her stomach meaningfully. "Tell him thank you from me."

"One last thing. We've got the drum. What happened to the swords and the armour?"

"Funny you should ask. I was thinking about that. I don't know."

"Why not?"

"I've never quite worked it out. It's all to do with a lad called Billy Bunter. I'll tell you the story some other time."

He watched her stand up. "And Gally?"

"Yes."

"What I said in the letter? Try to remember it yourself. Please?"

22

THE DELIVERY VAN driver, due Wednesday morning, precipitated another small crisis when he arrived late on Wednesday afternoon. Gally had finished the last of the small stock of fresh fruit and vegetables in the caravan's cupboard and as Penselwood had no shop she had been planning a long walk to Bourton and perhaps even a bus ride further on to Mere to stock up. Waiting for the driver knocked that one on the head. The builders were all off on another job. The plasterer had gone for fresh supplies and showed no immediate sign of returning, the plumber and electrician weren't due again until the next day and she had nothing obvious to do to occupy the time except some more gardening while she waited. What the driver, a balding rural chauvinist to whom she seemed almost invisible, eventually brought with him was the next problem. She had been expecting a fridge. She got a fridge and a freezer.

"This can't be for us," she said doubtfully.

The driver looked at his clipboard. "Says it is here."

"Where?"

"Whirlpool fridge and freezer. See? Matching pair. All paid for."

Mike's carbon signature, faint but undeniable, was on the delivery copy.

She sighed. "All right."

"Nice surprise from your old man, was it? If I'd have known I'd have put a ribbon round it."

"Not exactly."

He trolleyed both machines into the kitchen. "Where do you want them?"

"You can leave them there. I'll sort it out."

"Better wait 'til he gets here before you try and move them."

He went blessedly, leaving her in the silence to walk warily round the intrusive white boxes in the middle of the floor. The sketched layout they had made of the way the kitchen would be was pinned to a window frame. She took it down to look at it. The fridge was clearly marked but that was all. They had never talked about a freezer and it annoyed her that Mike had gone out and bought one without even mentioning it to her.

She'd never liked frozen food.

That thought came from nowhere and startled her with its truth and made her look again at the feelings the delivery had stirred up. In London she bought fresh food as a matter of course, but that required little conscious choice with open shops always close by. Ferney had said ignore the supermarkets, live naturally, stay in tune with what the seasons offered. She identified the seeds of her dislike of the freezer in those words, but the thought had opened a tiny, exciting window on the last time round. When did frozen food first appear? she wondered. She recognized the tingle of distant familiarity that marked an idea from before. So far they all seemed to feel like that, in that brief first stage before recognition brought them ballooning out. The life just past, the missing life between Cochrane's brutal act and this present time, must be the source of her feelings on freezers and she found that she very much wanted to be able to fill in that blank. Sitting on a stool, trying to quieten her mind and open it to memory's tendrils, she cast a mental hook baited with images of frozen food but nothing rose to take it.

Perhaps it's because I'm rooted here, she thought. This place fed and fuelled my other lives so I can find them again but not this last one. One day maybe I'll wander down the right road and the lock will open and I'll suddenly know. That held frightening suggestions that there were black holes dotted around the country with the power to pull her in and maroon her if travel took her in the wrong direction. The freezer went hand in hand with the idea of driving, two unpleasant and dangerous developments. Ferney manages, she thought, remembering his rooms with the videos and the tea-making machine—but he does it by being very selective about what he takes from the devices on offer. It's not that we're stuck in the mud—more that we've learnt enough to know what's good for us. We've had long enough to find out, after all.

Mike came back on Friday evening expecting praise for his thoughtfulness and generosity in ordering the freezer and, feeling it was unfair to do otherwise, she gave it to him. She made him a cup of tea and took him into the house where he was suitably amazed by the progress.

"Not long now," he said. "Won't it be nice to move in?"

"Oh yes."

"It's your birthday next week."

"We won't be moving in time for that."

"That wasn't what I was going to say. I've had this idea for a present, but I think it's something I'd better talk about with you first."

"All right, if you think so."

"I've just had a look at something I thought you'd really like."

His eyes were sparkling with suppressed excitement. She would have preferred the surprise and thought perhaps it was more that he couldn't keep it to himself than that he really needed her opinion.

"It's a little Citroën—a 2CV. It's a very nice one, red and white, hardly used at all. It would be brilliant round here."

She was instantly glad that he hadn't surprised her with it.

"Oh, Mike. I . . . I don't need a car." She tried to say it kindly, but his eyes showed hurt. "It's a lovely idea but I really enjoy *not* having one."

"It hardly counts as a car, you know. They don't use up much petrol. I just thought you could be so stuck up here by yourself. I mean, winter's coming up and if I'm away all week . . ."

"I'll manage fine," she said. A car meant risk. Could she have it and just drive it locally? No, there'd always be the temptation to go further afield. "I tell you what. Why don't you buy me a bike instead? I want something traditional, you know, shiny dark green with three gears and a basket on the front with handlebars that bend round at the end and one of those metal cases round the chain to stop my skirt getting dirty."

"You don't wear skirts," he said glumly. "I'm sure you'd find a car would make a difference. I mean look at this week, you could have gone to see the old man whenever you wanted."

"I'll go tomorrow in your car."

He stopped arguing and went very quiet, showing her just a corner of his sulk without displaying enough to prompt an accusation. She was left thinking about the triangular trap of cars, freezers and a village with no shops. It wasn't a question of convenience. There was no argument on that score and Ferney, she knew, would have been all in favour of cars if it just came down to that. It was the danger—that was the point—the danger of being out of range of this magnet of theirs when the time came. She had a wild vision of taking the Bag Stone with her strapped on the roof of a little Citroën, and almost giggled, but that would have made it worse with Mike and she managed to stop herself in time.

The next morning she drove carefully to Yeovil, shopped for Ferney's mixed bag of herbs and vegetables. Ironically she could only find fresh marjoram in the local supermarket after trying everywhere else, but she took the cellophane wrapping with its bar code off before she took it with her to the hospital.

Ferney was not alone. Mr. and Mrs. Carson, a dour elderly pair from Lancashire who were his neighbours, were there before her, paying a duty visit. Mrs. Carson had a face of astonishing narrowness under a frothy hairdo. She looked perfectly normal in profile but as soon as she turned to give Gally a fleeting acknowledgement, her face shrank to an axe blade.

"They don't give you much space for your things, Mr. Miller," she said with a sniff. "Mr. Carson wouldn't like that."

"Yes," said her husband.

"That's not what I call a pillow. We brought you a newspaper. Mr. Carson started the crossword for you."

"Mrs. Martin is repairing Bagstone Farm," said Ferney as Gally stood awkwardly at the end of the bed.

"Oh yes," said Mrs. Carson showing no interest whatsoever. She was a picture window person.

"It was kind of you to come to see me," Ferney said to them with a glance at Gally. "I don't want to keep you."

"You're not," said Mrs. Carson. "We bought a two-hour car park ticket. Mr. Carson only had a pound coin."

It was clear they had no intention of leaving before they'd used it up so Gally, marginalized at the end of the bed throughout a conversation of stilted awkwardness, didn't stay long despite the desperation in Ferney's eyes. In fact she was quite glad to have that excuse because she knew that, left alone, he would only have asked her the central question again and she had as yet no answer.

She spent the following week at the cottage, rooted as much in the present as was possible, making sure the radio was on during every waking minute, listening closely to every word spoken on Radio 4, even the repeats, as she moved along in the plasterer's wake, painting each room before it was really dry enough, glad that the hot weather was continuing.

All the time she was aware of the disturbing new tool at her disposal, the tool which should allow her to uncover whatever she wanted to know about her long partnership with the house, but she had all the anxiety of a new skipper taking a yacht out for the first

time into a sea that felt full of shoals just below the surface, waiting
to tear off her keel and capsize her. Once again something inside her
objected that Ferney had been unfair to introduce her so roughly to
this unexpected world, leaving her standing in front of a crumbling
dam of memory, fearing that a wrong move could cause a collapse
that would sweep her completely away. As long as she was vigilant it
was possible to avoid stirring up the memories, and most of the time
she was happy to resist the temptation. There were no more nightmares, though when, in safe daylight, she tested herself with the
burning car, the same old cold tendril of accusation clutched at her.

The following week, as signs of autumn started to stiffen the
leaves, the hospital rang to say they would be performing an ex-
ploratory operation now that Ferney was well enough to stand it. On
the Friday afternoon, when the clock told her the operation was
under way, she sat in an armchair on the bare boards of the upstairs
room that would soon be their bedroom. It was painted a soft yellow
and she knew it had long been a favourite place, but she did not wish,
for the moment, to dwell on that in case it transported her to unexpected times. As she sat there she felt an unfamiliar physical sensation, a convulsion inside her of tiny, intricate power—a deliberate
tickle from the wrong side of her skin. Until logic came to her rescue
she was startled, then she recognized the movement as her baby's first
kick and delight calmed her. Putting both hands on her swelling
stomach, she waited, wanting to feel another kick with a strong sense
that suddenly this was somebody inside her, but in the next breath
that thought brought apprehension. Ferney was on the operating
table. Did life's waxing here mean it was waning there?

The hospital were bland on the phone. They were running a bit
behind with the operation schedule. Yes, Mr. Miller was perfectly
all right. He was being prepared for surgery. Had anyone checked
him recently? Yes of course they had. There was an unspoken "for
heaven's sake" in the nurse's reply.

Gally couldn't stay in the house after that and the place she most
and least wanted to be was the hilltop. Present fear defeated past
peace. The hilltop carried Ferney's question with it and sufficient
unto tomorrow was the evil thereof. Mike wasn't due home until
after seven o'clock. Instead, she walked northeast, past the sloping
field called Kingsbury Bars, then where the road swung round left she
went straight on into the almost hidden mouth of the narrow muddy
path, Long Lane, which had been left alone when the age of cars selected a handful of the tracks for tarmac promotion. The lane teemed
with old experience, but to suppress its ghosts she thought resolutely

of modern plans, of moving into the house. Mike saw no reason to wait, though the builders had another three or four weeks' work downstairs, but she didn't want to share the house with anybody else, preferring to stay in the caravan until the night when it was really all theirs. For an appalling moment the thought crept in that she didn't even want to share it with Mike, but she pounced on that one, declared it alien, dismissed it as a bad joke from some dark recess and refused to think about it any further. Past Kite's Nest Farm, she reached the field path north to Pen Mill and turned onto it. The land fell to the wooded bottom where the Egbert Stone stood in the swampy spread of the river and teased her with changes and dislocations in its fence lines and borders that niggled at her without making themselves quite plain.

It came to her out of the landscape that it would not be possible to go on suppressing any of the events that made her what she was. Doing so gave her the constant feeling that someone else owned her values, someone else decided her attitudes, some locked-off past person had already made up her mind for her on right and wrong. She stood there quite still, looking round this border corner of her country, feeling it trying its best to speak to her, knowing she had to learn to listen to it all or else be constantly ambushed by it. To reclaim ownership of herself, she could see no other way but to learn to navigate through all the stacked-up varieties that preceded *this* Gally, not just the direct and pressing causes of distress but all the rest of it too. My life is an iceberg, she thought. Far more than two thirds of it is below the water and in the end I have no choice but to dive down to see what is there and if that is the case, then I suppose I had better begin now.

For need of a predictable starting point, which seemed the best of reasons, she went on walking until she arrived at the same spot by the hedge across the shallow valley from the castle mound where she had waited for Mike and met Ferney and where she already knew she had met the Breton Ferney, newly arrived from his epic Channel crossing. She even knew the words he had said again to her so recently. She failed to remember the tiny warning that had come unbidden earlier that same day just before Mike saw Ferney at work in the pit. Then, she had looked down at the open grassland valley below the old Norman castle where the water meadows had once been and where the Frenchmen had . . . Had what? She hadn't known the end of it then and she forgot the start of it now. The hermit crab trace of memory had withdrawn into its shell, pushed back by the

events of the rest of that day and now she failed to remember that
half-formed fear.

Sitting down on the grass by the hedge there seemed to be no hurry
at all. She looked out across the combe, dotted with sheep grazing the
short grass. A line of bushes marked the course of the stream that ran
along its bottom down to the Stour at its end, and on the far side the
roof of the house just below the castle mound showed neat and grey,
two small upper windows peering over its thick hedge under eyebrows of thatch. The trees were clustered around the castle. There
was an undeniable excitement in her at the idea that she could conjure up a world in which she would see for the first time, recognize
and immediately love a younger Ferney. She would find out what it
had been about the Breton boy that had identified him to her so
quickly and what it felt like to be of an age with him when all life and
all love lay ahead in delightful certainty. It felt almost as if she was
about to launch on an affair.

Bien sûr, c'est moi, she said and nothing came. That *was* what he
had said. *Bien sûr. Bien sûr. Bien sûr, c'est moi.* The litany felt thin
and pointless. Perhaps I'm thinking about it in the wrong way, she
thought. Cumulus clouds drifted to the northeast on the warm autumn wind and she stayed in French in her head, remembering a line
from a poem: *"J'aime les nuages, les nuages qui passent. Là-bas, là-
bas, les merveilleux nuages."*

There came an immediate harsh echo: *"Là-bas, là-bas,"* and she
looked down into a valley where the sheep had gone and the grass
was long and though she knew it was memory she was completely
and wholly there in it. The bushes were thicker along the stream and
out of them came a running man. The top of the hill across the combe
was bare, piled with fallen tree trunks. On its very end the rising
walls of the keep, already over a man's height, glistened with fresh-
cut facets of stone. Fallen tree trunks were piled by the saw-pit and
the hammering of the masons had stopped. The only movement up
on the hill was the slow heaving of an ox team dragging a litter along
its summit with more rough stone lashed to it for the masons to cut.
Everyone up there was looking towards her, down into the valley.

Stone used like this spread terror. Cut stone was only familiar to
her as the everlasting material of the worshippers of God, something
to be slowly assembled into walls with painstaking care in a time
measured in years, not days. What they were heaving into being up
ahead of her with forced, brutal speed was something new—military
stone—a stone promise that the tyranny of these Normans was no

passing evil. These Frenchmen were not like the invaders they'd known many times. They were no Danish raiding party fading away to the roar of burning roofs and the sobbing reek of blood: they were putting up their stone wall weapons as a sign that they were here to stay and all others were now subject people.

All this passed through her head as a chemical curl of fear and the man, gasping with effort, toiled up the gentle slope towards her as his pursuers burst from the bushes behind him. It was Ferney, gaunt and shock-headed, his useless arm dangling at his side while the other swung with his body, urging him on. Three Normans shouting their jabber at each other were racing up behind him and she could see they would reach him long before he got to her. She stood up out of her concealment, desperate for a way to alter the inevitable slow intersection below.

Ferney saw her. "Run," he shouted, but then the first Norman reached him, swung a sword across the back of his legs and he went down with a scream. Fear froze her and she despised this body which let her down so often with its flooding, involuntary, paralysing timidity. She'd been overpoweringly afraid in the morning when they had discussed Ferney's intention, sitting outside the house, looking at the Bag Stone as spiders' webs glistened white across it in the early sun.

"I must go and see," he had said.

"They might do something to you."

"They'll do something to Edgar otherwise."

The ox driver had arrived early at the house, stooping under the low doorway and rubbing his eyes in the cooking smoke inside. He'd told them that their son was ill and working slowly and that the Normans, who had pressed every able-bodied man and boy in the village into their service to haul the stone, would show no pity on him if he could not keep up the pace this morning. Ferney had sat there mulling it over.

"It's clear," he'd said in the end, "I have to go. I'll offer myself in his place until he feels well."

She touched his withered arm. "They won't take you. They've already said as much."

"Which would they rather have, a sick boy or a crippled man?"

"You're not allowed onto the hill. They said so. Only the workers."

The ridge in Selwood Forest was yet again paying the price for its geography. Five years earlier the news that the Normans had landed had taken several weeks to solidify from rumour into fact in the southwest, but it soon became very clear that this was not at all like previous invasions. These men believed that as a dominant minority, force should be used right from the start. Harold's military system had been broken on the Sussex Downs and there was no organized resistance at first as the Frenchmen moved through the land, but three times in the intervening four years the west had exploded into revolt. It was never strong enough nor organized enough to stand a chance of success against William's forces, for its commanders had no way of knowing what other men the French had in reserve within two or three days' march. Gally was frightened all that time, so frightened that the strong guiding self within her simply could not contain the flooding panic of her betraying glands.

So Ferney had gone and she had wanted to say, "You are so much more important to me than our son," but she knew what he would have replied as if he had spoken the words: "This son is worthy of our best efforts. You and I have much more time together. This is a boy above most boys."

Now she stood for once, refusing to fly as two of the soldiers held Ferney down and one raised a sword that caught the sun, red and silver, and hacked it down on his back and his neck once, twice, three times. For the first time in this life anger overtook the fear and she found astonished feet carrying her down the hill towards them as fast as she could run while an unfamiliar voice screamed hysterical threats at the soldiers. They looked at her approaching. The leader laughed, kicked Ferney's body, wiped his sword on the grass and led his men back towards the growing castle. The look on his face said he knew it was crueller to keep her alive than to kill her too.

Gally knelt by Ferney's head and saw his eyelids flickering. She forced herself to look at his back and from the pumping blood, oozing, bubbling out of the sword's deep slashes in his tunic she knew there was no help she could bring to him except final comfort. A sense came to her of all the other widows she had been, lined up to help her through this. She crooned over Ferney, stroking his forehead, talking to him as she had to her babies, then she saw from the lips that were moving, trickling more blood, that he was trying to speak. She had to lie down next to him in the soaking red grass to get her ear close enough because she could not hurt him more by trying to move him.

"Edgar . . . dead," he said in a wet whisper. "Laugh . . . at me." His eyes closed and reopened with a jerk. "I hit the man," he said in a stronger voice. "No good." A gush of blood came from his mouth and stopped him speaking, but his eyes were still fluttering. She had her forehead against his so that he would know she was there. "Next time," she said, "next time we'll not let anyone else concern us," but next time seemed a very long way away to her. She sang a song to him, the old song Alfred's men had sung around the stone, a song of strength and liberation: "We shall meet when the fighting is past, we shall sing when the battle is done, we shall drink when we've broken our fast, we shall sleep when our freedom is won."

He lay very still, the breath bubbling faintly and his eyelids, which were all she could see because she was so close, slowed their move-ment until the instant when the last tremor of life sagged out of him in a slow exhalation and then she still lay there, as if she could delay recognition of the fact so long as she did not move. Her reaction to all that fear was deep sandbagging fatigue and she subsided into a dull trance on the wet, red earth. Unknown time passed and she convulsed into wakefulness to find blood stiffening in crusts on her skin and her tunic and his terrible, cold body staring at her with set, dead eyes.

It was no comfort at all to think of next time. There was just lone-liness to face, loneliness and the uncertainty of when or how they would find each other. She wanted death and knew that she was too afraid to find it deliberately for herself. She wished the soldiers had killed her too. Then horror took her and she stood up on shaky, numbed legs, gave one last look at him and ran in the twilight away from the castle.

The path took her south to the buildings around Pen Mill which were too large in the deepening darkness and shone bewildering yel-low light into the evening as if on fire within. She found it harder and harder to go on running and was amazed at her weakness, she who for all her timidity had the body of a hunting dog and could run for miles if she had to. She stumbled into the lane, slumped down on an earth bank and huge eyes rushed at her out of the darkness.

23

MIKE, SITTING MISERABLY in the caravan, could find nothing to make the time pass faster or to calm his agitation. Water was cooling in the kettle next to a cup still containing an unused teabag which he seemed to lack the concentration or the will to bring together. He would have paced up and down had there been space. It was a bad end to a horrible week. Giving lectures, he had been flying by remote control. In tutorials he had been too distracted and uninterested to detect and pounce on the evasions, generalizations and misunderstandings of his students and in the weekly business meeting of department heads he had completely missed the psychological moment to make a firm defence of his next year's budget. He kept thinking back to Gally's rejection of the car he had offered her. It was to have been the biggest present he had ever given her and from the moment he had conceived it he had been expecting delight and pleasure. Her response felt like a final rejection of everything he had once assumed about their new way of life. A cottage in the country, he had thought then, would bring variety into their life—a choice of places to be. Mobility had been an essential part of that, based on the idea that they could never be bored if they had the freedom to alternate between the city and the country.

It seemed to him that Gally, egged on no doubt by the old man, had changed the rules by taking to this place so totally that she saw no need for the means to get out of it. A car would have given her the freedom to surprise him. He had already started to fantasize, returning to their cold, dark flat with a takeaway on a mid-week London evening, that she might have decided magically to travel up and the place would be full of the life she would bring with her. Turning down the car cut him deeply. She seemed to be narrowing and simplifying herself and her range of interests as she followed Ferney up some mad garden path. Mike felt helpless, hamstrung by the knowledge that he didn't understand the fragile processes going on before his eyes and held back from further confrontation by the dreadful consequences of the last one. Ferney's illness and his own part in it had put the old man temporarily out of bounds in Mike's inherited value system.

Gally not being there when he returned twisted the knife further. He always told her when he'd be back, always rang if he was going to be late, relying on her welcome to dump the week's baggage from his mind. There was no sign of her in the house or around the land and he'd been to the gate several times to look up and down the lane. It took a full hour for irritation and unease to turn to straightforward worry and in the next thirty minutes Mike started imagining an enormous range of terrible things that might have happened to his wife. He could see plainly her blood-soaked body lying in a ditch. He could have no idea that her own picture of herself coincided with his in almost every detail.

Ages ticked by in the next ten minutes as he tried to pick a course of action—a trip round the lanes in the car seemed the best first step, but then the phone might ring and they had no answering machine. He would have blamed Ferney if he could, but for the fact that he was in hospital. A logical solution struck him. The hospital might have called her to Ferney's bedside. She might have gotten a lift, or a taxi maybe. It might have been a sufficient emergency to make her forget to leave him a note. He rang Yeovil. Mr. Miller was still under the anaesthetic they said, in the recovery room. Mike had forgotten all about the operation and that was a relief because that surely explained where Gally must be. Was his wife there? he asked. This was going beyond the accepted scope of his call, but they looked because he sounded so strained and reported that she was not and that Mr. Miller was to have no visitors until at least the following day. More agitated than ever, he put the phone down and headlights swept the caravan as a car came slowly into the yard. He went outside, facing their dazzle, nervous of what bad news might come stalking from beyond the lights.

A figure got out of the driver's side and a man's diffident voice said, "I've got someone in the back. We thought it might be your wife."

Mike was at the door instantly, staring at the quietly sobbing figure curled up in the dim yellow of the interior light.

"Gally? What's wrong?"

She shook her head, didn't answer.

The woman in the passenger seat was middle-aged, concerned. "We thought it was," she said. "She was in the road by the Mill, sort of collapsed."

"Has she been hurt?"

"I don't think so. We couldn't see anything. She's ever so upset. Colin thought we ought to come here first."

"Yes, thank you. I'll get her inside."

He reached in and tried to help Gally out. She seemed to have no knowledge of the geography of a car's interior, thrusting wildly with her hands and looking around her uncomprehendingly. He had to pull her arm quite hard to get her moving in the right direction, murmuring encouragement which failed to reach her and feeling panic rising in him at the strangeness of her. Colin was standing by, embarrassed and awkward, and his wife stayed firmly in her seat. When Gally finally stood clear of the car, hunched over and swaying, Mike put an arm round her and guided her towards the caravan. Colin followed them to the door. Mike sat Gally down on the foam cushions.

"I could call a doctor for you when we get home," Colin said.

"Er, no . . . thanks. There's a phone here if we need it." Mike felt an explanation was needed. "She's pregnant," he said. It didn't seem adequate, but Colin wasn't going to argue. "Thank you very much for bringing her home."

"Well, let us know if we can do anything."

"I will. Thanks again."

He didn't even know where they lived, but they left him alone then and drove away. He bent over Gally. Her clothes were wet and muddy. The side of her face was covered in mud and lightly scratched. She was still crying.

"What is it, love? What happened?"

"It's Ferney," she moaned. "He's dead. He's dead."

"No he's not," he said gently. "I rang the hospital. He's in the recovery room."

She looked past him with blank eyes. "He is dead. I saw him. They cut him open. I left him there."

"Gally. He's not dead, I promise. I've talked to them. They operated on him but he's all right."

"NO." It was a loud cry and he flinched away from her. "They hacked at him, with swords, because of Edgar."

"Oh." The nature of the matter finally began to dawn on Mike and he looked at Gally in sudden understanding. "It's one of those."

She cried, silently now, wringing her hands.

"Gally. Come on, leave it. Gally. This is Mike. You're back in the caravan. Some people found you in the road. You're okay now."

It had no effect. He sat beside her and put an arm round her shoulders, trying not to mind as she shrank away. "You're imagining this, Gally. It's 1990. You're in the caravan with me, Mike. Ferney's in hospital. He's all right."

"It's his blood," she said, picking at her sleeves in a frantic gesture that spelt insanity to him. "All over me. All of his blood."

"There's nothing on your clothes except mud, love. Come on now, it's time to snap out of it. You're in the caravan." He went on trying to reach her, using variations on the same phrases over and over again, sometimes supplicating, sometimes stern and once almost angry. It made no difference. In the end, when phoning a doctor seemed the only other resort, he acted on some instinct, reaching out to press the play button on the tape deck. James Taylor's voice came on, halfway through "Fire and Rain" which seemed an inappropriate choice with its lyrics of violent bereavement, but it seemed to get through to her where his own words could not. She became very still, then sagged back against the cushions breathing deeply, her eyes blinking and refocusing. She passed a hand over her forehead. "Jesus," she said, then after a long silence, "I'm sorry." He hugged her.

Haltingly she tried to tell him what had happened to her, but she couldn't put enough words together to make sense and as soon as he was able to shed his fear that she had been physically harmed it was muscled aside by growing anxiety at the state of her mind. She became very tired and the gaps between her words got longer so he lifted her legs up on the foam mattress, put a pillow under her head then sprawled, fully dressed, on the cushion opposite her for a long time in sleepless, silent alarm. Sometime after midnight an owl hooted close by and the next thing he knew was the smell of coffee, a hand stroking his cheek and Gally's smiling face looking down at him.

"Are you all right?" she said.

"I am, yes." He was groggy. "What about you, though?"

She grimaced. "I'm sorry. I didn't mean that to happen. I got locked into it."

"What *was* it?"

"A memory."

"Of what?"

"Something pretty horrid."

"You kept saying Ferney was dead. About men with swords."

She shook her head. "I don't want to go back over it."

"All right." He tried for a safe approach. "It's not very good for you, is it?"

She didn't answer.

"You got yourself in a real state yesterday. Those people were really shocked."

"What people?" She looked at him in surprise.

"I don't know. The couple with the car. The couple who found you."

She had her hand over her mouth, looking at him. "I don't remember. I thought *you* . . ."

"Gally. This is getting a bit scary. I just wonder whether we ought not to get some help, maybe."

"What sort of help?"

"A doctor. Something like that."

"You mean a psychiatrist, don't you?"

"Maybe," he said defiantly. "I'm worried about you."

"Mike," she said, patting his hand, "I'm not going off my rocker. I can . . . I can remember some things all by myself now, but—I don't know—all the bad things seem to come back easiest. I'll just have to be very careful."

"It's not good for you."

"I think it is."

"How can it be?"

She gave him a look of pity which showed she knew how difficult it must be for him to understand. "It helps me navigate. It stops me bumping into some of the things that would trip me up if I didn't know they were there. It really is helping."

"I thought it was. That's why I haven't really butted in, but I've never known you to have so many nightmares."

"No, they've stopped, at least for the last few days. I think I know what they were now, where they came from."

"Can you tell me?"

"Not now. Do you mind?"

"Later. When you can." He was trying to give her some space, although he felt an urgent need to know everything. "Who was Edgar?"

"Edgar? I don't know any Edgars. What do you mean?"

"Last night you said whatever happened to Ferney was because of Edgar."

She thought but nothing came. "I don't have any idea."

He took a deep breath. "You can't be sure about these . . . memories."

"I think I can."

"Do you know what a palimpsest is?"

"No."

"It's a document that's been written over lots of times. A thousand years ago when parchment was pretty scarce, they'd wash the ink off a sheet of manuscript or rub at it with pumice stone and use it again. It all got a bit murky when they'd done that a few times."

"Umm, I assume there's a reason why you're telling me this?"

"Sorry. A historian's clumsy parallel. I did a bit of reading last week. About memory and things, and that's more or less the way memory works."

"Why were you doing this? For a lecture?"

"No of course not. For us. I was wondering about Ferney and it struck me it would be pretty impossible to remember so much. Even if you believe him, the fact is the memory doesn't work like that. It makes a palimpsest every time. When you remember something, what you remember next time isn't that thing itself, it's the memory of remembering it, so it's always changing. You can't trust memories."

"You'd have to be pretty rigorous then," said Gally, "making quite sure you remembered everything just right, wouldn't you?"

"You wouldn't be able to. It would gradually change every time, wouldn't it? It would pretty soon be pure fiction, don't you think?"

"Do you really want to talk about this now?"

"Yes, I do. Look, you frightened me yesterday. You can't expect me to believe all this stuff, Gally. Last night was something else."

"Mike, you've always believed everything I've said until now, haven't you?"

"Yes."

"So either you believe me now or you have to think I've got a serious mental problem, right?"

Mike didn't want to be hung on that hook. "No, it's just I think Ferney's got some way of influencing you."

"Ferney is in hospital. Yesterday I was by myself and I was able to remember every detail of something that happened hundreds of years ago."

"I wish you'd tell me."

"I . . . Can we leave that for now?" It was out there waiting to pounce again and the worst part of it couldn't be kept from her mind—the pain of losing Ferney from any of her lives, and for Mike's sake she couldn't let him tease that out of her. The pain of her cowardice, too.

"How can you ask me to believe that?"

"Well perhaps all I'm asking is that you accept it for now, because as far as I'm concerned it is completely real."

Mike looked distraught. "Gally. Don't you see? If I accept it, then I have to accept that you're much more Ferney's than you are mine."

It was out in the open and he had to press the point. Her silence forced him on.

"It's very hard. I know you've found comfort. I think maybe you've even found some sort of healing, but it's cutting me out and I won't be cut out. I just don't understand what's going on. You keep telling me he's an old man, but sometimes when I see the look in your eyes I'm bloody glad he's not younger and I'm not even sure that's much comfort really. I can't help thinking of him as . . . well, as a rival."

This was such dangerous ground.

"I wouldn't choose to hurt you," Gally said gently. "I can't lie, though. I know for absolutely certain that Ferney and I have . . ." she couldn't stab him with the word "love" ". . . that we've been close for such a long time. I know I say this a lot, but Ferney's a very old man, Mike. We haven't even rung this morning to see how he is. They're separate things, what's in the past and you and me, now. They have to be. You don't believe in all this. Well, just be patient then. If you're right, he'll soon be . . . gone and that will be an end to it."

"That's a pretty roundabout reply," said Mike. "A simple no would have sufficed."

He said it lightly as if it were a punch line, but the lightness was to cover up the ache. His tone brought a slight involuntary smile to her face which his suffering mind twisted to a further suggestion of rejection and she just had time to take in the tightening of his expression before he got up abruptly and strode out through the caravan door. She let him go as her own mind spun. She couldn't have given him that simple "no" for anything and her intractable honesty was pulling her apart.

I've never set out to do deliberate harm to anyone, she thought. How can I have got myself in this situation? A relentless inner voice insisted on giving her the reason: because until this year you were groping in the dark and now the light is shining through. The light that shows how much it hurts to lose Ferney.

Then she looked out of the window and saw Mike standing utterly dejected by the door of his car, unsure where to go and the balance swung back the other way. Nothing justified making him so sad. Driven by duty and fondness, but not what she would now honestly describe as love, she went out and held him.

That afternoon they both drove to Yeovil Hospital.

"You can come in if you want to," she said.

"It's better if I don't. I'll wait for you."

"I might be a while."

"I expect you will be."

She got out of the car and he wound down the window.

"Gally? Just remember who you are now. Just remember me."

She gave him a sad smile and walked inside.

Ferney was not too weak to welcome her, though he was still surrounded by monitoring instruments. They looked at each other appraisingly.

"So how did it go?"

"Don't ask me," he said. "I went to sleep feeling pretty good and I woke up sore. That's about the sum of it."

"Are you still sore now?"

"Nothing that won't pass."

"What did they find?"

"No. What's wrong with you first?"

She raised an eyebrow at him. "Who says anything's wrong with me?"

"I do," he said, "and I should know." His face twitched in pain which he rapidly controlled. "I could even make a guess what it is."

"What then?"

"Conflicting loyalties I'd say for sure, and why are they conflicting? Because something's happened recently that's made you think you have to choose."

She could only nod for fear her voice would catch.

"You've got that memory working more, haven't you?" he said. "And it took you somewhere painful."

She nodded again.

"Was it the promise? The promise you made on the hill?" He was watching her closely.

"No."

"I hoped it would be. Never mind what it was then. Probably something I wouldn't enjoy."

She found her voice though it was not as steady as she wanted. "I only seem to go back to the bad things."

"You're a learner driver, Gally. They're the easiest ones to hit. You've got a choice: either stop doing it or learn to do it better, and that's no choice really."

"Mike's outside waiting for me. I talked to him a lot this morning. Last night was dreadful, really dreadful, so I had to."

Ferney nodded encouragement and she went on. "I know what you'll say. You'll say that Mike is only a very small part of our lives, but he's been a very big part of this life and none of this is his fault. I have to think of him. What can I do?"

He stretched his neck, easing his head on the pillow, and considered. "I suppose you could say that these doctors are making it all a bit easier," he said. "They say this old carcass has just about had it." He was completely matter-of-fact. "A few months and that's it."

"How many months?" she said quietly.

"Three or four. Maybe a bit more with a lot of extra cutting, but I said I didn't want that."

"Oh Ferney, I'm too new to this not to be upset," she said and leaned forward in her chair so that her forehead rested against his chest.

"No need," he said. "I'll be back in a new set of clothes before you can say knife. Then just give me a few years to grow up." He stroked her forehead with lover's fingers. "You do realize," he went on quietly, "when I'm eighteen, say, you'll be in your forties."

"Stop it. I can add up." She sat up straight again. "I don't know what to do."

"I do." His voice sounded younger and stronger. "The way *he* sees life, I'm not going to be a problem for very much longer. Tell him what the doctors said. You can even tell him you'll stay away from me these next few weeks if you want to. If it helps him, it doesn't hurt us, does it? I know I'll be seeing you later, but he doesn't believe that, so that's all he'll care about. There's just one thing I ask in return."

"I can guess what that is." Her voice was sombre.

"Yes, you can. You've got to tell me you'll just try remembering one more time. Up on the hill. You've got to hear yourself out, Gally. You've got to hear your promise. You told me to say that to you."

"I don't know what will happen, Ferney. I couldn't stop yesterday. I couldn't get myself out of it."

"I can tell you why. Underneath you're worrying about that promise all the time, aren't you? You're thinking about remembering and you're fearing remembering and that's what's steering you straight into all the black bits. Don't do it like that. Just do what you know you've got to. Listen to yourself and that won't happen anymore. Use the words I gave you. They won't take you anywhere bad."

"But what happens *after* I listen to myself?"

"That's your choice, but at least you will have had your say."

She nodded agreement. "What about you? Are you coming home?"

"I plan to be out in a week or two."

"Who's going to look after you?"

"It'll work out. I'm not fading away in here, that's for sure. I'm going out on my terms, in my place. I'd be daft to stay here. Not right over a maternity ward with babies popping out ten times a day. You never know what might happen."

She laughed and as if that showed she had a sufficient reserve of strength to handle it, he said, "So what was it you remembered this time?"

"You. Being killed."

"There's a few of those. When?"

"By the Normans, down below the castle."

"Oh yes." He looked quite calm. "And?"

"And? Well, I was such a coward. I could feel it, all the fear."

"Gally, you were always troubled in that life by fear, but I saw you overcome it time and again. You couldn't have stopped them."

It was like the therapist all over again. You couldn't have saved your father. You were only ten. Your arm was broken.

"I always feel guilty, Ferney, terribly guilty. I always know that a man died because of me. I thought it was my father. Perhaps it was you."

She was hoping for some relieving, final word of absolution.

"I died because of the Frenchmen, not because of you. What could you have done, sent them back to Normandy? Some chance. No one died because of you." He smiled and pressed her hand and it didn't seem to help one little bit.

A NEW DREAM attacked her in the night when soft sleep had opened her defences. No one held her back this time. She smothered her fear and walked weightlessly towards the car, orange fire boiling through the coils of smoke, and pulled open the door with the immense power of her two strong arms. Her father's face turned gratefully to her and she was so pleased to see the fire hadn't yet charred it as she had feared. She pulled him out by his neck and the flames died, smothered in water, but immense sadness seized her as he slumped limply to the ground, knowing, despite or because of everything she'd done, that he was dead.

Mike woke her.

24

THE TREES WERE bare and a north wind pushed freezing sheets of air through the caravan's breached seams, its stiff curtains swaying inwards, needles moving on a dial of discomfort. Ever since they had first seen the house in the spring, it had been tucked inside the protecting fold of the trees. Now the landscape had been opened up, stripped of cover by the wind, but, just in time, the house was ready for it. Free of the scaffolding it was prepared to stand up for itself against anything the winter might bring.

The last thing to go was the builders' pile of rubble, but Gally was absolutely insistent, despite the frost on the inside of the caravan windows in the morning and the chill of damp in their clothes, that she would not move into the house until that final sign was gone. She bullied and cajoled Rick and his team into working overtime on the final Saturday morning to shovel all their leftovers of broken blocks, plaster fossils, cable off-cuts and plastic pipe into the back of their truck. As they were doing so she carried the remaining bedding and clothes into the house, and a £20 note persuaded Rick to hitch the caravan to the truck's tow-bar and take it with them to the dump.

Only then, when the smell of the truck's exhaust had blown off towards Shaftesbury, did she let Mike walk in through the front door with her, allowing herself the full sensation of ownership and appreciation. The house was sparsely furnished and they would need to find a lot more furniture to pad it with all the soft, comfortable corners she saw in her mind, but Gally had already found old carpets and armchairs in a local auction which looked as though they had always belonged. She wanted to be able to sit in comfort in whichever room suited her, chasing the sun as it swung through the house.

Curtains that had once been her grandmother's hung in most of the windows, providing another direct and familiar touch to help her root herself in this present time. When their silent, appreciative walk through the ground floor reached the kitchen, Mike opened the fridge and pulled out a bottle wrapped in tissue.

"Champagne to mark the occasion. Well, fizzy grape juice, actually, in deference to our tiny friend."

"We mustn't be late."

Mike looked at his watch. "No problem, we've got over an hour."

It had been his own idea that they should drive Ferney home from the hospital. Mike had offered it as a small consolation prize and a part of his personal penance on the day that they had finally left Monmouth's ring at the Taunton Museum, Gally handing it over with sadness and resignation after they had received a polite but pressing letter on the subject of legal requirements. Until then they had hardly talked about Ferney, but Gally could see that, of all Mike's conflicting emotions, the one that came out on top was his continuing feeling of guilt at what he saw as his contributory role in his collapse.

"When the old man's home, who's going to look after him?" he had asked diffidently.

"Oh, I gather there'll be a nurse popping in every now and then and Mary Sparrow says she'll help out too."

"Mary Sparrow?"

"You remember, 'my muffeties'? The one who laughs a lot?"

"Oh, *her*. Poor old Ferney. What about you?"

"What about me?"

"Well, you can help out a bit too, I suppose?"

You would pitch me, all unthinking, back into the maelstrom? The words stayed inside. It was a gift expressed as a duty and she must take it gingerly. "Every now and then, maybe."

"Look, I won't mind. As long as things stay on an even keel. We'd better offer to fetch him, anyway."

He knew exactly what the hospital had said about Ferney's limited time and, as Ferney had anticipated, it seemed to draw a bottom line under the extent of his hostility. Being a decent man he understood and was shamed by the knowledge that Ferney's coming death made him feel reassured. It made all the difference and was awful because of that, but it served to increase his new determination that they should be generous with their help in Ferney's remaining weeks.

"I suppose he'll have to go back in again at some point," he said.

"Why?" She was startled.

"Well, I mean. If it's cancer, he's going to get worse, isn't he? He can hardly stay at home."

Gally knew Ferney would not go back, not unless they strapped him to a stretcher. He would want to be home, of that she was quite sure, however he contrived it. If not, then she would have to be at the hospital with him.

They collected Ferney at half past two and he was able to walk quite well by himself out to the car although they were both ready near him in case. In the weeks he had spent in hospital the same thought had concerned him and he had been slowly pulling together his strength to try to outflank the enemy growing inside him for as long as he could. Gally had seen him in rationed, safe doses, taking contentment from simply being with him as they were now, refusing to take any of the complex backtracks available. The image constantly projected onto him by the hospital had made it simpler. All the staff saw him as an old man and concerned themselves with the dignity of his coming end. Left to herself Gally would have seen only his eyes containing the loving light of all their pasts and the promise of all the futures, but, surrounded by nurses tending him with such kind dismissiveness, she saw as well the body beyond the eyes and could play the nurses' game of supposing him to be almost at an end.

He hadn't referred to her promise on those visits. She knew that he only had to look at her to see she had not yet fulfilled it, but he seemed calm enough about that.

Mike was solicitous and formally polite with him. Gally was in the back of the car. Ferney's bungalow was warm, prepared and waiting for him, but he had other ideas. "You've moved in? You're in the house?"

"Yes. As of this morning," said Mike.

"Just as well. The cold's coming clipping in now. Can I see it?"

"You want to see the house?"

"If it's no trouble."

"We thought we ought to get you home."

"It won't do any harm."

From the back Gally could read Mike's double-talk. Ferney in the house might lessen his own hold on it. He was afraid that regained ground was about to be lost again. Ferney read him too and trumped him.

"I would really like to see it just once more."

Mike could not say no to that.

It was a new and delicious experience, coming into the yard for the first time with no caravan, no builders' vans, no scaffolding and with the Bag Stone leaning like a great tent peg to anchor the house. Loving satisfaction swelled through Gally as she leaned forward to look at it between the men in the front seats and to share it, to earth it, she reached out, one hand on Mike's shoulder and the other on Ferney's. To her discomfiture, Mike twitched his shoulder as if her hand was an unexpected irritation while from Ferney, her left hand tingled with an electric redoubling of the pure pleasure she felt.

She stayed in the car for a second to catch her breath while Mike came round to the passenger's side and helped Ferney out, then she followed them into the house and heard Ferney say, "You've got it about right, I think."

He walked slowly into the sitting room where the wide stone fireplace stood ready to feel its first warmth in sixty years.

"That chimney smokes when the wind's in the north. It comes down off the hill. You'll have to put a bit of a choke in, I expect. Best way's an iron plate up in there," he thrust his stick up into the wide mouth of the chimney, "an iron plate with a two-foot hole in it should do the trick."

Mike frowned slightly.

"Can I look upstairs?" said Ferney eagerly.

"Can you manage it?"

"I'd run up if my legs weren't out of practice."

At the top he stood on the landing looking in through the open doorway of their bedroom and she sensed that it would hurt him to go in and see the evidence of the bed she would be sharing with Mike that night, nor did she want him to see it.

"What do you think?" said Mike.

"I think it's back to its old self and it's been a very happy house," said Ferney. "Thank you for letting me see. I'll be off home now."

"Fine," said Mike. "I'll help you back to the car."

"Oh that's all right, I'll walk," said Ferney. "If you wouldn't mind dropping my bag sometime."

"No, that's out of the question. The hospital would never forgive us."

Protesting, they got him into the car, took him back to his bungalow and arranged a comfortable chair for him. Gally made him tea and Mary Sparrow arrived to fuss around him, bringing a huge pie in a china dish.

"I'm glad you're back," said Gally. "I'll come tomorrow," and bent to kiss him on the cheek. It was the first time she had done so in this oddly separate intimacy of their present lives and it was not at all like kissing a much older man. So much joy surrounded them for that warm second when her cheek was against his that it was a wrench to stand straight again.

They were about to get back into the car when a white police car drove into the close and parked behind them. The man who climbed out was in sergeant's uniform and he glanced at them briefly before walking up the path to Ferney's front door.

"He's only just come back," Gally called to the policeman, concerned. "He's been in hospital."

"That's all right," said the sergeant. "I won't bother him for long. I've just got something for him."

Gally stood in an agony of indecision. If this was, as she suspected, about the bones down at the roadworks, then she felt she ought to be there too, but no doubt the sergeant wouldn't see it that way.

"Can we wait?" she said to Mike. "Just until he's gone?"

He wasn't more than a couple of minutes and, seeing them waiting, gave them a rather more curious look this time as he went back to his car.

"I won't be a second," said Gally.

Mary Sparrow opened the door to her knock. Ferney was sitting in his chair staring into space.

"Is everything all right?" she said.

Mary was hovering behind her and it was clear Ferney didn't want to say much.

"It's fine. He just came to tell me they'd closed the file on the business down there."

"Was that all?"

"Let's talk about it later."

When she'd gone and when he'd finally persuaded Mary he could get himself to bed quite happily, Ferney sat quietly, thinking about the mystery of Billy Bunter.

The policeman had been quite happy about it all.

"We're satisfied. He ended up in Dartmoor, you know—the lad that did it. You knew he died in prison?"

"I knew that much. They wrote and told the vicar for some reason."

"He wrote an account of it while he was inside. It's all in the files somewhere. No mystery."

"Wrote? I didn't know he *could* write."

"Seems he did."

"How did he die? They never said."

"I don't know." The sergeant clearly felt that was inadequate. "Would you like me to find out?"

"I would."

"I'll see what I can do. It might take a while."

Poor Billy, Ferney thought when he was by himself again. He didn't ask much and he didn't get much. It wasn't right that they put a lad like that in Dartmoor, a lad who'd been so provoked and who wasn't really answerable for what he did. He'd never been vicious. Naughty maybe, but not on purpose. He didn't really know about closed doors. You'd always find him where you didn't expect him, nosing into things that weren't his. All kinds of stuff used to go astray when Billy was around, but you couldn't blame him. Monmouth's sword and the breastplates had probably gone that way. They'd certainly vanished after he'd been in one day.

GALLY AND MIKE went quietly back to Bagstone Farm and as evening came they lit a log fire and sat in the armchairs with the dim table lamps removing the evidence of modern repair from the sitting room. They sipped soup in mugs and gazed into the fire and a great gust of smoke swept out of the chimney as the wind raced across the roof.

"Ah," said Mike. "It's going to need a cowl or something."

An iron plate in the chimney opening was what it needed, an iron plate with a two-foot hole. Gally looked at Mike in surprise. She hadn't really noticed he was there. "I don't mind it," she said. "It covers up the smell of fresh paint."

He rose to his feet, smiled and bowed. "Mrs. Martin," he said, "shall we have an early night in our new bedroom?"

She suppressed a frown. It was as if a stranger had suggested making love to her here, in her house. The light was too dim for him to see her face and that gave her time to get back in control. She followed him up the stairs.

"I'm going to have a bath," she said. "I want to enjoy every bit of it."

"You've been using the bathroom for the last three weeks."

It was true. In the evenings, after the builders had gone, she had allowed that single infringement on the house.

"Yes, but I only painted it yesterday. I didn't want to spoil the feeling."

She lay in the long bath, soaking in luxurious hot water. The smell of the fresh paint made it easy to be modern and the room seemed to hold no great connections. Of course, she thought, there wouldn't have been a bathroom. Perhaps this will be a safe place when I need to be Mike's. This and the loo. The door opened and he came in with a tray and a bottle of Spanish champagne. "Ta-raah."

"Oh my goodness."

"You're allowed one drink, surely?" he said. "Why stop celebrating? It's a great day."

It was certainly a momentous day, a day of duties done and healing finished, but it was also a day in which she had crossed a threshold into a place where she had always been entirely Ferney's and now she had to find a way of sharing it. At that moment, only the bathroom seemed to protect her. "Stay and drink it here," she said. "Pull the chair over."

It was a good-sized room that had once been a bedroom and she'd found a lone armchair with a worn cover of green flowers on a yellow background that felt just right for it. Mike sat next to her in the chair, drinking and reminiscing about how they'd first found the house and all the stages on the way to this day. He left Ferney entirely out of his account and she was glad. If she pushed the old man out of her mind, too, she could make room for Mike and she concentrated on doing that.

"Why don't we drink the rest of this in bed?" he said as he filled up her glass. She knew that one glass had been quite enough, sensitive to the delicate balance of her baby's world, but she allowed him the pleasure of pouring it. She was frightened of getting out of the bath, frightened of what might follow if she left this insulating room that eased the dilemma of her faithfulness. She reached for his wrist as he poured and stroked it, understanding that he had a strong need to consummate this house with her, to declare it theirs. "It's a big bath," she said, "and it's still hot. Wouldn't you like it?"

"I'll share it with you," he replied, smiling and looking into her eyes.

"Yes," she said, sensing a way out of the trap. "Come on in."

He pulled his shirt over his head and she concentrated on his physical presence, the new muscles in his arms and shoulders, built up by the manual labour they'd done clearing the surrounding land. He turned half away, stooping and hopping to get his jeans off, and she deliberately lingered on the curve of his neat buttocks into his narrow waist. It felt very calculated, but she needed to guarantee him passion and she could feel on an animal level that her body was starting to respond to these messages she was force-feeding it. The champagne helped. He stood next to the bath wondering how to get in, and she sat up, water cascading off her swelling breasts down to the large seemingly independent convexity of her belly. She reached up to his neck and he bent to a long kiss which swirled their arousal together. She felt his hand on one breast, brushing her nipple, sending shivers down to her groin and then his hand stroked over her belly and down and she opened to him like a sea anemone in the warm water. After a long minute in which his tongue and fingers blotted out all else, she stood on trembling legs to make space for him in the bath and as he lay down in the water, she sat on his chest, meeting his unfocused gaze as his hands reached up to cup her breasts and eased herself back onto him, driven by urgency so that the bath water slopped backwards and forwards escaping over the rim in small splashes as she moved faster and faster. She came with him to a gasping climax that was entirely on a physical level, but strong enough to stop that mattering, then slipped down to lie squeezed against him by the constraints of the bath in a thought-free peace. Outside their slow time, the water seemed to grow rapidly colder and they got out together, helped to dry each other then went next door into the bedroom. As Gally rolled into bed, utterly at home, she felt for this one time she had been as fair as she could be to both men and avoided wondering what the future might bring. She and Mike were quickly asleep.

Three in the morning and the house's bones creaked as the first frost of winter crisped on its roof and tested its newly strengthened joints in slow contraction. Gally's calmer dreams had often in the past been searching dreams where she would be misled by places that at first seemed familiar, pushing through crowds, trying to catch up with people who always disappointed when they turned. Now, for the first time, her dreams were entirely delightful, putting her in the very centre of where she wanted to be, in a cocoon of comfort. In her sleep the lover who was the other half of her turned to her and put his warm arms around her and she flooded with acceptance so that her spirit and her body welcomed him into her, and where their minds melted together she wrapped her legs around him to crush them into matching physical unity. It was no dream, but she experienced every soft swollen movement of it through a filter of sleep and the end of it was a soaring harmony of spiritual perfection and physical ecstasy that she knew went as far as it was possible to go in complete sharing. But then abrupt movement chased it away and dragged her to a waking reality that was wrong and unexpected. A man was getting out of bed with harsh, angry movements and for that first moment of awareness the man was a stranger. In the second moment, he was revealed as Mike.

"What . . . what's the matter?" she said in a thick voice.

"You're the matter," he said bitterly.

"Why? What did I do?"

"You called out. Didn't you know?"

"No, I was asleep, I think."

"You called out 'Ferney.' "

25

AS THE WORLD turned towards a cold dawn, curled miserably alone in the big bed, Gally could not drive away a relentless voice that seemed intent on stripping away all the layers of pretence with which she tried to protect herself. If Mike had been there she could have calmed him down, forced him to listen to her apologies, kept him there and kept this voice away, but Mike was not there. Mike had driven off into the night, the engine reaching a crescendo in each gear until distance claimed all evidence of it, and in his absence the voice had started and it told her that she was running out of time for compromise. It was inside her, a grim questioner with no comfort in it that obliged her to sit in judgement on herself and would allow no inaccuracy in the statements it demanded.

"Is there space for Mike in your life?"

"Of course there is. There has to be. I married him. He wasn't happy before. I made him happy. I can't take that away."

"Is there space for Mike?"

"There has to be. I just can't find the right way to fit them both in."

"Is there space?"

"No. There has to be. No. There's not."

"What must you do?"

"Avoid hurting anyone."

"What must you do?"

"Talk to them both."

"Who do you love?"

"Both of them."

"Who do you love?"

"It's different."

"Who do you love?"

"Ferney, but I . . ."

"What must you do?"

"Be true to myself."

"What does that mean?"

"Be me. Get back in touch with all the other bits I can't reach."

"Can't reach?"

"Choose not to reach."

That won her a short reprieve of silence. She went to the bathroom wrapped up in a long sweater and a dressing gown to try to keep the voice away and sat there in the armchair for a long time, fearing sleep and worrying about Mike. He would have gone to the flat. He would drive too fast in his anger. He would be utterly miserable. At five in the morning, when he should have gotten there and the sky outside was still as black as it could be, she phoned, but the line was engaged and that must mean he had taken the phone off the hook. At least it meant he was there. She went back to bed with a cup of tea, propped pillows up behind her and unexpectedly found herself waking in that position, four hours later, with the tea cold next to her.

She had so looked forward to that first morning, had even planned ahead that she would bring Mike a tray of croissants and coffee and they would eat it in bed, taking shared pleasure in the unusual comfort of it all, but it seemed there was no pleasure to be had, just the faint echo of the unremitting voice. She phoned the flat again and even before it connected, she knew she would hear the engaged signal. Dressed, she went downstairs and suddenly wondered how many times she had been down those stairs. The woodwork of these treads might be new, but that made no difference. She had a pressing sense of all the streams of days that had begun this way, with that diagonal passage down from rest to action and before that, going back on this spot before there were stairs, when it was just one storey, then one flimsy room where rest and work were divided only by the action of standing up. She was still here. All the other bit players in their lives flared briefly and whirled away and there was nothing enduring except her and Ferney and the house and the stone and of those four only the stone kept its outward form unchanged. It was disturbing to think of Ferney, a mile away, dislocated in his temporary house.

I seem to be making so many mistakes, she said to herself sitting on a stool in the kitchen and a more friendly voice answered her.

"You have forgotten too much."

"Remembering doesn't seem to help."

"How could it not help? You know so much if you let yourself re-member it."

She had to go to Ferney. Mechanical duties called her, duties dis-cussed with Mike before the night's involuntary cry of betrayal. They had agreed she would check if the old man had managed to get himself breakfast. Prompted by the house or by the voice, for she could not tell whether they were the same thing, she was filled with resolution and, before she left, she went down the slope to the hollow tree where the plastic bag, ignored these last weeks, now showed clearly in its hole in the bare trunk to anyone who might look. With it in her pocket she walked along the lane, jacketed against the breath-fogging cold, and when she came to the gate up to the hilltop she turned off with no further conscious decision and didn't slow down until the top of the rise opened all the land below to her gaze. Frost pockets showed white streaks through the misty exhalations of the ditch-drained fields and the colours of that winter landscape were grey and a metal green that was mainly blue. The seat was damp and cold and she sat on a scarf that had been in her pocket, folded back and forth across the stone. She found she was shivering and the cold gave her an excuse, but making excuses was not part of her plan for the morn-ing so she admitted that she was frightened. She got out the letter and read it again, then despite the cold she imagined herself in the pale blue cotton dress he described, pink rosebuds in the pattern and her long blond hair hanging over her shoulders, and as she did the cold-ness left her. Summer warmth struggled to superimpose itself and the leaves came back, ghostly green on the bare branches.

"We can do it," she read from the letter. "We can if we set our minds to it. No more of this hit-and-miss." Nothing came and she made the dress as vivid as she could, the pattern developing in her mind's eye then shifting and disappearing when she lost concentra-tion. She ran her hand over the denim of her jeans, feeling only thin cotton print, and the pattern came back. In this other time she was standing by the stone seat, looking down at her leg, feeling the rent in the dress, looking up again in horror at Cochrane who was holding her wrist tightly.

"Let me go," she shouted. "You've torn it." She wrenched her wrist free, turned and ran down the hill towards the lane, knowing he was coming after her, praying Ferney would appear, shouting for help when she could spare the breath. Then the ground lurched up to meet her as she stumbled in a hole, knocking the wind out of her as she crashed down, but when she rolled over, hands up ready to fight him, it was cold winter and she was in her padded jacket and jeans and the year was 1990 again and she was alone on the hill.

As soon as she could breathe normally, she hurried down to the lane trying to compose herself and by the time she reached Ferney's house and saw through the window, to her relief, that he was moving around his sitting room, she was in shaky control. He opened the door to her and then opened his arms when he saw the look on her face and she stood there in the hall, suddenly finding peace, with his arms tightly around her and his cheek against hers. After some time he led her into the sitting room and they sat down side by side on the sofa.

"I tried to do it," she said, pacing her words carefully to avoid the fear. "I went up to the hill and I said the words and I imagined the dress the way you told me, but that man came, Cochrane. He was there on the top of the hill and he tore my dress. I ran away and I fell . . ."

"You *really* fell," he said, looking at the mud on her jeans.

"Yes, I did, but I knew I was falling in . . . in the memory and I knew he was going to catch me and do something terrible to me."

"Cochrane grabbed you, up on our hill?" He sounded incredulous, catching up with what she had said.

"Yes, he did. He was beside himself, bright red. His eyes were bulging." She shuddered.

"He got you there. I had no idea." Ferney's voice was grim. "All I knew was you disappeared. That must have been the day. Was it summer?"

"It was, yes."

"July the tenth, 1933. I'm so very sorry."

"It's not your fault."

"It is though, isn't it? I got you to walk back straight into it. I didn't remember that was the same dress you were wearing. I should have. It got driven out of my head, I suppose. It's not only that though, is it? There's more worrying you."

"Why do you say that?"

"Gally, love. Listen to me. We've got extra sight, you might say, you and me. We've had thirteen hundred years to get to know human nature. There's only a certain number of things that happen, of ways that people feel, and we've seen all of them a thousand times, you and me. We're good at people, have been for ages and ages. We can see what they really mean in every little twitch of them. We always know it when the words go only halfway. It keeps us out of trouble and ahead of the game." He smiled. "You may be a bit cut off from it at the moment, but it goes without saying we're best of all at reading each other. You used to say you could tell my thoughts. I don't know about that but I can certainly read your face."

"Last night. I seemed to be talking to myself, giving myself a bit of a going-over."

"Why?"

"I upset Mike."

"Oh dear. Have you made up?"

"I couldn't. He left. He drove off to London in the middle of the night."

Ferney sighed. "That was quite an upset, then. What happened?"

"We were . . . in bed and I called out your name."

"Oh no." He looked down. It sounded as if it hurt him and she thought it was the idea that she and Mike had been making love. He shook his head as if irritated with himself. "Then you say you started talking to yourself."

"I don't know what it was. It was just this voice in my head that wouldn't let me off the hook. It kept forcing me to say what I really thought about everything."

"It was you. It was all your wisdom, I expect. You've got it there, all locked away, and it knows when it's needed and I would say it sounds like it's definitely needed now."

She nodded. "I think I need all the help I can get. How can I get at it?"

He turned and gazed out of the window. "You mustn't think I'm saying this for my own ends."

"I won't."

"I think you've got to go back and try again, up the hill. I think you've got something big blocking you off there. Just do that and you'll know how to play it, I'm sure."

"But I'll see Cochrane again." It was almost a wail.

He turned back to her. "No, listen," he said. "This time you've got to take me along."

"Ferney, you can't possibly go up the hill today. You're fresh out of hospital."

"I don't mean like that. I mean take me along in your head. It was both of us were there, you know. That last time when Cochrane caught you, I wasn't there, was I? If you put me in your head too, you can't go wrong. I'll keep you safe from him. I only wish I could have done before."

She thought about it and nodded. "Well . . . tell me about it. Give me a bit more to go on. How were we sitting?"

He moved a bit closer to her and put one arm loosely round her shoulders. "Like this, more or less. We were a bit out of breath."

"What were we doing?"

He looked at her and a slow smile spread across his face. "You might get a bit of a shock if I told you that."

"Ah . . ." she leaned her head against his shoulder.

"How does that make you feel?" he said gently.

"Like I did last night when I was more or less asleep and I thought it was you, like it was the best thing in the world."

"I'd like you to know how it should be. It's a bit undignified being an old crock. When we're both young together, it's so good."

"I don't see an old crock," she said. "I look into your eyes and that's all I see, the inside, not the outside. You don't need to feel ashamed of anything."

"You were wearing the garland ring. Remember that. Get the feel of that around your head."

"I didn't have that on when Cochrane . . . No, of course." She answered herself. "If I'd been wearing it then, you wouldn't have still had it."

"No," he said. "That will keep you safe. There was nothing to worry about that day. Everything we said and did was about love." Then he sighed again.

"Fifty-five years," he said calmly. "That's too long between the two of us. It makes no sense like this. It would be so good to be young with you again. I want that so much."

She got up. "I'm going back to the hill. Right now, while it's fresh in my head."

"You're a brave girl."

"I've got to do it. I know that now. There's no other way."

UP THE SLOPE she made sure she kept the image of Ferney beside her and, sitting down on top, she waited until she felt calm then thought of the slight pressure of the garland ring around her forehead, the smell of the flowers woven into it. She put Ferney beside her in her mind and she wrapped the floral print of the dress around her. A strong physical thrill passed through her so that she went no further for a while but was content to enjoy it with her breath coming longer and deeper. Then she tried the words and there seemed to be more of them.

"We *can* do it," she said again. "We can if we set our minds to it. No more of this hit-and-miss." Ferney was beside her, his arm round her and his hand on her breast, the finger and thumb gently rolling her nipple between them. She was flat-bellied and her slim body was still singing from the love they had just made there on the hilltop, sure that no one would interrupt them. She carried the immediate memory of hugging him face to face, straddling his lap as they moved in perfect, scorching unity under the dome of their sky.

He kissed her neck below her hair. "It seems a terrible thing."

"We've done it for illness."

"Some illnesses. The ones we know there's no getting better from."

"Let's do it for joy."

"I know you're right. It will be so much better. There's never been joy with anyone else. It's only worth it when you're here."

"Are we agreed, then?" She had her face close to his with a wide, joyful smile. "Shall we swear to it, swear we'll always, always do it whatever?"

"Yes. What if one of us forgets?"

"Then the other has some reminding to do, that's all." She laughed and ran her fingers through his hair.

"And if both of us forget?"

She stopped laughing. "Well, maybe that will just have to be that if both of us forget. But we won't, we mustn't. Other folks have God. We've only got us."

He shook his head, amused. "You don't know they've got God. You can't be sure. Could be we're luckier than them. They just stop, maybe." He stopped talking then, holding her at arm's length, looking at the woven hoop of flowers in her hair.

She let the silence spread for a while before she spoke again. "I think they might have. You know what it's like when we die. The feeling that you're going somewhere and there's the light coming at the end only we never get to see it. I like to think the others do get there."

"Doesn't mean it's God."

"Doesn't mean it's not. It's something. Maybe one day we'll find out."

"So long as we find out together."

He stood up suddenly, staring at bushes down the slope of the hill.

"What is it?"

"Someone there, maybe. I saw something move."

"A rabbit?"

He stared for a long time. "No, it was too big for a coney."

"What then?"

"I don't know."

She got up, put her arm through his and they started to walk back down to the house. A lark was singing and as she turned her head to it she saw movement out of the corner of her eye. The smith, Cochrane, unmistakably. He was creeping away behind the hedge from the hiding place where he must have watched them. Watched them as they made love? The thought sickened her. She opened her mouth to tell Ferney, but shut it again. Three times already Ferney had clashed with Cochrane, having it out with the smith after his drunken propositions to her. Three times he had taken damage at the smith's brutal hands. The man was wrong in the head and she did not want Ferney to be hurt again, but she knew Ferney, for all his abhorrence of violence, would not shirk the issue if it came to it so she stayed silent, and the present Gally, knowing the tragedy to come, could do nothing to change that. She found herself able to separate herself a little from this remembered twin, and in doing so she was able to get a sudden sense of the depth of understanding she used to have at her command.

They were heading down the hill to the gate and beyond it the track was rough, potholed earth and stone. She was still submerged in this past time but now she made a bid to exert herself, swimming to the surface of this joint person and reimposing the present. The road was tarmac. She was in control and her body had changed to enfold the baby kicking inside her. For the first time she had managed the transition back to the present deliberately by herself, but it still came as a shock to lose Ferney from her side, to know that same man had gone on to a lifetime of loneliness. She wanted him back. She stood, irresolute for a moment in the road, then turned towards his bungalow.

He knew as soon as he saw her that this time it had worked.

"The nurse will be here soon," he said. "We haven't got long. Tell me how it was."

"I learnt there was something I didn't tell you that day," she said. "Cochrane was up there on the hill watching us. You thought you saw something. You were right."

He frowned, trying to remember. "Was I?"

"I saw him afterwards and I didn't tell you because I thought there'd be another fight. I should have done."

"It might not have made a difference."

"Oh yes it would. If we knew what sort of things he was prepared to do we'd have been more careful."

"He wanted you from the moment he saw you. It would have

made him even madder to see you and me like that. So what are you thinking, that if you'd told me then maybe you wouldn't have died?"

"I'm thinking that you wouldn't have spent all this time by yourself." She took his hand. "I'm so sorry."

"We could spend all our time looking back. No use doing it unless it helps you look forward. Tell me what else you learnt."

"I heard it all through. I know it was my idea and I know what it's like for us to be together and to be young. I know the difference it makes when our bodies match each other like our minds do and I know the house doesn't matter a bit except as the place where we are both happy together."

"But can you handle it?" he said.

"That's the bit I don't know." She gazed at him and the part she saw was the same young man who made her mind and body exult together. "I have a sense of a way that seems right."

He just waited.

"I think I must do it," she said and he let out a long breath. "I can't talk to Mike about it. It wouldn't be fair. I think I'll know for sure when the baby's born. If I know it's you then I'll know it's what you want, more than you could want me there as a mother to you."

"You'll know it's me."

"Yes. But there's another thing. That promise was about a simpler situation. The fact is Mike's there and I have to think of that too. I had a feeling of wisdom up there. It's faded away a bit now, but I think it was telling me I couldn't prejudge it, that I would know when the time came what I had to do."

"I can't argue with that," he said, and looked out of the window as a car drew up. "I think the nurse is here."

It wasn't the nurse. It was Mike.

26

EFFIE MULLARD WAS carrying a large shopping basket completely full of parsnips and it was not immediately clear whether she had just bought them or was perhaps trying to sell them. Gally had taken Mike Christmas shopping in an attempt to get some seasonal spirit into their life. Three weekends had passed since his midnight departure and miserable return—weekends in which he had skirted the issue, keeping the conversation on male, practical lines. On each of those nights he had said different variations of "I'm tired," put out the light and gone to sleep as soon as he got into bed, and in truth he did look tired. If he was keeping his outward emotions under tight wraps Gally could see there was a battle going on inside and she wished it were in her power to help, but there was an equally powerful struggle going on in her own mind whenever she allowed it.

It was now the Saturday before Christmas and the start of Mike's holiday. Every day during the week Gally had been to check up on Ferney and usually she would spend an hour or two reading to him, which was safe and which he seemed to enjoy.

"These eyes are getting a bit past it," he said. "I'd rather listen to you."

She wouldn't touch the history books which were his first preference. She offered him novels from a selection she brought with her, but he usually chose travel books from the large number on his own shelves.

"Why do you like these so much?" she asked one day.

"I can't go there, can I? Nor should you. France put me off all that, but I'm curious." He had videos too, neatly filed on his shelves in alphabetical order, exploration, adventure, nature—all of it overseas.

Gally thought of the foreign trips she had made, of a near-miss on a motorbike in Greece, of the snake she had all but stepped on in North Africa, and thought how worried he would have been had he known. It was perhaps the reason she had felt so reluctant to go to live in America.

Every time the postman came Ferney seemed disappointed with what he brought.

"Are you expecting something?" Gally asked him one day.

"Not really. That police sergeant said he'd send something, that's all."

"What was it?"

"Just something the lad wrote in prison."

"Billy Bunter?"

"That's the one."

"I know he killed Cochrane, but is there something else that's worrying you?"

"I sometimes feel like I failed him, that's all. I shouldn't have let them put him in prison."

"You could hardly have stopped them."

"Maybe not, but I'd like to know how it was for him at the end."

Sadness seemed to fill the room as he spoke.

He listened to the news on the hour every hour. It was dominated by the response to Iraq's invasion of Kuwait and he listened to the buildup in the Gulf as if he were taking the pulse of the fevered world. They both knew they could go no further for the moment in the direction of what would come next for them, but with that decided and left deliberately aside, Gally found she loved nothing more than sitting in that quiet room, offering him the sentences that took his mind off the pain—and he was in pain. There were times when he hid it, though she could still tell, and there were other times when it twisted his face for a minute despite himself. He had a liquid painkiller to dispense to himself and had given the doctors a terse answer when they'd enquired whether he felt confident to do that. It would be dangerous, they explained, if he took too much. In fact it took a lot to persuade him to take it at all.

At one bad moment when he had clamped down on a groan so that it came out as a snarl, she put down *A Short Walk in the Hindu Kush*.

"Shall I get you the bottle?"

"I'd rather not. I can get on top of this without it." He started breathing in long, controlled breaths but then grimaced again. "All right," he said. "Get it, would you?"

He took a spoonful and sat back and she watched for signs that it was starting to ease the pain. "Ferney?"

"Um?"

"Why don't you like taking it?"

"We've had a lot of pain come our way," he said, "and we didn't used to have stuff like this. I think if you start leaning on it, you lose something and there's no stopping then."

"Why do you feel you have to fight it?"

"You mean why don't I just take the whole lot?" He indicated the bottle and there was an unexpected anger in his voice which was, she knew, the product of the pain.

"You could if you wanted to. I'd understand."

"The time's not right," he said more gently. "I'll know when it is. Let's not talk about it."

She had a glimpse of what he really wanted to say, that he was still unsure what she would do when he died, and she left the bungalow that day feeling that all she seemed able to do was cause pain to both her men. When Mike came back that weekend with bags under his eyes and tried to greet her with a perfunctory kiss, she held him in a long hug which finally let his stiff body sag in relaxation. She had decorated the house with holly, filled it with candles and set a roaring log fire for his return.

He sat in front of the fire with a glass of Scotch and looked around the room.

"Very pagan," he said. "No Christmas tree?"

"No car to get one."

"Whose fault's that?" but he was smiling. "Do you want a tree?"

"Not really."

"Well, it's a recent custom. All Prince Albert's idea, you know."

"I'd rather have the holly and the ivy." She sat on the floor leaning against his knees and he rested a hand on her shoulder.

"That's pagan too, of course," he said. "I got together a lecture on Christmas history for the students' last day, just for fun. The evergreens were sacred, you see, because when the other trees lost their leaves they were the only place of refuge for the spirits of the woodland."

"That's why they put holly in cowsheds, so the cows would do well indoors."

"I never heard that one," he said and she heard in the tightening of his voice all the dangers of freely speaking what came into her head.

"I expect I read it somewhere," she said. "What else was there?"

"Lots of things," he said, his voice warming again. "Unmarried girls would have to go and fetch logs in from the woodpile last thing at night and they wouldn't count them until the next day. The number of logs told them whether the girl would marry in the next year. I'll bet they cheated. It can't have been that hard to count in the dark." He looked at the roaring fire. "Logs have always been a big part of Christmas, fire and light. The Romans celebrated the same day, you know. They called it *Dies Natalis Invicti Solis*."

"Which means?"

"You should have had a classical education. 'The day the unconquered sun is born.' Of course it wasn't until the fourth century that the Pope decided to make it Christ's birthday."

"I didn't know that."

"He had his reasons. Taking over a Roman festival was a neat trick."

"I'm amazed he got away with it. It must have seemed a bit strange for the first few years."

Mike smiled. I hope it can just go on like this, she thought.

"People forget quite quickly. I mean there's a far more recent example of that. What colour's Father Christmas's robe?" He fired the question at her.

All colours was the answer that came into her head, but a Christmas card on the table in her line of vision anchored her. "Red and white."

"It didn't used to be. Until some time in the thirties it was usually green or sometimes it was a mixture of colours, then do you know what happened?"

"No."

"The Coca-Cola Company decided they'd put him in their corporate livery and they plastered America with posters and cards and heaven knows what and in no time flat we had a red-and-white Santa."

"That's terrible," she said, but what was really terrible was that a sudden sliver of pure memory, unlike anything she had known before, had flashed through her mind, gone before there was time to hold on to anything except the faintest flavour of it. A memory of the red-and-white Santa, the new red-and-white Santa and a bleak feeling of desperate sorrow. The 1930s.

She got up quickly, took Mike's glass. "I'll get you some more," she said and went to the kitchen to give herself time.

"It's here," he called in surprise. "The bottle's on the table."

"Oh, of course," she said, but the moment was past. The thirties, she thought: 1938, '39? It's lurking there. That was the missing me. Whatever Christmas held then, it wasn't nice.

THE GILLINGHAM TRIP wasn't a great success. The shops were limited and Gally wished she'd suggested somewhere bigger, Salisbury maybe or even Bath. They bought various bottles of the sort of thing you're supposed to drink at Christmas and were about to stow them away in the car when a well-remembered voice said, "Major Clapham, what a nice surprise. I was just coming to see you."

Mrs. Mullard, dressed in an army greatcoat that brushed the ground, stood there smiling benignly at them with her basket of parsnips.

"Hello," said Mike gamely. "It's Martin, actually."

"Oh, go on with you," she said. "I know that, Martin, and how are you, Mrs. Clapham?"

"Fine. Nice to see you," said Gally. "Did you say you were coming to see us?"

"I've been trying to for such a long time but I don't know where the bus goes from these days, you see? They keep changing it. Still that's all right now."

"Oh good," said Mike. "Why?"

"Because you've got the car," Mrs. Mullard cried with a laugh and climbed into the back of the Toyota parked next to them.

"God almighty," said Mike as she closed the other car's door. "Let's run for it."

"Shush," said Gally, appalled. "We can't."

The door opened again and Mrs. Mullard climbed out looking indignant, addressing herself to the man sitting behind the wheel of the Toyota. "Well, you shouldn't be in Colonel Johnson's car." She straightened up and looked at them with pursed lips and defiant eyes. "Man doesn't know what he's talking about."

Mike opened the back door of their own car in defeat. "Here you are. Climb in. Would you like a lift home?"

"Thank you."

He drove out of the town in the Wincanton direction. "Er, let's see, Buckhorn Weston, that's left isn't it?"

"Straight on," said Mrs. Mullard. "I thought you knew."

Straight on was to Penselwood. "I thought perhaps you wanted to go home?"

"That's it. That's right. Straight on."

Mike glanced desperately at Gally, who stepped in. "Perhaps Mrs. Mullard would like a quick look at the house, then we could run her home afterwards."

Mrs. Mullard looked puzzled. "What house is that, dear?"

When they got to Bagstone Farm, she seemed to see nothing remarkable in the transformation and Gally, understanding that the old lady had never let herself see the dereliction, was pleased that nothing in the re-creation surprised her either—not at any rate, until she got inside.

"Who's done this then?" she demanded as soon as they got into the hall.

"Done what?"

"Put paint over everything. It'll have to come off. That's good wallpaper under there."

"Would you like a cup of tea?" Gally asked tentatively.

"I'll get it. You shouldn't have to," said Mrs. Mullard and marched off into the kitchen.

"She thinks she still lives here," Mike hissed at Gally, then there was a scream from the kitchen. They went into the room, alarmed.

"Someone's stolen all my things. Where's it gone?" Mrs. Mullard was standing in the middle of the room looking frantically all round her. "There's white things everywhere."

"No, it's all right," Gally said soothingly. "Come and sit down. I'll light the fire." She nudged Mike. "Do you mind making the tea?"

He was glad to stay out of the way.

The sitting room went down better and the old lady slipped back into the present day without a noticeable join. Gally knelt to light the fire.

"It smokes, you know. When the wind's in the north." She craned her head to peer up under the lintel. "Needs an iron plate across there, like it used to have."

"I know," said Gally. "We'll get one."

Mrs. Mullard looked at Gally's bulging stomach. "I wish I'd had my baby here," she said. "My Bessy. She's not quite got the full set, poor lamb." She tapped her head meaningfully. "I always say it was being pushed out of here like that did it to her. If I'd stayed on here, she'd have been as right as ninepence. I could feel it, you know." She leaned over conspiratorially. "It was your husband's fault, I'm sorry to say."

Gally knew she didn't mean Mike, but she couldn't tell whether the old lady's grip had slipped again or whether she perceived the deeper truth.

"What do you mean?" she said cautiously.

"You know what it's like. You can tell how they're getting on inside there, can't you? It was all fine while we were here, but when we had to move so suddenly I could feel it affecting her. The poor thing left a bit behind her." She looked around the room as if she might see Bessy's missing faculties scurrying behind a chair.

Mike brought in a tray of tea and occupied Mrs. Mullard with all the ritual questions concerning milk and sugar which are always inflected as if they are most vital and have never been asked before. Left to herself for a blessed moment, Gally's head whirled with frightening possibilities. Could her baby be harmed if something went wrong, if Ferney was taken off, perhaps taken off to hospital so that he was first there and then not there? Was it because of the stone, perhaps? The water and the stone. He'd diverted the water. Had that done it, left Bessy half-baked?

"I was just telling Gally," said Mrs. Mullard. "It was your father's fault."

"What was?" said Mike equably, but there was a loud knock at the front door and the old lady sprang up.

"That'll be the butcher," she said. "I've got a bone to pick with him."

Gally followed her as she rushed to the front door and dragged it open. Ferney stood outside, leaning on his stick. He gaped at her. "What are you doing here, Effie?"

"Opening the door," she said. "Come in you old rascal, I've got your wife here for tea."

"Ferney," said Gally anxiously, "have you walked here? You shouldn't be out."

"Why on earth not?" he said. "Best medicine there is."

"Come on in."

"Have you seen the butcher?" asked Mrs. Mullard, peering out into the yard. "He was here just now."

"He hasn't been here these fifty years," said Ferney. "You're getting soft in the head."

"Oh, go on with you." The old lady twinkled at him, then stared. "You're looking a bit old."

"I haven't been too well," Ferney admitted.

"Are you looking after him properly?" The old woman turned on Gally.

"I try to."

"Well you must both come here for Christmas," she said triumphantly, as though that were the obvious solution to the whole problem. "We'll have parsnips."

"It's not for you to invite me," said Ferney. "You don't live here anymore. They do." He nodded at Gally and Mike.

Mrs. Mullard seemed to falter as she looked round at the two of them. The spark went out of her. "Oh," she said, then she brightened again. "Well that's all right. They can have you. Anyway," she looked at Mike, "who are you?"

They had another cup of tea all round and then it was Ferney who with some firmness persuaded Mrs. Mullard to get back in the car to be taken home. He wouldn't accept any lift. "I've only done half my walk," he said. "Got to put in another mile or two."

"Have you got your painkiller?" Gally said quietly, looking at his face.

He slapped his pocket, but she wasn't convinced.

They put Mrs. Mullard in the front of the car and she chatted happily all the way to Buckhorn Weston about a score of people they had never heard of. Gally wasn't at all sure anybody else would have heard of them either. At least half of them sounded as though they only existed in the old lady's head. When they got to her gate, she said, "Let me out here. I've got to feed the chickens," and began to stump off without a backward glance.

"Hold on," said Mike. "You've forgotten your shopping. I'll get it." He went to the back of the car and offered her the basket of parsnips. She came back a few steps and shook her head.

"Never seen that before. It must be yours or perhaps it's Mary's."

He stood there undecided and Gally got out to join him. "Do have it," she said. "It's a present."

Mrs. Mullard took it doubtfully. "Funny present." She looked at them. "You give him parsnips—when he comes for Christmas. Ferney likes parsnips."

"My God, she's got a lot worse," Gally said uneasily when they were back in the car heading home.

"You're not kidding. What are we going to do now?"

"About what?"

"About old Ferney. She's as good as invited him."

"It was her, not us," she said judiciously.

"Yes but it looks awful now, doesn't it? I'm sure he'll expect us to say something."

"It doesn't matter how it *looks*, Mike. It's how you feel about it that matters."

"Well, fine, but I suppose that's it. Now it's on the table, it makes me feel bad. I know it's all been very difficult but it *is* Christmas and I suppose it's our duty."

"You mean you'll feel bad if you don't ask him over?"

"I suppose that's what I do mean. It's not as if we had any family coming down."

Mike's parents lived their remote existence in a retirement bungalow on Anglesey. They had shown no interest in seeing the new house and Gally's austere mother saw no point in Christmas.

"All right. I'm very happy to have him over, but it's your decision, Mike, so it's got to be you that invites him, not me, and you've got to mean it."

Mike thought for a while.

"All right."

"And if he starts talking about, you know, old things, you've got to remember it was your idea all the time."

He just nodded.

27

MIKE COLLECTED FERNEY at eleven o'clock on Christmas morning and the old man was waiting for him, dressed in a soft tweed suit and carrying a basket containing wrapped parcels. Gally, anxious to preserve the point that this was all Mike's idea, stayed at the house making sure everything was ready. She was on tenterhooks and went to a window as soon as she heard the car come back, wanting early warning of how it was going between the two of them. They seemed to be talking cheerfully enough as they came in. Mike was standing straighter than usual, very much the host. Ferney seemed more bent and she suspected they were both playing roles to make it easier for her and perhaps for themselves, too. She met them at the door and Ferney clasped her hand, looked her up and down and said, "May your house stand fast against the storm, may winter treat you kindly and the New Year bless your increase."

"And Merry Christmas to you," she said, with no mention of the New Year. She wanted to ask him where the words came from but didn't for fear that in telling her he might snap the thread of Mike's tolerance, so she ushered him in after showing him the shining green bicycle, complete with chain guard and basket, that Mike had presented to her that morning.

The men had a glass of sherry, sitting comfortably around the blazing fire. Gally, in deference to the demands of the baby, stuck to tomato juice.

"Did Gally warn you?" said Mike. "We have a vegetarian Christmas lunch."

"She did," said Ferney, "and I'm very much looking forward to it," and Gally blessed him for not saying that he was vegetarian, too, and of course always had been.

There was in any case no need to apologize. Gally had made a cashew nut and mushroom roast with a rich gravy. It even had mashed parsnip among the ingredients, though that was an accident of the recipe and had nothing to do with Effie Mullard's doubtful urging. They served it with chestnuts, Brussels sprouts and cranberry sauce and Ferney ate heartily to start with but soon slowed down. Gally and Mike could both see sudden signs of pain on his face and he stopped eating completely for a minute or two while they gave him space by talking to each other. At that visible sign Mike seemed to realize for the first time the scale of the pain Ferney was going through and his whole demeanour changed from forced formality to concerned friendliness. The moment passed and Ferney began to eat again, but his appetite had gone and when Mike took the plates his was still half full.

"It was very good," he said. "I'm sorry I couldn't manage more. Not used to it, I suppose."

"Don't worry. There's just some fruit salad. It's fresh. Would you like some?"

"A little would be nice."

They went into the sitting room to drink coffee and Mike looked questioningly at Gally, who nodded.

"We've got something for you," Mike said, picking up a parcel from the table.

Ferney took it from him with a smile of acknowledgement. "Thank you," he said. He opened it to find a box of cassettes, talking books. They had searched for and found his favourite subjects and he looked through them with a pleased expression, taking each one out for inspection, then turned to Gally questioningly. "This doesn't mean you're going to stop reading, does it?"

"No, of course it doesn't. It's for the times when I'm not there."

He reached into his basket and brought out parcels for each of them. Mike opened his to find a bottle of port. "It's not quite the one I asked for I'm afraid. Mrs. Sparrow shopped for me and I don't think she understood the difference."

Mike was pleased anyway.

Gally's package contained a pen and ink drawing, faded and framed in ebony, and it prompted a cry of delight when she recognized it for what it was—their house, drawn a long time earlier when it had thatch on its roof instead of slates, smaller without the later additions at the end.

"I thought that belonged here," he said, watching her as Mike crossed the room and sat next to her on the sofa to look at it. "I've had it put away for a while until there was the right wall for it to hang on."

"The front door's in the middle, too," she said. "It must be quite old."

"Last century sometime."

Gally, looking at the picture, saw tiny initials in the corner, GA or maybe GR, and, recognizing the similarities to her own style, silently wished for Mike not to notice them. He didn't.

"I've got another present, too. It's meant for both of you," Ferney went on and lifted the last packet out of the basket. It was quite small but clearly very heavy. He hesitated. "I just have to say something first. I want you both to have it, so that it's safe, but it wouldn't do to go taking it to any museums or anything like that. It would only cause trouble. Is that all right?"

Mike and Gally looked at each other.

"That's hard to say without knowing," said Mike slowly. "You make it sound a bit . . . dangerous. It sounds like you're not sure it's yours to give. Is it . . . is it something like the ring?"

"A bit like it, but it's mine as much as it's anybody's. Until I hand it over, then it's yours," said Ferney wryly. "It's something I think you would appreciate. There's quite a story to it."

Mike nodded and Ferney held it out to him. He seemed reluctant to take it.

"Give it to Gally," he suggested.

"No, you take it," said Gally.

He unwrapped it carefully. Inside the red and green paper with its pattern of holly leaves was a mass of white tissue and he turned it over and over, hefting the weight as he unwrapped it. What came out of all the paper was puzzling, a thick, grey, metallic object shaped like a flat, blunt dagger, maybe nine or ten inches long, covered with patches of white powder. Mike studied it curiously, holding it gingerly by the handle. It meant nothing to Gally.

"Turn it over," suggested Ferney, "and round the other way."

That revealed two things. With what he'd taken to be the handle now furthest away, the dagger stopped being a dagger and revealed itself as a crude, stubby cross. The foot and the arms were straight-sided, but the topmost part splayed out, widening into a segment like a pie slice. The second revelation was what made them both stare. The surface was covered in deeply incised lettering.

"I know this," Mike said suddenly, "I've seen it. What on earth is it?"

"Can you work it out?" Ferney asked, watching him closely.

The letters were large crude capitals, running across every inch of the cross with no regard for where the words began or ended. "Hici," said Mike, "no, Hicia cet." He frowned, working it out. "Oh, I see, it's a J not an I. It's 'Hic jacet sepultus'. . ." He put it down on his lap and looked up at Ferney, shocked, then read it all off: " 'Hic jacet sepultus inclitus Rex Arturius insula Avalonia.' "

"Which means?" asked Gally.

He shook his head in wonder. "You won't believe this." He looked at Ferney. "You know what it means, do you?"

Ferney nodded. "You say it, if you know."

It took Mike a moment or two to get it out, looking down at the cross in wonder.

He shook his head and looked at Gally. "It's something like 'Here lies the tomb of the renowned King Arthur in the Isle of Avalon.' At least, I think 'inclitus' is renowned." He turned back to stare at Ferney. "I've seen pictures of this," he corrected himself. "Well, drawings anyway. That's all there is, just drawings. This thing has been missing since God knows when. Wait a minute."

He crossed to the half-full bookshelf by the fire and searched it quickly.

"Here we are."

It was a dark green book: *A Field Guide to Somerset Archaeology.*

"I'm sure it's in here. Now, what am I looking for?" He ruffled through it.

"I've got that one," said Ferney. "It's good. I expect it's under Glastonbury."

Mike nodded. "Yes, of course. Here it is. Here's the actual drawing of it, for God's sake. Look, Gally. The caption says 'The lead cross supposed to have been found with the burial of King Arthur at Glastonbury.' Now, let's see," he skimmed down the page. "It says the monks found it in 1191, but it disappeared later on."

Ferney nodded. "About 1540, I think."

Mike held the cross up in one hand and the book in the other, looking from one to the other. "This must be a copy," he said and added quickly, "Very beautiful for all that. Where did it come from?"

"Out of the pits. Where you saw me digging the other day."

Mike stared at him. "You dug it up? Out of the pits? But Ferney, we must tell *someone*. It could be a cache. There could be all kinds of other things there."

Ferney looked a little sheepish. "It was in the tin box, you see."

"The box? The box you dug up?" Mike was having trouble with this, though to Gally it was all quite obvious. "But who put the box there?"

"Well, I did, of course," said Ferney. "A fair old time ago, though."

Mike looked at the book and at the cross and put the cross very carefully down on the table. "Oh good Lord," he said, and rubbed his forehead. "Would you tell us the story? The whole story?"

"It's a funny old tale," said Ferney. "Tells you a lot about the religion business. I'll tell it if you really want to hear. It's not exactly a Christmas story."

"Tell us anyway. Please?"

He was about to start when he heaved up in his seat, turning white, and clutched at his waist, blowing out a fierce breath of pain. They were both by his side in a moment, but he got it back under control.

"Ferney, you really must take some of your stuff," said Gally.

He nodded with his eyes shut. "It's in the basket."

She poured it for him, watching anxiously as he drank it down. "Sit there and relax for a while," she said, recognizing he needed a bit of time to himself. "We'll just go and clear the table."

Mike followed her into the kitchen and only managed to keep silent until he got the door shut. "I've never seen anything like it," he said. "It's got to be a copy, hasn't it? I hope it's a copy. I mean it must be old, you can see that. It's got oxidization all over it. For heaven's sake, what if it's not a copy? We can't just hang on to it, can we?"

"We agreed we would."

"Yes, but . . . it's not a copy. I'm sure it's real. You can tell, can't you? It's got an atmosphere."

"Either way we agreed. Now are you sure you want to hear the story?"

"Why?"

"Because I don't want you getting all upset. It's going to be about, you know, other times."

"But there's the cross. It's sort of inevitable. You can't get away from it."

"You mean you're prepared to believe him just because there's a solid object?"

"It helps."

"Come on, we'd better go back."

Ferney was sitting in his armchair leafing through the archaeology book, looking better. "There's some stuff on Cenwalch's castle in here," he said, "and Stavordale."

"I haven't read about Stavordale," said Mike. "It's a priory, isn't it?"

"It's not far away," said Ferney. "Private house now. Best condition it's ever been in. It was always a poor sort of a place. Costs money to keep up stonework, and those monks never had any. There were a lot of shenanigans about who should have it when Henry shut down the monasteries. They pinched a few bits and pieces from it to put in the church here, you know."

"Do you feel well enough to tell us about the cross?" Gally asked.

"That stuff works," he said. "Though I expect it wouldn't if I used it all the time." They sat down and he smiled. "Now, if you're sitting comfortably, then I'll begin.

" 'Course, you know about Glastonbury," he said, "I'm sure I don't have to tell you. Started out with the Irish monks. They were simple in their ways, lots of praying and singing, and then it got bigger and bigger and like things usually do it all started to be about something else. Rich families started sending their kids there, like a boarding school, and they had money sticking to them so the monks kept on building bits and pieces to make the place grander until the Vikings came and stopped them, pretty much put an end to it. They got it going again, though. It was a busy old place, drew in the pilgrims like nobody's business. Then they had a bit of a setback in the year 1184." He glanced at Mike. "I looked it up to check. In a book. In 1184 they set fire to it. There was some young kid who'd been beaten for not sweeping properly and he put a torch to a chest full of manuscripts they kept in there, back of the altar."

"What book's that in?" said Mike, interested.

"Oh that bit's not in a book. That was just local talk at the time. Anyway it was a hell of a blaze, you could see it for miles."

Gally swept off on Ferney's words. A warm, windy evening in May and she was anxious. Her uncle had been summonsed to Bruton, charged with clearing his plot deeper into the forest than it was meant to be. Her father was brooding outside on the bench. She knew he was worried that if the fine was too big they'd all have to help pay, which would mean selling a cow and they'd only been able to keep three over last winter. They needed calves to build up again before the November slaughter. There were six other children to feed, though the baby, like the one before, wasn't going to last long.

"Why don't you go and play with the others," said her mother. "You don't seem to do it anymore. You spend more time with that boy than you do with your own flesh and blood." There was a call from outside and her mother ducked her head through the doorway. "And there he is. I suppose you'll be off?"

The news Ferney brought was just for her, but she had to tell the others, still feeling a member of the family despite his stronger call on her, and it set them all rushing off with most of the rest of the village too. They hurried past the little wooden church to Pond Hill and there away to the northwest was a great red glow in the sky and even, now and then, a tiny individual uprush of flames that carried across the miles. There was no doubt what it was. This was no small hut burning. Such events were commonplace, but in the sparsely populated flatlands below they would make a brief flare, a little local tragedy. This was a blaze feeding on massive volumes of wood to make such a mark from far on the dark horizon. They all knew their bearings well from this hill.

"It's Glastonbury," they said to each other. "It must be all of it."

It was a day's walk there and a day's walk back and she remembered the sense of disappointment when her father wouldn't let her go with Ferney when he came to ask the following morning.

This won't do, she thought. I mustn't drift off. Mike will hate it. And with an effort, she lifted her drooping head and brought herself back to Ferney's present voice.

". . . losing loads of money. All those relics and stuff, bits of saint's toe bones and other rubbish they'd got from travelling con men, all gone up in smoke. They couldn't do a thing about rebuilding unless they got some money coming in so they needed something fresh to bring in the crowds again." He laughed and the pain seemed forgotten. "The first thing they did was really pretty silly. They suddenly announced they'd dug up Saint Dunstan. I expect they chose him because he'd been taught there as a boy, so they say. He'd even built part of the church, so he must have seemed to be a pretty good rabbit to pull out of the hat. They hadn't done their homework, though. They shouldn't have claimed they'd found him because he wasn't missing in the first place. Someone pointed out that old Dunstan only had one body and the remains of that were still tucked up snugly in his tomb in Canterbury. They tried some cock and bull story about rescuing his body when the Vikings were raiding, but it didn't wash so they left it a year or two then they tried again."

He paused, smiling, and said to Gally, "Can I have a glass of water? My throat's a bit dry."

"I'll get it," said Mike, springing up.

"Is this all right?" whispered Ferney as soon as he was out of the room.

"You can't stop now. He's enjoying it."

Ferney sipped the water Mike gave him and carried on. "Like I say, they left it a year or two then they started digging again and guess who they found this time? King Arthur and Queen Guinevere, no less, and how did they know? Because with the bones in their coffins was that little lead cross with those Latin words on it and everyone took it for gospel truth, being a bunch of simpletons."

"So it wasn't true?" said Gally.

Ferney snorted. "No more true than if someone said today that they'd just dug up Mickey Mouse and his wife Minnie. The whole story of Arthur was flim-flammed up by some fanciful Welsh writer. He got everyone going about the Avalon business. Now those old boys in Glastonbury were pretty smart when it came to cashing in and they'd seen the way the Arthur story had caught on, so something that turned Glastonbury into Avalon was bound to be pretty good for trade. Still is, come to that." He chuckled. "I went there a couple of years back. There was a coach outing. I don't usually like those things, but I wanted to take a look at the place again. Crawling with New Age magic shops, Avalon this and Arthur that. This cross must have helped to bring in millions over the years."

"That's a bit disappointing," said Gally. "You *are* a cynic. I always thought Glastonbury was somewhere special." She regretted the words as soon as they were out of her mouth. Please don't say yes, you always did, she begged silently, but Ferney just gave her a short look and Mike didn't notice.

"I'm not saying it wasn't," he answered. "What with the Tor and all those Irishmen early on. You have to take a place like that a bit seriously because of what they believed even if you don't agree. It was that lot that came later who spoilt it. They got into this competition, you see, about another sixty years on. Just pure advertising, that was what it was, our saint washes whiter, that kind of thing. The people that ran Westminster Abbey started claiming St. Peter laid the foundation stone or some nonsense like that, so good old Glastonbury had to go one better. Joseph of Arimathea founded theirs, they said. Some poet, you could always rely on poets to come up with a good slogan, made up a story about how Joseph took the Holy Grail there, then they said he planted his staff and it grew into the Holy Thorn. Now they sell you crystal balls and King Arthur tee-shirts."

He fell silent and took another sip of water. Mike picked up the cross again. "So this has got a lot to answer for?" he said.

"Well they didn't know, did they? They took it for what they were told it was. In some of the books that have that drawing in them, they say it should have been obvious. Those letters are twelfth-century style, but who knew that at the time? Not even the monk who carved them out, I'll bet."

"How did you find it?" Gally noticed the tone of wonder in Mike's voice which showed he accepted it.

Ferney looked hesitant.

"Go on," Mike said. "Just tell it. I won't mind, at least I think I won't."

"Well let's say, there was this man. We're talking about the six-teenth century now." He screwed up his face in thought. "You know what was going on. Fat Harry knocking six bells out of the monasteries and giving them away to his mates. Have you ever heard the story of little John Champernown?"

"No."

"He was a decent enough man by all accounts. Went up to London from Devon on urgent business of some sort and when he got to the court, he saw a whole bunch of people kneeling down in front of old Henry so he thought he'd better kneel down too, just to show his respect, you know. He didn't realize the others were all queuing up for goodies and before he could get up Henry's men gave him some Cornish priory as a gift—St. German's, I think it was. He tried to explain it was a mistake so he could give it back, but they wouldn't have it." Ferney wheezed with brief laughter.

"Anyway, when the dust settled everyone started looting whatever they could. The king's men were pretty quick at grabbing all the gold and silver, but there was still the lead on the roofs and there'd be people up there taking all kinds of risks, pulling it off. Now to start with that was the way the king wanted it, because it would let the weather in quicker and bring the stones down, but after a bit he realized he was missing out on quite a lot of money, lead being valuable stuff, so he set his commissioners to grabbing what was left and shipping it to London. His cronies were building their own palaces wherever they'd been given the monks' lands and they were keen to give him a good price for stuff like that. Anyway a bit down the road from here there's this place Montacute and a man called Wyatt . . ."

Montacute. Mons acutus, the pointed hill. Gally had heard of the hill long before she ever saw it. The story had gone round the countryside as fast as travellers could carry it of the black flint cross that was dug up there, the Holy Cross that Harold worshipped, the cross whose name his troops shouted as they stumbled to defeat at Hastings. It was a weary way to Montacute, but she'd been before, once for the old fair on the hill when the Normans' castle, disused now, still stood. The next time she went the castle had seeded other buildings, stone by stone, so nothing was left there but a small chapel, and down the hill the French monks had built their beautiful monastery. The third time was when everything was changing.

Ferney tied their horses' reins to the ring on the leaning door and they walked, awestruck, arm in arm into the desecration of the old priory church. It was newly vandalized, open to the sky at one end where the fire had burnt through the roof timbers. A great heap of wood, curled and sectioned grey-black by the fire, was piled up below the hole. Around the edges they could see from surviving, part-charred boards that they had been pews, the fire extinguished by the pouring rain that came once the flames had breached the roof. Soaked, smoke-blackened hangings drooped down from the walls and the smell of wet ash spread through the desolation as the priory's final incense. A crow flew in through the stone tracery of the west window, where a few glass shards missed by the stone throwers gleamed. It swerved as it saw them, cawing loudly, and clattered out.

"It feels like a crime," she said to her brother.

"They've destroyed beauty that took time to make. That's the crime. There's nothing so destructive as belief."

"It's all right for us. How are other people meant to know what to believe?"

"Follow your sovereign," he said wryly. "That's what we're told, isn't it? We're not sinning if we do what royalty says, even if they change their mind every other year. Do you know what I mind most about all this?"

"No."

He waved his arm at the land outside the windows. "No more vines. No more wine. Do you realize they've driven out all the wine-makers? Without the priors there'll be nothing to drink but ale and that's a dreary prospect, my sister-love."

They went to the door and looked down the hill to where the men with the ropes and the sticks were laying out their geometric patterns. "It's going to be one of the greatest houses in the whole country when it's finished," said Ferney as they remounted, "according to Sir Thomas Wyatt."

His voice, older, echoed the words "Sir Thomas Wyatt" and she pulled herself out of it for a second time like a tired driver fighting off sleep. Brother and sister? How had *that* been? My God. They'd been rich that time round, it was clear, but brother and sister? How on earth would they have managed that? There wasn't time to get to grips with it now.

"So Wyatt bought a whole load of the Glastonbury lead for his new roof. There hadn't been nearly enough at Montacute Priory," said Ferney, "and this man I'm talking about came across the wagons on the road. One of them had a collapsed wheel, so they'd had to shift all the lead off it before they could take the wheel off and get it all sorted out. He got there just as they were putting the last of it back on and he spotted this bit of lead they'd missed lying in the mud. He wasn't a poor man so he wouldn't have been tempted to keep it, but when he picked it up and saw the writing, he couldn't bring himself to throw it on the wagon, knowing it would go in the melt with the rest, so that's how it turned up, you see. Wyatt never built the house, mind—lost it when his son joined the revolt against Bloody Mary, then it got sold on two or three times before the Phelipses finally took over the whole project. I expect they were glad to have the lead ready and waiting."

It begged every question there was. Ferney made no attempt to explain the cross's history in the four hundred years between that moment and the present day, but Mike accepted that.

"And now you really want us to look after it, do you?"

"Yes please. That and the drum, two of my special things. They'll be better off with you." The unspoken words "when I die" hung in the air.

There was a short silence and Mike seemed to feel a need to break it. "The Reformation," he said, "it's unimaginable really—the change it must have made to life."

"There's changes men bring about," said Ferney, "and there's changes that come anyway and sometimes they're better. King Henry and the Catholics, that was all about power. You know, whenever they get the chance there's always strong men, or women come to that, who'll start turning everything to their particular advantage. Before you know it they'll have a hold on everything. It takes a hell of an upheaval to break that. Do you know what it took to get rid of slavery in this country?"

"Slavery?" Mike shook his head.

"Well, peasants and that. The feudal times. It took the Black Death. Plague was the only thing that could loosen man's stranglehold on his fellow men. The Wars of the Roses were the same. All right, maybe men started that on purpose, but it soon got out of hand. It was real gang warfare, but at least it got rid of the barons, thanks be. They slaughtered each other. You know, when they're left to themselves men have always found ways to dominate their fellow men. Good men come in from time to time, but the difference they make usually crumbles. It takes natural disasters to undo the strangleholds of power. Disasters are the only things that work long term and that's a terrible thing to have to say."

"You don't have much faith in human nature," said Mike.

"The humans you can have faith in are the ones who see things every other way as well as their own. The ones who just see it one way have it so much easier. They can grab the reins without having to stop and think. It takes a few of the horsemen of the apocalypse to stop them usually—and faith? Now that's a truly dangerous thing." Ferney stopped talking as his face screwed up in pain again.

They did what they could. He wouldn't take any more of the painkiller and it seemed best to take him home. Mike insisted on doing that and she sat by the fire waiting for him to come back, looking at the lead cross. She thought if she tried hard enough she probably could remember the cross itself as well as the surrounding circumstances, but enough was enough and it didn't seem a good idea to push her luck now that Mike seemed to have taken to Ferney as never before. He also seemed to believe.

He was away for a surprisingly long time and when he finally came back, he looked thoughtful.

"I didn't really like leaving the old boy," he said. "He had another bad go when we got there and he still wouldn't take any more of that medicine." He sat down and picked up the cross again. "What a day."

"What do you make of him now?"

"I'm trying not to think about it. It goes against everything logical I believe in."

He turned to her and there was clearly something on his mind. "Look Gally, I stopped on the way back to think about all this. I don't think he should be at home in the state he's in."

"Mike. It's his choice. He really hates being in hospital. I'm quite sure he wouldn't go back there voluntarily."

"No, I wasn't going to say that." He looked nervous. "I wonder . . . whether we shouldn't ask him if he wants to come here."

"He can come here. He's just been here."

"I don't mean to visit. I mean to stay, if you feel you're up to looking after him, that is."

It should have been a moment of joy but to Gally it felt as if a trap had just snapped shut around her.

28

THEY MOVED HIM in on Sunday the twentieth of January after spending a busy Saturday putting the finishing touches to a bedroom for him at the other end of the house to their own. It had become impossible, in the ever-shifting shape of their triangle, for Gally to communicate to Mike the scale of her feeling about this. It was not straightforward fear, more a solemn apprehension at the weight of the destiny which he was unwittingly loading onto her. It seemed to her that he had just stacked the cards to hand Ferney a huge advantage in a game where she was the one who stood to pay the final price. If, however, she let him see the slightest loose end in her, he might start to unravel it and then she knew he would be horrified by what was revealed. He seemed to have left her no way out except to confront the situation in which Ferney would pass the last days of his life and the last days of her pregnancy in the closest possible contact with her in this house where their long bonding forces were the strongest. The old slanting stone drew her eye every time she looked out of a window like a finger pointing to a descending danger in the sky. Was it a friend? It felt like one, but if so it was an implacable friend who would tolerate no disloyalty. The stone had its silicon finger in her soul now and there seemed to be no denying it.

Mike had an occasional streak of stubbornness which only needed the wrong person to goad him to bring it out and the wrong person in this case was a pompous doctor who was very doubtful indeed about Mike's plan. Dr. Killigrew was absolutely certain that the best place for Ferney was hospital, possibly followed by a place in a hospice if he could find somewhere suitable, but he made the mistake of implying that if Mike only knew as much about these things as he did then he would see the overwhelming strength of his case. That was a put-down of the type Mike was well used to in the academic world and it was like a red rag to a bull. From that moment on he was absolutely determined that Ferney would come to Bagstone Farm whatever any-one said. Caught on the undeniable hook of the artifacts the old man had produced, he was looking after Ferney as if he were some elderly example of an endangered species.

"I don't really understand why you're not keener on this," he com-plained to Gally as they struggled into the bedroom with a set of shelves he had bought for Ferney's books. "Let's put it over there, near the bed."

"I . . . just don't know if we'll be able to cope," said Gally.

"A bit further over. Do you think the work will be too hard? The nurse is coming twice a day and Mary Sparrow says there's two or three others will come and help if you want."

"I'll manage. Here?"

"That's fine, I'll just get something to put under this corner. It's rocking a bit."

He went downstairs, leaving Gally wondering at the perversity of events. I suppose I just have to look on the good side, she thought. They'd be taking him back to hospital otherwise and then wouldn't I be equally bothered? It didn't help. It still felt as though she was set-ting out on an extremely hazardous venture. The coming birth felt re-mote and the issue it would bring seemed so theoretical that at times she could choose not to think about it. The coming death, too.

They went to get him together, loading the boxes of books Ferney had selected into the boot of the car with his clothes and making a collection in the hall of all the other things he had earmarked for his comfort—a radio, the TV, the video, piles of tapes. He had been wait-ing in his armchair and while Mike was outside, packing the stuff away, Ferney beckoned Gally to him. His voice had become notice-ably weaker.

"I know it's not what you want."

"Oh, Ferney. I do really. I'm just . . . worried."

"Don't be. It will be the way it has to be."

The baby kicked hard and she put her hand on where its feet had made their presence felt.

"Ferney, there's a date in my life that I can't avoid. My body's counting down to it. The middle of February is coming whether I like it or not."

"That's all right, isn't it?"

"No it isn't. You know that. It gives you a date too, doesn't it? It feels like I'm sentencing you."

He shook his head. "It's not like that. It's just the way of things. Neither of us lives forever, not in one go." He nodded towards her belly. "Anyway I wouldn't miss this one for anything. Not unless they drag me off to hospital."

Gally looked out of the window to check that Mike was still busy. "Effie Mullard said she thought her daughter was a bit doolally because she had to move out of the house before she had her."

"Could be."

"So . . . if anything goes wrong and you did have to go to hospital . . ."

"What?"

"I'm asking if my baby . . . you . . . if my baby might have something wrong with him because you ended up in Yeovil."

His mouth twitched with a sudden pain. "I see what you're getting at. No, I think just so long as *you* stay there in the right place, the stone will see you through. There'll be nothing wrong with the baby."

"But if you've been taken off somewhere else, it might not be you?"

"Then we'll just have to see, I suppose. Maybe I'll miss out. Maybe I'll be back some other way, but that's not what's going to happen and even if it did, I'd find you."

"You don't know that."

"I think I do this time."

Mike came back into the hall and she was left in an unexpressed hollowness of doubt.

They moved him in and it was clear to Gally straightaway that for Ferney, any slight difficulties that resulted from the separation from most of the familiar objects of his life were swamped by the huge comfort of being back in the most familiar place of all. He settled into his bed and his armchair which gave him a view out of the window at the back of the house, down the slope of the hill to the open lands. The pain was now coming at increasingly frequent intervals, but the move seemed to have given him a new serenity in dealing with it.

On the first Monday morning, after Mike had left at the crack of dawn to drive off to his week at work, Gally lay in bed seeing five days full of unchaperoned danger ahead. It started from the first moment of silence after the car's line of noise had dwindled into the startling pink of the striated horizon, and in her half-sleeping, half-waking state the window asserted itself for a moment as smaller, its bars thicker and the glass carving swirls of bright distortion out of the dawn. She sat up sharply, rejecting it, slamming the newer window back into place with a force that jolted her to her soul, then she sat there for an hour reviewing the certain unmistakabilities of her life and they seemed to add up to a shorter list than she would have liked. At the end of the hour, she heard Ferney shuffle to and from the bathroom and then she went downstairs, made him a cup of tea and, wrapped in a long dressing-gown, went to confront the issue.

When she knocked there was silence and she pushed the door cautiously open. He was half-sitting up in bed gazing towards the window, his books neglected on the bedside table, and it took a few moments for him to register her presence. His face as he turned it to her seemed at first to have nothing of him inhabiting its diminished skin and bone, but then he came back from somewhere and animation slowly returned to the muscles around his cheeks, jaw and brow so that his eyes, tired and pained though they now were, came back to life and made him Ferney again.

"How kind of you," he said as she put the teacup beside him.

She crossed to the armchair and sat down with her own tea.

"How did you sleep?"

"So well that I don't remember."

"Are you awake enough to talk?"

"Yes. What's bothering you now?"

"I think I need some sort of code of conduct."

He knew what she meant without her having to say another word.

"Haven't you noticed?" he said.

"Noticed what?"

"I haven't led you back to anything for weeks now."

"You have. When you were telling us about the cross, the Glastonbury cross."

"You went back then?"

"You know I did."

"I thought maybe you did. I wasn't quite sure—but that wasn't me, Gally dear, that was *you*. You know the trick now."

"But . . . okay, but when you talk about things like that it pulls the feet out from under me."

"I know when to push and when not to push. Whatever happens now is between you and the rest of yourself. I've done what you asked. I've helped you back to all that. It's not for me to do any more than that."

Gally knew it was true, knew that she was looking for him to make it all safe for her when the real danger was at large within herself.

"Will you help me?" she said. "I understand all that, but will you try not to trip me up with things that take me back there? I know exactly what the question is, but I don't want to answer it bit by bit. I want to answer when the moment comes, otherwise I think it will get harder for me to know what I've got to do."

She was amazed that she could speak so calmly. Certainly she knew what the question was. The question was death.

He sighed and she couldn't tell if it was pain or not. "I'll do my best," he said. "It's difficult to be sure I can get the boundaries right, but I will try."

He came downstairs for a while during the morning and she made sure the fire was kept stoked up for him. She read to him for an hour, then the grim pain undermined his concentration and he went back to bed. The nurse came in the afternoon.

That evening she sat in his bedroom armchair again watching him sitting up in bed, eating a tiny meal as the television launched into the six o'clock news. It was all about the Gulf, the Scud missiles, the air war. Ferney watched intently.

"What do you think about it all?" she asked when the news finally turned to lesser events. It was the first time all day she had asked him for an opinion, given him the invitation to delineate the boundaries she had requested.

He gave her a look that said he was grateful for that trust. "The history books I've read make me wonder," he said. "It's all a long, long process and I think the geography has got in the way of the history so the whole thing's a bit stuck right now. Did you want a long answer or shall I stick to something short and pointless?"

"A long one, please." The sound of his voice in this warm, familiar room set up little currents of satisfied pleasure just under her skin. It was rich and companionable and she didn't want it to end.

"The books tell you what's happened so far, don't they? Go right back and there were tribes, hating and fearing and preying on each other most of the time. Then you get towns and cities doing the same sort of thing until there's a bigger threat and they get together. Then it's little states. Then it's big states and all the time it's all those separate fearing, hating groups joining up into bigger groups and finding another foreign rival to hate. Do you see what I mean?"

"I suppose I do. It sounds horrible. I thought you were going to be cheerful."

"Oh, but I am. That's the point. Just look where we are now. That whole process can't have suddenly stopped dead in its tracks, surely. I read a book on Switzerland last year. They were all separate groups living in the valleys just like tribes, you might say. The mountains gave them the ignorance to let them hate the people on the other side. Then they crossed the mountains. Now they're a nation. We've just got to keep on crossing the mountains, haven't we? Like England, Wales and Scotland stopping fighting and getting together. That's got to go on."

"How can it?" Gally asked gently. "Look at America. It runs right to the ocean all around."

His face lost its colour and she watched, feeling sympathetic pain as he struggled for breath for a whole minute, pushing the pain down. It subsided leaving him visibly weaker, shrinking in the bed in its backwash. After a long silence he pointed at the television and said in a smaller voice, "That's a bridge. That thing. It's got a lot wrong with it, but it lets you visit and when you see enough of a place it's harder to hate it. We'll get beyond the oceans somehow."

"You're an optimist, then?"

"Oh, that's another question completely. All I'm saying is this nationalism business—it changes all the time. There wasn't any nationalism in this country until Napoleon came along—not the sort of nationalism that had everyone spouting slogans and singing. That's quite new really. Before that wars were just things the nobs organized, nobs and mobs." He fell silent perhaps feeling he was getting a bit near the limits they'd agreed. "That's in books," he said and she smiled.

IN THE NEXT two weeks they quickly fell into a gentle pattern in which she pottered about the house, gradually tackling the small jobs that fine-tuned it to her vision. With each day, Ferney was less able to sustain a long conversation without breaking off for long moments in which he would wrestle with his cruel, multiplying invader and she would have to sit there in her own minor harmony of pain wishing she could help with more than words. If she had to go out, pedalling down from the ridge to the nearest shops for supplies, she would try to do it when the nurse, a capable and sympathetic woman, was there or else she would ring for Mary Sparrow to come over, but on those occasions Ferney would make a face and ask her not to be too long.

In the evenings he would go to sleep early. She knew the nurse had left tablets he could take to help him sleep, but she let him have

the dignity of making that decision without her interference. She
would sit downstairs by the fire, certain that if he needed her she
would know. On one such evening, early on, she found herself deeply
aware of the new life inside her in a more direct way than she had
been before. At the same time, she felt a faint finger of Ferney's pain
feel towards her from the room upstairs and as she put down her
book, disturbed by it, the pain hardened inside her into an uncomfortable muscle spasm that tightened and pulled into cramping discomfort low down in her guts. It caught her off balance, just as she
was reaching out towards Ferney's pain, and as she was wide open it
magnified her own and had her gasping and confused with its twisting squeeze until it had its way and started to subside. Then she recognized it as a contraction and curled up around her belly to protect
it, feeling the muscles gradually return to their normal state. She
waited for a long, suspended time, staring into the fire. A log tipped,
its balance eaten by the flames, and overbalanced, coughing sparks,
but no more pain came. Braxton Hicks, she said firmly to herself, just
a Braxton Hicks contraction—not the beginning of the end, not yet.
It made her think, for all that, and the experience looming in the fog
of the near future seemed more like a reef than a harbour.

In the firelight she took an inventory of herself and her resources
and had a sense of the progress she had made in the months since that
panic attack down by the roadworks. No more boilman, no more
burnman. They were history now, not horror. The old nightmares
had gone. The new one hadn't. She didn't understand the change, but
perhaps she would in time. Guilt went with it still. She felt less irrational fear now, a touch of claustrophobia maybe. I am getting better,
she thought, it's wisdom I'm still short of.

Her thoughts were interrupted by headlights turning across the
window with the descending growl of a car entering the gate and it
was then for the first time that she realized this was Friday and the
footsteps approaching had to be Mike. They met in the hall and
he studied her as if he were not sure what he would find.

She kissed him on the cheek and he raised an eyebrow.

"That's a bit formal."

He put his arms round her and kissed her on the mouth and she
had to suppress the reaction that it felt an intrusion.

"Have you had a good week?"

"All right in parts. How's it been with Ferney?"

"He's going downhill."

"Have you been able to cope?"

"Oh yes. The nurse is pretty good."

He looked round the hall. "You've painted the doors."

"Do you like them?"

He thought the green she had used was too dark and said, "Yes," with just a shade too much enthusiasm, so she knew he didn't.

The weekend passed quietly with her inhabiting the no-man's-land between the two men. Each day as Ferney diminished in tiny stages which could only be noticed, like the movement of an hour hand, by looking away, she found herself more and more in touch with the new life inside her and able to imagine it taking on the mental outlines of a person. On Sunday morning she took Ferney his breakfast as Mike prepared hers downstairs. Ferney's face was stretched on a bony rack of pain and she stood by him, holding his wrist in support, feeling a one-way flow of life between them that she knew would now be evident whenever she stepped into the inner circle of his presence.

When he recovered and even smiled a little, she had to bend to hear him.

"I want to pay my keep," he said.

"No, that's fine."

He frowned. "I don't want you to say that. It isn't fine. Listen to me."

She saw it mattered to him and kept silent.

"Go to the bungalow for me. There's a room at the back—before the one where the picture is?"

Gally remembered the quick glimpse of shelves and a row of clocks, Ferney's odd storeroom. "Yes."

"Go in there. By yourself, if you can. There are some tobacco tins on the right, under a green cover. Bring me one."

Mike wanted to come too when she said she was going to get something for Ferney.

"I'd rather we didn't leave him by himself," she said. "Do you mind staying?"

It was raining; she would have walked anyway, but he made a big thing about her taking the car and so as to limit the disagreement she gave way. She picked up the mail from Ferney's mat—it was mostly junk apart from two magazines, an electricity bill and a rather official-looking white envelope—then, with a sense of keen anticipation, she went into the room at the back of the house.

It was not nearly so full, she was sure, as when she had glimpsed it previously. All but one of the clocks she had seen had gone. The remaining one was an old bracket clock shrouded in a clear plastic bag which contained a sachet of crystals inside it, marked "desiccant."

Another shelf, she could see, held a few toys in boxes, from Dinky cars of the sixties through to modern plastic. Most of the rest of the shelves which had previously been piled high now contained only folded sheets and rugs except in a corner where one sheet covered several lumpy shapes. Though she felt trusted by Ferney to use her eyes, she respected his privacy too much to lift the covers. She knew perfectly well without having to risk any journey into her memory that what she could see was the remaining currency of his squirrel-caches of objects, the means by which he had learnt to transfer wealth between his generations. He must have been busy putting them back in the ground.

She followed his instructions, lifted the cover and found two square Navy Cut tobacco tins. They were heavy for their size and she took one, covered up the other and returned to Bagstone Farm after checking that all was well with the rest of the house.

When she gave the tin to Ferney he was clearly pleased. He held it in both hands and had trouble managing even that moderate weight. He fumbled with the lid, failed, sighed and she took it from him again.

"Shall I do it?"

He nodded.

Inside the tin was a folded plastic bag and inside the bag were twenty coins, heavy coins carrying inscriptions and Queen Victoria's head. They shone golden.

"Sovereigns," Ferney whispered. "I've got a number you can ring. There's a man at Ilminster gives me a good price for them. They'll help pay the bills."

The man arrived with cash on Tuesday. Gally dreaded his questions, but he didn't seem inclined to ask any. He wore a fur hat and had thick glasses and his car was a highly polished old Rover.

"It used to be the Queen's," he said as he got out when he saw Gally looking at it. "Mr. Miller's staying with you, is he?"

"Yes, he's not too well. He asked me to fix it with you."

"I've done a lot of business with him over the years. He's a good man. Give him my best wishes."

That was the extent of his curiosity. He peeled £20 and £50 notes off a large roll and left without a backward glance.

THE CRISIS CAME in the form of Dr. Killigrew on Wednesday afternoon. He arrived unannounced, which was quite rude enough, but it was clear to Gally from his whole haughty approach that he saw her as an obstacle that simply had to be swept aside. Even before he'd seen Ferney he started laying down the law that he thought they'd come to the end of what they could hope to do at home.

"We *are* coping," said Gally defiantly, keeping him from going straight upstairs.

"It's not within your realm of competence. He needs a proper regime of pain management," said the doctor. "He's got to be in a suitable place for that."

"This is a suitable place. He's very happy here."

"But you're not even family, are you?"

"What's that got to do with it?"

Upstairs he behaved as though Ferney were an imbecile, speaking loudly and slowly to him.

"Mr. Miller. We're going to see if we can't move you to somewhere nice. I think you need a bit of special looking after. How would that be?"

"I'm staying here," said Ferney.

"Yes, yes. I'm sure Mrs. Martin's seeing to you very well, but it wouldn't be good for you. We'll have to see."

"No we won't," said Ferney, summoning fresh strength into his voice. "It's got nothing to do with you. I want to stay."

"Look, Mr. Miller, I've got your best interests at heart and I do know what I'm talking about." The words were caring, but the voice betrayed them. "We can do a lot more in hospital to help you through this than we can if you're here. You should listen to advice."

"I know what it'll be like."

"With respect," said the doctor, with no respect, "I don't see how you can."

Ferney's face, so pale lately, flushed with more colour than Gally had seen in it for weeks and she was afraid for a moment that he would tell the doctor exactly what was wrong with his presumption. All he said, with slow-paced controlled fury, was, "You are a fool and I am staying here. Now bugger off." Then, paying the price of his emotion, he gasped in pain.

Dr. Killigrew chose to see only that and left the house with the arrogant speed of an insecure authoritarian, leaving Gally fuming in his wake. She kicked the door hard as he drove away without once looking back towards her, then went slowly upstairs.

Ferney's eyes were closed but they flickered open when she closed the door softly behind her.

"You can't get through to people like that," he whispered.

She found she was crying. "We'll stop him," she said.

"There's something I want to tell you." His voice was so faint she had to lean closer. "The policeman. He sent me Billy Bunter's . . ." He gasped then clenched his teeth in pain and it was all forgotten as she found the liquid for him, spooned it down and then sat there holding his hand until he went off to sleep.

That evening she tried to ring Mike, but the phone rang and rang and he hadn't come back at ten o'clock when the emotion of the afternoon turned to exhaustion and she fell asleep, fully dressed on her bed.

The dream was heading for its conclusion, her hands around her father's neck, when she woke at four in the morning to the immediate and certain knowledge that Dr. Killigrew's plans did not matter one bit. A great silent voice was crying through the house. All the ranked generations of Ferneys and Gallys seemed to be there with her in the room, reaching out to her, helping her up from the bed with an intensity of love and pain. In the room at the other end of the house, she knew immediately, Ferney was dying.

29

IN THE DARK the house was a stone organ sweeping her to him down the wooden tube of its corridor in a whirl of inaudible music. Her skin trembling, she paused for courage outside his door, then pushed it open to enter the stage for his final act.

He lay, head arched back a little like a bishop on a tomb, straight and white on the bed, and she inched towards him in fearful reverence. He breathed in a light rhythm, slow and shallow, and his eyes were closed. They opened as she bent over him, focused beyond her, and in a remote breath of a voice he said, "Gally?"

"Yes, I'm here."

"It doesn't hurt anymore."

"I'm so glad."

"Stay here."

"Of course I will."

There was a long silence and she kept still, bending over him while his eyes flickered shut then open again. The room was warm and the house was utterly quiet now that its summons had been met.

"Don't be afraid." She could barely hear his words.

Pulling the armchair to the side of the bed, she tried sitting down, but he moved his head, looking for her, and though she could see his lips moving, the faint words weren't clear.

"I'm here," she said softly and with tremendous effort he summoned up a full voice, timeless and devoid of age. "Lie with me," he said.

The bed was wide and she carefully lay down next to him, on her side, facing him with one of his hands clasped between both of hers. She had to lie curled, aslant, to make space for her full belly. The effort past, he had only a whisper left, but it was enough at this short distance.

"I can see so much," he said in tones of delight.

"What do you see?"

"Maypoles. When the maypoles came back." The remains of his voice changed pace, becoming less deliberate—the accidental outer manifestation of what was passing in his mind. "Cheer for the king. Gally, there's a king again. I don't care for kings but we can dance now and that's worth cheering for. Let's dance. I love to dance with you. Come with me." He gave a small cry of delight and in her mind's eye for a second she saw striped, fresh-painted maypoles, people whirling in cavalier joy. High poles, tall people. She and Ferney holding each other, scampering in their midst, so small, so happy, so complete.

"The killjoys are gone." One of their voices said it but she did not know whose it was.

"Kings," he whispered. "So few good men. Must tell the old stories. Who keeps the place right if we don't? Who listens? Who listens now?"

"I'm here. I'm listening." The countryside was listening, too. Beyond the house Gally felt the ridge crouched like a faithful dog sorrowing at the deathbed of its master, its protector, the articulator of its life story.

"I knew you the first second. Standing in the house with him." He was back in the present. "It was like being kicked. I knew who you were, but I thought I must be wrong until he spoke your name. Why's he there, Gally? Why's he in the way?"

She wanted to curl away from the question, but there was no possibility of escape from the stark truth his death was demanding.

"I didn't know. That's why. You know that's why. He's good to me. He's good to us. He was the most special person I'd met until I met you again."

The echoes of "until" started tears springing in the corners of her eyes. This was her man dying here. Her only man.

He was silent. His eyes closed again. A moth took off from the lampshade, swirled twice round their heads and settled on the wall. With his eyes shut he spoke in a voice that made no more noise than the moth's wings.

> "Let not our divided hearts be sworn to any other,
> There's love that stays and love that parts and love of sister,
>   brother.

Our halves are nothing on their own but half and half make one,
And halves divided stand alone when the adding's done.
Half-hearted I should never find my matching half elsewhere.
Without your half, my sister kind, my sum will be despair."

The sun grew bright and the room spread out. He finished with a theatrical groan, then sprang up off the couch and she laughed with delight.

"That's what you get when your tutor insists on teaching you mathematics and all you have in your soul is poetry," he said. His eyes twinkled and he was beautiful in his doublet and hose and she thrilled to the verve of him. "I do mean it, though," he said. "Our father has a husband up his capacious sleeve for you, Gally my sister-love."

"Do you know that? Who is it?" she asked, afraid.

"Thomas Phelips who will have the Montacute estate when the time comes, as well as that great house they're planning if they ever get round to building it."

It was inconceivable to her.

"I shall tell him I will not."

"And he will say it is not for you to decide."

"This is dreadful. I'm sure it has never happened before."

"We have never been brother and sister before."

"Nor have we both been born into fortune."

"I don't call this fortune," said Ferney impatiently, striding to the window and, putting one foot up on the window seat, he leaned on his raised knee as he looked out at the formal gardens. "I call this prison. Sneaking to your room, knowing what they'd say if we were found together. This isn't fortune. When we're poor nobody else owns our hearts. Everything else maybe, but not our hearts."

"And no one does now."

"But they think they do."

"I can't be told to spend the rest of my life with anyone else," she said, as the idea he had planted doubled and redoubled into its full enormity.

"And nor can I." He sprang away from the window, ran and slid to her on his knees, burying his head in her lap. She stroked his hair, loving him with the full love that results from having no fear of ever being denied or rejected or cut short.

In the present, silent room where Ferney lay sharing the faint echoes of it through antennae extended by the altered brain chemistry of his approaching death, she called in her sixteenth-century voice: "What will happen to us?" and a whispered answer came back with the certainty of history behind it, "The Sweat."

Words danced in her head, sweat, sickness, sweat and under them another insistent interloper—skimmington, the skimmington.

"He's dead," said her brother beside her bed in the middle of the night. "The sweating sickness."

"Dead? Father?"

"Yes, dead. The servants have run from the sickness. We must go. Come with me."

"Where?"

"Back home to the Bag Stone. The cottage is empty."

"You know that?"

"I went back there to see. We can be there together. No one will know who we are. We can be properly together, sister-love."

The skimmington skirled its sinister sibilance.

"Come with me."

Come to what? She scented distress down that road and Ferney's death reverie rescued her, turning them both away to a hilltop road of dressed chalk and stone on a dreamlike day in sparkling January where a laughing man in a stovepipe hat beckoned, shouting, "Come Ferney, come Gally. Now. The *char volant* will wait no longer and the wind is rising, my beauties."

"There are fresh miracles every day," said Ferney, running hand in hand with her to the spindly carriage. "Good morning, Captain Hudson."

"Good morning to you. Get in, get in," he cried back. "You shall be the first."

The horses were grazing, uncoupled from the traces, and long cords led from the captain's hands where he sat ready on the box to the great frames his men held a hundred yards ahead. "Have you been eating well?" he roared. "It's weight I need, weight at the back there." Gally and Ferney were laughing too much to answer, settling themselves on the plank that served as a seat across the back of the platform.

The captain glanced over his shoulder. "Get ready now," he bellowed to his men. "She's running up astern. Launch when she's on the beam."

Behind them the London stage coach, paint and varnish shining, swayed out of the trees onto the plain.

"Stand by for the maiden voyage of the *char volant*," bawled the captain. "Wait for it. LET GO!"

The men thrust the unwieldy frames up and the wind took them streaming into the sky with long tails steadying them as they climbed. The captain, strapped to his seat, had his arms braced against wooden posts. Holding the kite cords like reins, wrapped round his wrists, he was pulled forward by the strength of their tug and the carriage began to roll with increasing speed, Ferney cheering loudly from the back. In seconds they were barrelling across the plain, yawing as the wind took the kites crazily off to one side, the captain fighting with the lines to pull them straight again. Passengers on the stage coach looked across at them, astonished, and the driver thrashed his whip across the backs of the startled, nickering horses to take on the outlandish challenge or perhaps simply to try to get clear of this alarming sight that was racing along beside him. The *char volant,* towed by the soaring kites, accelerated to the speed of a galloping horse and then beyond into a sensation of bucketing, breathtaking pace that was completely new to Gally, exhilarating and terrifying in equal measure. The kites were primrose yellow against the winter-blue sky. The coach was dwindling behind them.

"This is the future," shrieked the captain. "Gurney's steam coach will never beat the horses. The *char volant* will double their speed. We can fly with the wind."

"So long as it's blowing the right way," Ferney shouted back, but the captain, letting go of both cords as the track ahead turned sharply to the right, took no notice. The kites whirled off, tumbling to the ground, and the carriage bounced to a halt.

They were walking back to the house. "There's always something new," Ferney said, his arm comfortably around her.

"Not always something quite so new as that."

"No, thank heaven, but the more I see, the more I learn to see."

She understood. "Every sunset, every flame."

"Infinite variety."

Back in the house they stood admiring the new painting, still bright in its bold colour, commanding the wall. She loved to see the image of the pair of them standing by the gate—the house and the stone completing their triangle. It was a record of themselves that they had never had before and she wondered how they could preserve it for their futures. In that transported state, all her reticence suspended, she finally understood how completely she belonged to Ferney and he to her and that what was between them ran very much deeper than any love she had previously imagined or heard described. They were indeed two halves whose joining produced a state of ecstatic understanding that was entirely unique. Nothing could go wrong for long unless they lost each other in the crowded speed and distance of this new time.

The joint dream was broken then, as his hand tightened convulsively on hers. She came back to the bedroom in its stillness with an answering spasm inside her and stroked his hand, murmuring comfort for them both. When she saw his lips move she had to put her cheek almost alongside his to hear.

"I wish they hadn't burnt the colours. Colours were joy. They burnt the colours in the churches. Didn't like the churches, but I liked the colours. Henry made them. They burnt them or they covered them with paint. Colours are fear now, not joy. Painters are afraid of colour. Pictures should be bright. Our picture should be bright. It *was* bright."

"We can clean it. It will be bright again."

"Clean it so you can always see us there."

"I will."

"Say the prayer for me. Alfred's prayer."

She said it in a low voice which trembled just a little: "Thou art the end and the beginning. Thou carriest me. Thou art the way and the journey's end. Even so, God, be my companion today."

"Gally?"

"Yes, my dearest?"

"Be my companion."

"I am. I always will be."

"Come with me."

He turned his head slowly and looked at her and all she could see was the light in his shining eyes which was the sight she knew best and loved most in the world and as she looked at it, the light seemed as much in her as it was in him. A moment came in the pin-drop quiet of that room when all the light was within her. Then she looked at him with a full feeling of life inside her and his eyes were uninhabited. She bent and kissed his forehead and a strong swelling pain told her that in this moment when life had left him, her time had come too.

Outside the window a faint line of pink showed on the horizon and she tried to be sad that Ferney had missed the dawn, but knew that this *was* his dawn. She left the room as the contraction passed and went carefully down to the telephone knowing she held a powerful life within. The phone at the flat rang six times before Mike's sleepy voice answered.

"Umm, hello?"

She didn't know how to announce herself because Ferney seemed to own all the available aspects of her and she could not be disloyal to him.

"It's me."

"Gally? What's happened?"

"Ferney's . . . gone."

"Oh God. When?"

"Just now."

"Was he . . . were you with him?"

"Yes."

"By yourself?"

"Yes."

"Are you all right?"

"Yes, I think so."

"Oh, Gally. I'm on my way."

"If you want to. There's something else."

"What?"

"The baby's started."

He told her to call the hospital, the doctor, the police, Mary Sparrow and everyone else he could think of. She got him off the phone as soon as she could and went back to the bedroom to sit next to Ferney's body.

His voice called from corners of the room or perhaps from corners of her head: "Come with me."

Another strong contraction took her like an earthquake of the flesh and she heard him again: "Come with me."

What was here next to her on the bed was a mockery of what he had been, a meaningless husk. What was to come was a child. Of course she would love her child, all the more because it was Ferney, but what comfort would there be for her? What she yearned for was to have him there, strong and young and with her so that they could share each other in every way. She found herself crying and once she had started the tears came stronger and stronger until she was pouring aching tears at the loneliness that faced her. It felt at that moment as though this next childhood were a prison sentence, an emotional separation laid out in years and tens of years from the man she longed for. She went in her head back to the top of the hill on that day with the garland in her hair when she had told Ferney what they must do and this time she found herself astride him, united in love and pure delight and she could feel every atom of him and every spark of his soul and she knew she must have this again, that she must do this deed and she could not deny the inevitability of the solution she had herself invented.

She quietened down then, became purposeful, shutting Mike out of her mind and considering the ways. As soon as the baby was born she must do it, before what pretended to be normal life caught her in its deceiving grip. Ferney's painkiller was on the table and beside it stood the almost unused bottle of his powerful sleeping tablets. She took them in her hand, went down to the kitchen, stopping on the way to sit on the stairs with another powerful contraction, and then she crushed the tablets into the mixture, pouring the result into a small bottle which she topped up with brandy. Putting the bottle in the bag she had packed for the onset of birth, she began to climb the stairs to Ferney's room.

This time the voice was within her: "Come with me."

The contractions were coming faster now, so she turned back to the telephone.

The 999 operator answered immediately and asked her which service she required.

"I'm sorry, I'm not sure whether this counts as an emergency or not. I'm having a baby and the contractions are coming quite fast now."

"We'll get you an ambulance. Don't worry. Where are you?"

Gally told him.

"Are you alone?"

"Well that's the other thing. There was someone else here but he's just died. That's what started the baby."

"Mrs. Martin, if this doesn't count as an emergency, I don't know what does."

She went back up to the bedroom to wait with Ferney and sat, nursing the contractions for a timeless space. She saw the white envelope open on the bedside table and knowing what it must be, picked it up, sitting irresolute, holding it. It was the police sergeant's letter about Billy Bunter. She knew it had mattered a great deal to Ferney and felt glad that it had arrived in time. She considered reading it, but tyres on the gravel stopped her before she could reach a decision.

The police beat the ambulance by a minute or two and took over. Gally was in hospital within half an hour, beyond concentrating on anything by this time but the coming birth, making sure all the time that her bag was beside her. Between shuddering, gasping contractions, she prayed that Mike would not arrive in time—the whole thing would be simpler that way, and she found herself able to block out all thought of his reaction. The immediate process involving her, her body and this special life which was now locked and limited inside her commanded all the imagination she could spare.

It was a rapid, forceful business. A midwife encouraged her, doctors came and went, a nurse held her hand, smiling sincere wishes that she was sure her hubby would be here at any minute. The huge impossible pain set new boundaries with each contraction until she felt she must tear apart, but there was no stopping this immensely powerful pumping that her body had never told her it knew how to do.

"I can see it," said the midwife. "I can see the head. Nearly there."

I want the bottle, Gally just had time to think. I must have it as soon as he's born. Another screaming heave blotted out the thought. Can I reach it, she wondered in the short gap when thought was again possible. Better not to linger on the baby. Or maybe I should take it as soon as I can rest, then they won't think it's odd if I sleep. This was it. This had to be it or she would die of pain. Die of pain. Come with me. Pain. Come with me.

"It's here," said the midwife and Gally knew she needed no bottle, that now at this moment of physical chaos she had the power to simply cease to live and that was what she *would* now do. The baby slipped wetly from her into the midwife's hands and she felt her speeding heart accelerate to burst.

The midwife changed all that with four absurd words just as Mike rushed into the room.

"You have a daughter."

30

ON THE MORNING of 7 February, Rose's second birthday, Gally got up early and walked to the church to put fresh flowers on Ferney's grave, because this was also the second anniversary of his death and she owed it to her beautiful daughter to put the sadness out of her mind for the rest of the day.

She squatted in front of the grave, staring at the headstone as if it might hold the clue to what had happened. It was easiest to go along with Mike's view that they had both fallen under some temporary persuasive madness, though she guessed he only used the word "both" to avoid it sounding like an accusation. She knew that wasn't what had happened and she didn't need any of the pieces of solid evidence—the ring, the Glastonbury cross, or the drum now shrouded in their attic—to confirm that. When her guard was down, fresh insights into her long past would come creeping in, although she rarely sought them out deliberately, and that was all the proof she needed.

The great fear that ambushed her if she woke in the early hours was that Ferney's worries about the modern world had been borne out, that he had been torn away at that critical moment, hijacked perhaps by some passing ambulance carrying another imminent mother towards delivery and was, even now, adrift out there in a foreign world, aching dimly for comfort he could not find. She sometimes considered going round the hospitals, or sorting through the public registers to find out who else had been born around that same time and one day soon she might even be driven to do that.

There was a practical and moral problem driving her in that direction. A week after Ferney's death they had been asked to come to the offices of a Wincanton solicitor who had told them that Ferney had left the bungalow to Gally to be disposed of as she thought fit. The solicitor was clearly puzzled by the rest of his instructions. Ferney had left the rest of his estate including "his possessions wherever they might be" to Gally's first-born. Rosie was now therefore the owner of Ferney's furniture and books, the contents of his cupboards and some £80,000 in various investments. She was also the owner, Gally realized, of a vast hoard of tins and boxes, buried who knows where, in which Ferney had concealed his caches of treasure and to which perhaps, one day, a young unknown Ferney might return. Knowing that, as things had turned out, this was a mistake, Gally felt a powerful responsibility to make sure it was set right if it were possible to do so. This was not something she could ever discuss with Mike.

In other ways she had done all she could to rebuild her old life with Mike, avoiding the danger areas as much as she could. They had a life, centred around Rosie, that worked better than she could reasonably have expected. She respected and at the very least liked Mike enormously and that was as much as most people had, wasn't it? As she looked at the headstone, it was clear to her that it wasn't enough and she heard again Ferney's voice, deep and powerful now.

"Come with me."

She shook her head, blinked back tears and turned away.

On the way back she tried to remember the words of Ferney's poem as she had tried many times in the past two years. It always seemed blocked by fear. Two lines came back:

> Our halves are nothing on their own but half and half make one,
> And halves divided stand alone when the adding's done.

Now that she finally understood the fear and the guilt, now that even the last variant of her nightmare had been wiped away by knowledge, it seemed possible that she could retrieve the rest of his poem, which was precious to her beyond belief. In the background to that poem there had always been this familiar, unfamiliar word—the skimmington. A few weeks earlier she had discovered what it meant. They had gone to Montacute House, because Mike wanted to. Rose was in her pushchair and they had wandered past the portraits and the fine Elizabethan panelling. In the Great Hall they paused in front of a high-mounted plasterwork panel and a guide, with a group behind them, began to intone an explanation.

"This panel is a lively depiction of an old country tradition known as a Skimmington ride," he had said and Gally, about to move on, had frozen to the spot. "You'll notice the man riding backwards on the donkey, facing the tail while the others heap ridicule upon him. This was a custom used to force henpecked or cuckolded husbands to stand up for themselves for fear they would be paraded round in this manner if they allowed it to continue. The skimming ladle, normally used for skimming milk in cheesemaking, was used to beat the man and the Skimmington ride was also used to punish other offences against sexual standards of the times."

Gally had stood there transported to a cold, violent night when she and Ferney had been dragged from the house—brother and sister living as man and wife, beaten round the village, lashed to a horse. Beaten although no one knew the real truth and if they had, they would have beaten them twice as hard. How could they ever ask for understanding outside their universe of two? Ferney had failed to warn her that it could be so hazardous, she thought, but knew that was hardly a failure. Ferney had had neither the time nor the opportunity to go through all the rarer problems they had occasionally faced.

The solace in her life was Rosie and she loved Rosie so deeply that it hurt. As soon as she had heard those words in the delivery room, they had freed her to stay alive, to bond with this familiar, completely unexpected stranger, but that decision carried its own burden of guilt. She looked out from the road across the flatlands below and felt guilty that she *could* love anyone else while Ferney was marooned somewhere out there, building strength for the day when his legs were big enough to carry him back in search of her and Penselwood. She needed to know what he was going through. Would *he* even know? Had he been carried too far away into madness? The great gap in her own last life threatened and taunted her with its message of oblivion. Was he suffering the same?

She thought again about the price the world could exact on them, about the savage beating of the Skimmington ride, and the thought of that beating carried a faint harmonic, some other memory resonating with it. It was whisper-faint, but it immediately touched her deeply. She tried to grasp it, failed, felt it slip away then deliberately blanked her mind and when all was quiet she let herself go further back into the Skimmington, the sharp-edged pain as cudgels broke her arm, the terrible fear as the metal ladle slashed sideways into Ferney's unprotected neck.

The blows hit her in the face, in the stomach, inside now, not in the open air. She grunted, fell sideways off the bench in a hell that was dimly perceived and a boot caught her hard between the legs.

"In the balls," she heard the Gorilla's voice. "Whack 'em in. I'll have no more lip from this one." She doubled up as the boots slammed into her, in her face, in her side. She felt a rib go and clutched her hands into the fiery agony of her groin. Why didn't the warders come?

"That'll learn him not to cheek me," said the Gorilla.

She had no idea. All she'd said was his name. The men called him that when he wasn't there. Wasn't that his name then, Gorilla? Why was he doing this?

"One more for luck, Billy sodding Bunter, and don't ever call me that again."

The last boot brought blackness with it and in the half-life, caught between that claustrophobic prison cell and the cold February graveyard, the words of the police sergeant's letter came back to her.

"Dear Mr. Miller, this is all there was. I hope it helps."

A photocopy of a torn sheet of paper.

"My friend Ivan is writing this for me because I do not know how. I did what I did because the man Cockran deserved it. He killed a woman. He killed me."

There were brackets with a note from Ivan: "(This is what he wants me to write. He is very muddled here.)"

It ended with one line: "They call me Billy Bunter. They never call me my proper name. My proper name is Gary."

She opened her eyes on grey stones and a dusting of frost as the church bell called the hour. Ivan had written Gary, but she knew that wasn't what poor, damaged Billy had said. Gally was what he'd said. It was awful and immense and she had to push its meaning away until Rosie's special day was done.

The cottage welcomed her in and she stood in the hall listening for any sounds from upstairs. None came. She went into the sitting room to fetch Rosie's presents, meaning to pile them on the breakfast table, smiling as she imagined her excitement. She stood in front of the picture and, as she often did when no one else was there, stared at it for a long time, needing something familiar to comfort her.

The picture was another issue that Mike felt they had to resolve and she preferred not to. The restorers in Salisbury had phoned her the week after they had delivered it for cleaning.

"Mrs. Martin, this is John Colman."

"Good morning, Mr. Colman."

"I've just started work on your picture."

"Oh good. How's it going?" She thought he was probably going to announce bad news, revise the estimate upwards. If so she had already decided she would pay without asking Mike, pay out of the proceeds from Ferney's bungalow. His words were very clear to her still: "Pictures should be bright. Clean it so you can always see us there," and, like a faint echo, "Come with me."

"It's going very well. It's mostly the effects of smoke, you know, open fires and candles. There's no technical problem at all. It's not that. I'm just not sure I should be doing it."

"Why on earth not? We can hardly see it at all the way it is now."

"No, no. Look, we're very good at cleaning. I'm not saying we're not, but we're perhaps not the most famous firm in the business and I wonder if you shouldn't take it to London, just to be on the safe side."

"Why should we do that? You're not going to ruin it, surely?"

"No, of course not. Look, this may come as a bit of a surprise to you, but now that I've got it partly clean, I'm pretty certain it's something quite remarkable."

"In what way?"

"I know it sounds absurd and I may be making a fool of myself, but it looks to me very much as though you have a Constable here. It's nowhere in the catalogues, but if it's not Constable it's the best copy of his style I've ever seen."

Gally laughed. "No, I'm sure it's not. John Poorman, that was what my . . . my family always called him."

"It's been in your family? It has a provenance?"

"Oh no, not exactly. No, only, er, rumours I suppose you'd say."

"It's not mentioned in any of the books or any of his letters, I've checked, but of course he painted a great deal around Salisbury and Gillingham."

Gally saw the pitfalls of notoriety looming up. "Mr. Colman, if it's not mentioned, I'm sure it's just someone who followed his style. Let's not get too worried. You finish the cleaning and maybe later on we'll take it for someone to have a look at. I appreciate your thoughtfulness."

When she put the phone down she had crossed to her desk and taken out the dry yellow slip of paper that had come unstuck from the back of the canvas before they had taken it in. It was itself heavily stained and the ink had faded. She held it to the light.

"Nov. 1823. For F and G, with affection JC."

She had decided not to show that to Mike.

Now she looked at the painting, wishing Constable had put more detail into the tiny faces, wishing also that the poor hard-pressed artist had found more fortune during his lifetime. She cherished this proof that the ancient ties could not be easily unbound.

Rosie enjoyed her breakfast, spending as much time playing with the wrapping paper as she did with the toys. Mike watched with a benevolent smile. Her vocabulary was expanding in leaps and bounds, though it was often a struggle to work out what she meant. She unwrapped a giant rabbit from Mike's sister and yelled with delight. "Connie, connie."

"It's a rabbit," said Mike. "Bunny."

"No, connie. Like it. Coney, coney."

"It's a bunny, you funny old thing."

"Funny, funny, funny," said Rosie insistently, turning to Gally for confirmation.

"Very funny," said Mike, though Rosie wasn't laughing.

"You think *everything's* funny, don't you, Rosie?" Gally exclaimed, as she turned towards her daughter, smiling. Her smile slipped.

"Funny, furny, furny," her daughter maintained, waving her hand forcefully and it was quite clear she was pointing at herself.